Down, But Not Out: Breaking Chains

CHERYL BARTON

BARTON PUBLISHING, LLC

Published by:
Barton Publishing, LLC

*This book is a work of fiction. Any references or similarities to
actual events, real people, living or dead, or to real places, are
intended to give the novel a sense of reality. Any similarities in
names, characters, places and incidents is entirely coincidental.*

Barton Publishing, LLC
P.O. Box 962
Reisterstown, Maryland 21136
www.bartonbookpublishing.net

Ordering Information:
Quantity sales. Special discounts are available on quantity
purchases by corporations, associations, and others. For details,
contact the publisher at the address above.

Orders by U.S. trade bookstores and wholesalers.
Please contact information@bartonbookpublishing.net

ISBN-10: 0615887627
ISBN-13: 978-0615887623

Down, But Not Out: Breaking Chains

Dana Carr believed she had the perfect marriage until her husband of seventeen years moved out declaring he needed space. She'd spent her life making her family her one and only priority, forgetting about her own goals and desires. A chance meeting with handsome stranger, Hunter Gray, opens her eyes to what's been missing in her life, including being cherished like a woman should; unconditionally.

Terri Bryant thought she had to have a man who was older and successful in order to find the kind of love she desired, even if she had to deal with being mistreated and disrespected. Into her life walks a much younger man, Kerrion Lee, who she thought didn't measure up to her requirements She's caught off guard when he shows her that his age and status have nothing to do with showing her the respect she deserves by helping her see her true self-worth.

Karina Joseph can't let go of the past that has set the tone for her present, leading into a bleak future. She's a young mother of two, living in the hood and finding the only way to survive is to use her body to get what she wants, even if it means attracting some of the seediest men around. A minor run in with a car and its driver, Dr. Mykel Tanner, puts her on a new path to independence, a better outlook on life and a man she never thought would be within her reach.

OTHER BOOKS BY CHERYL BARTON:

BACHELOR SERIES:
Bachelor Not For Sale
A Designed Affair
A Perfect Combination

AMOROUS OCCUPATIONS SERIES:
The Artist
The Bookkeeper
The Chef

NON-SERIES TITLES:
Holly for Christmas
Second Chances: Three Valentine Novellas

ABOUT THE AUTHOR:

Cheryl Barton lives in Maryland and in her spare time she enjoys reading, writing, spending time with her family, line dancing and eating Maryland steamed crabs.

To contact and connect with Cheryl Barton:

Website: http://www.cherylbarton.net
Facebook: Author Cheryl Barton
Twitter: @mscbarton
Instagram: @crbarton30

You can get all of Author Cheryl Barton's books by visiting her Author Central page on Amazon at www.amazon.com/author/cherylbarton or on her website at www.cherylbarton.net

DEDICATION

To my brother John, III who is always in my thoughts. I'm
thankful for the memories.
John Barton, III
December 26, 1962 – February 24, 2013

~~

To my cousin, Andrea D. Gentry who departed this life on
October 2, 2007, I miss you! I know you would be proud of
the journey I'm on. I can almost hear the words of
encouragement from you to stay the path no matter what.
Rest in His arms.

Chapter One
DANA

"Mom, stop! I think I saw daddy and Reese."

The last thing Dana wanted to do was stop her car for an impromptu run in with her husband James and his latest girlfriend. They may be separated, but the sight of him with Reese was more than she could stand.

There were occasions when she knew she would see them and she'd prepare herself for the encounter. Today wasn't affording her the opportunity for any type of preparation, which happened when they ran into each other by happenstance. The situation with her marriage was bizarre to say the least and a stronger woman would have divorced her cheating husband by now, but not her. She was, as the saying goes, stuck between a rock and a hard place, which is a place she never thought she'd be in.

After seventeen years of marriage, James Carr, the man she'd given up her life and family for, moved out of the house they shared with their two children, Jamie and Jason and into his own condo. He did so claiming he needed space to think through the problems in their marriage; problems that were unbeknownst to her. Every couple had their disagreements and arguments and she and James were no different, but nothing occurred that warranted his moving out and shacking up with his very young girlfriend Reese, someone Dana couldn't stand the sight of.

The one thing she wasn't, was a Reese fan. She had issues with any woman who slept with a married man, whether he was separated or not. Being separated still meant being married until they were actually divorced. Still, Reese wasn't the blame, her husband was.

James was handsome and married or not, women flirted with him all the time. She had to admit even to herself that he could be irresistible to the opposite sex. He was six foot, four inches tall with a sexy, athletic body, kept up by weekly workouts. His bald head added to the sexiness of his demeanor and style. James was often mistaken for the actor Morris Chestnut.

That same gorgeous hunk of a man that she'd married years ago was also the same one that cheated on her several times, that she knew of. James was also hard to resist with not only his good looks, but his charm. He could talk a good game, making it hard to say not to him. She should know because it was that charm that had worked on her years ago.

The mentioning of Reese's name by her daughter made her skin feel like someone was pricking it with pins. Reese was in her twenties and like herself, at an early age, had been blinded by the good looks, the money and the lifestyle that was James Carr.

Trying to pretend like she didn't hear Jamie as she again shouted, asking her to stop, may have worked if she hadn't been caught by a red light half of a block away from where James and Reese were sitting at a table outside of a restaurant. Just her luck, she thought.

Before she knew it, Jamie had opened the car door while they were stopped, slammed it shut and ran back in the direction of the restaurant. She tried to scream for Jamie to stop, but as usual she was ignored. Once her son Jason noticed his sister had made a run for it, he opened the door on his side of the car and jumped out, slamming it shut. That left her with no choice but to go around the block to wait for them.

On the drive around, Dana thought about what her reaction would be seeing her husband and Reese together. It bothered her a lot and James knew it. He'd told her she needed to get over it because he had no plans of hiding Reese like some dirty little secret simply to help her deal with the fact that they were separated.

The separation wasn't the only problem considering it bothered her more knowing they were living together. She and James had spoken about the living together situation because she was concerned about the confusion it would cause their kids. James reassured her that he lived alone, though Reese was there often. She didn't believe for one moment that Reese wasn't living with him. She only hoped they were being discreet around the kids.

She hated the whole situation, but there was nothing she could do about it and that angered her. Angry or not, this was her life and with all she'd gone through being married and separated from James, she was barely holding on enough to keep up with thirteen year old Jamie and sixteen year old Jason's needs for her time and attention. She had none to waste on a man who walked out on his family during a mid-life crisis and hooked up with someone a mere eight years older than his son.

Finally coming back around the block, she pulled up to the curb right next to where they were sitting and noticed the kids had already taken seats and were engaged in conversation.

She may have had to pull over, but getting out of the car was out of the question. She would sit and wait on the kids to finish talking, which she hoped wouldn't take long.

A tap on her window startled her. Thinking it was one of the kids, she turned around and looked into the face of a smiling James.

'Just great,' she muttered to herself while rolling the window down.

"Hey Dana."

"Hi James," she replied looking over at him and then turning her attention back to nothing in particular out of the front window. She hoped he would get the message that she didn't want to be bothered and walk away. When he leaned further into the window, she knew she had no such luck.

"The kids were talking about coming by next weekend. I want to be sure it's okay with you," James said.

Turning around to him, she made sure her face showed how upset she was.

"James, I was planning to surprise the kids and take them to see my family that weekend. I told you about this a few weeks ago."

"Yeah I forgot about that. I've already told them yes so take them to see your family another time. They're not going anywhere so reschedule the visit," he said nonchalantly.

"Neither are you. Why can't you do another weekend?" she retorted.

Dana shifted in her seat, feeling uncomfortable that another conversation between them had gone from zero to sixty in no time at all. She made sure her irritation with him was obvious, not only by her look, but by her body language too.

The smile that greeted her was now gone from James' face and what stared back at her was far from happiness.

"I'm doing the weekend I told you and I've already agreed to next weekend with them. I don't want to disappoint them so change your plans. Besides, you already said it's a surprise so they don't know about it. They aren't close to your family anyway so a change won't really matter."

"Whose fault is that?" Dana uttered before she realized she'd actually said it out loud, especially when the look on his face said that he'd heard her loud and clear.

"I'll pretend I didn't hear that. I'm not about to argue with you and visit an old conversation about how my children don't know your family and how it's all my fault. You should be tired of bringing that up because I'm tired of hearing it. Like I said, change your plans and pick another time to visit your family. I'll pick the kids up from school that Friday so make sure you have their stuff ready. I'll stop by during the day to pick everything up," he said sternly.

Dana was about to continue pleading her case, not wanting to lose yet another argument with him, when he turned and walked away, dismissing her and whatever she was about to say. Though she was shocked, she knew she should not have been because his reaction was how he always responded to her. He enjoyed intimidating her and reminding her that he was still in charge. He'd ruled their marriage like that and now that they were separated, he still did.

What was she to do? Of course if she told the kids now that they couldn't go with him that weekend, they would mope around until she changed her mind. It was a lose-lose situation for her as usual.

She looked over at the table where they were all talking and knew the moment he told them he'd confirmed with her that they were coming with him for that weekend because Jamie did her usual happy dance, spinning around and jumping up and down with extra excitement.

Her plans to take the kids to visit her family had just changed.

~~

James couldn't shake the conversation he'd had with his wife. She'd had a lot of nerve, he thought as he settled in for the evening. The conversation with her at the car had disrupted the rest of his day and even now as he prepared for bed, thoughts of it still lingered, making him feel stressed. He was tired of always arguing with her when it came to what he wanted to do with his kids. So she mentioned to him something about taking the kids for a visit to see her family; he didn't care. He didn't care for them and if he could continue to keep his kids away from them like he had done all their lives, he would do so. He wouldn't settle for them poisoning his kid's minds against him as they tried to do with Dana when he'd first met her.

"What has you so tense baby?" Reese asked walking into the bedroom in nothing but a barely there pink thong and a sheer pink lace tank top. Seeing her, he forgot all about his problems with Dana and focused on the sexy sight before him as he watched her walk over to the bed to join him. He liked that she didn't just join him, but she slowly crawled up on the bed from the bottom like a cat stalking her prey. He watched as she moved slowly up their king-sized bed with a look that said she had something sexy in mind for them for the evening.

"Nothing now that I see what you have in mind," he said, trying to relax in the moment and not stay in the earlier conversation with his wife. This moment was so much better.

"Are you sure you're not still worked up over your conversation with you know who earlier?" Reese asked finally reaching him and coming up to straddle his lap, like she knew he liked for her to do.

"Well I was a little distracted, but not anymore. You have a tendency to help me clear my mind of anything but you, baby," James said, reaching to pull her as close to him as he could.

"That's good because I want your mind on me and not that mean old woman you were married to."

"Reese, I'm still married to her and we're going to have disagreements, especially when it comes to the children and I have to learn to not let her get to me like she did today."

Reese reached up to caress his face to smooth out the stress lines that were there and he melted under her touch.

"That's right baby. I don't like how she talks to you and treats you. I don't want her hateful attitude coming into our home and disrupting our lives."

James heard nothing Reese was saying. The last thing he wanted to do was talk about his wife with Reese. Reese had a purpose in their relationship and she was now miring it with talk of his wife, ruining his mood.

He tried to change that by pulling her closer, planting soft kisses along the column of her neck and when she continued to talk, he stopped his efforts, about to lose patience with her.

"James, honey, when are you going to divorce her anyway? You know that should be you and I living in that big house with the kids and not her. She doesn't deserve that house and she doesn't deserve you still paying for everything for her. She needs to get a job and take care of herself. What grown woman stays home and doesn't even think about working?"

James began to tense up even more. He didn't mind the way he thought about Dana, whether it be good or bad, but he didn't want to hear anyone else talking about her, especially not Reese.

"Don't worry about it. You just worry about keeping me happy and I'll take care of Dana and her issues."

"Okay. I want you to be happy and the longer you stay married to her, the more miserable you'll be. I'm always coming to the rescue and saving the day after she's upset you."

"That's why you're my little stress reliever, so how about a little de-stressing?" he asked, letting her know that he was done talking.

He wanted to end all talk about divorcing Dana, something he had no plans of doing. Why should he when Dana had no problem letting him do what he wanted without making any real demands for him to choose to stay or not to stay with her? Right now, he had the best of both worlds and he had no desire to rock the boat.

He pushed all thoughts of divorce, Dana, kids and everything else from his mind as he focused on Reese and her de-stressing techniques.

~~

Dana contemplated how to handle the conversation with her mother about her visit that no longer included the kids. She'd spent the day cleaning which often helped her clear her head, but today it didn't provide much of a reprieve.

She looked around at all of the shining stainless steel appliances and sparkling wood floors and knew that spending her day doing housework didn't help her figure out how to explain things to her mother. She'd put off the conversation long enough and needed to get it over with.

She picked up the phone from the kitchen counter and dialed, feeling anxious as soon as she heard the first ring.

"Hey mom, how are you doing?" she said when her mother answered.

"Hi Dana, I'm doing fine. How are you and the kids doing?"

"We're doing great mom."

"That's good. Your father and I were talking about you and the kids. We're excited about your upcoming visit. Your sisters and their families will all be here and we're planning on having a big family cook-out. I know the kids are getting bigger every day and I can't wait to see them."

Dana could hear the exhilaration in her mother's voice. She'd only seen them a few times over the years, so going home for a visit was a big deal. She felt bad that she was about to disappoint her mother once again.

"Mom, that's why I'm calling. It looks like we won't be coming, or at least the kids won't, but I'll still be there. I completely forgot that James has the kids that weekend. I didn't check the date with him before I made the plan to visit. I'm sorry because I know you've put a lot of planning into the kids' visit and I really hate to do this to you."

She waited through several dreadful moments of her mother's silent disappointment. The assumption, as usual, was that her mother was picking her words carefully to keep the peace, but to also let Dana know that she was able to see through the lie. Even though for years, she had little to no contact with her mother, it amazed her how she was still able to read right through any lie Dana told.

"I'm sorry to hear they won't be coming, but I'm glad you're still coming because I miss you; we all do. I was hoping to spend some time with my grandchildren since I've missed so many years with them already. I feel like they don't know me and your dad at all," her mother said despondently.

She felt worse hearing how her mother's tone changed to one of disenchantment.

"I know mom. I promise you'll get to see them soon. James reminded me about his weekend plans with the kids that couldn't be changed."

"Dana, you know I love you, but never lie to me for James. Don't forget I know him very well. He's kept you and my grandchildren away for years due to his own selfishness. After what he's put you through, you're still covering for him. You and I both know you did not mix up the dates. What happened this time? Did you tell him you were bringing the kids here and he suddenly came up with something else for the kids to do? When will his obsession with controlling every move you and the kids make end? I guess being separated didn't change that." The tone in her mother's words cut deep.

Her mother was right, but what could she do.

"I'm sorry mom, really I am. The kids asked him if they

could spend that weekend with him while I was planning to surprise them with the visit home, so I hadn't told them yet."

"He knew though didn't he? He could have told them another weekend would be better since he knew you had plans, but he chose to manipulate the situation to his benefit to keep them away from us and let's not forget to also control you. You don't have to admit it because I already know it. He's done it their entire lives and his control over you has been going on since the day you met him. If he was able to get you to stay away from us for this long, I know he already has his hold over the kids too. You're not even together anymore and he still controls your every move. Speaking of that, when are you going to file for divorce? It's clear he's not coming back and it's been a year of separation. He gets to live the playboy life like a single man and you're still bound by your duties as a wife."

Dana couldn't handle her mother right now. She never sugar coated anything. She knew her family meant well, but she was doing what she needed to do to keep the peace. Besides, who said anything about James never coming back to her? He was going through something that a lot of men go through. Eventually she believed he would see that his place was with her and the kids and he would come to his senses. Her only hope was that by the time he did, she would have been able to repair her relationship with her family and the friends she'd lost contact with over the years.

"Mom, I hear you. I'm not filing for divorce. If I do that it would only make James angrier and if you remember he still takes care of the me and the kids. I'm still solely dependent on him, so without him and his support, I would have nothing. You know I don't work so I have to keep the peace. The one time I mentioned divorce, the conversation turned into a shouting match and he threatened that he would only give me what the courts say he has to give me, which would be a lot less than what I currently receive from him. We've been married a long time and I'm not willing to give up on it yet."

"Dana, do you mean to tell me that his girlfriend isn't enough incentive to divorce him? You could sell the house and move closer to us and we could help you with the kids. You don't have to be treated this way."

She regretted telling her mother about the separation and how James had taken up with a much younger woman. She hated having to explain herself and her marriage to anyone.

"James would never allow me to move the kids out of state away from him. He would sue me for custody and he'd win because I have nothing to fight him with and I don't feel bound. I'm making my kids my priority. I'm thinking about them and what divorcing their father and moving away would do to them and I can't do that."

"You mean you're making James your priority. The kids are old enough to understand an unhappy environment. You think it's good for them to see their father with other women while still keeping his grips on you? What is it that Jamie is seeing when it comes to how a man treats a woman? What about Jason? Is he admiring his father and pitying you? Will that be how he treats women as a man? You have to think of that and what they're being exposed to."

Her mother was hitting way below the belt. Her remarks stung, no matter how right she was. It still hurt to hear her say them.

Tears threatened to fall as Dana began to feel defeated.

"Mom, I can't do this with you right now. This entire situation is hard enough for me. Do you still want me to come for a visit without the kids?" she asked.

She heard her mother sigh, an indication that she knew how much her words were hurting and not helping.

"Dana I'm sorry. Of course I still want you to come. It's been a long time since the family was all together. We'll plan something with the kids another time. We have some celebrating to do. Your sister is about to open up her own dental practice and we're all excited for her. I love you Dana and I can't wait to see you," she heard her mother say happily, removing all signs of hurt, anger and pity from her voice.

She felt a little better. She missed her family as much as they've missed her.

"I love you too mom. I can't wait to come home to see everyone. I'll see if James will keep the kids a few extra days so that I can stay a little longer."

"That sounds great. I'm already excited," her mother said.

"Okay, that's great mom. I wanted to let you know of the change in plans. I need to get dinner ready for the kids so I'll talk to you soon and tell dad I love him. Make sure you tell everyone that I'm looking forward to seeing them."

"Dana, why don't you call your sisters and let them know how you're doing? It would be good if you could connect with them before you get here. That way you can have time to play catch up before everyone is around and you may not have time for one on one talks. I know they miss you too."

She more than missed her sisters. She'd picked up the phone several times to call them over the past year, but couldn't. For years, her sisters made attempts to connect with her and would invite her, James and the kids for visits, but she gave them one excuse after another of why they couldn't. She didn't tell them the truth which was that James didn't want any connection to her family. Now she was alienated from them. She wanted to be within the folds of her family again and she was going to make every effort to make up for lost time and beginning a sisterly dialogue with them was a great start.

"I will do that mom. That's a great idea. I really could use some girl talk with them. I hope they're not mad for the years I ignored their calls and declined invitations from them. I really do miss them."

"Nonsense," her mother said vehemently. "Your sisters love you and no matter when you reach out, they'll always embrace you."

"Thanks mom. I needed to hear that."

They talked a little more and by the end of the conversation she was almost in tears. She not only missed them, living so far away, but her mother reminded her of so many aspects of her life that she'd let happen that contributed to her current situation. She wasn't surprised to hear any of it because she was living it.

There was no doubt that James is controlling, but he is still her husband and for now, she had to deal with it whether she liked it or not. He held all the cards and she had to play along. She wasn't happy about it, but she was only a homemaker, which meant she had no income coming in. She and the kids depended on James to provide for them and as long as that was the case, she had to keep quiet and do things his way.

On the other hand, she also knew her mother was right about the lie she told her about the kids' visit. James knew about her plans and he could have made up an excuse for them not going with him that weekend, but he didn't because he still had issues with her family.

In the year since they'd separated, she was able to take the kids to visit her family only once and even then, he called constantly wanting to talk to the kids, purposely intruding on the visit.

Throughout the seventeen years of their marriage, he wouldn't let her have anything to do with her family or any of the friends she'd had back when they'd met. He did it out of spite because of her family's dislike for him. They were against her marrying him and told her that her life would be nothing as long as she was with him. Her mistake was telling him back then that her family felt that way and because of that, he wanted nothing else to do with them from the day they got married. Once he had her in his grip, he was able to control her contact with everyone around her. It's obvious he was still trying to have that control.

She had to think of Jamie and Jason. Her kids were her life and she wanted the problems she and James had to be seamless to them. Since they wanted to spend the weekend with him, she decided to let it go. It wasn't often that they requested to stay with him and he wasn't too busy to accommodate them. It was important to her that they continue to have a great relationship.

Her family meant everything to her and no matter how long they'd been separated, she still held out hope that if she played her cards right and went along with things,

James would come back and make them whole again. Maybe then she could unite her family with James and the kids so that they could continue to be a part of her life now that she was in contact with them again.

Chapter Two
DANA

"Hunter it's good to see you again."

"Hey Jeff, it's good to be seen."

Hunter greeted his best friend as soon as he walked into the house where Jeff's birthday party was in full swing.

"Thanks for coming out. I wasn't sure you'd show up."

Hunter couldn't believe he'd shown up himself. He looked around at a room full of friends he and his ex-wife traveled and hung out with in the past. When he received the invitation to the birthday celebration, he thought about not showing up wondering if his ex-wife and her new husband were also invited. So far he saw no signs of them. The fact that they lived out of town may be the reason, but Hunter still wasn't sure that they wouldn't show up.

"I wouldn't miss a chance to come out and celebrate your birthday."

"Great. Did you come by yourself or did you bring a date."

Hunter didn't miss Jeff's search of the space behind him as he looked around for anyone he didn't recognize.

"No date. I came by myself."

"Cool. You know you don't have to worry. Casey and I didn't invite your ex and her new husband. I told her that you and I were friends before you were married to Trish and if I had to choose to keep the peace, I wanted to invite you, so we didn't send her one."

Hunter wanted no special treatment. His marriage had been over a long time ago so there was no reason for any of their friends to feel awkward.

"It's not a problem. You could have invited them. You do realize the marriage ended a long time ago right? The awkwardness of running into each other ended along ago."

What Hunter didn't say was though the awkwardness of seeing his ex-wife and her new husband had ended, it still wasn't something he looked forward to doing.

"Whew, that's good. How about a beer? There are some out back on the deck."

"Sure."

Hunter followed his friend and he waved and nodded at a few of Jeff's family members and friends that he knew. He and Jeff had been friends since their college days and through the years they'd remained close. They even had kids who were the same age. His daughter Coral and Jeff and his wife Casey's son Ethan were the same age and both were in college. Hunter missed his daughter while she was away at school, but unlike some father's, because she lived with him and not her mother, he got to spend time with her when she had breaks from school.

Following his divorce from Trish which ended badly, Hunter fought hard to get custody of Coral. Trish had become unhappy in the marriage saying she felt it was stale and started hanging out late at night with a new group of friends that Hunter didn't know and didn't like. She had begun drinking heavily and doing illegal drugs. Initially when they'd first separated, Coral moved with Trish into an apartment. He had offered to let them have the house and he would move out, but Trish wanted a clean break from their old life and wanted a new place.

He'd gone to his job as a college professor one day and when he'd returned, Trish had moved all of her and Coral's belongings out. They worked out an agreement for when Coral would be with him and things worked out fine in the beginning. After a few early morning phone calls from his then twelve year old daughter saying Trish had not come home the night before and Coral had been home alone, Hunter sued her for custody. After failing several drug tests, the judge awarded sole custody to Hunter with visitation to Trish.

Looking back on his life with Trish as he grabbed a beer from one of the coolers on the deck, Hunter knew that the best decision he'd ever made was to let Trish go and not fight her on the divorce. He started off playing the game of staying together for the sake of Coral and thought that he could get Trish to stay, but knew that it wouldn't be fair to Coral in the long run and he had been right. Once his daughter had moved in with him, they were back to a life of normalcy and he was happy with the close relationship he had with his daughter.

Before he could get a good gulp of his beer down, Jeff's facial expression changed to one of caution as he turned to face him.

"Listen, I need to warn you about something," Jeff said.

Cautious was an understatement compared to how Hunter was feeling. He had a feeling he wasn't going to like what Jeff had to say. The look on his face was sending out all kinds of warning signs.

"Spill it Jeff," Hunter said petulantly.

"Casey invited a friend of hers to the party. She sent me over to you not long after you'd arrived to see if you came alone so that she could introduce you. Now don't shoot the messenger, I thought I would warn you."

It was worse than Hunter thought. He hated when anyone tried to set him up as if he couldn't find a woman on his own. He may be divorced, but he was still in impeccable shape. He worked out several times a week and he's always had the market cornered when it came to looks. He made the decision that he didn't want to date and bed a lot of women. He wasn't into using women in any way and when he was ready to settle down, that's the woman he'd make a move with. He would know when he met her and so far, that hadn't happened, especially since he'd been focused on being a good dad to Coral, making sure she had everything she needed, including all of his time if she wanted it. He dated, but there was nothing serious going on. He guessed that Jeff's wife had her own plan in mind for what she thought was Hunter's happiness. He wasted no time in telling Jeff what he thought of Casey's matchmaking.

"Man you know better than to let your wife set me up with someone. You know I don't have a problem in the female department and the last thing I need is for anyone to set me up, especially if I didn't ask."

"I know that and I'm sure she knows that too. She's always telling her friends what a great guy you are. We feel terrible about how your marriage to Trish ended, you know with her cheating on you, the drinking and drugs and everything.

Really? Hunter thought. He came to his party to hear about his ex-wife whom he'd divorced years ago. Did they really think he was still hung up on her simply because he had not married again or because they didn't know of anyone he was seeing?

Hunter tampered down his anger and tried to turn the conversation back on the party and not his dating life.

"Seriously Jeff, this is a party for you. I really don't want to stand here and talk to you about my ex-wife or my dating situation. What are we teenagers?" he laughed.

"You know how Casey can be. I wanted to warn you ahead of time."

Hunter was about to respond when he looked over Jeff's shoulder and saw Casey coming in his direction followed by a beautiful woman who he assumed was the woman Jeff mentioned.

"Hunter!" Casey said embracing him in a hug.

"Casey, it's good to see you again. It's been a long time."

"I know it's been way too long. How have you been? How is the life of a college professor treating you?"

"I've been great and work is fine."

"Good. I want to introduce you to someone."

Hunter laughed as he watched Casey stepped back from him and jump right into matchmaker mode, moving her friend closer to him.

"This is a co-worker of mine. Her name is Sara and she's recently divorced."

Too much information Hunter thought and Casey's friend looked as embarrassed as Hunter felt for her.

"Hello Sara, it's nice to meet you."

"Hello Hunter is nice to meet you."

"Jeff, I need your help with something for a minute," Casey said, obvious to everyone that her plan was to leave him and Sara alone.

When they walked away, Hunter felt the need to apologize.

"I'm sorry for that. Casey means well."

"Yes she does and I'm sorry too. Until a few minutes ago, I had no idea her purpose for inviting me was to set me up with someone, which is something I didn't want nor would I ever ask her to do."

"Don't worry about it."

"Can I let you in on a secret?" Sara asked.

"Sure."

"I'm thinking maybe if I had revealed to Casey that I'm divorced because I told my husband I was a lesbian, she never would have put either of us in this situation."

Hunter was first stunned by the admission and when Sara laughed lightly, he laughed along with her.

"Well you changed the whole game for her. I can see her looking at us over your shoulder and she looks like she's patting herself on the back. I'll tell you what, I won't tell her if you won't. That way for the rest of the night, if she thinks things aren't going well between us, she won't try to change things up and introduce us to two different people."

"That sounds like a great plan to me. Shall we make our way over to the food table and really have her jumping for joy?" Sara asked.

"Definitely; that's something I'd like to see."

Hunter spent the rest of the evening talking and dancing with Sara until he noticed the hour. He had an early morning game of golf he didn't want to be tired or late for. After thanking Sara for a fun night, he went in search of Jeff.

"Jeff, I'm out of here. I have an early morning game of

golf. Thanks for the invite."

"I'll walk you out and I'm glad you came through. So what did you think of Sara?" he asked when they reached the door.

"Jeff man, your wife needs to stick to selling houses. Her radar on a woman's availability is not working and even if it was, I don't need to be set up. Oh, and Sara is a lesbian. That's why she and her husband divorced."

Hunter laughed at the surprised look on his friend's face.

"The two of you were cozy all night though," Jeff quipped.

"True. That's because she's actually a nice person and I figured if I didn't go along with acting as if a connection was made, Casey would try and set me up with someone else here tonight. Please tell her I said thanks, but no thanks. Like I said, I don't have a problem with women. I got this covered."

"Does that mean you're seeing someone?"

"Not at the moment. I date like any other single man, but have I met the woman that I'd like to be in a relationship with? No not yet."

"I know the divorce was hard on you. You know Casey means well and I should have stopped her antics the minute I knew what she was planning."

"It's all good and there was no harm done. It was actually fun watching your wife act like she should hang a shingle outside of your house for a profession in love connections. That was priceless."

"Well you know how I feel about things. Trish really messed up with you. You deserve much better than that."

"Trish wasn't the only one at fault in my marriage, no

matter what anyone thinks they may know about it. We both had our faults. If nothing else I learned a lot about myself and how to handle problems in relationships. Trish and I spent a lot of years unhappy, and we probably stayed together as long as we did because of my daughter. That was one of the many mistakes we made. You have to be happy with each other for any marriage to work. Without that, eventually, it will falter."

"So does that mean you haven't given up on falling in love and possibly getting married again?"

Hunter never doubted he would embrace love and marriage again.

"I look forward to both when it happens. I don't want anyone setting me up though, so be sure you pass that along to your wife. When I meet that woman who will steal my breath away, I'll let you both know. Thanks again for the invite."

Hunter headed off in the direction of his car and even though he didn't like that Casey tried to set him up, he'd had a lot of fun hanging with Sara most of the night and it did make him realize how much he missed having a more steady relationship with a woman. With Coral now away at college, he had more time for him and it was time he invested as much time in his personal life as he did in his professional life.

Chapter Three
DANA

Dana's front door opened and she knew it couldn't be anyone else but James coming by to pick up the bags she'd packed for the kids for their weekend with him. She'd spent the morning trying to come up with a way to bring up the weekend visit without causing a big blow-out.

Even though she'd finally given in, she still wanted him to know that she wasn't happy about having to change her plans, especially after talking with the kids about their plans with him for the weekend and they revealed information to her she's sure James wouldn't be happy that she knew.

During a casual conversation with them, she learned that they had not asked him if they could spend the weekend with him.

When they went over to the table that day at the restaurant to say hello, he mentioned he and Reese were going to the new carnival a couple of counties over and wanted to know if they wanted to go. He lured them in with promises of junk food, staying at a hotel for the weekend and shopping, which was something they both loved to do.

It hadn't been their idea to spend the weekend with

him; it was his, which angered her. He led her to believe the weekend with him was the kids' idea. He deliberately set out to sabotage her weekend away with them to Seattle to visit her family. She tried to hold her anger in check when she heard him enter the house because she didn't need another fight with him, though this time it really was warranted.

"Dana are you here?" she heard him yell.

"I'm in the kitchen," she said through gritted teeth.

James appeared in the doorway in a black business suit, crisp white shirt and one of his many bright colored ties, something that was a staple for him that added to how good he always looked in a suit. Even as angry as she was at him, he was still the best dressed man she knew.

Putting his appearance to the side, her anger surfaced before she could hold it back. She gripped the edge of her brown marble countertop to hold on to the little bit of control she did have.

"Why did you lie to me about the kids wanting to stay with you this weekend?" she said without any warning.

James paused before coming back at her with an attitude of his own.

"I never have to explain anything to you when it comes to my children, remember that. Where are their things? I have a meeting I need to get to. I didn't come here to have a fight with you. It's too early in the morning for attitude," he said crossly.

She refused to back down. His deliberate deceit was intolerable. This time he had crossed a line with her.

"James explain to me why you did that? You knew I had plans to visit my family and yet you consciously planned for something else that you knew the kids wouldn't be able to say no to. A carnival James? What kid wouldn't want to go to that? Why would they say no to anything that involved carnival rides and junk food for an entire weekend? I won't even bring up the shopping spree you threw in for good measure. You know Jamie would never resist an opportunity to shop for new clothes and Jason for new video games. Then to top it off, you lied about the whole thing. Why?"

She was fired up. His hatred for her family was evident, but trying to use the kids as a pawn in his scheme was beyond belief. Still, he didn't seem to be backing down.

"You can take the kids to see your family anytime. The carnival is only here for this one weekend. I thought it would be a great weekend to spend with them since I've been so busy lately. Why are you trying to make this such a big deal? They don't know your family anyway so there's no loss. Stop being so over-dramatic about everything and it doesn't matter whether they mentioned spending the weekend or I did, it's done. Where are their bags?" he demanded.

Dana couldn't let it go. He purposely set the weekend up so that her plans would change and she would once again have to disappoint her family. She pressed on.

"We need to be a united front when it comes to the kids, James. You could have talked to me about it before you talked to the kids about it. It was obvious you knew what you were going to do because our seeing you outside the restaurant was a coincidence. We should have discussed this or maybe that carnival would be at another location in another county not far from here on another weekend that would have been more convenient for me."

The look on James' face told her that she'd gone too far.

She watched as he loosened his tie and she knew that his patience had worn off.

"Dana, like I said, when it comes to my kids, I don't have to clear or discuss anything with you. This weekend was convenient for me so it was the weekend that I chose. I don't have to plan anything around what is a convenience for you. Every day is convenient for you because you don't work or do anything except take care of this house and look after the well-being of my kids. You have nothing, but time on your hands so what's the big deal? Going to visit your family is not a priority when it comes to them; spending time with me is. Now, as far as I'm concerned this discussion is over."

After his loud response, they stared at each other, both boiling with anger.

This was not Dana's plan. She didn't want a fight with him. For now, she figured it would be best to let the subject go and bring it up another time about how they should work better together when it comes to plans for the kids.

"Fine James. Their bags are in the living room. I'm not trying to make this out of anything. I wish you would consult me when you have plans with the kids, especially if you know I already have something planned. I always discuss my plans for them with you so that we can work together. I only ask that you do the same in return out of courtesy."

She waited, hoping he would calm down and see how rational she was being.

"I suggest you continue doing that," he said. The level of disgust in his tone did not escape her.

"Suppose I had already purchased the airline tickets? I wouldn't have been able to get that money back. All I'm saying is talk to me. I don't think that's asking too much," she said calmly, trying to diffuse what was now a volatile situation. The venomous look he gave her let her know that there would be no calming him down. She watched as he stepped even further into the kitchen.

"Whose money would have been lost?" he said in an even tone that was laced with antagonism. When he did so, he also turned his head so that his ear was closest to her.

Dana felt belittled when he pushed his ear out at her as if he was listening, waiting for her to respond knowing what he meant. She knew he wanted her to understand that since he still took care of her, it would have been his money lost and he didn't care.

She remained silent, not letting him treat her as if she didn't matter.

When she didn't respond, he edged her on.

"I don't think I heard your answer," he said flippantly.

She wouldn't give him the satisfaction of responding.

"Let me answer for you since all of a sudden you've lost the ability to speak and run off at the mouth. My money!" he shouted. "That's whose money would have been lost and I don't care. What I do care about are my kids, not about money you may have lost buying them plane tickets to visit a family they know nothing about. Buy new tickets."

She stood grounded as she watched him head in the direction of the bags and the front door. She had no fight left in her and was embarrassed that she allowed him to once again talk down to her.

She followed him as he reached for the bags and it reminded her that she'd packed a few extra days' worth of clothes for them and it dawned on her why she had done so.

When he reached for the door, she stopped him.

"Wait, I forgot to ask you something. Do you think you could keep the kids a few extra days? I was hoping to spend a little extra time with my family by staying until Wednesday instead of coming back on Sunday evening. My sisters and their families will be there and I thought the extra time would be good with them."

She watched James as he stiffened and turned slowly toward her.

"How inconvenient of you. Did you just realize that you wanted to stay a few extra days or did you already plan for that by packing extra for the kids hoping I would say yes? Wait, did you just talk to me about convenience?" he said shrewdly.

James was right. She should have asked him prior to today, but she was upset with him and didn't feel like talking. She'd given him a speech about this very thing.

"I'm sorry. Yes I knew I wanted to stay a few extra days and yes I packed a few extra things for them. Can you keep them until Wednesday or not? I'll be back in time to get Jamie from school and Jason can take the school bus. I can pick up their clothes from you when I get back on Wednesday or you can drop them off."

She didn't like the look that crossed his face. She could see that he was up to something.

He stepped a little closer to her with a cunning look on his face. She knew that look. It was his deal making face. She'd seen it many times over the years when he had business deals to make. She didn't like the direction she thought the conversation was about to go in.

"So, if I agree to keep them a few extra days, what do I

get for the inconvenience?" he asked, cleverly.

She should have known that it would cost her to get his agreement. What that cost would be had her fearing his closeness. Maybe for once, she'd stand up to him and win, she thought.

"More time with your kids is not an inconvenience James. They're old enough that you don't have to look after them around the clock. They even know how to cook for themselves."

James moved close enough to her that she could feel his minty fresh breath on her face.

"You didn't answer my question with the right answer. What do I get if I say yes?"

She remained quiet and tried looking away until his hand reached up and turned her face back so that they were almost nose to nose.

She tried to respond, but nothing came out. There was no doubt about what he wanted and she couldn't get her mind to come up with a way out of it. Before she could, he spoke again, this time moving so that he was talking directly into her ear with an even deeper voice.

She hated that his closeness still did things to her. She didn't want him, but it was clear to her that he wanted her. She knew that Reese was probably fulfilling every sexual desire he had, so why he still came to her for sex she didn't understand. She guessed he did it because he could.

"You need to answer me or my answer is already no, unless you can think of something that might persuade me to change my no to a yes," she heard him say with no hint of anger. What she heard was a deep, guttural seductive tone.

She knew what he meant. She was hoping it wasn't

true.

"What do you want?" she asked, sheepishly.

Trying to step back from him, not liking how close together they were standing, apparently was fruitless when James used his hand to draw her back to him, this time pulling their bodies flush against each other so that she could feel his intent which was now pressing intimately up against her.

"Well, how badly do you need the extra days with your family?" she heard him say, while he also began removing the tie that he had loosened earlier.

This wasn't good, she thought. She nervously tried to talk her way out of the inevitable.

"It's only a few extra days James. Why do we need to make some kind of deal? You are not at the bank sealing some big deal for work," she said, trying to dissuade him with logic.

He then stepped back from her. She'd been married to him long enough to know he would not give up easily.

"Okay, fine. Then I suggest you find your way back home sometime Sunday evening because I'll be dropping them off and you need to be here. I don't like the idea of them being here by themselves, especially overnight."

She watched as he went back to gathering the kids' things as she nervously thought of how to fix it so that she could have the extra time away. She'd already bought the return ticket for Wednesday morning from Seattle. This was the second trip home to her family in a year and she really wanted time to spend with them.

It was obvious what he wanted and it was that want that she hated giving in to when he held the upper hand.

Her heart started beating faster when he moved toward

the door to leave.

To get what she wanted, she knew she was going to have to give in.

As he was about to open the door, she grabbed his arm stopping him. It's not like sex isn't something she was foreign to many times over their marriage and the year since they'd separated.

He turned around with a look on his face that said he knew that she was going to stop him.

"Fine James," she said curtly.

"Fine what Dana? I suggest you say it nicer."

James placed the luggage back down on the floor and looked at her waiting for an answer.

Dana calmed her voice.

"I'm saying okay to what you want."

She turned toward the stairs that led to the second level and began walking up. When he didn't follow her, she stopped.

"You're saying okay to what?"

"Stop it James," she said feeling conquered.

"You know what I want to hear so say it. All that mouth you had when I came in and now you can't seem to form the words you know you need to say?"

That wicked look that she hated was back in his eyes. She wanted to cry, but she wouldn't give him the satisfaction he lived for. Keeping her composure while holding back her tears, she obliged him so that she could get what she wanted. Looking in the face of her husband, the negotiator, she gave in.

"I want you," she said, trying to sound convincing.

He smiled like a little kid who'd found where the jar of cookies had been hidden.

"That's what I thought," he said, now moving to follow her.

She turned towards the bedroom once again.

"Suddenly I think my whole morning is about to free up," he said smiling a smile that Dana couldn't see, but she still knew he had.

She was bound as her mom said she was. Her wifely duties didn't end because he'd left her and taken up with a much younger woman. He still controlled her using sex as a negotiation tool to get what he wanted and like other times in the past, it was working today.

"Now you see how easy it is to change my no to a yes," he said deceitfully as he removed his suit jacket and hung it over the banister on his way up the stairs to the bedroom.

Chapter Four
DANA

"Mom, I told you I needed my uniform cleaned for today. I have practice after school. I looked for it and it's still in the dirty laundry. Now what am I supposed to do?" Jason said angrily.

Her son at six feet tall was an exact replica of her husband. From the tone of his voice, he apparently had the attitude of him too. Dana didn't like that he was becoming more and more like his dad every day, especially his demanding attitude.

"Jason, you never said anything about needing your uniform for today. I would have remembered that and I would have made sure it was washed."

Morning productions of drama never failed when she was trying to get the kids out of the door and off to school. She'd barely begun making Jamie's lunch before Jason began the morning's encounter.

"Well I need it today. You can wash it and bring it to me at school. My practice isn't until three thirty."

Dana watched her son finish his breakfast without one hit of recognition that he may have spoken to her in an arduous tone. She guessed his attitude was her fault.

Maybe he did mention needing his uniform and she forgot. She couldn't blame him for being a little upset. At sixteen, sports were important to him. He was a member of the varsity football team and though his grades were not that good, he did excel in the sport. She ignored his insolence for now and continued making Jamie's lunch.

"I'll have it at the school before your classes end so don't worry," she replied.

The kids outside screamed that the school bus was coming so Jason jumped up from his seat, not bothering to clean up his mess or to thank her for agreeing to have his uniform cleaned and at his school as he requested.

He simply ran out of the door, not saying a word. Dana assumed that meant, as usual, that she was expected to put his dirty dishes away.

"Mom, where is my short red skirt?" Jamie screamed down the stairs at her. She could hear her moving around on the second level preparing for school.

"I don't know Jamie. I didn't realize you had a short red skirt," she hollered back up the stairs.

"Dad's girlfriend bought it for me and I want to wear it today," Jamie said finally coming down and entering the kitchen still in pajama bottoms.

Dana turned to see her standing apparently waiting for her to find it. Dramatic production number two, Dana thought.

The mentioning of James' girlfriend made her skin crawl. Jamie knew how much of a sore subject for her it was to discuss Reese, but apparently the red skirt meant more than her mother's feelings.

"Mom, are you going to help me look for it or not?"

Dana lived for her kids, but it was days like today that

made her realize she was as much a doormat for them as she was for their father. She ignored her daughter's moodiness, knowing it would be best to help her find the skirt than to let her stand there waiting. If she did, it would be on her if Jamie were late for school.

"I'll look, but I don't know what it looks like. Let me put your lunch in the bag and I'll come up and help."

"Don't worry about packing my lunch today. Dad gave me money because I wanted to buy my lunch this week."

Dana should have known. If there was a glitch of any kind, it usually involved James.

"Jamie, I already made it. You said you wanted turkey this week and I went out last night to get it. You never said a word about buying your lunch."

Dana noticed she was no longer talking face to face with Jamie, but to the back of her head as she watched her walk away to head back upstairs to search for the skirt. She followed closely behind to help search for the infamous garment.

"Jamie, I don't see a red skirt. When did you get it?" Dana asked as she looked through Jamie's closet while Jamie looked again through her dresser.

"A few weeks ago when we stayed with dad while you were out of town. Reese and I went shopping and she bought it for me. Oh, wait. I know where it is. I didn't bring the bag upstairs. I think it's still in the family room downstairs."

Ugh, there goes that name again, Dana thought to herself. She hated how the kids said Reese's name as if their father having a girlfriend was a natural thing.

"Here it is mom. I'll be ready in a few minutes."

She went back down to continue cleaning the kitchen

when Jamie appeared again a few minutes later now ready to leave.

"Let's go mom. I'm supposed to be at school a little bit early today. I have a rehearsal for the play before first period class."

Dana heard nothing Jamie was saying because she was too focused on how short the red skirt was that her thirteen year old daughter was now wearing.

Jamie, who was tall for her age, was beginning to fill out and with the shape that was developing, the short length of the skirt she had on made Dana wish for the days of the past when her daughter was happy wearing clothing with animals all over them. It was obvious her teenager was growing up, but into something as short as the red skirt, Dana wasn't about to accept.

"Jamie, you are not leaving this house with a skirt on that short going to middle school."

"Mom, don't overreact. It's a skirt and dad thought it was fine when I tried it on and showed him. He didn't think it was too short."

Dana could care less what James thought because it was obvious he had no clue about what's appropriate for school and for a girl Jamie's age. This red skirt clearly was not it. Dana responded calmly hoping to not anger her daughter while convincing her to change her clothes into something else.

"It's too short Jamie. Why don't you go change into something more appropriate for school?"

"There is nothing wrong with this skirt mom. You are so old fashioned and I don't like long skirts like you wear. Maybe you should wear skirts a little shorter. Dad likes Reese in short skirts. He says they show off her legs."

Dana stood with her mouth wide opened and stunned at her daughter's attempt to get her way by intimidation. Obviously something learned from her father.

If it was Jamie's intention to deflate her mother this morning, it worked. Dana didn't know how to respond to that. She should be raging mad, but she discovered since the separation from her husband, that her children were becoming mean kids and have recognized the way to get her to accommodate whatever they wanted, they only needed to bring up their father or Reese and she would shut down, as she was doing right now.

It seemed as if lately she was always on the defense with everyone around her and today she wasn't in the mood. If Jamie wanted to go dressed like that, then she would let her. She figured Jamie would be more embarrassed when she got called to the office and would have to call home to get something else to wear.

Today, she didn't feel like fighting with anyone. She smiled to herself, encouraging herself to shake off everything that was trying to mess up her day and her happy mood. She was still thinking about the wonderful time she'd had visiting her family in Seattle a few weeks back.

Even her kids' early morning issues couldn't take away the smile that crept on her face thinking of how good it felt to be around them again.

One night she and her sisters had stayed up all night talking and catching up on all the years they'd missed being a part of each other's lives.

Even though her family disliked James, her sisters still genuinely told her that they were sorry for the current state of her marriage. They didn't judge her when she told them that deep down she wanted her marriage back intact and that she was letting James have his space, hoping he would soon get over whatever he's going through and come back home.

If either of her sisters thought she was crazy for feeling that way, neither said anything to her. She was glad because even though it made her sound desperate, she didn't want anyone telling her so. She wanted to deal with her problems her way.

It didn't even bother her anymore that she'd lost a little bit of her own self-respect when she'd given in to sleeping with James the Friday before her flight to Seattle. That entire day it weighed heavily on her mind that she was so susceptible to his wishes and demands. Her reasons for doing so always came down to one thing; she wanted her family back the way it was and if playing along is what it took for that to happen then that's what she would do. What other choice did she have? James and the kids have been her whole world for the past seventeen years and she didn't know anything else but being his wife and their mother.

She smiled knowing at least one part of her life was coming together and that was closing the distance gap with her parents and her sisters. She'd also connected with a few old friends while she was home visiting. She didn't realize how much she'd missed having others in her life besides James and the kids.

Her parents and her sisters didn't deserve her deserting them over the years and she would make it up to them. Her happy thoughts were disturbed by the shrill of Jamie hollering at her once again.

"Mom, come on. Let's go already. You're going to make

me late for my rehearsal."

She knew she had to pick her battles and today wasn't the day to start one with Jamie. They were already running late.

"Don't forget your lunch."

Jamie ignored her and didn't bother with the lunch.

"I have money. I don't want to take my lunch," Jamie said as Dana watched her leave the kitchen and enter the garage to wait for her ride to school.

Dana stood perplexed. When did her life become dealing with children with smart mouths and attitudes who ignored her? She didn't want to make Jamie late so she grabbed her keys, after placing the lunch she had prepared for her in the fridge. She then rushed to get her to school before she was late for her rehearsal.

~~

The life of a homemaker was as hard as working a full-time job. Jason was involved in every sporting event ever created and she was already running him from one practice or game to another with not much time for herself.

Jamie was heavily involved in acting and singing and if she wasn't spending her time at sporting events with her son, she was running to plays and musicals that Jamie was performing in, again, no time for herself. Even when they were in school all day, she was still busy tending to something they needed done. Today was an example.

First she ran to the store once Jamie discovered while she was out shopping for skirts that were too short, that she forgot to pick up the book for her English class that was needed by third period. Off Dana went to the bookstore after dropping Jamie at her school. She then received a call from her son telling her to also grab his cleats because he'd left those at home when he found his uniform wasn't clean and in a rush to not miss the bus, he forgot them. That reminded Dana that she needed to get back home to wash and dry his uniform and get it back to his school before the end of the day.

She longed for days when she did have some time to herself. On those few rare occasions she'd shop for things for the house or the kids. She sometimes volunteered at the kids' school, which was also for them. So in other words, even when she had spare time, it was used up doing things for everyone else.

Now back at home and finished with her tasks, she'd hoped that today, she could have a moment to herself. Both kids had after school activities and she wasn't scheduled to pick them up until after six. Maybe checking out one of the latest movies at the local theater could be a good relaxing afternoon. She checked the local listings of movies before taking a shower to prepare for enjoying a free afternoon focused on her and found a good Tyler Perry movie that she hadn't seen.

She exited the shower and had begun toweling dry when she heard the door downstairs open and close. She quickly grabbed her robe when she heard James' voice calling out for her. She hated that he still, not only had a key to the house, but used it whenever he felt like it. He was still paying all of the bills so to him he was entitled. She didn't know how to counter that since it was true. She was about to meet him on the lower level when he showed up in the doorway to her bedroom. His appearance startled her as she tried desperately to tie her robe tight around her.

"James, what are you doing here in the middle of the day?" she asked.

Seeing the look on his face as he stared at her from head to toe, she wished she'd had time to dress before he'd shown up. He had a habit of doing that every now and then, especially when the kids weren't home. Usually that meant he wanted sex. Today, she wasn't for it. Whenever he did this to her, she felt used always giving into him and then he left to go back to his latest young fling; in this case the scandalous Reese.

"I came to see you," he said. "I decided to take a late lunch and when I drove by and happened to see your car in the driveway, I decided to stop in and say hello."

Dana didn't believe him for one second. The house was located in a cul-de-sac so he wasn't driving by and noticed her car.

"Go home James," she said turning around, ignoring his presence, hoping he would get the message. He didn't.

"I am home, Dana, or have you forgotten I still pay every bill around here."

She knew better than anyone that he did; she hated that she was still so connected and vulnerable to him.

"Okay, fine. So you're here because this is your house. I know that. You remind me every time you come by and every time you write me a check to cover the household bills. You sound like a broken record and I don't want to argue because I have things to do so if you didn't want anything, the kids will be home later if you want to come back when they're here."

Dana watched as he came further into the room coming right up to her.

"I told you, I came to see you. When the kids were over recently, they told me you seemed sad all the time so I thought I'd stop by to see if you were okay."

When he reached out to rub his hands up and down the sleeves of her robe, she knew this situation wasn't good.

"James, since when do you care about what I'm feeling? That's not something you've cared about lately so why don't you state the real reason you're here so that I can get on with my day." She was losing patience quickly with his antics.

Even though she was trying to be rude, subtly, it wasn't having the effect on James that she wanted. Rather than his usual response of getting angry and turning away, he spoke softer with a hint of a smile on his face.

"Now don't be like that. Why are you so aggressive? I came here with good intentions and you're trying to pick a fight. Come on now Dana, you know I still love you. Being separated doesn't mean that we stopped caring about each other."

There was that gentle, soft, seductive tone he used whenever he wanted something from her.

His words combined with how good he smelled, she felt herself being drawn in once again. She couldn't understand why she was trying to pick a fight with him because she didn't mean to. She didn't like that they were standing in her bedroom and she wasn't dressed.

James had a way of getting her to do whatever he wanted, even if he commanded it. Technically, he was still her husband and though he'd left her, she was still in love with him. She hated that she was, but she didn't have anyone else and every time he came around, she was reminded of that.

She said nothing as she felt him lean in closer and closer until his lips touched hers in a sweet kiss that melted her hard manner even more.

"Now you know you don't want to fight with me. I didn't come here for a fight. I came to see if you were okay and to brighten up your day a little," he said, placing an even softer kiss on the side of her neck. "Don't you like when I drop by sometimes to see you? I have to say I enjoy it very much. What do you have on under this robe?"

There used to be a time when the way James touched and kissed her that her body would be set on fire with want for him, but that wasn't the case anymore. It did feel good, but it didn't arouse her like it used to. Visions of him with Reese were turning her as cold as ice and she came to her senses quickly and tried to step back from him.

"I don't think this is a good idea," she said drawing her robe even closer around her body, knowing she was completely naked underneath.

His voice became more intimate and he closed the gap between them that she'd made.

"Don't you miss me, Dana? I know we're having some problems and I'm not here anymore, but I still love you; you know that."

This was leading where it always led, she thought. He must have sensed her hesitation when she didn't respond.

"Come on Dana. I know for a fact you're not seeing anyone; at least that better be the case. I don't want men around my children. Aren't you lonely for a man's touch? Let me give you the relief I know you need."

She looked at him wondering what to say to get him to leave her alone. She hated that he made her sound lonely even if that was the case.

She had to fight back. She had to stop giving in to him.

"Where's Reese at James?" she said tersely. "I'm sure she's not happy about your impromptu visits to me in the

45

middle of the day, unless she doesn't know you're even here."

If she thought her comment would deter him, she was wrong. He wasn't deterred one bit. If nothing else, he pressed even more toward her, letting her feel how hot and hard his body was for her.

"She's where she's supposed to be and I'm here with you, right where I want to be. No matter what we're going through, I still love you. I think given a little more time, we'll work things out and I'll be back here with you and the kids and we'll be a family again. I'm trying to find that spark with you again, but I can't do it if you're always fighting me. Show me how much you love and miss me. I need to know that if I'm ever going to get myself together and realize with my family is where I should be. All this tension between us all the time isn't helping us find our way back to each other so you need to lighten up. I'm being nice and sweet and you're trying to be callous and hateful. Don't be like that," he crooned, pulling her closer to him.

She heard his words and was torn with believing him or not and she wanted to believe him more than anything. Seventeen years is a long time to be in love and married to someone and give up on any possibility that things could really work out. She wanted that, not for herself, but for her children too. She wanted her family back together again, the way it should be. She'd spent her life committed and dedicated to them and she deserved to have her family back together and happy like it should be. He'd won again, she thought.

Lowering her hands slowly, she wasn't surprised when he reached down to untie the belt holding her robe together to expose her nakedness.

She saw him look his fill.

"You are a beautiful woman with a knock out body, even after seventeen years of marriage and having two children. You stay in shape very well. I bet younger women are jealous of this gorgeous, voluptuous body you have."

No other words were exchanged as she gave into him once again. She no longer resisted as he removed the robe completely from her body. He then removed his clothes and took her to bed on the promise that things will work out for them. She had to trust and believe that.

~~

The day didn't pan out as she would have liked. Dana was finally getting dressed with enough time to get dinner started before she had to pick both kids up from after school activities. She never made it to her movie. After spending two hours in bed with James, faking her way through so that he would be done, all of a sudden he remembered he had to be someplace and expeditiously got dressed and made a hasty exit, promising her that he was going to find a way to break things off with Reese very soon and he'd be back home with them for good. She'd heard that before, many times.

In the past, she believed that, but now, after he got what he came for and she felt like a doormat, she knew it was the same words he always used to keep her hanging on. She never learned how to fight and resist him. He had no plans to be with her again, other than sexually, but she wasn't strong enough to believe it and let go. The same hold he'd had over her since she was eighteen years old, he still held over her now.

Seventeen years ago when they'd gotten married, she

knew that they would have a wonderful life. James was on the rise in the banking business and he'd promised her the world. She was eighteen when they met and he was quite a few years older. His father was president of the bank where he worked and he was being groomed to one day hold the same type of position his father held. The day she'd met him was one of the best days of her life. She'd never had an older man interested in her before.

She had graduated from high school and was planning to take a year off before going off to college. She and some friends were spending an afternoon at a local McDonald's planning some trips for fun that they would take since they were all taking a year off before college. James had been there the same day having lunch. He was gorgeous and every woman who passed by him gave him a second glance and added an extra wiggle to their walk.

While sitting with her friends, she kept looking over at him and noticed that each time she did, he was also looking at her and each time, he would smile.

Dana had been through experiences with boys before, but that had been the first time someone older had shown any real interest in her. At the time she wasn't sure how much older than her he was, but it turned out that he was seven years older than her. One of her friends dared her to go over and say hello and she never lost on a dare. She nervously got up to throw away discarded trash, even though she hadn't finished eating her food. It happened that James was sitting right next to one of the trash cans. It wasn't the one that was closest to her, but she needed a reason to be closer to him.

As she slowly put her trash in the bin piece by piece, she looked over at him and sure enough, he was staring at her.

She wasn't sure what to say and hoped he would say something before she went back to her seat. As luck would have it, he did. He told her how pretty she was and made her laugh when he told her he was praying that she was eighteen years old because if not he was embarrassed. She reassured him she was and they began to talk. She laughed even more when he asked her to produce identification that proved she was eighteen. Once she did they talked until he had to leave to get back to work.

Dana went back to the table with her friends and the first thing she told them was that she was in love. She and James had been inseparable from that day forward. Her family tried to keep them apart, but since she was eighteen years old, there wasn't much they could do.

They didn't like him because he didn't like that she wanted to have a career of her own. When the time came for her to prepare for college a year later, James proposed. Her family told her he'd proposed to keep her close to him and to keep her under his control. She didn't listen to them then and now she saw what they saw. She was disgusted that it took her so many years to see that they were right, but at this point, right or wrong, she believed her dedication was to her husband and her children. This was the life she'd chosen and no one was to blame for that, but her.

She and James married right after her twentieth birthday. He'd promised her that they could have children right away that she could spend all of her time with them because she wouldn't need to work. After watching her mother work as hard as her father, she didn't want that for herself and her children. It was true that her mother spent a lot of time with her and her sisters, but Dana knew there were times when her mother wished she could have been home more, especially when they were very young. Dana wanted to have kids and if she could spend time not missing any of their growing up, she wanted to do that. She could always take college courses when time permitted or after her kids were older and in school all day. She made the decision to say yes to James' proposal and for a lot of years, she was happy she did.

It wasn't until he started spending more and more time away from home, hanging with friends, going to strip bars and meeting outside women that she knew it wasn't the life she had signed up for, but she loved him. He was her first and he had done exactly what he said he would do.

Working his way up in the banking business, he was a bank president and sat on several boards of other corporations which netted him a lot of financial freedom that he used to splurge on her and the kids. She didn't realize the sacrifice for living a good life would be her peace of mind and her self-respect.

She knew early about the other women, but she let it go because he was a great provider. They lived in a big beautiful home and she always drove a top of the line car with plenty of money to do whatever she wanted. Her kids longed for nothing that money could buy and being a stay at home mother, she was always around when they needed her.

Reflecting on her life, she saw that outside of James and the kids, she didn't have any close friends and she didn't stay in contact with any of her childhood friends. James made sure he found something wrong with every friend she had or tried to make, telling her that her first priority was to take care of him and the kids and being the loyal wife and she went along with that. She had a great life and didn't want to make unnecessary trouble in it.

Keeping her away from her family was another part of his plan. He felt that her family always intruded on the life they were trying to make, so two years after getting married, James moved them from Seattle to Chicago, clear across the country. He said it was a business decision, but she knew that he didn't want her family in her ear giving her any advice or any ideas about the life she was living. He wanted to be the only person in her life and she gave that to him.

The few friends she did try to connect with once they moved to Chicago, James always found something wrong with them too. He wouldn't be cordial to them and therefore, they would come around less and less. He made it clear to her that she needed all of her free time to focus on keeping her family happy and making a nice home for them. She had done that and the years of getting satisfaction out of that had died years ago and now she felt trapped.

One regret she had was that she never went to college or held any type of job. She loved volunteering at the kids' schools and that fed more and more into her desire to become a teacher. There was a time when she wanted to take classes to pursue a degree in early childhood education, but never got the opportunity to do so. Every time she would bring the idea up to James he would shoot it down, telling her she had all she needed taking care of him and the kids and because he said it, she believed it, whether it was true or not.

Dana spent year after year doing what was natural, which was taking care of the kids, cooking, cleaning, taking care of James and making sure whatever they needed, she took care of because she was the homemaker. It was now starting to feel like it wasn't enough, especially after James walked out on them.

She thought back to that day a year ago and she'd known something wasn't right. James had been distant for months and had been spending less and less time at home. It was no longer work or other women. She could tell he was making plans to leave. When he finally did, he told her that he didn't know what it was, but that he wasn't happy anymore. He needed some time to figure out what it was and while he did that, he would live elsewhere. He left it to her to explain to the kids and they immediately blamed her. They said it must have been something she'd done that drove him away.

James was a great father and a great provider and the kids' lives didn't change much, other than the fact that their father didn't live with them anymore. He made up for that by spoiling them with whatever they wanted and as long as they were happy, she let it slide.

She didn't remember the day she started allowing the kids to treat her with a lack of respect like their father, but it did happen and she allowed it. Things had to change. She couldn't go on like this. That was her last thought as she ran out the door to pick them up.

Chapter Five
DANA

"Your usual, Mr. Hunter?" the cashier asked from behind the counter.

"Actually I think I'll try something different today. How about a turkey club with extra tomatoes and two bottles of water? I appreciate it Kim," Hunter Gray said as he paid and stepped to the side to wait on his lunch. He looked around the deli and didn't see any empty tables. There were plenty of tables with one person, but none were empty. All of the counter seats were also full. He came into the same deli twice a week before work for the great sandwiches and most days the crowd was smaller. The classes he taught at the local college didn't start until after three in the afternoon, so he always stopped in prior to heading to campus. He was close enough to the school that he didn't have to rush as time drew nearer to the start time and he didn't have to worry about rush hour traffic. Today the deli was especially crowded. Looking around and then out of the window of the deli, he understood why there was a larger than usual crowd; the new bookstore across the street was having a grand opening.

While he waited he looked around for a table mate that wouldn't mind him sharing their table. He felt awkward asking a guy so he looked for a woman that wouldn't think he was trying to hit on her or who looked friendly enough that she wouldn't find him sharing a table with her as intrusive of her space. Hunter grabbed his food, looked around and noticed one woman looking as if she were about to leave and he headed toward the table where she sat alone.

"Excuse me, are you leaving? I'm in search of a table," he asked.

"No, I'm not leaving. I was getting up to get another bottle of water, but feel free to share if you like. I really don't mind."

Wow, what a beautiful woman. He would be crazy not to sit across from such a gorgeous woman and enjoy his lunch, so he took her up on the offer.

"Are you sure?" he asked.

"I'm sure, have a seat," the woman said, waving him toward the empty seat as she left to get her bottle of water.

Hunter watched her walk away and loved the gracefulness of her walk, making it look like she was gliding. He took a moment to admire her exquisite beauty. She looked to be about five foot seven or five foot eight inches tall. Her skin was the color of coffee after placing a small amount of cream in it. Her tone was gorgeous and blemish free. Her hair was long and cascaded around her face where it then rested on her shoulders. It was a beautiful shade of light brown with gold streaks throughout. Her body was voluptuous and rounded in all of the right places. Hunter wondered if she was married and he was glaring at another man's wife. It had been a very long time since he'd had an instantaneous response to a woman and that was saying a lot considering the number of women he encountered on any given day. Besides her obvious beauty, there was an aura about her that had him drawn to her after only a few seconds of conversation.

When she returned he was already enjoying his sandwich. He stood to help her with her chair before retaking his seat again.

"Thank you," she said and Hunter felt like he'd died and gone to heaven. Her voice was soft and it matched her glowing smile.

He distracted himself from staring by taking a bite of his sandwich.

"Hello, my name is Dana."

After swallowing, he finally said, "Hello Dana. I'm Hunter; Hunter Gray. Thank you for sharing your table. It's a big crowd in here today."

"No problem and you're right. I think the crowd is because of the grand opening of the bookstore across the street. I came from there and it's packed with people."

They settled into idle chatter as they ate.

"Did you find any good reads at the opening?" he asked.

"Actually I did. More than I wanted to. Normally I do most of my reading on my electronic reader, but there are still times when I need the feel of an actual book."

Hunter understood that, being an educator.

"I tell my students that all the time when they wonder why I won't let them use electronic readers in class. I want them to get used to having a book in their hands. I love the accessibility a reader or a tablet provides, but I never want them to forget what it feels like to touch and read from an actual book."

"Students? You're a teacher?" Dana asked.

"Yes, I'm a professor at the college up the street. I teach

English Literature courses."

"So I already know you love books."

He couldn't believe how lovely Dana was. They had been talking long enough that they had finished eating, but neither moved to get up to leave.

"Are you coming from teaching for the day or are you finished already?" Dana inquired.

Hunter looked at his watch.

"I have two classes this evening, with the first starting in about an hour."

"What about you? Did you take off today to attend the opening or heading to work yourself?" he asked.

"Actually, I'm waiting to pick my daughter up from school. She goes to a middle school not far from here so I figured I'd relax and enjoy lunch until it was time to go get her. I'm a stay at home mom so when I can find time to get out of the house and enjoy a bookstore opening or other daytime activities, I try to take advantage of that since the opportunity seems so rare."

"Is your daughter your only child?"

"No, I also have a son who's sixteen going on twenty-five," she said, laughing at the thought of her smart mouthed teenager.

"Your husband isn't going to walk in and think we're on a date or anything if he sees us is he," Hunter added while smiling at Dana.

"Husband?" Dana asked.

Hunter looked at her bewildered. He was looking right at the large diamond wedding ring on her finger. He was disappointed when he'd spotted it, but figured he would still enjoy the conversation while they ate. He saw no harm done.

Dana saw the direction of his gaze.

"Oh, no not at all. I'm separated at the moment," she said sadly.

"I'm sorry to hear that. I hope things turn out well."

"It's okay. It's actually been a year since we separated and I haven't taken my ring off yet."

"Oh," was all Hunter said. A woman separated a year and still wearing her wedding ring is a clear sign that she's not over her husband yet and he knew that feeling. It took him a while after his wife left him to finally get used to not wearing his ring, so he could relate to her struggle. He also noticed that the mentioning of her marriage made Dana seem uncomfortable and he didn't want that.

"I'm sorry if the subject makes you feel down. I wasn't trying to pry and I apologize if it seemed as if I was."

When she looked over at him and smiled, he knew she was okay.

"There is nothing to apologize for because there was no way you could know. I suppose it's crazy to still have it on. I feel that until we are actually divorced, I'm still married. I don't know."

She felt a little awkward talking to a complete stranger about her marriage or lack of one. He didn't seem to mind, which was good. She liked talking to him. He was easy to converse with and besides being extremely handsome, he made her feel very comfortable.

"So since we're digging, how about you? Do you have any children or are you married?" she asked, even though she didn't see a wedding ring on his finger.

"I have a daughter Coral who is away at college enjoying her freshman year and I am divorced."

Dana leaned in a little closer to him. "Should I say I'm

sorry that you're divorced or is it a good thing and I should say congratulations?"

Hunter didn't know how to respond and wasn't sure how serious she was until she laughed so loud, others in the deli turned to look at them. It caused him to laugh.

Saying congratulations in this situation will suffice. We are both in a much happier place now. We stayed married a few years longer than we probably should have because of my daughter, but once it was finally over, it was definitely over."

Dana sat, listening to him and knew that's exactly what she was feeling. It was time she understood a divorce was inevitable for her too. Her wedding ring began to feel like a ton of bricks resting on her finger. She too would probably be much happier if she and James called it quits and divorced. Being in limbo had no benefit for either of them and especially not to the kids. It only gave James a ticket to come and go as he pleased leaving her to feel like sometimes she's still his wife and other times, someone he came to see when he needed additional sexual gratification. She allowed him to feel that way because he knew he held the strings to her life.

"Well, it looks like my lunch is over," Hunter said, not really wanting to leave. He was really enjoying talking to Dana. Though he could see a sadness in her eyes, he knew that behind that, he was looking at a remarkable woman. He only wished she could see that for herself. He had encountered enough women who didn't understand her worth to know what it looked like when it was staring back at him. He wished men understood the negative effect their bad treatment of women had on them. It left many women as damaged goods and when the next man came along, they didn't see him. All they could see was how the last man treated them. He'd dated several of those types of women since his divorce and no matter how he tried to explain to them that he was not their former spouses or mates, they were too deeply scarred to see the forest for the trees. He actually saw something different in Dana which made him want to know more about her. He wished he had the time, but class was starting soon.

"Well it was nice to meet you Hunter," Dana said with excitement in her voice. She surprised herself at how good it felt to sit and talk to a man and enjoy the time. James had been the only man in her life for so long that she'd never experienced a fun and open conversation with another one.

"The feeling is mutual. Can I throw any of your trash away for you before I leave?" he asked.

Dana felt like a kid in a candy store. Someone was asking if they could do something for her for a change and that never happens.

"No thank you. I'm going to finish these chips before I head out and I'll toss everything out then."

She watched as he stood to get rid of his trash. Hunter was intriguing and extremely handsome. Something about him had her longing for real attention from a man, something she hadn't gotten from James in years. She felt a twinge of guilt as she twisted the wedding ring on her finger. She knew she shouldn't be feeling an attraction to another man, especially since she was still married and had scolded James many times about his wayward eyes.

She let her gaze follow Hunter and she admired the amazing specimen that he was. He was taller than her with a lean, toned body and what added to his allure was how impeccably dressed he was in a pair of black dressed pants with a black pullover sweater. Sitting across from him while they ate, she was embarrassed every time he caught her staring at him. She couldn't help herself because he was beyond handsome. His hair was a cut close on the sides with more on top and with his light complexion and handsome features, he reminded her of the singer Maxwell.

There was something about him that seemed irresistible. She liked how easily they flowed from one conversation topic to another. She hadn't given any man the time of day since James had moved out and none had really approached her which was probably due to the wedding ring she refused to take off. Maybe it was because she was still too glass eyed for a husband who didn't really want her anymore. All she knew for now was that she was captivated by the handsome stranger and wished they'd had more time to talk.

"Dana, the pleasure was all mine. Thank you for making my lunch more enjoyable than it has been in a long time. I hope I run into you again," Hunter said hopeful when he returned to the table.

"Well with the bookstore across the street from here, you just may."

"Take care Dana and don't stop smiling. Yours is a beautiful one.

She blushed. It had been a long time since a man told her she was beautiful and meant it. She could see in his eyes that he really meant those words. James said it all the time, especially when he was trying to get her in bed.

She watched as he grabbed his black leather bomber jacket off of the back of the chair to put it on and she held her breath when she noticed his muscular physique through his shirt when he reached to put his arms in the sleeves. Dana felt warm all of a sudden and wondered where the flash of heat was coming from.

Hunter said one last goodbye as he exited the deli and turned to wave at her. She waved back and hoped that she would see him again. She was about to turn back around in her seat when she noticed Hunter coming back through the door.

"Did you forget something," she asked, looking around the table they were sitting at to see if he'd left anything.

"No, I didn't leave anything. I wanted you to know how much I enjoyed talking to you today and I wanted to leave you my card in case you want to get together for lunch again or maybe coffee. No pressure at all, if you feel comfortable with that. I'll leave it up to you."

Dana hesitated before taking the card. Was he asking her out on a date, she wondered? Should she take it or would she be inviting trouble? Would taking it mean she was being unfaithful to James? Maybe she was making too much out of the gesture and he was only being friendly. She didn't know, but she wanted to find out and she wouldn't if she didn't take the card.

She took it and said thank you. She didn't want to acknowledge that she would call, but in case she got up the nerve to, she wanted to have the number to do so.

Hunter didn't say anything else; he left after she accepted his card.

She stared at the card not knowing how to react to accepting it. She was still a married woman, separated or not and her attraction to another man is as bad as what James was doing with other women, without the sex of course. Was she really wrong for accepting the card?

Probably, but she decided to keep it anyway. She wasn't planning to get romantically involved with him. She glanced down at her wedding ring once again. She had spent about an hour having lunch and talking with Hunter and for the first time, she said to herself that her marriage was in fact over. If she was feeling the kind of attraction to Hunter that she was feeling, there was no way her relationship with James would ever be the same. Her short interaction with Hunter told her that she needed to once and for all move on. She wasn't sure how she'd go about it, but it was over. It wasn't because of Hunter that she was now realizing that. He happened to be the vessel by which she saw herself in the mirror and didn't like what she'd seen. Her life had been at a standstill for a long time and she no longer saw herself. She only saw herself as Jamie and Jason's mother and James' wife. She'd forgotten what she wanted and needed, but the little card she held in her hand told her it was time to find Dana again and figure out what she wanted for herself.

Chapter Six
DANA

"No sleepover Jamie, absolutely not."

"Why can't I have a sleepover mom? You're not doing anything. You never go anywhere so you'll be home so why can't I have some friends over for a weekend sleepover?"

Dana was getting tired of arguing back and forth with her daughter.

"I said so," she finally replied, hopefully ending the conversation.

Jamie stomped around her room cleaning things up muttering under her breath.

"Dad would let me have a sleepover," Dana heard her say.

Her anger boiled over.

"What did you say?" she asked even though she knew she'd heard Jamie quite well.

Louder now so that Dana could hear her Jamie repeated herself in a sarcastic tone.

"Dad would let me have a sleepover. He said if you wouldn't that I could stay at his place this weekend and I could have friends over."

Here we go again, Dana thought. Everything was about what James would do.

"Did he really?" she asked.

Dana wasn't falling for it; not anymore. She was tired of her kids playing her and their father against each other, trying to get their way. He'd taught them the game of manipulation well. Defending her actions and decisions to him and her children was getting old for her. If they want to continue to make her the punching bag, this weekend, they'd all do it from a distance.

"Well you know what, call him then because like I said, you're not having a sleepover this weekend. You had one a few weeks ago. Whether I'm going to be home or not, you aren't having one."

Dana was furious.

"Go right now and call your father and tell him to come and get you so that Reese can supervise your sleepover because I'm sure he has no desire to hang around a bunch of thirteen year old girls. Let me know what time he's coming to get you. When I say no about something that's exactly what I mean, so if he's willing, then go there because I said no sleepover here this weekend and I mean it."

Dana stomped off into her room and slammed her door. She had also had the same conversation with her son a few hours before when he asked to invite the football team over for movies and pizza. She said no to him also. She wanted a weekend at home in peace without other people's kids running around. If they both decided to spend another weekend with their father, she would gladly open the door and lock it behind them on their way out because she could use another break. In fact, she didn't want to wait to see if either child would call James, she was going to call him herself. She grabbed the phone and dialed him before she calmed down and changed her mind.

"James, can you pick up Jamie and Jason for the weekend when you get off?" she said into the phone when he picked up, not giving him a chance to say hello.

"Why? They were just with me."

"What are your kids limited on visits now?" she asked with a little more force behind her voice than she'd intended.

"That's not what I said Dana. Apparently you're upset about something from your tone so don't turn this around on me. What's going on?" he asked.

"They both claim that if I don't let them have friends over this weekend that you told them they could come over to your place and do it. I've said no to anyone coming over, so come get them. They'll be at the door waiting and if you don't show up, I'll bring them over and drop them off. The choice is yours." She didn't wait for his response. She hung up in the midst of his retort.

For the first time in a long time, she was tired of them all and needed a break.

She went to Jamie's room first.

"Get up, get dressed and pack a bag for the weekend. Your dad is coming to get you."

The look of shock on Jamie's face gave Dana the satisfaction she needed. It wasn't often she shouted demands at either of them and took the necessary control over situations with them always trying to keep the peace and make them happy.

"Why? I didn't say I wanted to go over to his place. I didn't even call him. I've decided it's okay if I don't have a sleepover."

The nerve of her, Dana thought. Not this time though.

"Oh, you've decided did you?" Dana asked, tossing all patience with her daughter out the window.

"Yeah, I'm fine here at home this weekend with you."

She was a consolation prize? No more patience with her teenager existed.

"Don't test me Jamie. Get up, get dressed and packed *NOW* and don't make me tell you twice." she shouted, loud enough to wake the dead.

She then went in search of Jason and barked the same orders to him.

In less than an hour, James was at the door, using his key to enter. She didn't stand around long enough for conversation. She told both kids she loved them, because she did and she went to her room and again, slammed the door shut. A few minutes later, she heard the front door shut and looked out of her bedroom window to see her husband usher both kids into his car and they drove off.

~~

It was Friday night and for once, Hunter didn't have plans to hang out with his buddies. They were all going to a baseball game and he wasn't in the mood. It had been a long work week and he wanted to relax at home. He was planning to spend the evening working on his business plan to open an evening tutorial program for high school students. He wanted to do his part to help them prepare for the transition to college. It was disturbing to him how unprepared a lot of the kids were for classes on the college level. Many of them were failing because there was a gap in their learning from high school to college. He had been thinking for a few years about opening an after school program for high school juniors and seniors to focus on what they will need to be successful their first few semesters of college.

For the next upcoming semester, he was planning to move all of his scheduled classes to daytime hours so that as soon as he found a location, he could open up his tutorial center.

Before settling in, he waited to hear from his daughter before ordering a pizza and spending the rest of the evening working. His phone rang right on time.

"Hey Coral," he said answering on the first ring.

"Hey dad!"

"How are you? How's school?"

"I'm fine dad. School is going really good; better than I thought. There is so much to do on campus everyday besides classes, so I'm staying busy and making lots of friends."

"I'm glad to hear that."

"What are you doing dad?"

"I'm about to order a pizza, relax and do a little more work on my business plan for the center. I'm looking to be up and running right after the spring semester ends."

"On a Friday night? Really dad? You live a very boring life."

"Boring? I don't live a boring life at all. Fridays are my busiest days at work and I didn't feel like doing anything. You'll understand when you get older. Life isn't about being out and about all the time."

"I know dad. What about a date? You know a woman? Remember those?" she said laughing.

"Very funny Coral. No I don't have a date tonight, but don't count your old man out because I still got it!" he said laughing along with her.

"TMI dad. That is way too much information. Well I

don't want to keep you from your pizza and work. I wanted to call and say hello, tell you I love you and thanks for being the best dad ever! I'm also going to email you the homecoming schedule if you plan to visit me for the game. I know you said you wanted to."

"Yes, I'm coming for homecoming. I'll print it out and make flight arrangements so I won't have to make the long drive after a long work week."

"Okay dad. I'm going to email you right now. Mom said she's not coming."

Hunter could hear the sadness in his daughter's voice. "I'm sure she has a good reason for not coming Coral so don't be too hard on her. She probably has a work thing. You know how that can be."

"Dad, don't make excuses for her. If she really wanted to be here she would make sure she was free. She knew like you that it was coming up. I think she's still mad that I chose to live with you and not her. What do you think?"

"Coral, it's been years since you came to live with me and your mother loves you very much. No, I don't think she's still angry about that. I think she really understood that you didn't want to be uprooted from your life and your friends to move a few hundred miles away and besides the struggles she had back then, it wasn't a good environment for you. She's remarried and happy now and I believe it's a work thing, so go easy on her. I'll be there with bells on. You know I will never miss anything. I'm sure your mom will figure things out so that she can be supportive too. You still have more years of college and events that she can come to. Give her a little wiggle room okay?" he asked.

"Sure dad, anything for you."

"Okay, let's move on. I'll print the information and book

my travel. I'll see you in two weeks. Love you sweet pea," he said right before hanging up.

After logging in to his email, he didn't see an email from her yet, but what he did see was an email from a DCarr. He didn't recognize the name, but smiled when he saw the subject line that read, 'Bronson's Deli Turkey club.' That was the place he loved to eat lunch and he had only had the turkey club once, which was the day he'd met Dana a few weeks ago. He hadn't been able to stop thinking about her since then and every time he went into the deli, he looked around for her, but never saw her there again. He tried not to focus on it too much since she apparently was still struggling when it came to her marriage and he didn't want to be any kind of a distraction for her. He did enjoy talking to her and hoped that if she ever became a free woman, that she would perhaps look him up. It had to be her he thought as he opened the email and read.

Hello Hunter. It was nice meeting you and talking to you at the deli. I wasn't sure if I should call or not and I thought an email would be appropriate for contact. I know it's been a few weeks and I hope that you remember me. I don't know the etiquette for emailing someone as opposed to calling them on the phone. I wanted to reach out and say hello and to thank you for the business card and the great conversation over lunch. I also wanted to thank you because as strange as this may seem when you read this, you opened my eyes to something that day. It was refreshing talking to you and that was something I had not felt in a long time. After you left, I struggled with the feeling that I was doing something wrong when I accepted the card from you. For a while I felt like I was no better than my husband. I wondered what kind of signal I would be sending if I actually called or emailed you knowing I'm still married. Is it wrong to do, even though I'm separated? My way of thinking is that until a couple is actually divorced, you are still married so any contact with someone could be dangerous to the marriage vows taken. I knew I was still living by marriage vows that only existed because I refuse to remove the last symbol of a marriage that I know is most likely over. I don't know what I'm trying to do by emailing you, but I wanted to let you know that talking to you that day was invigorating and it made me smile in a way that I had not done in a very long time. I decided to email you when I made the decision to take off my wedding ring and to find the fun side of life again. I don't know what happens now, but I wanted you to know I didn't forget that I had the card and again, I wanted to reach out and say hello. Now that you have my email address, feel free to use it. Have a good night. Dana.

It was her and he was glad she'd contacted him. He didn't care whether it was by phone or email, he was glad to hear from her. Perhaps she wouldn't mind meeting him for another sandwich one day soon. He wasn't a pushy guy and didn't want to seem that way with her. If her marriage was truly over and she was willing to move forward from it, then he would respect that without adding his own agenda. He wanted to see her again. He didn't want to wait to reach back out to her. He responded immediately with an email of his own.

Hi Dana. I'm glad you reached out and email is fine if that makes you comfortable. There is no etiquette; do what feels comfortable. I wasn't sure you would contact me. I'm glad you did and I hope you'll continue to do so. I would love to continue talking to you if you are even open to that. I'm sorry to hear of the struggles you went through after our chat at the deli. I didn't want you to feel like you were doing anything wrong by either still wearing your wedding ring or by accepting my card. I would never push you in any direction when it came to how you handled your situation. You seemed like you could use someone to talk to and if that works for you that works for me too. Whenever you are ready, let me know and maybe we can meet at the deli and enjoy more conversation over sandwiches. I will leave it up to you. Until then, keep smiling. Hunter.

~~

Saturday came sooner than Dana wanted it to. She had enjoyed a nice evening the night before. She normally worked out in her family room, but last night, after her husband picked up the kids, she got dressed and went to a local recreation center to do some line dancing. She'd heard some women talking about it earlier in the week when she went supermarket shopping and wanted to get out of the house. She'd had a great time and the women even invited her to come back again. It felt great to do something that didn't revolve around her children, though she loved them dearly. She needed to find more time to do things for herself.

She also knew it wasn't a coincidence that she'd met Hunter, a college professor that day in the deli. She had longed for a life as a teacher, which was something she'd given up on years ago. After talking with him and hearing about his classes and the students, the desire to become a teacher was stronger than ever. It had been weeks since she'd run into him at the deli and when she came in from the gym, she went in search of the card he'd given her. She wanted to thank him for the conversation that helped her to think clearly about a lot of things in life.

She had been nervous after sending the email to him. She was too nervous to wait around for his response. She'd never shown any interest in any man since before James. Was she actually interested in Hunter? She wasn't sure, but all she knew was she had enjoyed talking to him at the deli and she wanted to reach out to him to connect again. Perhaps he could offer her some help on where to start if she wanted to take some college courses.

Her nervousness over what his response would be sent her back out for the evening. She decided to stroll through the local mall and grab a bite to eat. It was the only way to stay away from her computer and to keep her from checking her email. She shocked herself at the impression her brief encounter with him had left her with. He had no idea that the words he'd said told her a lot about herself. When he mentioned that he and his ex-wife were happier after the divorce, she understood that she too was in a dead space in her marriage. She didn't know how to remedy it.

Her daughter Jamie saying she never went anywhere or did anything stuck with her also. She didn't need to sit at home, especially when the kids were gone. She shot that email to Hunter and then ran right out the door.

For the first time in a long time, she took a long look at her life and didn't like the direction it was going in, just as she hated all of the wasted years of doing nothing for herself that would make her happy.

She'd come in after her trip to the mall and couldn't resist checking to see if Hunter had responded. When she saw he had, she couldn't stop smiling. That was new for her. He wanted to see her again. She didn't know why, but he did. He had to know that she was a lost cause. His last impression of her was of a woman still pining for a man who clearly didn't want her. She hadn't even bothered to stop wearing her wedding ring, though James had stopped wearing his even before he moved out. She looked down at her hand where her wedding ring once sat and loved the new ring she'd bought for herself at the mall. She already felt like a new woman. It was time to move on.

She didn't respond right away, but went to bed smiling after reading his email. Smiling was now her favorite thing to do in spite of what direction her life was going in.

Now in the light of the next day, she had plans to do house cleaning and laundry since the kids were still with their father. That was the plan until her cell phone made a sound letting her know she had a voicemail. She played it and felt disgusted when she heard James' voice telling her that the kids were having a good time and that Reese was chaperoning them all at the diner near his condo so he was going to drop by the house to see her. She knew exactly what that meant. He wanted sex and she wasn't waiting around to be used again. She quickly showered, dressed, grabbed her phone and purse and got out before he showed up. She wasn't sure she was strong enough to stand up to him right now and knew it would be best if she wasn't around when he showed up.

She had been in her car driving around not sure what she wanted to do. She decided to go see the movie she'd wanted to see a few weeks ago. Checking the listing, she saw that it was still playing in the theater, so she headed for the afternoon showing.

Her phone vibrated several times while she was in the

theater. She wasn't answering anyone until the movie was over. It wasn't too often she got time to herself and she needed it.

When the movie was over and she'd laughed so hard at the latest comedy from Tyler Perry, she exited the theater and reached to check her messages. There were several from both kids with a list of things they needed her to do for them. There were also a few messages from James asking where she was and why she wasn't answering his calls. He had been by the house a few times and she was nowhere to be found.

She wasn't ready to venture home yet and decided to take a leap. She pulled out the card Hunter had given her and was about to send him another email when she decided to call instead.

"Hello, this is Hunter," she heard him say when he answered. She liked the sound of his deep voice that reminded her of the singer Barry White.

She hesitated at first; never being sure of herself and this was one of those times where she wondered what she was thinking calling him. Separated or not she was still a married woman. No time to back down now, she thought.

"Hello?" Dana heard him say again.

"Uh, yes, hello Hunter. It's Dana Carr from the deli?" she said, nervously.

"Dana, hello, how are you?"

He sounded genuinely happy to hear from her.

"I'm fine. I hope I'm not interrupting anything? I can always call you another time." she said, pacing around the inside of the theater.

"Now that you've called, I have all the time in the world. I've been checking my email to see if you'd replied to my message. It's nice to hear from you."

"I was out and about and thought I would call to say hello."

"I'm glad you did," he said.

And then there was silence. She didn't know if she should invite him out for coffee or what she should say. She didn't know the decorum. She had never entertained the idea of another man in all of the years of her marriage, including this last year of the separation. She wasn't sure what to do next since she'd called him.

Hunter could tell reaching wasn't familiar to her so he helped her along, knowing it probably took every ounce of strength to call him.

"Listen, Dana if you're not busy, would you like to meet for a sandwich at the deli?"

"That would be nice," she heard herself saying before she had a chance to digest that she'd said yes.

"Okay, I'll grab a quick shower and meet you there in about thirty minutes? Are you near the deli or do you need longer?"

"No, I'm actually not far at all, so thirty minutes is good. I'll meet you there."

She hung up and exhaled the breath she had been holding in the whole time. She was having lunch with a man. A man who was not her husband and where she thought guilt would set in, happiness showed up. She smiled all the way to her car.

Once at the deli, she grabbed a table and waited for Hunter to show up.

"Hello beautiful."

Dana looked up into the deep, dark and alluring eyes of Hunter.

"Hello," she replied, bashfully. She gazed in admiration at how good he looked. Unlike that day that they'd met when he was dressed in all black work attire, today he was dressed down in jeans that were made for his body. He wore a t-shirt that was taut across his chest and the leather bomber jacket he wore gave him a rugged look that made him look casual yet sexy.

"I hope I haven't kept you waiting too long. I got a call from my daughter as I was about to walk out and I had to log into my laptop to get an email she was sending over. Did you already know what you wanted to eat? I'll go up and place our order."

"Yes, I'm going to have the shrimp salad sandwich with coleslaw. I already have my drink," she said holding up a bottle of water.

"I'll be right back," he said as he removed his jacket and went to place their orders.

Dana was nervous. She wasn't sure what she was doing. She watched Hunter as he placed their orders and while he did so, she shifted nervously in her chair and removed her own jacket to get more comfortable. In the back of her mind, she was still questioning her decision to meet him for lunch. This was new to her and she was still questioning herself when he returned.

"Dana, are you okay. You look a little worried about something."

She didn't know how to tell him that she should probably leave.

Understanding crossed his face.

"It's okay Dana. I want you to know that I understand if this is a little uncomfortable and new for you. Look, no pressure here okay? It's only a few sandwiches and some friendly conversation and if at any time you feel out of place, let me know. I told you, I've been where you are, caught in a marriage not sure what direction it would go in, so being here with me is leaving you confused. Believe me when I say, I'm not trying to get anything from you other than your company. If that makes you uncomfortable, please tell me because that's not my intention. I can just as easily change our order to take-out."

She heard nothing, but sincerity. She wasn't accustomed to that and she liked it. She liked being told the honest truth from the heart and she felt like she was getting that from him. He really cared about her level of comfort being with him. She needed to relax.

"No, Hunter. I'm fine. I was questioning myself a little, but it has nothing to do with my level of comfort being here with you. I'm okay. So, tell me about your daughter," she said.

~~

Dana walked back into her quiet house and thought over the great time she'd had with Hunter. They sat for hours eating, talking, laughing and joking. Being around him was stimulating.

She had been with James for so long, she didn't realize other men were charming and honest with their thoughts and feelings. He even seemed interested when she shared with him her desire to go back to school to teach. She wasn't sure how to go about doing so with the busy schedule her kids had that consumed her day.

Many times she'd told her dreams of going to school to become a teacher to James and he'd shot her down, giving her no support. When she mentioned her desire to teach to Hunter, he told her to let him know if there was anything he could do to help her reach her goal. After getting nothing but rejection from James for years and years, it was uplifting to hear Hunter say she should go for it.

He told her a lot about what happened in his marriage that made it end badly. The best thing for him that resulted from his marriage was his daughter Coral. Dana could tell they were very close and unlike her relationship with her own children, Hunter's relationship with his daughter was built on respect.

She felt like she'd lost the respect of her children the moment her husband walked out on them. Apparently her children were suffering as much as she was by her not being able to break free of her husband's grasp. She should have filed for divorce already. She knew he was never going to come back to her and the kids one hundred percent. She would never have her life back and even if she could, she wasn't sure she even wanted it back. Her life with James was not a happy one and she spent years unfulfilled and blaming James when the blame was solely on her. She loved him and her kids, but life had been strictly about them. Not much of it was about her.

During her visit home with her family they confirmed what she already knew; her life needed to change. The moment she saw everyone again, she cried like a baby. She never wanted the hugs between her and her three sisters to ever end. They each had children who were strangers to her and none of them knew much about Jamie and Jason either. It was time Dana brought her family back together again. Her kids had cousins who longed to get to know them and she needed to make that happen. This was something she did by allowing herself to be manipulated by James for years.

She tried stopping by to pay a visit to her high school friend while she was home, but she wasn't there so she made a vow that she would call her and if they could gather up some form of a friendship again, she would do that.

Her talks with her family and with Hunter made all the sense in the world. She needed to figure out how to find herself again.

The biggest step forward for her was that out of her conversation with Hunter, he'd left her with information on how to enroll in college courses. She already felt like a new woman.

Chapter Seven
DANA

"Mom, we're home."

"Hi kids," she replied when they were all in the same room. "Did you have a great time with your dad this weekend?"

"We had fun. I really wanted to come home though," Jamie said sadly.

"I know, but you were being difficult so you needed to stay with your dad. No more back and forth and no more trying to get your way by playing the daddy card. I've had enough of that."

"Whatever," Jamie said before leaving the room, obviously mad.

Jason disappeared too.

Dana was glad because she still had a lot to do. It was Sunday and she'd been in all day doing research online.

Hunter had given her a lot of great leads on taking courses and she had been checking out websites where she could get a degree from the comfort of her own home. She'd discovered some promising leads and looked forward to following up on them Monday after the kids were off to school. She'd have the entire day to make phone calls to register for her first set of classes.

Somewhere her phone was ringing. Her heart raced when she picked it up and saw that it was Hunter calling. She didn't want the kids to hear her so she went to a private spot in the house to take the call. The kids were getting their baths for bed so she should be out of their ear range.

"Hi Hunter."

"Hey there. I was calling to say hello and to see if you'd done any research on the sites I gave you."

"I did. You gave me a lot of good information. I'm going to make some calls tomorrow to see if I can register for classes. I didn't realize you could get a degree in such a short period of time and that semesters started all the time, especially on line. I'm excited about the possibilities. I guess I needed a boost and some information on where to begin. How was the rest of your evening?" she asked.

"Filled with thoughts of you," he replied.

She didn't know what to say. This was all new to her. Her husband had stopped saying nice, sweet things to her years before they'd even split up.

"Dana, did you hear me?" Hunter queried.

"Yes I did, I'm sorry. I heard you and I've been thinking about you. I enjoyed our time together yesterday at the deli."

"I hope you have some free time to talk tonight. I know you said your kids were coming back home tonight. Am I interrupting?"

"No, you're fine. They're getting ready for bed. They have school tomorrow and I was doing a few things around the house that can certainly wait for another time."

"Good," Hunter replied. "So tell me more about your plans once you get started with your classes. Did you know you could also get some classroom hours by volunteering at one of the local schools? You could even volunteer at either of the schools your kids go to."

"Oh goodness no. They would both have heart attacks if I stepped foot in their schools without it being to bring them something they needed or if it wasn't for something special. I've volunteered before, but it's never been on a consistent basis. I probably could do one of the elementary schools for a few hours each day. That's the age range I'd like to teach anyway. The classes I'm thinking of taking can be done any time of the day which works out good. I won't have to sit in front of the computer at a specific time of the day each day. I may have time to stop in at one of the local elementary schools tomorrow to check into that. Thank you for giving me some great ideas. I haven't been this motivated in a long time."

"I'm glad I could help and if you have any questions about anything, let me know. I'm available when you need me. I look forward to hearing from you about your progress. Don't give up no matter what."

"Thank you for the encouragement Hunter. It really means a lot to me."

"Great, now let's talk about something not child, school or career related."

"I'm all for that," Dana said, sinking further down into one of the comfortable chairs. She could talk to Hunter for hours and never get tired.

Dana was sad that she had to finally let Hunter off of the phone. He had an early morning of meetings and she needed to get to bed also. She took time to put her last load of laundry in the dryer before cutting off all of the lights and heading up to bed. As she reached the top landing, she could hear her children talking. She looked at the time and it was after eleven at night, past their bedtimes. They both should have been asleep already. She headed into her son's room to break up whatever they were doing and was stopped when she reached the door, hearing that she was the topic of discussion.

"I'm going to be like dad. I'm going to marry a woman like mom who doesn't do anything but wait on me all the time. I won't let her work either. I want her to stay at home cooking all of my meals and keeping my house clean. I may even get me a girlfriend or two on the side like him," Dana heard Jason say. "Mom doesn't seem to mind so it must be okay."

"Why would you need a girlfriend if you have a wife, stupid," she heard Jamie ask.

"Dad always did. He's had a girlfriend on the side for a long time; even before he moved out. He told me so and he said women were created to do whatever we men tell them to do. They don't have to think or work or do anything except whatever the husband says. Dad says men are smarter and are the providers. Look at mom, she doesn't do anything but laundry, cooking and looking after us. You don't hear her complaining because she loves it."

"Well maybe I'll be like mom then. I'll find me a husband that won't want me to work. I can sit around all day watching television and cooking. That doesn't seem like such a hard job," she heard Jamie say.

"That's what women do. The few that do work aren't really smart according to dad. Those are the women that no man wants so they don't have a man to take care of them like mom has, so they have to work."

Dana couldn't believe what she was hearing. Is this

really the kind of image her kids had of her? Was James really filling her son's head with foolishness like this? The thought that he was doing so angered her beyond anything she'd ever experienced before.

"All you'll need to do is grow up, get married and have some babies. You don't even have to worry about going to college, especially since you don't really like school," Jason said. "Look at mom. She lives in this big house and drives a nice car. She always has plenty of money that dad gives her and we still have everything we want. She never went to college."

"Yeah, you're right Jason. Why waste time with that if I'm going to marry a man who'll take care of me."

Dana had heard enough. She wouldn't take it out on the kids. She would talk to them another time. She first needed to deal with James. Strangling him for filling their son's head with a bunch of mess was the least she wanted to do to him. She would not see her son grow up and turn into her husband, treating women the way she allowed James to treat her. Major changes were needed in the Carr household.

All these years, she didn't realize how much of her life with James her children had picked up on. She didn't want them to think it was the thing to treat a woman like a doormat. She had allowed it for many years, but no more. She had her kids' future to think about. She wanted them both to have healthier relationships with the opposite sex. Her life with James would not be the example of the life to have. It would be a sign of what not to do if you want real happiness and real love.

She needed to put a stop to the conversation, but not let on that she had been listening. She went back to the stairs as if she was coming up and called out to them both.

"I know I don't hear conversation still going on after eleven," she hollered. As soon as she did, she heard Jamie run across the floor of the bathroom that separated her room from her brother's.

"Sorry mom. I'm in bed now, good night," she heard Jamie say.

"Good night Jamie. That means you too Jason," she added.

"Good night mom." She saw the light go out under his door and headed into her own room. She was too wired up to sleep. The conversation between her kids played over and over in her head. Her son actually praised his father for treating her the way he did and Jamie had dreams of being like her. Dana couldn't have that. She wanted Jamie to be a successful wife, mother and career woman. She needed Jamie to know that she could have it all and still have a great life. She needed to be a better example than the one she'd been for the past seventeen years. She didn't realize how closely Jamie was watching her life. Even though there was nothing wrong with being a housewife, the wrong part was if Jamie thought it was the thing to do because it was what she thought all women did. She also didn't want her thinking that she couldn't have a great career and still take care of her family one day when she had one. If Jamie did decide to be a housewife, Dana would celebrate that, but she wanted to make sure it wasn't because she thought she didn't have any options. There were plenty of options and women did it every day.

Being a housewife was like having a full-time job. There was a lot involved in it. It was too bad that all her kids took from it were the bad parts; the parts where she allowed their father to treat her as less than an equal partner in the family. Dana had even noticed the tone of her children's voices had become like James'. It border lined patronizing her. She had overlooked that for a while, giving them the benefit of the doubt that they missed their father. Her letting things slide wasn't beneficial to her or them.

She reached into her night stand and pulled out a pad and began writing out a plan to secure a better future for herself and her children. It was time she did more for her own life. She didn't have to continually settle for James pulling her like a puppet on a string. She would take control of her own life and it would start with the conversation she knew she needed to have with him. For now, she would write out what she wanted to do and would start working on it the next day. She already knew she was going to sign up for college classes. She would also seek out one of the elementary schools to volunteer at to see what it would be like being in the school helping the kids. She then wanted to plan a family gathering at her house and invite her family to come from Seattle for a weekend. It was time she put more effort in getting her relationship with them back to where it should be. Dealing with James would take much more thought. She needed to finally get him straight because enough was enough. Hearing her kids talking tonight was the wake-up call she finally needed to break away and do something she should have done a long time ago. It was time to file for divorce. It was time to let go of her loveless marriage.

~~

After dropping the kids off at school, Dana called James at the office. His secretary told her that James was flying out of town for a week long business trip. That angered her because he could have told her he would be out of town for a week. Suppose there was an emergency with the kids. She hung up and called his cell to leave him a message and was surprised when he answered instead.

"James, I thought I would get your voice mail. Your secretary said you were flying out someplace for business today. You couldn't have let me know?" she asked.

"Dana, I didn't think of it. I don't normally see the kids until the weekend and they both said they were staying home with you this coming weekend so I figured I'd check on them when I got back. They know to call my cell during the week if they need me anyway. Now, to what do I owe this early morning conversation?" he asked.

"I need to talk to you about the kids and a few other things, but it can wait until you get back."

"Or you could tell me now," he interjected.

"I'll wait until you get back. Let me know when you have some free time. What day will you be back?"

"I won't be back until next Monday. I'm on business this week, but I'm staying over a few extra days for some relaxation and to play a few games of golf. I should be free Monday afternoon or anytime Tuesday."

"That's fine. Let's shoot for Monday afternoon to talk," she said.

"Okay, I'll come by the house."

She didn't like him coming by the house because she knew what that meant and the days of his drop in sex are over.

"No need to do that. I'll stop by your office to talk. The conversation won't take long and I'll already be out after dropping the kids off and getting a few errands done."

"Fine, whatever. I'll see you next week. Is that it?" he

asked as if she were wasting his time. .

"Bye James," she said, hating the tone he often took with her when she didn't agree with something he wanted. It was obvious he wanted to come by the house and she wasn't having any of that. She would be sure to let him know that his key soon would no longer work because she was changing the locks and she didn't care what he thought about it. It didn't matter how many bills he continued to pay for the house, he no longer lived there and he needed to knock or ring the bell like every other visitor does.

Dana felt rejuvenated. After talking with James she then called her mother about a visit.

"Mom, hi," she said when her mother answered.

"Hi Dana. It's so good to hear from you."

"It's good to hear your voice too and I won't keep you long. I was thinking about having the family come out to Chicago for a visit. Do you think dad would be up for that? I'll call Melanie, Lana and Carrie to ask them." Dana couldn't wait to talk to her sisters about coming out with their entire families.

"Oh Dana, I think your dad would be on a plane today if I told him. When do you think this will be?"

"I haven't had time to think of that. I actually thought about doing it and thought I would see how you felt about it. Let me work out the details and I'll call you back about it. I think it will be good for the kids and you've never been to my house. It's time I remedied that."

"Dana, what about James? How do you think he'll feel about that?"

She couldn't wait to answer that.

"James has no say over what I do and who I have in my home because he no longer lives here," she said with power.

"Well that works fine for me then. Let me know and your father and I will be there. I know your sisters will too. Your father and I were talking about how nice it was to have you home a few weeks back. He will be ecstatic when I tell him we've been invited to Chicago for a visit."

"Oh, I also want to tell you I'm registering for college classes today. I'm planning to get my degree in childhood education and I'm finally going to be a teacher. You know how I've always wanted to do that and I'm finally going to make it happen for myself."

"What's gotten into you? I'm happy to hear the excitement in your voice and I can't wait to hear all about your classes. I'm proud of you Dana."

"Thanks mom. I appreciate the support. I'm going to go, so tell dad I said hello and I'll call you in a few days with more details about a visit. I love you," she said before hanging up.

She was already excited about her family's visit. What she didn't care about was what James' reaction would be. It was her family and she wanted to see them. Her mind was running a million miles a minute thinking of all she wanted to do when her family came to town. She would make sure they had a lot of fun. It was also time her kids learned more about her side of the family and interacted more with their cousins. Distance shouldn't keep them from getting and staying close. First she needed to call her sisters and let them know of her plans too and then she'd turn her attention to doing all of the things for herself that she wanted to achieve for the day.

Chapter Eight
DANA

Hunter waited impatiently like a teenage boy waiting for his first girlfriend to show up. He and Dana had agreed to meet at their usual spot. They had been in touch several times over the past week and he was anxious to hear about the progress she'd made in signing up for classes. When he called to invite her to lunch, she'd also told him she had lots of other new developments to share with him. He asked if she'd like to take in a movie and she joyfully agreed.

He was glad when he looked up to see her coming through the door.

"You made it," he said.

"Of course. Did you doubt that I would show up?" Dana asked.

"I wasn't sure if something had come up with your kids," he said.

"No, everything is good with the kids and in fact, everything is good all-around for me these days. The kids are at home eating pizza and watching movies or playing with one of their many electronic games. I told them I would be out for a while. Did you want to eat before or after the movie?" she asked.

"Since we haven't ordered yet, let's do after and let's do

a nice restaurant this time. I think we can graduate up to the next level of dining," he added.

"I agree."

They were in walking distance of the local theater so they decided to walk rather than move their cars. They still had plenty of time before the movie started and were walking when Dana suddenly stopped. Hunter looked perplexed when he saw a look of concern on her face.

"Dana, what is it? Are you okay?" he asked.

"I want to say one thing before we head off. I told you I had a lot of developments in my life lately that I wanted to share. Since we've decided to do a movie first, I'll save most of it to talk about later. For now I want you to know that I went to see a lawyer yesterday and am filing for divorce from James."

Dana looked up into Hunter's eyes for any reaction. What she saw was attentiveness, allowing her to finish her thoughts before he commented, so she continued on.

"I don't want you to think that I did that because of you; I did it because of me. I have known for a long time that my marriage was over, but I let James convince me time and time again that was life was to be at his beck and call. What I didn't want to do was be like James. I was hurt when I discovered he was seeing other woman and I lived with it hoping he would stop and that I could figure out what it was that made him stray and fix it. I have enjoyed our talks and I appreciate all of the advice you've given me about classes and volunteering at a local school. I'm not sure where any of this is leading and I don't want to be presumptuous or anything. I want to be sure that I am free and clear to pursue something with anyone of my choosing and not be bound by a ring and a marriage that isn't working for me anymore."

Dana didn't want to feel guilty about any feelings that may develop between them. Meeting with an attorney who will file the necessary paperwork opened up a whole new world for her and she already felt free. She continued looked at him hoping he would say something. His silence was scaring her. Maybe he wasn't interested in anything and saw her as a damsel who needed a push. When he didn't say anything, she queried.

"Hunter? Are you going to say anything?"

He smiled a bright smile and Dana's heart melted.

"Of course I am. I wanted to be sure you were done with all you needed to say. I have a lot to say, but I'll reserve most of it for after the movie. What I will say now is that, whatever decisions you make I will support you one hundred percent. I also want you to know that you aren't being presumptuous about anything. I haven't said anything or done anything to let you know how interested I am in you because I wouldn't feel comfortable doing so if there was a chance you were going to give your marriage a try. I would never stand in the way of that, but now that I know you will soon be a free and clear woman, I plan to put all of my energy behind showing you how much I like you and would love being able to pursue something more with you at whatever level you are comfortable with."

Dana's smile couldn't be brighter. She feared her face would crack if she smiled any harder. She was glad he felt that way because the more interaction they had, the more she was being drawn to him. She appreciated that he never pushed her or made any move on her, but he remained a true gentleman and allowed her to handle her business her way.

"How was that for a response?" he asked.

"Perfect," she replied. "Now that we have that out of the way, shall we make our way to the movie?"

"We shall," he replied. Dana's blood rushed to her head when Hunter reached out and joined her hand with his as they walked to the theater. It felt so natural walking and holding hands with him.

"So let's talk about light stuff and save the heavy stuff for dinner conversation. Tell me something fun and exciting that you've been doing that's not about working or school?"

Dana couldn't wait to tell him all that she'd done, thanks to him, but she'd save that for later. She wanted to tell him about her family coming to visit.

"Well for the first time, my family is coming for a visit in a few weeks. I invited my parents, my sisters and their husbands and kids to come for a weekend and I'm more excited than I've ever been. None of them have ever been to visit. They're actually coming in on a Friday morning and staying until Monday. I'm planning a cookout at the house and some fun activities for the kids. My kids are also excited about the visit. After a few phone calls with my sisters this week, we introduced our kids via Skype and now the kids stay in contact with each other on their own."

"That's good news Dana. I'm happy to hear that things are looking up with your relationship with your family. Family is everything and you only have one set of parents so make sure you always cherish them. I travel to California a few times a year to visit my parents, especially with them getting older."

"I don't plan to lose contact with them ever again," Dana admitted.

They were almost at the movie theater when a young man stopped them.

"Mrs. Carr? Is that you?" Dana heard someone say. She turned around to see one of her son's friends.

"Yes Michael, it's me. How are you doing?" she said.

"I'm doing great. Is Jason with you?"

"No he and Jamie are at home." She noticed Michael had been eyeing Hunter and made sure to let them know he saw that they were holding hands, knowing Hunter wasn't Jamie and Jason's father.

"Okay, tell Jason I said hello," Michael said walking off, still keeping an eye on Hunter.

"I guess this means Jason will soon hear about me," Hunter said.

"I'm afraid you're right. Michael is probably calling him right now."

Dana did notice Michael taking his cell phone out to make a call. She wasn't worried at all. She was entitled to a life and now that she was officially filing for divorce, she had nothing to hide from anyone.

"Do you want to forget about the movie and dinner and go home? I'm sure if that kid is calling your son, you'll have to explain a lot to them."

Dana wanted to do nothing of the sort.

"No, I'm Jason's mother and I don't answer to him; he and Jamie answer to me. I've been looking forward to this time with you all day. My kids will be fine," she said. "Let's go and enjoy our movie."

After the movie, they settled in for a nice dinner at a local seafood restaurant. While they waited for their food, Dana filled Hunter in on her very busy week.

She started by telling him about the conversation she

overheard Jamie and Jason having and that she'd planned to talk to James when he returned in a few days from out of town.

"Talking with James is a good idea. I can't believe as a man, he would actually want your son to have that outlook on how to treat his wife, let alone wanting him to think so negatively about you. You don't deserve that; no woman deserves that. Women everyday make great contributions to society and most of those women are stay at home mothers too. There is nothing negative about wanting to make sure their husbands and kids are taken care of daily. He's getting a false impression and that won't go over well when he becomes a man. He will only learn to look down on women and not see their true worth. As for your daughter, it's important that she understands your decision to be a stay at home mother and that it's not something she should look down on. There is nothing wrong with it if it's what she wants to do, but if it's because of what you overheard, then she definitely needs to be reprogrammed and soon, before it sinks in too far."

"I know and I agree. I have no idea what James was thinking talking like that around my son. I've had a week to get over being angry so that when I talk to him, it's with a level head and not out of anger."

"Great, so tell me what else you've been dying to tell me about your week. I know we've talked almost every day, but since our conversations stayed away from kids, work and school, I want to hear about everything else now."

Dana was excited to share all of her news.

"Well, I signed up for my first three classes on line and they start next week. I also spoke with the local elementary school and they are looking for more volunteers. The good part about that was after speaking with the principal, she called a few hours later and said she'd mentioned me to a few of the teachers and they all knew me from a lot of the work I do working with the kids in girl scouts and boy scouts over the years and a lot of the activities my kids are a part of. She called to tell me that they actually have a paid part time position available in the first grade classrooms as a teacher's aide. There are a few classes I have to take that deal with children in the classroom and I'd have to have a background check, which I'm not concerned about. I've already had first aide training so that's one class I won't have to take. I only need to bring my certification in when I fill out the paperwork. She's giving me a few days to think about it, but I already know I'm going to take it. It's another step leading to my independence," she said.

"This is all wonderful Dana," Hunter said.

"Thanks to you. You told me a lot of things about finding my own way. I know you were trying to help and some of the things you said were harsh, but they were definitely needed. If I hadn't told you some of my dreams for myself, I assume you never would have known to use those words of encouragement that you used to put a fire under me."

Dana remembered the many talks they'd had since they'd met where he encouraged her to do what she needed to do for her and her kids and no one else. He also told her if it meant giving her marriage another try then she should do that, but to make sure she is as happy as she is making her kids and James. He also told her she should never, ever settle for being cheated on. In his opinion it was one of the worse things you could do to a woman, especially one who is also the wife. She deserved better and she should expect and demand better from James. Dana didn't worry much about that. She had every intention of breaking free of being bound by James.

Hunter had the kind of talks with her that she was sure, if she had any real close girlfriends, they would be saying the same things. James ended up with the few friends she had after they split. They were married to men who were friends with James so she became the casualty.

"I'm thankful for who you are. You were unselfish in your comments and I appreciate that."

"I'm glad I could help," he added.

Dana couldn't believe how happy she was whenever they talked or were together. Hunter treated her with so much respect and kindness. She didn't feel tense or anxious around him and she looked forward to more time with together.

"I'm here for whatever you need, Dana. If you need a sounding board, call me. If you need a friend, call me. If you need some help with your classes, I think you already know to call me. I am a college professor, of course, so what better friend to have when you're in school than a teacher," he said.

"That's very true."

"Can I ask you something?" Hunter asked.

"Sure. You can ask me anything."

"You are a wonderful woman and I've listened to you say that the few friendships you had here in Chicago you no longer have because they pretty much took James' side with the separation since their husbands were already friends of his. Do you do other activities to build up your own friend base? I say that because it's always good to have a good friend or two to bounce things off of. I have my best friend Jeff who I can count on for any and everything and I don't know what I'd do without him."

"I know what you mean. I went line dancing recently and the ladies invited me back to join them. I plan to do that on a weekly basis. One of the other ladies in the class invited me to a wine and paint ladies night out she's having next week and I'm going to that too. I've also been talking this week to a friend I had back in high school and we actually talked about taking a girl's trip away to an island to catch up and have some fun. I'm finding what it's like to have my life with my family and a life outside of it. You are right in that I do miss having friendships for the sake of having friends."

After dinner, they shared more with neither one of them wanting to get up to leave. It was getting late and Hunter wanted to touch on one last subject before they left.

"Where do we go from here Dana?" he asked clearly startling her.

She didn't know how to answer. She knew where she wanted things to go, but she wanted to get to that place slowly.

"I see you struggling with your answer so let me begin first. I'm enjoying being with you and I don't want that to change so unless you tell me that you don't want me around, I'm not going anywhere. We do need to figure out how we're going to do this friendship thing. I'm enjoying our friendship, but I also want you to know that eventually I'd like this to be more when you're ready. I have no problem waiting because I know you're worth it. I want to know what you're thinking. Am I worth the wait?"

She wasn't struggling with her answer. She wanted to

be sure the words she chose represented her true feeling.

"You are more than worth the wait Hunter. I find myself thinking about you all throughout the day. I'm enjoying the friendship we're developing and talking to you is another highlight of my day. I'd like us to continue on the path that we're on and I thank you for being patient with me while I sort out my life. It's nice to know you're not running scared of all of my drama. It was time I did something about it, not to be with you, but so that I am happy with myself again. I've looked in the mirror for too long, not liking what I saw. I'm in a good place and thanks to you, I know that I am still desirable in the eyes of men. I like you a lot and I'm thankful for the day you asked to share my table at the deli. Does that help in answering your question?" she asked, hopeful.

"I'm assuming after today, your kids will know a little about me, since I'm sure that kid Michael we saw has called or texted Jason by now. I want to continue seeing you and when you're ready, I'd like to be more than friends. I think we have something special here and I want to see where it goes. I'm not going anywhere."

Dana was happy to hear that.

"Now that I know you, I don't want to stop seeing you either. I know my situation is tricky so if you can be a little more patient with me, it will all workout," she said, hopeful.

Hunter smiled knowing those were the words he wanted to hear.

"Beautiful, I'm not going anywhere. I will be as patient as you want me to be as long as I know you're here with me."

"I'm right where you are," she said.

"Those words are music to my ears. The hour is getting late and I want to be sure you get home okay. Let me walk you back to your car and call me when you get home."

"I will."

They reached Dana's car and she was a little sad that their evening was coming to an end.

"Have a safe trip home and a wonderful night, sweetheart," Hunter said before pulling Dana to him and kissing her lightly on the lips. "I'd like to share a more intimate kiss with you, but I know we'll have time for that when the time is right. I'll talk to you tonight."

Dana was more than enthralled by him. She couldn't wait to see where things would go.

~~

"I hope you had fun mom," Jason said, not with cheer, but with disdain as soon as Dana walked through the front door of her house. As she'd suspected, his friend Michael had called and told him he'd seen her holding hands with a man that was not his father.

"I had a great time," she said, not paying his tone any attention.

"When were you going to tell us you were seeing some guy? Does dad know? He won't be happy."

She took a few steps closer to him getting right up in his face so that her message was clear.

"Jason, I don't answer to your father. I am my own woman."

She knew her anger was evident in the grimace she sure was showing on her face.

"Not according to dad. He says you do answer to him because he pays for everything we have."

Dana stood shaken at not only her son's words, but at

the way he was speaking to her. Now she'd had enough. Her patience had worn off and it was time to clear the air and make sure it was clear to him that his place in the family was that of a child. Dana chose her worlds carefully and made sure the tone was one of seriousness at his delving into how she decided to live her life.

"I'm only going to say this once so pay attention. I don't care what your father pays around here. I don't answer to him and I certainly don't answer to you. What I do with my time is my own business and who I spend my time with is not your business or anyone else's. Paying the bills around here and taking care of this family is what your father is supposed to do. You and Jamie are his children and it's what a father does. If for any reason your father has issues with me, I'll deal with that because that is something that's not your concern either. Now you get one free pass in your lifetime to have that tone with me and that free pass has come and gone. If I hear it again, you won't appreciate my reaction, so I'm telling you to control your tone and not forget your place. I am *YOUR* mother. I expect you to respect that no matter what."

"I wasn't trying to be disrespectful," he said.

"You may not have been trying, but you were. Now, the other night I overheard you and Jamie talking. I don't want you filling her head with any of that crap your father is filling your head with. I stayed home and took care of my family because that's what I wanted to do. Whatever your father did or didn't do throughout my marriage to him should not encourage you to be the same type of man. His treatment of me and other women is not something you should admire. I want you to be better and I want you to treat women better. If you marry a woman, she deserves your love and commitment to her and only her. There is no room for other women in the marriage bed. You're old enough and I know you know about sex. It disgusts me that your father has told you about his extracurricular activities with other women because that's not something to admire and you should be ashamed of him, not sitting in awe. You have no idea how horrible it makes a woman feel to know that her husband feels the need to go outside of his marriage to get something he can get at home. It's not something a man has to do; it's something he chooses to do."

She saw the look on her son's face and could see the impact of how she allowed her husband to treat her all the years of their marriage. It wasn't just James' fault, it was hers also.

"Now I don't know nor do I care what Michael may have said to you, but know this, my personal life is of no concern of yours. Again, yes I did have a good time today. His name is Hunter and he's a nice man, but we are just friends. Stay in your place as my son and we won't have to have this conversation again. Do I make myself clear?"

Dana was breathing hard by the time she was through and she saw the moment her words finally sunk in for Jason. His shoulders dropped and he looked down at the floor ashamed of what he now knew she'd over heard him saying to Jamie.

"Yes mom and I'm sorry. I'm sorry for what I said to you and how I said it and I'm sorry for saying those things to Jamie. I didn't really mean them. I'll go apologize to her too. I know it's wrong how dad treats you and I don't like it either. I may have said those things to Jamie, but I swear I didn't mean them. I would never treat a woman badly and I don't like how dad is. He treats Reese the same way. I would never do that, I promise."

Dana felt better. She could tell her son was sincere in his apology and she could see that he knew he'd crossed a line, never to be crossed again. She still had to have her talk with James because now that she's gaining control of her own life, it was time to relinquish him of any remaining control he thinks he has. She needed to reach out to her lawyer to ask how long it would take for the initial paperwork to be completed for her divorce. She needed to break the cycle of misery in her family and get them all a fresh start. They needed to be in a much healthier space.

"Go down and clean up the family room. I expect better from you from this point on."

She watched as her son shook his head in agreement and went to do as she asked. For the first time, she took control of a situation like she should have many times in the past. For too long everyone walked all over her. It's now a new day. There's a new sheriff in town and her name is Dana Carr, she thought as she walked away with a little extra boldness in her steps.

Chapter Nine
DANA

"What happened with your conversation with James about what you overhead Jason saying to Jamie?"

Dana was still upset about that conversation and even more upset that for a week, James had been avoiding her since he got back in town. She'd called him and even stopped by the bank headquarters to speak with him, but as usual he was unavailable. She knew he'd been in touch with the children, but he had yet to return her phone call. She assumed the last conversation they'd had alerted him to the fact that what she wanted to talk about wasn't something good. Sooner or later they'd see each other and he wouldn't be able to avoid her then. For now she wanted to wipe all thoughts of James from her mind and focus on Hunter. The kids were at friends' houses for sleepovers and Hunter invited her to his home for a quiet evening.

"We haven't spoken yet. I think he's avoiding me. When we last spoke I think he could tell something was different in my voice. I'm not worried though because it will happen sooner than he thinks. I did have a talk with Jason and have made a lot of things crystal clear to him. He knows the things he was saying to Jamie were wrong and he apologized. As her older brother I expect more from him in the way of respect for women, especially his sister and I.

If he doesn't respect us like he should, there is nothing that would prevent him from disrespecting other women. I'm good with how my talk with him turned out last week. Now, tonight I'm hoping to not spend it talking about any drama with James."

Hunter couldn't agree more. He never wanted her to think that any conversation was off limits, including discussions about James and her kids. He wanted them to be able to talk about any and everything.

He invited her over so that they could have a quiet evening and not have to spend it at a restaurant or at a movie. He wanted some quiet time alone for them. Tonight he'd cooked dinner for them and hoped to have a Netflix kind of night.

"We don't have to talk about anything you don't want to talk about. I want you to know that if for any reason you wanted to talk about it, I'm always here for you. No subject is off limits. Now, how about we move this conversation into the dining room so that I can set the table for dinner."

"Why don't I go set the table while you finish getting the food ready? I feel like you're doing everything. I could have cooked us a great meal tonight you know. You didn't have to do this."

"You really don't know how to let someone cater to you do you?" Hunter asked, curiously.

Dana didn't know how to answer because he was right. She'd spent most of her life taking care of others. No one ever wanted to do something as nice as cook dinner for her where she didn't have to lift a finger. She felt out of her element when she wasn't cooking for someone else.

"I guess I don't. Am I really that predictable? You knew I would offer to do everything didn't you?" She laughed at herself. She was always taking care of everyone else.

Hunter loved the innocence in Dana, not knowing how to relax and let a man do things for her for a change. He walked over and gave her a comforting hug.

"Dana, I knew you would offer and I appreciate you for that, but you've spent a lot of years taking care of everyone else and for tonight, I want to take care of you. Tell me what you need."

Dana's heart started beating faster. She didn't know what to say. No one had ever asked her what she needed and she was speechless. Hunter was so different than what she was accustomed to. He was obviously serious about his request. He was still staring at her waiting for an answer.

"Dana?"

"I need to be here with you enjoying a quiet evening with nothing on my mind, but you and this incredible meal you've cooked tonight. I want to be held and told that all of these new things I'm doing in my life are going to work out. Right now I need you. Thank you for making dinner for me tonight and showing me that I can be catered to sometimes too. Now, how about I help you get things all set up? Can I at least do that?" she asked.

"Absolutely. I'll grab the dishes from the cabinet and we'll both set the table and bring the food in. I also have candles I want to set out. After that we're going to settle in to watch some Netflix movies and I don't care if it's a chick flick, you pick whatever you want us to watch. Tonight is all about you. How does that sound?"

Nothing sounded better as far as she was concerned.

"That sounds incredible."

Hunter had made a lovely meal for them. He cooked baked trout, steamed vegetables, sautéed shrimp and scallops and twice baked potatoes. Dana was in heaven.

"This food is delicious!" She exclaimed tasting some of everything on her plate. "You are a wonderful cook."

"Thank you. As a bachelor before I got married, if I didn't learn how to cook, I wouldn't have eaten. I can't eat at fast food joints all my life," he chuckled.

"Well I'm certainly impressed. I've never had a meal cooked for me before."

"If you'll let me, this won't be the last time I'll cook for you. I hope I get the chance to do a lot of things for you. Tell me how your plans for classes and working at the school are coming along," Hunter asked.

"Well, classes are about to begin. On line classes are very convenient. There is no set time that I have to be someplace or spend my day in the classroom. It's self-paced and I like that. I've ordered all of the books I'll need on line and I'm waiting for them to arrive. I can't wait until I start that first class. It's very exciting and I think my kids are even excited for me. They've been asking a lot of questions. Jason even told me he thought I'd make a great teacher. They told me they would help more around the house so that I can have extra time to study."

Hunter could see the exuberance on her face as she talked. He was as happy for her as she was for herself. He loved that she had begun to understand that she didn't have to depend on anyone in order to reach out and grab a hold to her dreams. He saw a brand new spark and he loved being a witness to it evolving.

"That's wonderful. I knew everything would work out great for you. What about the elementary school? What happened with that?"

Dana held that great news for last.

"Well, I'm starting next week at the school. They originally asked if I was available to do sixteen hours a week. The other day I got a call from the Principal asking if I was interested in working more hours than that. She saw my scores from the classes I had to take in order to be an aid at the school and she was impressed. I'll be working four days a week, six hours a day and I cannot wait to start. I owe you a debt of gratitude. I knew all along that I had it within me to pick myself up and out of my situation with James, but it was your extra encouragement and all of the resources you gave me that pushed me on to actually make the steps. I'm happier than I've been in a long time and a lot of that has to do with you. Thank you for helping me see me in my future. I have to admit, I see myself looking pretty good!"

"Dana, I knew when I met you that you were something special and I'm glad that I'm around to see how things are unfolding for you. Now, since we've finished dinner, I'm going to put these dishes in the dishwasher and put the extra food away. Why don't you go into the other room down the hall there where you'll see a big screen television? Find something good for us to watch and relax. I'll join you in a few minutes."

"You are so good to me," she said happily.

"Hearing you say that puts a smile on my face. Before you go, I need one thing from you."

Dana didn't know what that could be. Maybe he needed her to bring her dishes into the kitchen. She reached for her plates and he stopped her.

"That's not what I meant; I got this. I need this from you."

Dana wasn't sure what the "this" was he was talking

about until he came up close to her, caressed the side of her face with the palm of his hand and then leaned down and brought his lips in contact with hers for a kiss. The kiss was powerful and exploded in her brain. She leaned into him to show him she wanted the kiss as much as he did.

Hunter felt the kiss in every part of his body. Once his lips touched Dana's, he felt an electric spark that seemed to energize him. He had planned for the kiss to be short and sweet, just enough to let her know that he appreciated her, but it turned into more than that. Before he knew it, he was pulling her body until it was lined up against his. He reached down to grasp her hips lightly to pull her as close as he could get and then he deepened the kiss. He knew the kiss was the right move when he felt Dana's arms come up and surround his neck, drawing him even more intimately against her. The kiss was as close to perfect as any he had ever experienced. As their lips caressed each other and their tongues tangled for dominance, it was as if nothing else mattered, but the two of them and the feelings the kiss was generating in him. He moaned into her mouth, letting her know the enjoyment he was getting from it. When he felt his body hardening in a place that he didn't want known to her, he ended the kiss. They were both breathing heavily as they pulled away.

"Any more of that and I think we both would have burst into flames," Dana expressed through breaths as she tried to regain some composure.

"You won't get an argument out of me. I felt the fire as much as you. You had better go get the movie started while I stick my head in the freezer to cool off," Hunter said comically.

Dana stood stunned by how good kissing Hunter felt.

She couldn't seem to get her feet to move. When they finally did, she headed for a place in the house that was anyplace other than where she stood. He felt so good in her arms, she wanted to throw caution to the wind and jump him right in the middle of his dining room. Before she did that, she moved so that they could both get a little space.

After Dana was gone, Hunter stood staring at the empty space where she had been standing. He really didn't mean to take the kiss as far as it had gotten, but he certainly didn't regret it. Holding Dana was something he'd wanted to do for a while and kissing her was the number one thing on his to do list. He didn't want to push her into anything; he wanted to share a little bit of intimacy with her and boy did he. He needed to get his head together before joining her for the movie. If he didn't, there was no telling what they would do next. He wanted her, but the time wasn't right. He'd made a promise to himself that he would hold back until the mess with her husband was resolved. It wasn't yet, so he needed to work on containing the beast in him that wanted to break free and make sweet love to her. There hopefully would be a time for that in the future. For now, he needed a cold drink and some major lessons in restraint.

Dana sat staring at the television screen before she even turned it on. She shocked herself with the notion that she'd kissed another man. She did it and she liked it. Even now, she felt no guilt. Yes, she technically was still married to James, but that was a mere detail and they had been living apart a year. It was beyond time to move on. She wouldn't, however, go any further than a few kisses until her marriage was legally over. She didn't owe anything to

James; she knew that if she were going to have something more than friendship with Hunter, she wanted to be clear and free to do so. She heard him coming in the distance so she quickly turned on the television and searched for a movie. She hummed happily while doing so, loving the place she was at in her life. She knew that the best was still yet to come.

~~

Dana pulled into her driveway and was exiting her car when she looked up to see James had pulled up behind her. She was coming from dropping Jamie off at school and when she returned, here he was, waiting for her.

After avoiding her, he finally shows up unannounced. She got out of her car and waited for him to do the same and catch up to her.

"Hi James. What are you doing here? The kids are still in school."

"Hi to you too. I know where they are. What is it that you wanted to talk to me about?" he inquired. He'd done enough avoiding her and whatever issue she had with him. He wanted to get it over with.

"I wanted to talk to you about how Jason perceives your actions and your behavior."

"Well, can we do this inside the house? The neighbors don't need a show."

Dana wasn't falling for that. She knew what his middle of the day drop-ins were all about.

"We can have this conversation right here. There are no neighbors close enough to hear anything we talk about assuming this doesn't turn into a shouting match. I'm sure we can have a conversation like two civil adults without raising our voices. Like I said, my concern is the negative way Jason is viewing women, mimicking your actions thinking treating women like property is the proper way to treat someone. I caught him telling Jamie that she would be better off marrying a man who would give her a house, a car and money and all she had to do was whatever he commanded her to do. He even told her she shouldn't worry about college because you've told him that women aren't smart in business and should just be homemakers. I think you need to be more careful of what Jason and Jamie hear you say and do. They are like sponges, soaking up everything."

"Sponges huh?" James asked, snickering. "Are they soaking up you and your boyfriend's actions too?"

Dana was at a loss for words. It was apparent James knew about Hunter.

"You look shocked Dana. Is there a cat around here holding on to your tongue or something? You have nothing to say? You're worried about what I'm doing around my kids and they live with you, so what are they seeing around here? Jason told me one of his friends saw you hugged up and holding hands with some guy. Who is this guy? Are you messing around with someone and bringing him around my kids?" James said in a challenging manner.

"I have not brought anyone around Jamie or Jason. Yes one of Jason's friends saw me with someone which is really none of your business."

"Oh it's not? Now that you've stopped wearing your wedding ring, it doesn't mean you're not still married to me. What do you think people will say when they see you around town with some man and you're still my wife?"

Dana looked down at her wedding ring finger where the

new ring she bought for herself now sat.

"Yes, I noticed the missing ring the minute you got out of the car. Since I heard you had been out with a man, I was wondering what kind of man would date a married woman."

Dana assumed she must be in the twilight zone. James couldn't have made mention cf dating while married. He brought attitude so she gave him a lot in return.

"I know you did not say anything to me about dating while married. How many women were there before Reese, huh James? Don't even go there with me. I took my ring off before I went out with Hunter and not to hide the fact that I'm married, but to acknowledge for myself that the marriage is over. As far as I'm concerned our marriage ended the day you left this house and bought a condo. It may have taken me a long time to come to terms with that, but once I did, I knew it was time to move on and stop living in the past or on the notion that what I wanted was my marriage back; a marriage that you have no respect for, so don't you dare come up to my house and accuse me of anything. I went to a movie and had dinner, not that I even owe you any type of an explanation because I don't."

Even though their tempers were flaring, Dana was glad they were able to control the sound level of their words. She kept her tone low as she continued.

"I know you're not talking about us still being married, mister I'm living with a twenty-four year old? Listen; don't come around here questioning what I do with my life. Like I said, I haven't brought Hunter around here. I'm not saying that I won't, I'm saying that I haven't. He and I are just friends, again, not that I have to explain anything to you."

"Make sure you don't. No matter what you think or what this Hunter guy has planned, you're still my wife, ring on your finger or not. What's this I hear about you taking classes and working? I thought we agreed that you didn't need to work. I provide for you and the kids well enough that you don't have to work. The kids need you here at home so what do you need to take classes for anyway? All of a sudden you have a dream?"

Anger and sarcasm. She could do that too.

"Don't belittle me James; it's not attractive. I decided for me that I wanted to work. I have the opportunity to work at an elementary school while the kids are in school, so at that time of day, they don't need me to be here at home. If something comes up in the middle of the day and they need something, they have two parents. If I'm not available, they can call you. As far as the classes, I've decided I want to get a degree to teach which shouldn't be shocking to you. I've been saying that since before we got married, but the only difference now is I don't have you in my ear daily telling me it's a waste of time. You don't need to worry about what goes on in this house. Don't forget, you chose not to live here."

"I chose? I didn't choose not to be here. You pushed me away. You nag, you complain and you have issues because you are unhappy with your own life. I was tired of being a party to it."

Dana could hear in his voice that all the things in the past that he would spout at her to hold her in place were about to come out of his mouth and the last time he did that was truly the last time. She wasn't taking it anymore. She put her hand up to stop any further words he was about to say.

"Save it James because I don't want to hear it. Take that mess home to Reese since I understand you have a way of talking down to her too. Unlike her, I no longer have to take it. This is my house and I'm about to turn around and go inside of it. I contacted you not to have an all-out argument with you, but I want you to be more discreet about what my children hear and see when they are with you. You can save your insults for your tart. Taking that from you is her job now, not mine."

She was fired up and she could see that James was too. This was the first time she'd actually stood up to him like this and it felt good. She could tell by the look on his face that he didn't know how to respond to the woman he was now standing in front of. When she thought he would come back with more to say, she watched as he turned around and headed back to his car, not saying a word. She didn't stand around to watch him pull off. She walked into her own house, hearing his car as he sped off down the street. She knew for once in her life, she'd experienced a win-win situation in her favor and it felt good.

Chapter Ten
DANA

"Hey dad," Coral said when Hunter answered his ringing phone.

"Hey baby girl. How are you?" he asked.

"I'm fine. I was thinking of coming home next weekend and wanted to check with you about getting airline tickets. There is a sixty-nine dollar sale going on for flights into Chicago."

"You're coming home? That's great. I'll go on line and get your tickets today. What day are you thinking of leaving to come home?"

"Thursday afternoon because I don't have classes next Friday and my last class on Thursday ends at noon."

"Okay, I got it. I'll email you the confirmation in a little while. I can't wait to see you."

Hunter was more than excited Coral was coming home. He hadn't seen her since homecoming when he went to visit her.

"Thanks dad," he heard her say. "What else has been going on?"

He didn't know whether to tell her about Dana or not. They were seeing each other, but were keeping it on a friendship level for now. She was still very special to him and he didn't want to have to keep his distance from her because Coral would be in town. Besides, he really wanted her to meet Dana. He was planning for their friendship to be a lot more eventually and he knew Coral would be happy for him. He decided to go for it.

"Well, I've been seeing someone."

He was about to continue when she threw a million questions at him.

"Coral, slow down. It's not serious and for now she's a friend. It's a strange circumstance. I didn't want to keep it from you in case her name comes up or anything while you're home. Now to answer a few of the questions you asked, she's a wonderful woman, her name is Dana, she's a mother of two children, a boy and a girl and she's someone who is special to me. I'll tell you more when you get home. For now I wanted you to know."

"I'm happy for you dad. You deserve someone really nice. One day I won't be living at home anymore and I want you to be happy with someone and not be home alone or lonely. Do you think I can meet her when I come home for the weekend?"

"I don't know yet. I would have to check with her. Right now, she hasn't told her children much about me and we were trying to keep things simple for now. You're an adult so I can tell you this; she's still married though she will be divorced soon. We're friends and we want to wait to see how things go before we bring you kids in on this. On my end, I decided I didn't want to keep this a secret from you. Dana's situation is a little different, so I'm respecting her wishes."

"Okay dad, but just so you know, you have never told me about any other woman you've been interested in since you divorced from mom, so I know this one is really special. As long as you're happy, then I'm happy too. Well I have to go. I have a class. I'll call you tonight after I get the flight confirmation. Love you dad!"

"Love you too," Hunter replied before hanging up and then picking the phone back up to call Dana. He had no doubt Coral would be worrying him to death about meeting Dana when she came home and he wanted to give her a heads up.

"Hey you," she said enthusiastically when she answered his call.

"Hey yourself. Were you busy?" he asked.

"No not really. I was doing some research for one of my classes. How is your day going?"

"It's going fine. I'm about to head out to teach my evening classes, but I wanted to call and say hello and to hear your voice. I also wanted to see if you're still okay after your argument with James two weeks ago in front of your house. I know you said you were fine with it, but I was worried about you after you said he keeps leaving you messages on your cell."

Dana loved how much he truly cared about her.

"Hunter, I'm fine. For the first time after an argument with James, I didn't leave it defeated like I have so many times in the past. He's leaving me messages saying he wants us to do counseling and get our marriage back on track and that he's thinking of putting his condo up for sale. I've ignored every message because I'm not entertaining any of that. He's only doing that because he knows about you and he never thought there would be anyone for me other than him. He's been by here twice to pick up the kids and didn't even get out of the car. I guess he's giving me the silent treatment since I haven't responded to his many messages. I found out from my lawyer today that James is going to be served early next week. That's when the fireworks will start I'm sure, but I'm ready for it. My attorney thinks that I won't have to wait a long time for the divorce to be final considering James actually moved out a year ago and has even purchased a separate home. I'm happy that I can finally move on with my life and it will be a new beginning for the kids too. How are things with you?" she asked.

"I'm great, especially now that I hear your voice. Speaking of kids, mine is one of the reasons I'm calling you. I wanted to tell you that I mentioned you to my daughter today. I hope that was okay, not knowing if you even wanted her to know about you for now. I know we're taking things slow, but she's coming home next weekend and I don't want to have to stay away from you because we agreed to not broadcast to our kids that we were spending time together. What do you think?"

She had no issue with that. She was happy that he thought she was special enough to want to tell his daughter about her.

"I think it's wonderful. I will leave it up to you, but I would love to meet her and I think it's time Jamie and Jason met you. I know we agreed to be friends until things are worked out, but I don't want to have to sneak and see you or sneak and talk to you out of fear one of the kids will find out about it. The argument I ended up having with James stemmed from that kid telling Jason he saw you and I together. Jason had let it slip one day while talking to his father."

Hunter knew that things were rocky and was glad they didn't get more heated than they had for her.

"My personal life is none of his business, just as his isn't a concern of mine. I plan to tell Jamie and Jason a little more about you so that they understand what's going on. I do have an idea. What do you say you bring Coral and I'll bring the kids and let's get together while she's home. It's the holiday season and with Christmas coming in a few weeks, I'd like to be able to spend time with you and not hide it from the kids. I don't know what we can do, but before then I'll think of something. I don't want them thinking too much about what you and I are to each other. I think we should tell them we are friends and one day we may be more, but for now we wanted to be the ones to tell them what's happening. Is that okay with you?"

"That's fine with me. I agree, we should get everyone together. You won't be married forever and as soon as you aren't, I'm stepping up my game," Hunter joked, but serious at the same time.

"Well you won't have to wait long. I told my attorney to let me know the night before James is served with the divorce papers. I'm going to tell Jamie and Jason about it the night before so that they aren't surprised. I don't want to tell them too soon because I need James to be served first. I also care a great deal about you and I'm doing us both a disservice by not being in a position to openly be involved with you. I want to be able to do that so much," she admitted.

Hunter liked the sound of that.

"I want that too Dana. This friendship thing is fine for now, but I know I'm going to want more."

"You're not the only one feeling that way," she said.

"You are special to me Dana, more than you can even imagine. Well I'm going to head to my first class of the evening. Let me know what you want to do as far as the kids meeting each other when Coral comes home and we'll make it happen. I know Coral will be ecstatic. It'll be late when I get in so I'll talk to you tomorrow."

Dana hung up feeling like she was floating on air. For once, things in her life were working in her favor and really looking up. It felt good to be appreciated and celebrated by the right man.

Chapter Eleven
DANA

"So this is it huh?"

Dana turned around to see her husband standing behind her in the back yard of her house. She was getting the grill ready for a family dinner with her, the kids, Hunter and his daughter. Though it was freezing cold outside, everyone wanted grilled burgers, hotdogs and steaks so she quickly cleaned the grill to prepare it.

She and Hunter had agreed that rather than take everyone out to a restaurant for a public meeting that he and Coral would come to her house and they could all sit down and talk. What she didn't expect was to see James show up at her house. She kept forgetting to get the locks changed. That would be the first thing on her list for the next day.

She knew that he had been served with divorce papers earlier in the week. The process server said that he had to catch James at the airport to deliver them. After stopping at this office, the server had been told that James was on his way to the airport for a business trip. He knew how important it was to get the papers to James that day, so he went to the airport and using the photo of James that he had, he served him as he was entering the doors at the airport after being given the flight information at his office, telling them it was an important banking matter. She thought that she would have heard from him by now, but she guessed he waited until he returned to have the conversation in person.

She knew things had finally come to a head since he was now at her house, holding divorce papers in his hand. Any other time she would entertain him, but she didn't really want to at the moment. She was cold, busy and expecting company.

"Not now James. Whatever this is save it. I have a busy day planned and I don't have time to try and figure out this maze of a conversation with you."

"I know all about your busy day. So the boyfriend and his daughter are coming over? You do realize you're still married to me. We're not divorced yet, even though I was served with papers in the airport earlier this week. I needed the rest of the week to calm down and wonder what the hell you were thinking filing for divorce? Have you thought of the negative repercussions of you doing that? I've been leaving you messages and you've been ignoring them. You did this and we haven't talked about how we need to put our marriage back on track. Believe me when I say, you don't want to divorce me. You'll regret it."

Thankfully Dana was in the yard by herself so she didn't have to worry about what the kids heard. She turned around to face him to let him know, he had no power over her anymore.

"Don't even try coming up in MY house with any scare tactics. There are no negative repercussions from what I can decipher. I've been living in hell since the moment you decided to have your first fling. From where I'm standing, my life is looking up."

"So what, you've given up on our marriage ever working

out again now that you have a boyfriend? I received divorce papers from you, no warning."

"He's not a boyfriend, he's a friend. No warning James? Really? You've had a whole year to work out whatever issues were going on that made you leave in the first place. Was I supposed to sit around while you played house with every tart in a fifty mile radius? No more James. No more falling for your promises of putting this family back together because this family is already together. You chose to walk away from us and the life we had together and I, stupidly, waited over a year for something I knew was never going to happen."

"You didn't give it time to happen Dana. Instead you had me served with divorce papers without even talking to me about this first. What if I told you that I really do want to come home?" he said in a softer tone.

Dana wasn't falling for his game anymore, but she let him continue.

"I miss you and the kids and I miss our life together. I don't know what's going on with you working, going to college, dating someone. I don't think I know this Dana who's standing in front of me. I never thought you'd actually file for divorce. We haven't even done any real counseling or anything."

"Counseling? What kind of counseling would we need to do? It's clear you made a decision of what you wanted to do a long time ago and I'm just catching up and realizing that you made that decision and it was finally benefiting me.

"Dana, all I know is when I found out about Hunter and when I received the divorce papers, I thought about how much I really did miss my family. The papers made it real," he said shaking them at her.

"Hunter and papers are what made this situation real for you? It wasn't the day you walked out on your family? You're being ridiculous James.'

"It's all true Dana. I never filed for divorce from you because I was always planning to come back home to you and the kids. We've been together since you were eighteen years old. Can you really file for divorce now and walk away without giving us another chance? You said this Hunter guy is not a boyfriend, but a friend, so nothing is stopping you from giving this family another chance to be whole. You are the one now responsible for tearing this family apart. I broke things off with Reese when I got back in town today, telling her I wanted my family back. I called a realtor to put my condo on the market because I'm serious about making our family work again. I think instead of a divorce, we should do counseling to work out our issues. I don't think divorce is the answer, so call it off today."

Dana smile with satisfaction. His words meant nothing to her, nor did his demands.

"I'm not calling anything off," she declared.

"If you divorce me you won't get anything. I promise you that," he threatened.

Is he serious? She wanted to scream, but knew she had to keep her voice down, so she calmly walked right up so that they were face to face, like he did with her many times when trying to make a point.

"How dare you come here issuing orders? You come up in here trying to trick me into believing before you got the divorce papers that you'd planned to come back home. Well let me enlighten you to the reality of the state of our marriage. You were not and are not invited to come back here. That option is no longer on the table. Truth be told, that was no longer an option the moment you screwed your first tart outside of our marriage. At that time I wasn't strong enough to do what I needed to do for myself and my children. We don't deserve the treatment you've given us this past year and I especially didn't deserve having Reese thrown in my face all the time. I let you alienate me from my family and my childhood friends. My children didn't even know my side of the family, but thankfully I was able to remedy that and they talk to my parents several times a week. They are looking forward to a few weeks from now when my family will all come here for a great family weekend gathering. The kids are enjoying getting to know their cousins via Skype and phone calls. My life with you is over with. There is a brand new Dana in town and her name will soon be Dana Richardson again as soon as the divorce is final."

It felt good letting him know that she'll soon be going back to her maiden name. She no longer had a need for his. She was happy to be taking her life back and by the look on James' face, she knew he wasn't ready for the Dana he was now facing. Before he could respond, she cut him off and continued.

"You've strong armed me into being the little housewife so that you could hold all of the cards. Well not any more. I filed for divorce because I need my independence. I want to retain a level of self-respect for myself where I can look my kids in the face and they can see that I'm not a mat for you to walk all over. I was so happy being your wife and their mother all of those years that I lost myself somewhere in those years in the past, but not anymore. I plan to finish my classes, continue to work and live my own dreams out. That dream is to become a school teacher and nothing is going to stop that. I certainly won't let you and your broken promises or threats deter me from that. I am my own woman and I never could and probably never will be unless I get out from under you. We share two kids together now and that's it. You can use all the threats you want to try and control what happens here in my house or with my children, but you won't win. I love them, they love me and I'm a good mother. I'm not the one who walked out on them when I had a mid-life crisis. You're not a little boy anymore, you're a man. Take responsibility for the mistakes you've made. Own them, live with them and realize you took too long trying to fix them. Now, like I said when you first got here, I have a very busy day planned. I have guests coming and you're not invited. If you'd like to see the kids, feel free to do that, but make it short. I suggest the next time you stop by my house, you call first. I'm having a locksmith come tomorrow to change the locks so your key will no longer work and the alarm code will be changed today. Unless you have anything else you need to say, you can see yourself out. I'll see you in court and make sure you bring your checkbook. I don't plan to lose my house, my kids or the support you've been providing for them. I sat back as the dutiful wife while you pursued your dreams and now I plan to ask a judge to have you pay while I secure mine. Don't come here making a threat about cutting off support for my children. That's what you're supposed to do and not do it as a way to control their mother."

Dana turned back around to finish prepping the grill. She wasn't sure if James had more to say or not, but it was time he got a dose of his own medicine. She learned from him how to dismiss someone from a conversation. He'd done it enough times to her. She heard him walking away and was glad that was the decision he'd made. There was no telling what else she'd say now that she was fired up. All she knew was it felt good taking back who she was.

Chapter Twelve
DANA

Dana couldn't believe she was holding in her hand her final divorce papers. Her attorney was right in that it took only a few short months for everything to be finalized. In that time, life had changed for the better for them all.

After that cold day back in early winter when she and Hunter decided to let their kids meet by cooking some grilled food, they had all been inseparable. After her heated conversation with James, Hunter and Coral had shown up when she'd taken the last of the burgers off of the grill. It was too cold to eat outside so they set up a table in the family room where Dana thought they would all be more comfortable than in the kitchen or the dining room.

Jamie took to Coral immediately wanting to know all about college life, dancing and boys. Coral was on her college's dance and cheerleading teams and Jamie hung on every word of the many performances Coral told her about. As for the boys, Coral told he to wait a few more years and she'd tell her everything. She was even surprised at Jason's calm and almost charming attitude once he met Hunter and Coral. It turns out, unlike most Chicago fans, he and Hunter were both San Francisco Raiders fans, so that started a football conversation that was never-ending. That evening turned out well and after giving Jamie her email address and cell phone number, Coral promised to stay in touch before heading off later that evening to hang with some friends before she had to go back to school. She and Hunter were both pleased with how things turned out that evening.

She also found that after James consulted with his own attorney, he was advised to sign the papers since Dana was only asking for what he was already giving her including a little extra to cover her classes. His attorney knew that with the kind of money and holdings James had, she could ask for a lot more and didn't. Dana wanted to be free and wanted to be sure he would continue to take care of the kids and one day their college tuitions. As for her, she planned to take care of herself. James finally relented and gave in, signing the papers and ending their marriage.

"My divorce is final," Dana said out loud to herself. She couldn't stop looking at the papers that finally declared her a single woman again.

The kids were finally adjusting to the new Dana. There was no more talking back or raising their voices at her. She'd set some house rules and neither child wanted to deal with the consequences of not following them. They seemed to be happier now that she was happier. She knew she'd made the right decision in divorcing James. She needed to do it, not just for her own sanity, but for the sanity of her children. There was too much drama all the time.

She also found herself free to get closer to Hunter. He'd held to his word that he would wait while she sorted out her affairs with James and he had. They were closer than ever and now that the divorce was final. They needed to figure out what going to the next level was going to mean for them. They were enjoying a quiet evening trying to take it all in.

"Are you okay Ms. Richardson?" Hunter asked, concerned about the emotions she was probably experiencing and using her new last name since she'd decided to go back to her maiden name. He remembered the day his divorce was final and all the emotions he'd experienced. He wanted to be a shoulder for her if she needed it.

She smiled hearing him use her name for clarity that they were free to go the distance with each other.

"I'm actually better than I thought I would be. Thank you for being here for me through all of this. I know you tried to take a back seat to everything and to not be an influence on anything I decided to do. I appreciate you doing that."

Hunter was happy that she was free from the restraints of being married to her ex-husband. Now he wondered what was next for her and what was next for them.

"So what's next for you and what's next for us?" he asked.

Dana turned from her position of being enveloped in his embrace while they watched television at his house, so that she was facing him. She too wondered what was next for them.

"What would you like to be next for us?" she asked.

"Dana, you told me for years you had no control over your life. Everything you did, a decision was made for you. That time is over and done. Now is the time for you to assert your independence and speak about what you want. I don't want to decide what happens next. I want you to tell me what you want to happen next and if it involves me,

I want to do everything within my power to make that happen. So I'm asking you again, what's next?"

Dana wasn't acquainted with taking the lead on decision making, but she liked the feeling of being in control.

"Well as for me, I'm going to focus more on school while I continue working with the kids. I'm doing great in my classes and I love my job at the school. In the divorce settlement, I got the house and James has to continue paying the mortgage even though his name is no longer on it. That's a huge weight off of my shoulders which allows me to continue focusing on school without worry. He was also ordered to cover my school expenses for undergraduate only. The additional financial support he's required to pay will allow me to finish school, and work and I'm able to support myself and my children. I'm looking forward to fulfilling my dream of becoming a teacher. I never understood how much I was missing out on until I started working with the children. I'm excited about the future and as for us, I want our friendship to become something more. I've become accustomed to counting on you, not depending on you. I count on you to let me be myself around you. I love how comfortable you make me feel and how much I've learned from you. You don't try to control me or dictate to me how I should live my life and you let me be me. I still want to be me, but I want to be me with you, if you'll have me. I see something special when I think of us together. I don't think it was an accident that I shared my table with you at the deli because I believe it was meant to be. I needed that small push to get out from under my situation and you helped me with that without pushing your own agenda on me. What do you think about us being more than friends?"

Hunter was thinking the same thing.

"I think it's a wonderful idea. I think I'm falling in love with you, but please don't let that scare you away. I'm not going to move too fast with forcing my love on you. I feel like I've been given a second chance at love and I don't want to lose that. I made some mistakes in the past that I have learned from and I think you've done the same thing. I believe together we can grow into something very special. So what do you say as my official girlfriend, we go out and celebrate at the deli where we first met?"

"Girlfriend? Eww!"

Hunter and Dana both turned to see Jamie and Coral had come in the room. Coral was in the middle of her spring semester at college and when Jamie told her of the school play she was going to be in, Coral came home for the weekend to see Jamie perform.

"Mom, you're someone's girlfriend?" Jamie asked curiously.

Dana smiled realizing she was.

"Well, I guess I am. Hunter and I have decided that we really like each other and we want to be together."

"Mom, women your age aren't supposed to have boyfriends, they have husbands."

They all laughed, including Jamie.

"Well Jamie," Hunter chimed in, "one day if your mom ever decides that she's ready to have a husband again, I hope it's me. How's that?"

"I like that," she answered, smiling brightly.

"So do I," Coral added.

"Me too," Dana said.

"I like the idea of having a big sister," Jamie added.

"Well Jamie, whether they are ever husband and wife or

not, consider me your big sister anyway," Coral said. "What do you say you and I leave the two of them to their trip to the deli and let's go to the movies; my treat. Well, dad's treat because I'm broke."

Everyone laughed again when Coral held her hand out for money and Hunter slapped some into it.

"Don't do anything you're always telling me I shouldn't do!" Coral exclaimed as she and Jamie headed for the door.

Doing something Coral wouldn't do is exactly what Hunter had in mind for him and Dana. He turned his attention back to her.

"Now, back to my question. Dinner at the deli? Following that I was thinking you and I could pack an overnight bag and have some alone time at a suite in downtown Chicago. I know you said Jason was at his dad's place and Coral and Jamie will be gone for hours. I can call Coral and tell her to let Jamie stay the night here with her. I think they'd both like that. That will give you and me some much needed time to ourselves. What do you think about that plan?" he asked.

"I say you call Coral and I'll call Jamie so that she can stop at home to get an overnight bag which I'll pack while I'm there packing mine. Nothing would make me happier than spending a wonderful night, all night long in your arms. In fact, I thought you'd never ask."

"I'll go up and pack a few things, call Coral and we can be out of here in no time. In the meantime, call Jamie and let her know about spending the night. Do you think you need to call Jason even though he's at his dad's? You never know if he'll decide to come home early."

"Good idea. I'll do that and tell him if he needs me he can call my cell."

While Hunter was getting an overnight bag packed, he took the time to call the Ritz-Carlton in downtown Chicago to book a suite for them for the night. He also requested a bottle of champagne to have chilling on ice in the room when they got there and a nice dinner which he gave them a time for delivery so that it would still be hot when they got there. He would nix the deli and they would head for their special night together. He'd waited what seemed an eternity and he couldn't wait to fall asleep with Dana in his arms. He wanted the night to be special. It would be the first time that they would be spending the night together and he wanted everything to be perfect.

Dana called both of her kids to let them know that she could be reached on her cell phone if they needed her. Jamie was more than excited to hear that she would be spending the night with Coral. Jamie told her that Coral was going give her a facial and they were going to polish each other's nails and eat ice cream and watch movies all night long. Dana had never heard that much excitement in Jamie's voice before. She had no worries that Coral and Jamie would have a great time. She wanted them to bond. She planned to be a part of Hunter and Coral's life for a long time and was glad that Jamie and Coral were already close.

Jason didn't say much. She knew that he had pretty much figured out that she would be with Hunter all night and he told her that he was happy to see her happy again.

After Hunter came back ready to leave, they went to her house so that she could pack a bag for the night. While Hunter waited for her downstairs, Dana went through her dresser to find the right night gown for the evening. She selected a short black silk gown that she'd recently bought.

It still had the tags from the store on it. She thought it would be perfect; something new for a new beginning. Finally getting her bag and turning out the lights, she joined him.

"Are you ready to go?" he asked.

"More than you know," she happily replied.

~ ~

The Ritz-Carlton was a beautiful hotel. Dana had been to it several times for events, but she'd never been in the hotel suites before. The one she and Hunter were in was gorgeous. She looked around with amazement as she took it all in, including the expensive bottle of wine that was set up for them. With the wine were several cheeses, fruits and vegetables.

"Hunter, when did you do all of this," she asked inquisitively.

"I wanted this to be very special for us both. I called when I was packing my things for the night. I hope you like everything."

"I love everything."

"That's good to know because this is only the beginning for us tonight. I've waited a long time to be able to hold you in my arms all night. I'm hoping time slows down for the two of us tonight. I want to be sure we both savor every precious moment."

"I've waited as long as you have and I'm looking forward to this night and many others alone with you. Shall we order dinner?" she asked.

Hunter had other plans.

"Dinner is fine with me if that's really what you want to do," he said coming up behind her placing a kiss on the back of her neck while pulling her back into his embrace.

Dana moaned at the closeness and the desire that swept through her feeling the intimate kiss.

"If there is more from where this kiss came from then I would say I'm not hungry at all."

"Oh, I'm hungry," Hunter said softly, "just not for food at the moment. I don't want to do anything that you're not ready for, so you let me know how far we can go tonight and that's what we'll do."

Dana turned around in his arms and without second guessing, she reached up to pull Hunter by the shoulders until their lips met in a kiss that was scorching with promise and visions of much more than kisses.

Hunter could hardly contain himself with the way Dana was kissing him. If he had any doubts of how much she wanted him, they were gone. He picked her up and headed straight for the bedroom. After ending the kiss, he placed Dana back on her feet.

"Do you have any idea of how much I love you? My head is spinning right now and I want you to know that I love you Dana and if you will let me, I want to show you how a woman who is really and truly loved should be treated. First, I'm going to go back out to get our wine and tray of veggies and fruits so that we can toast to a wonderful relationship; one that I've waited a lifetime to have. Then I'm going to come back in here and we're going to have a night to remember."

"That's sounds like a good plan. I'm going to take the time while you're doing that to grab a shower and get out of these clothes I've been in all day."

Dana grabbed her overnight bag and headed into the adjourning bathroom.

Hunter grabbed his own bag after getting the wine and

cheese and placing it on the table in the bedroom. He went into the other bathroom to grab his own shower.

Returning to the room afterward, he noticed Dana was still in the bathroom. He took the time to uncork the wine and poured them both a glass. He found a radio station that played soft rhythm and blues music all night. He was about to dim the lights a little when the bathroom door opened. If he hadn't been near a table to brace himself for the sight before him, he would have fallen to the floor overwhelmed with pure delight. Dana was standing in the doorway in the sexiest black nightie he'd ever seen. Her hair that had been pinned up when they arrived was now flowing down around her shoulders. He couldn't take his eyes off of her. She was a beautiful woman and the see through black nightie added to her allure.

"You are one beautiful woman Dana. How did I get so lucky?" he asked making his way over to her.

"I'm the lucky one. You make me feel special since the first day we met."

"Let me show you more of how special you are to me," he said leading her away from the doorway and over to the bed.

Dana went without hesitation. Nothing pleased her more than to realize she'd waited what seemed a lifetime for love again and now that she'd found it, she was all in. When they reached the bed, she wanted to be sure to make one thing clear to Hunter before anything else happened.

"Hunter, I love you too. I want you to know that the love in this room is not one sided. I never thought I'd feel the way you make me feel or the way I feel about you and I wanted you to know that I love you very much."

Hunter didn't say a word. He looked in her eyes, smiled

and lifted her up to place her in the center of the bed.

"Your love is exactly what I need baby, so thank you. As long as I have that and you, I'm a happy man."

Dana's stomach felt like butterflies were fluttering around in it, not from nervousness, but from the sheer magnitude of the love she saw looking back at her from Hunter's eyes. Her breath caught the moment he leaned down and placed a kiss first on each of her cheeks before coming down on top of her, not using his full weight, but enough that she could feel his arousal for her. Her body became pliant when Hunter took her mouth in a kiss that was deep and all consuming, laced with love, passion and fulfilment.

Hunter wasted no time divesting Dana of the nightie that he loved so much to make them both a lot more comfortable and he couldn't think of a more comfortable state than being completely naked.

After Hunter removed all of their clothing, Dana was able to get her first look at his gloriously, naked body and her body instantly ached for need for him.

As he rejoined her, she didn't want him to waste any time joining their bodies. She'd waited a long time to feel loved again in the most intimate way.

"Love me Hunter," she whispered in his ear.

"I will always give you what you want and what you need baby.

Without any additional pleasantries, Hunter tested her readiness for him and upon finding she was more than ready, he joined their bodies and loved her slowly when she needed it slow and then deep and faster when she screamed that she needed that. They rode the crest of pleasure that continued taking them both higher and higher to a level of ecstasy neither had experienced before.

"You're finally mine baby," Hunter said, breathy.

"I'm all yours baby forever and ever," Dana replied, adding more words of love as she held on tighter for the ride of her life, racing for the cliff toward pleasure like none she'd ever known.

When he felt them both reaching the precipice of a mutual explosion, he closed his mouth over hers to make sure their bodies were not only joined below, but that they were sealing the moment with a kiss neither would ever forget.

As Dana gripped Hunter tighter, never, ever wanting to let him go, she heard his confessions of love over and over for her and the moment she exploded along with him, she knew that she was connected, not just intimately with his body, but also with his heart. The pleasure went on and on as they both whispered words of love that would last a lifetime.

TERRI'S STORY

Chapter One
TERRI

"Surprise!" the ladies shouted as the bride-to-be entered the room. It was an exciting time and everyone in the room could see that the bride, Jordan, was surprised to enter a room of family and friends who had gathered to celebrate this big, new and exciting time in her life. Terri Bryant was no exception. She and Jordan had met a few years ago at work where they both worked as senior marketing and public relations specialists. The huge smile on Jordan's face was proof positive that she was happy about her impending day. Terri watched as her friend made her way around the room hugging and thanking everyone, with tears of joy running down her face.

"Terri!" Jordan said embracing her with a hug of gratitude. "Thank you for coming. This shower was really a surprise. All of you sure know how to keep a secret. All week working together and you didn't even give a hint that there was a bridal shower this week," Jordan exclaimed excitedly.

"Now Jordan, I promised to not let the cat out of the bag and we really wanted you to be surprised. Stay tuned," Terri whispered in her ear. "The celebration for you is just beginning."

She watched as Jordan smiled brighter, then shook her

head in agreement and went on to continue to greet more of her guests.

Terri admired Jordan. She was having the kind of day so many women dreamed about leading up to their wedding day. It was a day filled with all of her family, friends and co-workers, gathered together to wish her well in her marriage. Terri herself had never been married or engaged, but hoped that one day, her prince charming would propose to her and she could have a celebration similar to this one. She would never tell anyone, but she secretly had her own bridal shower and wedding already planned out in her head. One day, she thought to herself, moving about the room to join in on the fun.

The shower was in full swing. Terri watched as Jordan opened gifts from sexy lingerie to body oils and even one package that contained a brand new, self-install stripper pole for the bedroom. Terri laughed knowing that Jordan's soon to be husband would love that gift most of all.

They were all wonderful and exciting gifts for a friend who deserved every bit of happiness coming her way. She was marrying the man of her dreams. If Terri thought about it, Jordan was marrying the man of every woman's dreams. He treated her like at queen. No one ever doubted that André adored Jordan and they were going to have a wonderful life together. Even when they were gathered with a small group of their closest friends and Jordan could tell all of her deepest darkest secrets, she had nothing but good things to say about her fiancé. That's how it should be. Every woman wants to marry the man of her dreams, not just the guy who proposes and the woman says yes because she's always wanted to get married and have the dream wedding that all little girls dreamt about.

Now as a woman and not a little girl anymore, there should be more to it than an expensive wedding and no real love.

Thinking about her own relationship Terri would say that she was in love. She wasn't preparing for a wedding or anything, but she was in love. He wasn't the perfect man like Jordan's fiancé, but to her he was a great guy. He was definitely successful, which was a major plus in her book. She had dealt with enough broke brothers that she was over getting involved with anyone who wasn't powerful and successful. A man had to be very successful for her to even be interested. She wasn't sure that he was head over heels in love with her, but she hoped that would develop over time. He was a great catch and whatever she needed to do to keep him happy with her, is what she would do. She had been on a search for a man with money and status and now that she had him, she was going to make sure they would have a future together by any means necessary.

"Hey Terri."

She turned at the mentioning of her name to see that another co-worker had arrived.

"Hey Mari. I'm glad you made it. I know earlier in the week you said you weren't quite sure you would," Terri said.

"Yes. I've had a sick child all week and his fever finally broke. Now that he's feeling a little bit better, I was able to come out for a bit and join in the fun. I wasn't going to make today until my husband practically shoved me out of the door because he felt like I needed a break; a little free time away from wiping up drool and runny noses day after day."

"Oh, I'm so glad he's feeling better. I know that you've been worried all week about his high fever."

"Yes, I'm feeling better now that he's feeling better also."

"It's good that your husband could fill in and give you a break."

"Yeah, he's good like that," Mari said. "He's definitely a great example of what it means to co-parent. He never leaves it all on me. I'm a lucky girl."

Terri agreed. Another friend who often boasted about the great man she'd married.

Hearing all of her friends talk about the great men in their lives had Terri secretly hoping that one day she'd be able to boast with honesty about how great Daniel is to her instead of the few white lies she often found herself telling so that she could join in the conversations they would have about good men. Her story was slightly different.

Her very successful, attorney boyfriend, Daniel Allen at forty-six years old was sixteen years older than she was and she felt lucky to have him, though he could use a little work in the caring boyfriend department. She liked him because he was older and more mature than most men she found interesting. She found that she preferred men who were much older. The guys her age were either major players, into other men or had babies by several different women. Daniel had a few short comings like any other person, but she could see a very happy life with him in the future. She could imagine them living in a gorgeous mansion with at least two beautiful kids running around and her being able to drive an expensive, fancy car while having help from a nanny with the kids. All of that would be worth the little bit of misery she suffered through. That misery consisted of Daniel complaining about her weight, often calling her fat. She dealt with it because she knew he didn't really mean to be nasty to her. He only did it when he was upset with her or if he'd had a bad day at the office.

She knew being an attorney was a very stressful job so she didn't mind him taking his anger out on her every now and then. She'd even learned to live with him trying to mold her into the woman he wanted her to be. She didn't mind changing for her man. He knew what he wanted and if she was going to keep him, she needed to make some changes. She wished he wouldn't talk down to her in front of friends. He embarrassed her, but she dealt with that also because he apologized to her when they were alone, telling her he didn't mean it and she believed him. If he did mean all of the terrible things he said to her, then why would he still be with her? She brushed it off and continued to work on being the woman he wanted her to be. He was the first man in a long time that she could see herself with long term as long as she played her cards right. She had to bide her time. When she proved to him that she could be what he wanted and needed, he would propose and they would be complete.

"Well I'm going to grab another piece of cake and check out the gifts I missed seeing Jordan open before I arrived. I'll talk with you in a bit," Mari said breaking into Terri's thoughts.

Terri was on her third piece of cake and really wanted a fourth, but she was trying hard to control the love affair she had with any and everything sweet. Daniel would be angry if he knew she'd consumed that many slices of cake, even though they were thin slices compared to other's she'd had. He'd recently commented that sweets were not her friend and that if she ever planned to be his wife, she'd have to stay away from sweets, bread and anything else that was preventing her from losing weight. She promised him she would work on it and thinking about those three slices of cake, she felt ashamed that she'd broken her promise.

All of her life she'd been overweight. A few times she'd tried several different diets and even tried working out sometimes, but nothing seemed to work because right after those attempts, she'd go right back to her old habit of indulging in sweet treats. There were times when Daniel would tell her she was sexy and voluptuous and he loved her like that and other times he'd come to her place with ads about quick scheme weight loss programs or some other information on the latest weight loss pills. She often didn't know what direction to go in. One day her weight was fine with him, others he hated it.

She herself was up and down when it came to how she felt about her weight. She knew that she could stand to lose a little weight, but on the other hand, she was happy with who she was most times. She didn't think she was a fat type of heavy. She was in fact voluptuous with rounded hips and a behind that turned heads wherever she went. She was a little thick around the middle, but it wasn't flabby or too unattractive. She dressed nice, always being told she was the best dressed of her group of friends.

Terri knew she was pretty and her long natural hair was something she didn't have to supplement with weaves, but she did because Daniel hated natural hair. He liked women with very long, straight, permed hair. Terri refused to put those chemicals in her hair so she kept her long black, streaked weave tight and looking good for his approval.

Her cell phone rang and it was the man she was

thinking about. Anyone looking at her would think that she'd won the lottery, her smile was so bright.

"Hi honey," she said happily into the phone, answering it before it rang too many times.

"Where are you Terri? I've called you several times," he said angrily.

She must have missed it while having fun at the shower.

"I'm sorry. My phone was in my purse and with the noise at the bridal shower, I didn't hear it ring. I picked my purse up and it started ringing."

"Suppose I had an emergency reason for contacting you. You should always keep your phone on you anyway when we're not together."

"I know you're right and I'm sorry. Is everything okay?" she asked, concerned that she'd upset him. Sometimes he would go days of being upset with her and not call. She couldn't stand times like that.

"No, everything is not alright Terri," he said. "I took the evening off to spend it with you and you're at some bridal shower."

"I told you about Jordan's bridal shower weeks ago. You remember Jordan, she works with me at the firm," Terri explained.

"Yeah, I remember Jordan. She's the one who's always trying to drag you out to clubs or to the gym making you think you're fat or something."

"Daniel you've been telling me yourself that you want me to lose some weight, so I figured going to the gym with her would be okay."

"Are you trying to throw my words back at me Terri?" he demanded.

"No baby, I'm not. I was explaining why I was going to

the gym with her."

"Yeah, well you don't need to go to the gym. The gym is a meat market where desperate women go looking for men. Are you looking for a man?" he asked.

Terri was frightened that she had indeed upset him. Of course she wasn't looking for anyone.

"No baby. You're all the man I need or want. I won't go with her anymore okay?" she said, hoping that would calm the situation down.

"I told you I don't like her. You could certainly do better in the friendship department. I don't like your group of so called friends. I know they don't think I'm good for you, but I don't care what they think. This relationship is about you and me right?"

"Yes Daniel, you're right and I'm sorry for upsetting you."

"So are you coming home or what?" he asked.

Terri hesitated before answering. She really wanted to stay, but it sounded like Daniel was going to have a problem with that.

"I haven't been here that long and they haven't started most of the games yet," she said.

"Games? Really Terri, how old are you? Well that's fine. You go ahead and stay at your little party. I guess Jordan is more important to you than I am. Maybe it's time I called some of the other women who are really interested in me. You know I don't usually date women as young as you, but I thought you were ready for a more mature relationship. I guess I was wrong," he said.

Terri didn't want that. She wouldn't be able to stand losing him. That would again make her the only one of her friends with no man and she was already thirty. She had to make her relationship a priority just as her friends who were all either engaged or married had done. She needed to do everything in her power to keep her man and make sure he was happy.

"No, you're not wrong. I love you and you mean more to me than anyone, you know that," she admitted.

"I can't tell Terri because right now, I feel like I have to convince you to leave and spend time with me. So are you leaving or am I going to find something else to do with my time tonight?" he asked.

Terri looked around the room at all the fun the ladies were having and loved the atmosphere, but she knew Daniel could find any other woman to spend time with, but he was choosing her. She knew any of her friends would make the same sacrifice that she was about to make.

"I'm leaving right now," she said heading toward the front door.

"That's what I like to hear. Since I'm not too happy with you right now, I'll wait here at your house for twenty minutes and then I'm leaving," he said.

"Daniel, I'm about a half hour away. I might not make it in twenty minutes. Please wait for me," she pleaded.

"Okay, thirty minutes, but not a minute more. You know you'll have to make this little episode up to me. I expect something very sexy, lacy and maybe a little dance added on."

"Okay, I will I promise. I don't mean to upset you. I'm leaving right now and I will make this up to you."

Terri hung up, grabbed her things and went to Jordan to apologize for having to leave.

"Jordan, I'm so sorry I have to leave. I have a family emergency," she lied.

Terri watched as Jordan's happiness was replaced with sadness.

"Terri, you're going to miss all of the fun," Jordan exclaimed sadly.

"I know and I'm sorry. You know I wouldn't leave if it wasn't important."

Jordan knew better.

"You can say it Terri."

"Say what?" Terri asked, not looking directly at Jordan, avoiding eye contact while fake straightening her clothes.

"It's Daniel right? He doesn't want you to be here. What did he do this time, make a threat of leaving you or did he use the threat of going out with another woman if you didn't leave right now?"

Terri knew that Jordan could read her like a book. She didn't like lying to her friend, but she didn't want to sound too desperate saying she was leaving because her boyfriend told her to.

"It's not like that Jordan. He's had a really bad day and he really needs me right now. Come on, you would do the same thing for Andre if it were him," she said.

"No Terri, I wouldn't. Not only would I not ditch my own plans, but I know that Andre would never ask me too. We are all adults and you are entitled to have a life not only with Daniel, but one that doesn't involve him dictating every aspect of yours. I know you love him and there is nothing wrong with wanting to please him, but he is controlling. You guys put a lot into this shower and you should be here to enjoy it with me. I would never make you choose and you know that, so go ahead and go make Daniel happy. You know I love you and I wish you would realize you deserve so much better. I don't care how much money he makes or how powerful he is, you still deserve to have a little girl time fun. I wish you would see that you are worth more than a string-puppet for that man. I'm not hating on you or your relationship and I love you like a sister. I want so much more for you and right now, your happiness is solely based on his and that's not how life should be. Well I'm sure he has you on some type of schedule so you better get going. At least grab some cake to take with you before you leave. Even take a piece for Daniel," Jordan said.

Terri knew that was hard for Jordan to say knowing that Daniel didn't like her. Despite that she still tried for Terri's sake, hoping to show her happiness and to be the friend that Terri needed.

"I better not. You know I'm watching my weight," Terri said.

"You mean Daniel doesn't want you eating cake."

Now Terri felt stupid. No matter what, she still had to leave and she didn't want to have this conversation with Jordan right now. She was already running out of time with having thirty minutes to get home to Daniel.

"Congratulations again sweetie," Terri said ignoring the little bit of tension between the two of them. "I'll call you tomorrow and you can tell me all about the things I'm missing out on tonight, okay?"

"Okay, we'll talk tomorrow Terri. Make sure you tell Daniel I said hello," Jordan said sarcastically, knowing that Daniel didn't like her.

"I will and thanks for understanding," she said giving Jordan a hug and going around her to go out the door before anyone else noticed her departure. She didn't want anyone to try and make her feel bad for leaving. She knew any of them would do the same thing. Even Jordan would, no matter what she'd said.

Chapter Two
TERRI

Daniel was lounging around on Terri's sofa watching television and watching the time. He told her she would have thirty minutes to get home and he meant thirty minutes. He had no doubt she would make it on time even if she had to run a few lights to make it happen. He had her in check like that, so there was no need for him to put his shoes back on because she would be coming through the door in less than ten minutes, probably out of breath from rushing. Sometimes he found it amusing watching her bend over backwards for him. He only had to snap and she would stand at attention if he wanted her to. It was nice having a woman at his beck and call because so many women these days didn't allow themselves to be treated like that by men. He liked the few that still did.

He, at first, had reservations about the much younger marketing specialist his firm had hired a year ago. He never found himself interested in younger women, but he'd caught her staring at him a few times while they were working on a marketing campaign for his law firm. He'd recently made partner and was looking forward to going to the next level adding on more clients.

The firm Terri worked for was the perfect firm to help him do that. Late nights of working with Terri had gone from all business to them having sex all over his office, on every piece of furniture. She was unlike the older women he encountered and dated. She was wild and did any and everything he wanted her to do. He'd found a way to use her naiveté to his advantage. He also never saw himself with a woman who was larger than a size six. Terri was a size six times three. Though she was a lot bigger than women he was used to dating, she still wore it well. She was thick in all of the right places. She had a luscious, big round behind, a reasonably small waist for her size and large breasts that he loved giving extra special attention to. She had a beautiful round face that was a chestnut brown and her make-up was always perfect, something he required. Her lips were gorgeous and he loved when she encased them in shiny, glossy lip gloss. The things she could do with those lips are what turned him on the most. He was looking forward to that tonight.

"Baby, are you here," Daniel heard as Terri came rushing through the door of her brownstone sounding very much out of breath.

"Yeah, I'm watching television. I was about to get up and leave. You made it under the wire," he said, not even turning around.

"I'm sorry. I only went to the shower because I thought you'd be working late again," Terri said apologetically.

"Don't worry about it. You're here now and that's what really matters. Aren't you going to come over here to the sofa and show me how much you missed me and how sorry you are for not being here at home when I got here?" Daniel asked.

Terri didn't hesitate. She went around and stood right in front of him, leaning toward him to give him the kiss she knew he was waiting for. She felt alive and desirable every time they kissed. She gave every kiss her all, wanting to show him how much he meant to her. He was her everything and she never wanted him to think otherwise.

"That kiss was exactly what I needed after a long day at the office. You have no idea what a crazy day I've had. I'm all tense and you know exactly what I need right now to relieve the tension," he said looking first up into her eyes and then down at his zipper.

She knew exactly what he wanted. As his woman it was her duty to make sure he was happy and satisfied at all times. If not he would find another woman to take care of his needs and she couldn't have that. She lowered herself to her knees as she helped him undress so that she could relax him.

~~

Terri lay in bed snuggled up to Daniel and looked at the clock noticing it was before nine at night. She was about to say something when she heard Daniel's stomach growl.

"Sounds like you're starving for more than the sex we just had," she said, jokingly.

"I am starving. What are you planning to make me to eat?" he asked.

"Do you want your favorite, grilled chicken breasts and a salad?" she asked. She knew that Daniel loved to eat light and never anything greasy or fattening. He had a gorgeous, body which came from hours a week of working out at the gym. He could give any young guy a run for his money in the body department. Daniel didn't have an ounce of fat on him.

"That sounds great. And some red wine would go nice with that," he added.

"I don't think I have any red, but I do have white," she added.

"I prefer red. You can take my car if you'd like to go get some," Daniel said before getting up and grabbing his pants from the floor.

Terri caught the car keys when Daniel tossed them to her before he headed off in the direction of the bathroom.

"You know the brand I like."

After he closed the bathroom door, she got up, grabbed her clothes and headed to the hallway bathroom to freshen up before running out to the store to get the wine. She convinced herself it was okay because she actually had a few other things she needed, so it was a great idea for her to go instead of him. She hurried so that she could get back to cook.

On the ride to the store, Terri sat back, comfortable in the plush leather seating of Daniel's Porsche. It wasn't often that he let her drive it and definitely not by herself. She loved the slick silver car and it spoke of the kind of money and stature Daniel had. She loved that she was his woman after she'd spent too much time over the past few years dating losers. Now was her time to get the kind of man she really wanted. She would show her family and friends that she could land a handsome, successful man. Everyone had been telling her that she would never get a man unless she lost some of the excess weight she was carrying around. She was told she would only get what was left over after all of the beautiful, skinny women were spoken for.

When she was younger and in high school, she was the one all the kids made fun of. No one ever asked her to any of the dances and so she would take a family friend or a distant cousin. In college, she'd dated, but most of those relationships were based on sex. That's how it was during those college days. When she really started looking for a serious relationship, she never found a guy who was committed to only her. There were always other women on the side.

Once she'd found the great job that she has now, that pays very well, she started attracting men who wanted to be with her because they thought she was financially stable. Many would hit her up for loans only to then disappear when it came time to pay her back. She'd learned her lesson. No more broke or guys starting out.

When she'd met Daniel, things had changed for her. He was wealthy, had a great job and had his own. She didn't have to worry about him taking advantage of her. She needed to make some changes in her life to make him happy. It wasn't until Daniel made mention of her weight that she thought about taking dieting and exercise seriously. Then Daniel would change his mind and dissuade her. He told her she was who she was supposed to be. Tonight was one of those nights. While making love he'd told her she was the most beautiful woman in the world and that he wouldn't change a thing about her.

She was glad that all thought of their earlier phone discussion when she was at the bridal shower had disappeared. Things were once again right in their world and Terri couldn't be happier.

Daniel showered and was glad for the small reprieve from Terri. She always liked to cuddle after sex and all he really wanted was a nice cold beer and some food. Knowing how much she loved to eat, he figured that would have been on her mind too. He was glad his stomach spoke up before he did. Now that she was gone, he needed to make a few phone calls. He had hoped to come to Terri's house earlier and be gone by now, but her being at that bridal shower put a glitch in his plans. He would have to push his original plans later into the evening. He'd come up with some excuse when Terri returned. For now, he had plans to make as he reached for his cell phone.

"Hey, it's Daniel," he said when the woman on the other end answered. "Listen, I'm going to be a little later than usual. What are you up to?" he asked.

"Nothing," he heard her reply. "I'm laying here in bed naked except for the red bottoms you bought me, waiting for you."

Daniel's body jumped with excitement at the thought of the twenty two year old, in-shaped woman on the other end of the phone. She was the daughter of one of his partners and he couldn't wait to get to her.

"So you made it to the room on time?" he asked.

"Of course, baby. You told me to be here so I'm here. I'm in town for the entire weekend from college to spend it with you. My parents don't know that I'm in town so I'm going to stay here in the room the whole weekend. I was hoping you would be here by now and that you'd cleared the entire weekend for me. I've got some new things I want to experiment with," she said seductively.

Daniel couldn't wait to find out what they were.

"Don't worry sweetie, I'll be there soon. I have a high profile client that has been arrested that I have to deal with tonight, but as soon as I'm done, I'm yours for the rest of the weekend," he said while getting dressed. He knew that Terri wouldn't be long, especially if she went to a nearby store. He would give her the same story about a client in trouble so that he could leave for the evening.

"Keep it hot for me," he said before hanging up. He heard Terri coming back in the door as soon as he'd put his phone away.

"Daniel, I'm back," Terri hollered throughout the house, hoping he was finished with his shower and ready to eat. She went straight to the kitchen to begin cooking. It wouldn't take her long to put a few chicken breasts on the indoor grill and to make a quick salad like he liked. She turned around when she heard him enter the room and was shocked to see that he was fully dressed and even holding his suit jacket in his hand.

"I'm sorry Terri," he began. "I have a very high profile client who called saying he's been arrested. You know I represent several professional football players and one of them has gotten himself into some trouble with a drunk driving charge. I need to get this taken care of before the press hears about this. I'm sorry because I know you were about to make us a fantastic dinner. Can I get a rain check?" he asked, straightening his tie and putting on his jacket.

She understood, knowing the kind of clients he had and how he worked his magic keeping them out of trouble.

"Sure I understand," she said. She was sad that he had to leave, but she didn't want to put a damper on the evening. "Do you think you'll be able to make it back sometime tonight? I can still make you something to eat and keep it warm for you."

"Probably not," he said. "I'm sure the team owners will want to meet with the player and me after I'm able to get him out and who knows how long that will take," he said.

Daniel walked over to Terri. "You know how much I

hate leaving you tonight. I was really looking forward to waking up next to you in the morning. I'll tell you what, I'll make it up to you. One of my friends is hosting a football party Sunday evening at his house. Why don't you come with me?" he said.

Terri was excited. Daniel didn't take her out often around many of his friends. He always said he was busy with work that when he was free, he didn't want to share her with anyone. This gave her hope.

"That would be great," she said happily.

"Good. Can you also make some of your world famous chili and those hotter than fire wings? There will be about fifteen people there. Everyone will love your cooking especially since I brag about it with the guys," he said, giving her a kiss on the cheek and not waiting for her to respond. He already knew she would do it.

"Sure, I can do that. What time Sunday should I be ready?" she asked.

"I'll pick you up around three and thanks baby. You always take good care of me. I'll call you tomorrow if I get a chance. I'm hoping this thing with the player doesn't take up my whole Saturday. If this takes all day tomorrow, I'll call you Sunday when I'm on my way," he added.

"Good luck with helping that player. You are too good to them," Terri said as she watched Daniel rush out the door. After she heard him lock the door back using the key she'd given him, she settled in to make a meal for one. She was about to put her dinner on the grill when her phone rang. It was Daniel. He must have left something.

"Hey," she said answering. "Did you forget something?"

"Yes, I need a favor. Do you think you could swing by the cleaners and grab my dry cleaning in the morning? It's been there a few days over. There is a suit I need for a big meeting on Monday. It's my power gray suit. It's the same one I always go to when I need a big win. They'll know you since you've done this for me in the past."

"Sure. No problem. That's why I'm here. To help when you need me," Terri said.

"Thanks. Talk to you Sunday," She heard him say. She assumed that meant he already knew he wouldn't be talking to her on Saturday.

Chapter Three
TERRI

It was Sunday and Terri was finishing getting dressed when she had to run to grab her phone before it stopped ringing. She grabbed it thinking it was Daniel saying he was on his way.

"I'm ready," she said into the phone.

"Ready for what?" Jordan said on the other line.

"Oh, Jordan, I'm sorry. I thought you were Daniel. I'm waiting for him to pick me up."

"Really? Where are the two of you going?" Jordan asked, curiously.

It didn't escape Terri the sound of surprise in Jordan's voice hearing that she and Daniel were going somewhere together. It's not something they did often.

"One of his friends is hosting a football party today for the game and he invited me to go with him."

"Wow, really? He's finally taking you around some of his friends?" Jordan said.

"Don't be mean Jordan."

"That's not being mean Terri. You know he never takes you anywhere around anyone he knows and you have been going out with him for a year. Let me guess here, he asked you to make something right? You've been cooking all morning I bet."

Terri knew she had to lie or the conversation would not go well. She looked at the spread of food she'd prepared.

"No he didn't. He told me what time to be ready so stop thinking so bad of him all the time because he's really a great guy. He can be very intense sometimes, but that's because of his job as a partner in his law firm," she explained.

"Whatever you say girl. I was calling to tell you all about the rest of the shower you missed on Friday. Why don't you give me a call later when you get in after the football party so we can talk?"

"Why don't we talk at work tomorrow? I'm sure I'm probably going to spend the night at Daniel's house tonight. You know he likes my full attention when we're together."

"Is that what they're calling it these days, full attention? You sure you don't mean wanting you under his complete control?" Jordan asked, seriously.

"Jordan, let me have this okay? I know you don't like Daniel, but I love him. Be happy that I'm happy okay?"

"Okay Terri. I'll do that only because we're friends and yes I want to see you happy. Is he coming with you to my wedding?"

Terri hesitated, knowing she hadn't asked him yet. She hadn't brought the subject up to him. He wasn't a fan of Jordan's even though he had only met her a few times. Daniel thought Jordan was too strong minded for a woman. He felt that women should be a lot more submissive than Jordan was.

"I'll ask him later tonight and let you know at work tomorrow, but I'm sure he will since I told him I was in the wedding. Besides, since we're seeing each other, I don't see why he wouldn't assume we would be going together."

"Okay, just let me know. Have fun today and I really mean that Terri. No playing housemaid to a bunch of men. Try to enjoy yourself too."

"I will and I'll talk to you tomorrow."

"Who was that you were talking to?" Daniel asked Terri as he came through the door as she was ending the call.

"Oh, that was my mother," she lied. "She missed me in church today and was checking on me."

Terri knew it was best to lie. He wouldn't be happy if she mentioned Jordan's name and she wanted to have a fun day with him. One thing did bother her; she was doing a lot of lying lately to keep the peace. That couldn't be good.

"This food looks good. You outdid yourself baby. I'll start putting the food in my truck while you go change," Daniel said, nonchalantly.

"Change?" Terry asked, looking down at her attire.

"Yeah, change," Daniel responded.

"Your top shows too much cleavage and don't you have jeans that aren't so tight?" he asked.

"Daniel, you can't be serious. I look fine. My cleavage is what it is and my jeans have plenty of room in them," she said showing him by pulling on the extra room.

"Terri, you are not going around a room full of men dressed like an invitation for sex. Where is the jersey I bought you? If you put that on you can keep the jeans on."

"I do have on a jersey. It's a jersey made for women, with a woman's cut," she said.

"I don't like it and you're going to make us late. Humor me and put on the jersey I bought. I don't want any other guy at the party ogling you. Ogling you is only for me," he said, leaning over to plant a kiss on her lips, no doubt to persuade her even more. "I promise later tonight, I'll let you model your jersey for me with nothing else on. I'll even wear my matching boxers for you, so do this for me," he said.

Terri couldn't deny Daniel anything.

"Okay. You load up the food and I'll put the other jersey on over this one," she said hurrying to change.

~~

Terri was having a good time at the football party. Daniel had very nice friends and the wives and girlfriends were also nice. The men were enjoying the game on the lower level in front of the massive screen while she and the other ladies were enjoying the game and some girl talk on the upper level in the family room. It was nice to be around some of Daniel's friends who welcomed her with open arms.

At one point in the evening, she was a little worried and upset when she went to the restroom on the upper level and was about to turn a corner to go into the bathroom when she overheard voices. Those voices turned out to be Daniel's and one of the girlfriends of one of Daniel's friends. They were in one of the bedrooms whispering, but not so low that Terri couldn't hear them. She couldn't make out the conversation because it sounded muffled. She didn't understand why they would have snuck off. She started to interrupt and then thought about that choice. If it were really innocent, it would only piss Daniel off and the night would be ruined. If it wasn't, the result would be the same so she turned and went back downstairs to use the one on the lower level. It was occupied before, but now it was empty.

Later when Daniel had come up from the lower level to grab more beer, she watched as he and the same woman had given each other a suspicious look. She wasn't the only one who noticed it either. She did, however, let it go. She came as his girlfriend and would leave the same way and she wouldn't let a little jealousy ruin that. Everyone there knows who she is. She decided to enjoy the rest of the evening and was happy the food she'd made was a hit.

On the drive to Daniel's house after the party, Terri decided to innocently inquire about what she'd seen and sort of overheard.

"So who was the woman I heard you talking to on the upper level of the house? I went to use the restroom and heard you two talking in one of the bedrooms," she said, smiling to let him know she wasn't trying to start an argument.

"There was a bathroom on the other two levels. Why didn't you go to one of them? Were you spying on me or something?"

"I know, but they were occupied and I was told to use one of the bathrooms on the top floor. I wasn't spying because I didn't know you were up there. I could hear you when I walked by," she admitted.

"Oh really? What did you hear?" he asked, continuing to drive, but tightening his grip on the steering wheel.

Terri could see asking him was not a good idea.

"Well nothing really," she said.

"That's because it was nothing. Are you becoming one of those jealous women that you hang around with? I thought you were more mature than that, even for your age. This is why I normally stay away from women younger women. You always think something is going on if you see your man talking to another woman."

A fight was not where Terri wanted this to lead. Now she wished she had never brought it up.

"It's not like that. I was just making conversation on the drive to your house. I'm not trying to accuse you of anything or start an argument so let's drop it, okay?"

"If you must know, we were talking about Phil's birthday. She's Phil's girlfriend and she wants my help in keeping him busy and bringing him to the surprise birthday party that's being planned for him. She wanted to tell me about the plans so that Phil couldn't hear us. The other guys know also and I was the only one not in the loop which is why we were talking," he lied, remembering his time in the room with a big breasted Tammy. He couldn't very well tell Terri that he was in that room devouring the woman. Tammy was gorgeous from the moment he'd first met her and Daniel liked her ever since then, a few months back when Phil first introduced him and his other friends to her.

His body, even now, began hardening remembering seeing her come into the house in her very low cut shirt showing every piece of flesh she had and the short denim skirt that showed legs that seemed to go on forever. He knew from the start that Tammy had a thing for him; most women did. He didn't think she was adventurous enough to let him take her up against a wall in the bedroom while everyone else was enjoying the game. He thought he was doing a good job muffling her screams of pleasure while they enjoyed a quickie, only to now find that Terri may have heard them. Luckily she didn't appear to have heard too much, so telling her the lie about the birthday planning was easy.

"Oh, that's nice. A surprise party will be a lot of fun. I'm sure Phil will appreciate you helping Tammy out," Terri said, trying to put the conversation to rest.

Daniel smiled as he looked out of the side window while they were stopped at a light. Once again, he was able to convince her that she was overreacting. Still his body was raging with want at the thought of what he and Tammy had done. They'd made plans to hook up again soon, but for now, Daniel needed relief.

"Perhaps I should take you home," he said, trying to seem angry and inpatient with her.

"No, don't do that baby, I'm sorry. I wasn't trying to insinuate anything at all. I was curious and like I said, it was simply conversation. I still want to model my jersey for you tonight while wearing nothing else. I have it on under this one."

Terri lifted her shirt to show him she still had on the other jersey.

Daniel looked over at her.

"Why don't you show me that jersey with all that luscious cleavage right now?"

"Now?" she asked. Daniel, we're in the car. We'll be at your house soon and I can show you then. Someone might see," she said looking around as if people were looking through the car windows.

"Well it must not be too much of a big deal. You were going to wear it around my friends tonight. I want a looksee right now."

This was crazy, she thought. They were in the car and he wanted her to flash him. Only for him would she even think of doing something like this. She reached for the hem of the big jersey and pulled it over her head.

"Nice," he said. "A little more," he encouraged.

"A little more what? We're in the car, Daniel."

"We're on a dark secluded street. There's no one around so take the bra off for me."

Terri looked around and didn't see anyone.

"Plus the windows on my truck are tinted; no one can see in even if they wanted to," he added, noticing her hesitation.

"Look, don't worry about it if you're scared someone will see. I'm an attorney and I wouldn't do anything risky that could get either of us in trouble. I'll pull over there," he pointed to an even darker area of the street.

Terri looked where he was pointing and didn't want to disappoint him.

"Okay," she said as he turned in the direction of the very dark area. When he did, she reached behind her and underneath her shirt to unsnap her bra. When she did, she tossed it into the back seat.

"Nice," he said, reaching over to caress the large globes. "How about we both get in the back seat with that bra?" he asked.

Terri bit her lip trying to decide what to do. They'd never done anything risky before.

"That or we could call it a night." He knew how this was going to go. She would do it. When he unlocked the car doors, he watched her reach for the handle to get out. When she was settled in the back, he got out to join her. He took a moment to let his head fill with pictures of Tammy and her tiny thong, slim body and supple lips and he joined Terri in the back for some fun.

Chapter Four
TERRI

"Kerrion, how is the progress on your gym coming along."

"It's going slow, but coming along Ma. How are you?"

"I'm fine son. I talked with your brother today and he asked me about you. Why haven't you been in touch with him?"

Kerrion knew that was coming up. He loved his family, but every time he talked to one of his brothers, they wanted to offer him money to speed up the process of fulfilling his dream of opening up his own gym. He loved them, but this was his dream and he really wanted to do it himself.

"Ma, Chase only wants to talk to me to discuss money and like I keep telling all of you, I got this."

"I know. I hate to see you working so hard. We all want to help make this easier for you. Besides, you work so much that you don't even have any kind of personal life. I was hoping to have grandchildren from all of my children before I leave this earth one day."

He knew that was eventually going to come up in their conversation.

"Ma, for starters, you're not leaving this earth any time soon and between Damon and Darren, your favorite twin sons, you have enough grandchildren to keep you busy for now. Don't start trying to plan out my personal or business life. I'm good on both fronts."

"Okay, well I hope I see you this week. I miss my baby boy."

"I promise I'll be over tomorrow. I'm working at the store tonight, but I have lots of time to stop in on my favorite lady tomorrow."

"Oh good! I'll take that for now, but don't forget what I said about the leaving the earth thing or the grandchildren thing."

"I hear you Ma. Love you," Kerrion said before hanging up the phone.

He loved his mother who was always reminding him that he focused too much time on work and not enough on having fun. He would make more time for fun if he could find the right woman to have some fun with. The women around his age of twenty-five weren't really checking for him, working several jobs trying to build a life for himself. They want the ready made money makers who could keep them draped in the latest expensive attire, something he couldn't afford to do. Everything he made he poured into saving up for his dream business.

He was tired of the women who thought that who they were was defined by how big their behinds were, how much hair they could have flowing down their backs or how good they could put it on him in the bedroom. He didn't want to get it twisted, he would tap that in a minute, but he was tired of tapping for tapping sake. He wanted to find a woman who was ready to settle down with a hardworking brother and who wanted to be showered with as much love and affection as she could stand.

Every woman he seemed to meet had the same first question. How much money did he make and what did he do for a living. When he told them he worked as a security guard at a supermarket, the conversation pretty much came to an end. He never got around to telling them that he was a college graduate who worked as a personal trainer during the day and a security guard at night because he had business goals for himself that he was working hard to achieve. All they heard was security guard and figured he wasn't about much. At that point, he knew that when the lack of interest on the females end happened, he wasn't interested either. He wanted someone non-superficial and less worried about money and more worried about finding a fulfilling relationship.

His friends and brothers called him an old soul. They couldn't believe at his age that he wasn't sowing as many wild oats as he could. They saw how women threw themselves at him all the time and he had to admit that he loved the attention, but it wasn't his looks alone that he wanted to be the draw for the woman of his dreams. He had learned to look beyond a woman's physical beauty alone to find what else she had going on.

He'd experienced his share of casual dating and casual sex and was ready for something more. His buddies thought he was crazy with talk of finding one woman to be involved with, but that's what he wanted. He loved the love he saw between his parents and that's what he wanted. Twenty-five or not he was ready. He hoped that he could find a woman who was ready also.

~~

Terri was having a busy week. Monday she and Jordan ate lunch together and Jordan filled her in on all the events at the shower that she'd missed. She was sad that she'd left early. She really wanted to have fun with the ladies that night because she didn't get to hang with them often.

Whenever she made plans to do so, Daniel always seemed to come up with something else for her to do. The conversation she'd had with Jordan earlier in the week came back to her mind as she sat at home thinking about her week.

"We're all going out this Friday night for a girl's night out if you want to come," Jordan stated.

"That sounds like fun. Can I get back to you and let you know on Wednesday? I think Daniel made plans for a play or something for us to see this Friday night."

Jordan didn't press.

"Sure, let me know because we need to get a head count for a VIP section with food and drinks. It'll be a lot of fun. I'm trying to say goodbye to my single days in style!" Jordan exclaimed.

It was now Friday evening and Terri had been in all evening after leaving work, waiting to hear back from Daniel. She had only talked to him once all week. He said his schedule was crazy and that he was planning something for them for Friday, so she went ahead and cancelled on the girl's night out with Jordan and some of their other friends. By Wednesday, Jordan was ready to give her the speech again about her putting her own life on hold waiting to see if Daniel had time for her. Terri listened as she always did and let it go in one ear and out the other. She loved Jordan, but she couldn't get Jordan to understand that she was showing Daniel that she would be a good mate.

The hour was getting late and any plans Daniel may have made were probably cancelled at this point. She decided to try his cell once again. This time he answered.

"Daniel? I thought we were going out tonight?" she

said.

"I'm sorry. This has been the week from hell. I got in from the office and crashed. The phone woke me up."

"Oh, I'm sorry baby. You sound very tired and I didn't mean to wake you," she said.

"That's okay because I needed to get up anyway. I came in and after being busy all week, I saw that my house was a mess. I haven't done any laundry all week, the dishes are piling up and there is a layer of dust so thick on everything that I think I could spell my name out in it."

Terri felt sorry for him. He worked so hard.

"That's awful. You work too hard Daniel," she said.

Daniel knew she was partially correct. He did work hard, but his hardest work was in the time he'd spent all week satisfying Tammy. She was an animal and he couldn't seem to get enough of her. He'd hooked up with her every night of the week which was why his place was a mess.

"I'm sorry about our plans for the night. I really wanted to take you out for a nice evening to see a play and have a nice fancy dinner. I'm so tired. I may have to hire me a maid to help out around here."

Terri had a better idea.

"Why don't I come over and help you get your house in a livable condition? I'm not doing anything tonight since we had plans and it's now too late. I could also stop and grab some food since I'm sure you haven't eaten either."

Daniel knew she'd bite. He loved that she was all about him. What kind of sad world would he live in if women didn't have low self-esteem, he wondered.

"That's a great idea if it won't put you out. I know you said you were invited out with some friends. You sure you don't want to go ahead and go with them?" he asked, not really meaning a word of it.

"No, I'd rather be with you. I can go out with them another time. Do you need me to bring anything else with me?" she asked.

"Can you stop and pick up a few cleaning supplies. I think I'm all out from the last time I cleaned," he said.

"Sure, I'll do that and I'll be right over."

"You are the best Terri. I couldn't ask for a better girlfriend," he said before hanging up.

~~

Terri drove by a few stores on her way to Daniel's, but bypassed them so that she could stop at one closer to his house. When she was a few blocks away, she pulled into the lot of a large supermarket. She grabbed a cart so that she could pick up a few extra things. Rather than pick up food, she decided to make them a nice dinner and needed to grab all the fixings. She entered the market which was very crowded for a Friday night. As she went from aisle to aisle grabbing what she needed, she noticed the security guard who had been near the door when she came in was now in her aisle. He wasn't really watching her as if she was stealing something. He was staring at her. Terri could tell he was much younger than she was. He seemed to be about twenty-one or twenty-two and he was fine.

He was light-skin with his hair neatly trimmed with a little facial hair. He looked a lot like the singer Drake. She could also tell, even through his uniform, that he was nicely built. Too bad she didn't go for younger men and was already involved. She smiled back at him when she looked up, catching him staring. She moved on to the next aisle. A few more aisles down, she encountered him again. Wasn't stalking illegal she thought?

"You might do better if you took a picture," she said to the handsome guard.

"Oh, I'm sorry that was very rude of me. I don't mean to make you uncomfortable," he said with a deep, gruff and very sexy voice.

"I'm not uncomfortable. I'm sure you wouldn't be wearing that uniform if you were some undercover stalker or something."

"Very true, but then again you never know. Wait, that wasn't a good thing to say, but no I'm not a stalker. I find you extremely beautiful and I tried to keep myself from following you and staring at you, but it didn't work out so well as you can see," he said, teasing.

"Thank you for the compliment."

"My name is Kerrion Lee. You are?" he asked, holding out his hand for a handshake.

Terri hesitated before deciding there was no harm in being nice.

"I'm Terri," she replied.

"Well it's nice to meet you Terri. Again, I apologize for staring and sort of following you. I haven't been able to take my eyes off of you since you walked in the store and for once I can say that to someone and it's not because I think they're ripping the store off."

"Now that's funny."

"Do you think it would be possible to call you sometime and maybe grab a cup of coffee or something when you're free?" he asked.

Goodness he was even more handsome when he smiled. Another time she may have actually said yes, but she had Daniel, so it wasn't possible.

"I wish I could, but I'm seeing someone. I'm actually

here picking up a few things to make him dinner at his place tonight," she said, signally towards the food in her cart.

She watched as Kerrion checked out the items in the basket. "So does he have you cleaning his place before or after you cook him dinner?" he asked, making reference to the large number of cleaning supplies she had in her cart. He was actually joking, but knew he had touched on something when her smile turned to a frown.

Terri felt embarrassed.

"Well he has had a very busy week and I thought I'd help him out. That's what girlfriends do," she said, trying to make light of it.

"That's not what my girlfriend would be doing on a Friday night if I had one," Kerrion said. "I definitely wouldn't have her out in the market this time of night picking up my supermarket items. Mine would be at home with her feet up, relaxing after her own long day, waiting for me to show up with a cart full of food to make her dinner and if we didn't live together, I'd clean my own place or hire someone to do it, but that's just me," he added.

Terri smiled. Now that's what I'm talking about, she said in her head. Where is that side of Daniel, she thought.

"That would be some lucky woman," she said. "Well I better get going. It was nice to meet you Kerrion."

"Nice to meet you too Terri."

She walked past him to head in the direction of the cash register. After she'd paid for her items, she headed toward the front door where Kerrion stood.

"I promise I'm not stalking you. I want to be sure you get to your car safely."

"Thank you. I appreciate that," she said as they walked to her car.

"Let me get those," Kerrion said reaching for her bags to place them in her trunk. When she turned her head for a second to reach for a lighter bag to place in the trunk, Kerrion placed a piece of paper that had his name, phone number and a small note on it in one of her bags. Listening to her talk about a man she would be waiting on hand and foot tonight, he doubted the dude would be helping her unpack the bags, so he didn't worry about him seeing the note.

"Have a good night Terri," he said, closing her trunk and grabbing the cart to take it back to the store.

"Thank you," she said getting into her car.

Terri waved at him through the window as she backed out and drove away. She could still see him standing outside the store watching her drive off as she turned the corner and was now out of his sight. He had definitely been very nice and she was intrigued by the story he told her about how he would treat his own woman, but she knew younger guys didn't really know anything about how to treat a woman. The generation that was coming up now was all about themselves. He was probably like every other younger guy she knew and a few she'd been involved with. He could probably sell a good story, but didn't follow through on any of it.

She turned her thoughts away from the handsome guard and picked up her speed getting to Daniel's house. She had her own man anyway and he was all about her. He was definitely starving by now, she thought as she drove on a little faster. When she reached his house, he opened the door as she reached it. He looked happy to see her, but she was disappointed when he turned around and headed in the direction of the kitchen, not bothering to offer to help her with the few bags she had in her arms. She closed the door behind her and followed him.

"I bought all the fixings for a great dinner. I hope you're hungry," she said.

"I'm starving. Did you remember to get the cleaning supplies?" he asked.

"Yes," she answered, emptying out the bags and prepping everything for dinner.

"Good. I'm going into the other room to watch television to get out of your way."

"Daniel, before you go I want to ask you something."

Jordan had once again asked her whether Daniel would be accompanying her to the wedding. She needed a final head count.

"What's up?" he asked.

"Well you know Jordan is getting married soon and I was wondering if you were coming to the wedding with me."

She hoped he would say yes. She'd done everything he'd asked of her and hoped he could do this one thing for her so that she wouldn't have to go by herself.

"I don't know Terri. I don't really like her."

"I know, but I want you to go for me, not for her. I don't want to go to the wedding alone."

She continued to empty out the supermarket bags, hoping he would give her this one thing.

"When is it?"

"Next month, the last Saturday," she answered.

"I'll let you know. I'm going to go sit down. Holler when dinner is ready."

Terri already knew his response meant he was going to come up with a reason to say no. She let him go before she said something that would cause an argument because she was angry. For once in their relationship, she wanted something to revolve around her. Once she'd like to be the center of attention and do something that she wanted to do. She knew from his tone that she was going to be going to the wedding by herself. He didn't have to say it, but she knew eventually it would be coming.

Here she was standing in the middle of his kitchen about to cook him dinner and then clean up his place. She always bent over backwards doing whatever he wanted because if she didn't, he held other women over her head. He had a habit of reminding her how lucky she should feel because he'd chosen her when he could have his pick of any woman. Maybe her friends were right; maybe she was being a big fool for him. Everything they did was all about him. She went where he wanted to go, did all the things he wanted to do, ran around doing things for him whenever he asked and during the entire relationship she'd barely asked him for anything. When she finally does, he needs to think about it.

She felt stupid and used. Did she really let him make her believe that she didn't deserve better? Her life and her every decision was based on what he wanted and how he would react. Was she this desperate for a relationship that she was willing to sacrifice her own happiness, wants and needs for his? That's not a relationship she wanted and she deserved more. When did she become this person who spent more time pleasing someone else and not thinking of herself? She couldn't let this continue. She needed to speak her mind. She walked into the other room to find

Daniel to let him know how she felt.

"Daniel?"

"I'll go."

Terri wasn't sure she'd heard him. "What did you say?"

"I said I'll go. To the wedding? Remember you asked?" he said.

"Yeah I remember. You're going with me?"

"Yes. I checked my calendar and I don't have anything going on that weekend so I'll go with you. Happy now?" he asked. Daniel knew she'd be happy and he'd reap the benefits of her happiness. He had plenty of time to come up with an excuse and not go, but for now he would say he'll go so that she'd shut up about it. By the look on her face, he could see that he'd made her very happy.

Terri ran over to him, jumped in his lap and covered his face with kisses.

"Thank you baby. Thank you so much!" she exclaimed. "I promise you'll have a great time."

"Anything for you," Daniel lied. "I'm still hungry Terri."

"Anything for you," Terri said, getting up and skipping into the kitchen to finish dinner. No more doubting her relationship, she thought before she started the fire on the stove to cook the man she loved dinner. She was happy and quickly forgot about any reservations she may have had about them.

Chapter Five
TERRI

The work week flew by. Terri spent the entire weekend at Daniel's house and loved every minute of it. She had cleaned his place from top to bottom and he'd taken the weekend off, which was something he never did. She let him rest while she cooked and made his place shine like a bright new penny. She loved taking care of him and he was appreciative of her. He promised her that they would take a trip away, probably to an island real soon once he wrapped up some big cases he had and then they would get some much needed time away for some fun and relaxation. He gave her the task of looking into places to go and activities they could do and she'd been busy all week doing that.

Jordan stopped by her office on Thursday as she was browsing vacation catalogs.

"Going somewhere?" she asked.

Terri smiled, happy to be able give Jordan the news about her plans.

"Daniel and I are thinking of taking a vacation to an island and I'm looking into places to go. Where are you and Andre going for your honeymoon?"

"We're going to Paris."

"That's sounds wonderful. One day when Daniel and I finally get married, we may do the same thing. I hear Paris is beautiful."

"You and Daniel are planning to get married?"

"No, we aren't planning it, but one day I'm sure we will. We've been together a year and I think we're getting close. You'll be the first to know."

Jordan didn't see things turning out that way for her friend, but she wanted to be as supportive as she could, even with a friend who was head over heels in love with a leech.

"Tell me when and where and I'll get my bridesmaid dress and get you down that aisle like you're about to do for me. What did you and Daniel end up doing Friday night?"

Terri was embarrassed to tell Jordan that she and Daniel didn't go anywhere and she actually spent the weekend cooking and cleaning his house. She played it safe.

"Nothing really. He'd had a crazy week and slept through most of Friday. When I finally reached him, I'd woken him up. We decided to stay in so I cooked us some grilled chops and spinach along with a couple of salads. We watched movies and chilled," she said. She decided to leave out the part about cleaning, knowing Jordan wouldn't understand that.

"Sounds like a great evening."

"Oh and guess what? I was at the market and this young guy tried to pick me up. Can you believe that?" Terri said.

"Yeah I can believe it. You're a beautiful woman Terri. Any man would be lucky to be interested in you. Was he cute?"

"Cute is an understatement girl. This brother was drop-dead gorgeous. He looked like that singer Drake. Girl I could have eaten him up. He did ask me out, but I had to shoot him down. I told him I was seeing someone, though he is quite persistent."

"Persistent how?" Jordan asked.

"When I got to Daniel's and unpacked the groceries, this guy had somehow placed his name and number in one of the bags. Suppose Daniel had seen it?" Terri said.

"Girl you know Daniel would not have seen it. He does not put food away I'm sure."

"I know, but still he could have and he would have seen it. He also wrote a note that said to call him if I ever change my mind and want to be on the other end of someone cooking for me."

"I like him already."

"Yeah well, that's not going to happen. I do not plan on calling him." She didn't add that she didn't throw away the note with his number on it. She instead kept it and didn't know why.

"Are we on for lunch today?" Jordan asked.

"Can I get a rain check for tomorrow?"

"Of course. I'll let you get back to your vacation perusing and I hope you find a good spot to go to. Talk to you later today."

Terri waited until Jordan had left before calling Daniel, whom she hadn't talked to since she'd left his house early Sunday morning. She wanted to stay all day Sunday, but she'd promised her mother she would be in church that morning and Daniel didn't do church.

"Daniel Allen's office, how can I help you?" the assistant asked when Terri dialed Daniel's office.

"Hello, this is Terri Bryant, is Mr. Allen available?" she asked.

"Sure, hold on."

"Terri, hi," she heard Daniel say casually as if they'd been in contact since Sunday.

"Hi yourself. I thought I would have heard from you by now. How is your week coming along?" she asked.

"Busy as usual. What's up with you?" he asked.

"Well I was hoping to do lunch with you today," she said.

"I can't because I'm tied to this office today with cases that have me under lock and key."

"I can bring you lunch and we could eat in your office. I miss you and I want to see you."

"Thanks, but that's not a good idea. I told you before I don't want people in the office whispering about us. They know you work for the marketing firm we hired for the promotions we've been running. I don't want anyone to know that we've mixed business with pleasure," he said.

"Are you telling me the people at your firm don't know all this time that we've been involved? It's been a year Daniel. Why have you been hiding it from everyone? Is that why you never want me to come to the office? They all still think my visits have all been about business?" Terri asked, unhappy.

"Terri, it's not like that at all. I do admit that no one knows we're involved and it's important for my career that I keep my work separate from my personal life," he explained. "When the time is right I'll tell them."

Terri couldn't believe what she was hearing. The break in the conversation was very revealing to her. Now she knew why she had never been seen with him at any of the functions associated with his work as anything more than the representative from SR Marketing & Associates. He never took her as his date to any function and whenever they showed up at the same ones, he always introduced her as the brains behind the brilliant marketing campaign that helped increase the number of clients the law firm has. Come to think of it, the only people outside of his office that she'd ever met were the friends she'd met at the football party. None of those people worked for him either. They were all friends from the gym he frequented. Others were a part of a baseball team he played for in his old neighborhood when he had time. She had never even met anyone in his family before. It never clicked because she was so wrapped up in making sure he was happy with her.

Daniel claimed he wanted their time to be special and about the two of them because work kept him so busy all the time. She never questioned him because she was happy to be with him. Hearing him dismiss her today was a wake-up call. When she thought back over the time they'd been together, he'd kept her secluded from his surroundings like a dirty little secret. They never took any trips together, although he'd made promises from the start. They'd been out plenty of times to movies and dinner, but never with another couple and never to any family gatherings. He spoke of them after he'd already gone, saying they were impromptu affairs, not giving him time to ask her to go with him.

She'd asked about his family plenty of times and he always had one excuse after another of why she'd never met them. She again brushed it off because she couldn't see past the fact that he wanted her. She was happy that he had no problem meeting her family and being around them. Now she felt ashamed and invisible and more used than she had been by any other man in her past. She didn't want to talk to Daniel right now. She finally saw herself as her friends saw her and she felt sick.

"Ok, well lunch another time Daniel. I have a lot of work today myself so I'll talk to you later," she said.

"Great. Maybe we'll do something fun this weekend. I'll let you know," he said.

Terri saw right through that too. Another tactic to keep her at his beck and call sitting by the phone waiting to see if he was planning to make time for her.

"Right, call me," she said before slamming the receiver down.

Terri sat in her office feeling more exposed than she'd ever been. She bet when she wasn't around her friends, they talked about her and how dumb her behavior was for a man who didn't feel about her the way she felt about him. She got up from behind her desk which now felt confining and paced around her office. All the time they were together and he was never really serious about her. She needed comfort food and that meant cake, which always did the trick. She grabbed her purse and went in search of it.

As she walked through the open floor of the office, she caught the eye of several women whom she considered friends and wondered what their real thoughts were about her. She walked faster to get away from all eyes.

Terri made it to the corner bakery, but couldn't make herself enter. This was how she'd gotten herself in trouble over the years. She always turned to food when things didn't go well for her. She needed to change that habit. She turned back around and called Jordan to see if she was still free for lunch. No more bad behaviors when it came to comfort food and no more foolish behavior when it came to men.

~~

"Ms. Bryant, you have a call on line two from Mr. Allen. Shall I put him through," her assistant said.

"No. Please apologize to him for me and let him know I'll give him a call as soon as I'm free," she said. She spent the entire weekend avoiding Daniel. His messages were sweet and wonderful and apologetic, but she wasn't falling for it. That's what he always did when he screwed up. Normally, she fell for it. She, however, was waking up from a year-long sleep.

"Avoiding Daniel now are we?" Jordan asked when Terri looked up to see her standing in the doorway to her office.

"It's a long story and one I don't feel like talking about right now. What's up with you?"

"A few of us are going to the gym after work. I know you don't go with us anymore, but I didn't want to not ask you since it's a group of us from work who are going. Would you like to go?"

She'd spent a lot of time avoiding her friends for Daniel and never hung out with them. She also had been thinking a lot about getting into the gym. Not for anyone else, but for her.

"I'd love to go. What time are you going?"

The look on Jordan's face was priceless. She'd finally said yes to some time with the girls. In a few weeks Jordan would be getting married and Terri had missed every single outing that had been planned leading up to her big day. She even slipped out in the middle of her bridal shower.

"Right after work," Jordan said.

"Great because I was planning to leave a little bit early today anyway, so I'll have time to run home and change into some workout gear and meet you there."

"Now you're not going to flake out on us again and stand us up are you?" Jordan asked.

"No. I promise I will be there."

Terri meant it.

Chapter Six
TERRI

Terri pulled up to her house and saw Daniel's car parked a few doors down. She wasn't in the mood for him today because she was still very pissed at him. She walked into her house ready for a showdown.

"Where the hell have you been all week?" he asked the moment she entered.

"Hello to you too," she replied, walking in, being nonchalant about his presence and his anger. She placed her bag on the sofa and started browsing through the mail she'd brought in with her from the mailbox.

"Terri, stop playing with me. Are you still angry about lunch last week? It's been a week. You're being ridiculous and childish. This is what I try to avoid. Your age is once again becoming an issue so please stop acting immature," he said, angrily.

"Then why are you with me Daniel," she asked calmly. "If I'm so immature why are you here now? I can't do this right now with you. You haven't been able to reach me all week and now you know how it feels. I call you and call you and you don't even think to take a minute to call me back. You make plans with me and you know you're going to cancel, but you wait until it's too late for me to do anything else. I don't do anything that doesn't involve you.

You on the other hand have a whole other life that you keep me from being a part of don't you?"

Her anger stunned him, according to the look on his face.

"Don't bother responding because like I said, I can't do this with you right now. I'm meeting some friends at the gym. We can talk about this later," she said heading up the steps toward her bedroom to change.

"You're going to the gym? What for? You look fine. You don't need to work out," he said following her into her bedroom.

"I'm going for me because I think I need to work out. I'm also thinking of starting this new diet I heard about that involves mainly vegetables and fruit."

"What the hell for? So now you're going to starve yourself? For what Terri? I like you the way you are. Who are you changing for? I know it's not some other guy so it must be those damn friends of yours," he said, getting angrier and angrier.

Terri couldn't believe he'd just insulted her.

"What, do you think no other man would be interested in me? Is that why you don't want me working out or going on a diet? One day you tell me I'm fat and then you change up and tell me I'm fine the way I am. You want me to lose weight and then you change your mind and want me to stay fat. Is that so no one else would want me so that you could control me? Isn't that what you've been doing?" she asked while continuing to get dressed in her workout gear.

Daniel took a few moments to calm down. He was only making her angry and that was not his intent. He didn't like this new combative Terri. Where was the submissive Terri that liked?

"Terri, listen to yourself. I've always told you how beautiful you are the way you are. I'm sure other men find you beautiful too. I do admit that there are some things that need to change and I guess I need to stop taking advantage of you and be a better boyfriend, so I admit that okay. Why don't we forget about the gym and go out and have a nice dinner tonight and get beyond this. I'm sorry about lunch last week okay? I'm sorry."

Terri knew that this was normally the time where she would give in and this time she wasn't doing it. She'd made a promise to her friends and to herself. She wanted to go to the gym because she wanted to go and not for anyone else.

"Daniel, we can do dinner tomorrow night or any other night, but not tonight. Tonight I have plans," she said, lacing up her sneakers, grabbing her keys and heading back downstairs with Daniel in tow.

"Okay, go have your time at the gym. Why don't you come by my place afterwards?"

She turned toward him before going out the door. "I'll call you later. I think the ladies go out for drinks afterward and I want to go and if it's late, I'll call you tomorrow. Lock the door when you leave," she said over her shoulder, leaving Daniel standing in her doorway looking like he had been shocked by the paddles hospitals use to resuscitate a dying patient. She felt exhilarated and she liked it. It was time to take her life back. Maybe there was hope for her and Daniel and maybe not. If not, she would move on because she was better than the treatment she was getting from him.

~~

The gym was exactly what Terri needed. She thought she

would be out of breath and out of shape to the point where she would not be able to keep up with everyone, but she was proud of herself. She did a lot of cardio on the machines and was about to do some light work on the weights when she turned and walked right into a massive wall of t-shirt covered flesh.

"Excuse me," she said, not yet looking up. "I wasn't watching where I was going."

"No problem, Terri."

Hearing her name she looked up into the chocolate brown eyes of the gorgeous security guard from the supermarket.

"Oh hi," she said, recognizing him instantly and remembering his name with no problem. "It's nice to see you again Kerrion."

"The pleasure is most definitely mine."

Terri smiled. "Don't tell me you're back to stalking me again. Now this is taking stalking to another whole level," she said, lightly.

"Not at all. I actually here five days a week.

Terri looked at him and could tell it showed.

"I've never seen you here before," he said.

"I've never been here before. I'm here with some friends. One of them is getting married and is trying to get rid of those last few pounds and I decided to join them today."

"Ah, so no cooking dinner or cleaning houses today for you?" Kerrion said joking, making reference to what her plans were the first time they'd met.

Terri laughed along with him remembering their conversation in the market.

"No not today. Today is a day about me."

"Well we could all use some type of workout. You look beautiful, by the way, even all sweaty."

Shyly, Terri thanked him.

"So where are these friends you came with?"

Terri looked around and pointed them out.

"I recognize them. They come in once a week and have been for several months. I'm glad you decided to join them today."

Terri was more than happy she had also.

"So am I. I don't want to keep you from your workout," she said.

"You're not keeping me from anything. I'm enjoying standing right here talking to you."

She could not look away from his piercing stare. It was intoxicating to be so close to him. He was all muscle and glistening from sweat. If only he were a few years older and she wasn't involved with Daniel. Even though they were having some problems, she was still involved with him. That didn't mean she couldn't look and she was getting quite an eye full, especially when she looked further down. The rest of him was just as massive. She bashfully looked away, ashamed at how she was standing in the middle of the gym gawking at him.

"Well I was about to figure out these weights," she said.

"Would you like some help?"

She hesitated at first, but then saw no harm in getting his help.

"Sure. It's been a long time since I've been to a gym. I guess I should get some help with managing the weights."

~~

"That's it, three more and you should be good."

Kerrion was wrapping up helping Terri lift the weights

a few more times. He didn't want her to overdo it since she hadn't worked out in a long time.

Terri was now done and though her body was beginning to ache, it was a good ache. She needed this workout and she was definitely going to continue.

"Thank you for your help today. I really appreciate it."

"No problem. Like I said, I'm here five days a week. If you see me and you need my help, let me know."

Kerrion smiled hoping she'd take him up on his offer.

"Won't the people who run the gym be upset that you're helping me instead of me going to one of the staff members?" she asked.

Kerrion hit her with a big bright smile that made her heart melt. She watched as he leaned in closer toward her.

"I am a staff member. I work here before working the late shift at the supermarket where we met. I'm here later on Wednesdays and Thursdays because I'm off from the market those nights, but usually you can find me here all week until about seven."

"Oh, I hope I didn't take up all of your time from the other guests here at the gym."

She looked around to see if anyone else was waiting for assistance from him.

"Not at all. So listen..."

They were then interrupted before he could complete his thought.

"So what do we have here?" Jordan said as she and Terri's other friends walked up on them.

Terri was nervous and stumbling over her words before finally getting them out.

"Umm, this is Kerrion. He works here. He was helping me with the weights."

"We know who Kerrion is. Remember, we come here once a week," Jordan said.

"Right and we were finishing up so thanks again, Kerrion." Terri said attempting to walk away with her friends. She wasn't walking fast enough.

"Before you go, I was wondering if I could speak with you for a minute, Terri, if that's okay with your friends."

"It's alright with us," they all said together.

Terri gave them a look that said they shouldn't have done that, before turning back to Kerrion.

"I wanted to see if you would like to get a smoothie with me before you leave. We have a great smoothie bar here in the gym that serves up the healthiest smoothies you've ever had. I was hoping we could sit and talk a bit."

Terri knew she should say no. She was planning to hang with the ladies after the workout.

"I think we're all going out for drinks after this, right ladies?" she said loud enough for them to hear her.

"Nonsense," Jordan chimed in. "Go ahead and have your smoothie. We're glad you came out with us tonight. I'll talk to you tomorrow at the office."

The ladies walked away, waving at her as they did and leaving her standing with her mouth open at their sudden departure.

"Still busy?" Kerrion asked, seeing his opportunity.

"No, I guess I'm not. Can I ask you one question?"

"Sure," he replied

"How old are you?"

"I'm twenty-five. Is that a problem for you?" he asked.

"I'm thirty Kerrion."

"Okay, let me ask it this way. Is your age a problem for you? It's not a problem for me. Listen, it's just a smoothie and some conversation. Whenever you're ready, I'll walk you to your car. Remember how well I did that the night at the market?" he said with humor and a blazingly hot smile.

She knew she shouldn't because somewhere in the back of her mind were lingering thoughts of Daniel. She also thought of his treatment of her and she brushed any more thoughts of him off.

"Okay, a smoothie and some conversation it is."

~~

"I had a wonderful time talking to you. I hope we can do this again," Kerrion said when they reached Terri's car.

Neither of them noticed the late hour. They'd sat talking over smoothies for over two hours and were having a good time and time got away from them.

"I had a great time too. I loved hearing about all of your plans for your own personal training business and gym. I was wondering why you were working so hard here at the gym and at the supermarket. You are very driven and that's admirable."

"I appreciate that, but being driven and working hard should be the norm for all men, not the exception. There is never a time when a man shouldn't be planning for a better life for himself," he said.

"Well, I better get home. It's getting late and I have some work to look over for a big meeting in the morning."

Kerrion was watching her get in her car and didn't want to pass up the chance to see her again, boyfriend or not.

"Terri, I know you never called me after I slipped my number in your shopping bag. You mentioned over the smoothie that you got the note. Were you ever going to use it?" he asked.

"I honestly don't know. All I can tell you is that I didn't throw it away."

"Okay, fair enough. Will you at least call me when you get home so that I know you're in safely since I kept you out so late?"

Terri smiled, really feeling connected to Kerrion. He seemed to be a genuinely nice guy, even if he was only twenty-five. She couldn't really squawk too much about age because she was involved with a man who was sixteen years older than her. Though she believed older men were more her style, she liked Kerrion's style, even though it was packed in a twenty-five year old body.

"Yes, I'll call you when I get in."

"Are you sure you still have the number. Why don't you put it in your phone to be sure," he said.

Terri grabbed her phone and typed in the numbers he read off to her.

"Thanks again Kerrion."

"Thank you Terri and have a good night."

He stood making sure she'd driven off the lot and into traffic before turning back to the gym. He felt sorry for the guy Terri was involved with because he didn't know it yet, Kerrion thought, but he was going to have to find himself a new girlfriend. Terri was going to be his.

As he walked back into the gym, he thought about the great conversation they'd had. He learned that she was a marketing and public relations specialist. Hearing her talk about business, he could tell she had it going on and he liked it. He loved how she lit up when she talked about her family. She even commented to him that she loved hearing all about his family.

Two thumbs up that family meant everything to them both. He'd also shared with her his plans for building his own business and how hard he was working to make his dream a reality. She'd given him a few pointers from a marketing perspective and the more they talked, the more he liked her. It didn't escape him that she was gorgeous. She was beautiful inside and out and she was someone he wanted to get to know better. He was quite sure the man she had didn't treat her the way she should be treated. He knew that from the moment he knew she'd be cleaning his house. The fact that a man would take advantage of her like that pissed him off. He didn't want to come in between whatever she had going on with her boyfriend, but he was ready to show her how a woman should really be treated.

Chapter Seven
TERRI

Terri was beat and her body was aching terribly from the gym workout the night before. She couldn't even get her legs to walk steady on her usual high heels. She wore some that were much lower and when she could get away with it throughout the day, she slipped into her sneakers. She knew it was normal for the body to feel like this, especially since she didn't work out often. She'd soaked for over an hour the night before after talking with Kerrion on the phone. The brief call she made to let him know that she was home safe had turned into an hour long conversation. She'd learned a lot about him at the gym and even more once they spoke on the phone. He turned out to be a very interesting person.

He'd graduated from college with a degree in health fitness. His plan was to start his own personal training business which would include a gym. He had been working at the gym for a few years learning all he could about the business and working on his personal training skills with the gym's clientele. He was working at the supermarket to earn extra money to put towards purchasing the equipment he would need so that he could get a loan to rent a spot for his gym. He told her all about his plan and she was impressed.

Being in marketing and promotions she could see that

with the right public relations specialist, his business could flourish in no time.

He told her that he was raised in a great home with two loving parents and that he was the youngest of five children, a set of older twin brothers and an older sister and one brother who was the oldest of the bunch. He'd started working at the supermarket his sophomore year in college and was able to save most of his salary because he had plans for his gym. He was closer than ever to seeing his dream come true because he patiently waited.

When the conversation turned more personal, she discovered that he wasn't involved with anyone at the moment. The last relationship he had was with a young woman who didn't understand his drive. She wanted him to party and hang out like her, but he remained focus on the education his parents were paying for. He'd done a lot of casual dating, but was tired of that and was more interested in a woman who wanted something long-term. Loyalty and commitment meant everything to him and even though he and his last serious girlfriend had been so different in their thinking, he was still willing to give things a try with her. That was until he saw her one morning coming out of the room of another guy who lived in the same dorm he lived in and he hadn't dealt with her since. Once trust was breached, he didn't give his trust back to the same person again. If they did it once, they would do it again, he'd told her. Wise words, she thought.

Before ending the phone call, she shared with him a little about her relationship with Daniel and how he was making her feel. Surprising to her, Kerrion didn't tell her to leave Daniel nor did he talk bad about Daniel. He listened and let her unload and told her that she shouldn't sacrifice her happiness for anything or anyone.

They hung up agreeing to talk soon, especially after she offered to help him with a marketing plan for his gym. He'd offered to pay her for her time since it's what she did for a living, but surprising to him, she wouldn't hear of it so they compromised. He would help her in her effort to work out and lose weight and she would help him get the word out about his business.

After their conversation, she couldn't believe how much she'd enjoyed talking to him. He was nothing like she expected for a twenty-five year old. He was mature, wise and determined, all of the features she admired in men. They had agreed to meet for breakfast Saturday morning at a local deli and he would share more about his plan with her so that she could begin working out a marketing plan for him.

Terri was still thinking of Kerrion at the end of the week when she looked up to see Daniel standing in the doorway of her office.

"How long have you been standing there?" she asked, surprised to see him in the middle of the day.

"Long enough to realize you were daydreaming about something. Whatever it was must have been good. You were smiling the whole time."

"Not really. I was thinking of a friend I'm helping with a marketing plan to start a business as a personal trainer."

"Him?" Daniel asked. "Who is this guy because I've never heard you mention any male friends who were opening up gyms?"

"He's someone I met; nothing major. He was telling me about his plan and I offered to help him with it. You know I'm everything marketing."

"Well I hope he's paying you handsomely for your time and information," Daniel said coming further into her office.

She didn't immediately respond because she knew everything was all about the dollar to him and she was beyond that.

"Anyway, I was wondering if you wanted to have lunch today. I have a big break in my day before I have to be back in court. I didn't like how things ended with us the other day and we need to get the air cleared and get back to a better place without all the tension."

"Sure," she said. "I'll get my things."

Over lunch they tried idle chit chat, but Terri wasn't interested. Every topic had been about Daniel. Any time she tried to interject anything about herself, he turned the conversation back to himself so she stopped trying. She sat there and listened while he rambled off about how much money he would be making in the next year and how much prestige he was gaining. She was sick of hearing that too. She faked interest and continued to enjoy her glazed salmon topped salad.

"I see you're serious about this healthier eating," Daniel said. "I've never seen you eat salmon before. I didn't even know you liked it. I was hoping we could go out for some steaks tonight. I haven't had one in a long time and I know how much you love them with mushrooms and onions."

Terri was surprised that she had no interest in spending her evening with Daniel. She was excited about seeing Kerrion on Saturday and if she spent the night with Daniel, she wouldn't make it to her breakfast in the morning.

"I need a rain check Daniel. I'm going over to my mom's house when I get off. She wants me to go with her to get a dress for Jordan's wedding and to do a few other things. I'll probably hang over there until later this evening. I haven't really spent a lot of time with her lately."

"You're always claiming I never take you anywhere, especially around my friends. A few people from the office were going out this evening and I thought you'd like to join us," he said, trying to convince her to change her plans.

"I appreciate it, really I do, but I already made plans with my mother," she said, feeling alive and free that for the first time since they'd started dating, she was putting herself before him and she liked it.

Daniel looked at her as if he didn't know who she was. She knew that he was used to getting his way so he didn't know how to react when she didn't go along with his plan. She knew he was angry and the rest of the lunch was eaten in silence.

~~

Kerrion arrived early at the deli and waited for Terri with all of the information for his business in hand. He'd spent the evening before pulling everything together like Terri had asked him too. He was grateful for her help and even more grateful that he'd get to see her again because of his attraction to her. He'd never felt an instant connection to any woman like he did the night he first spotted her at the market. When she walked in, she had an air about her that drew him in. He knew he was wrong for following her around the store, but he couldn't help himself. Customers should never be made uncomfortable, but he couldn't walk away. It was obvious she was a bit older than he was so he had to choose his words carefully if he planned to speak to her. Women were already more mature than men so he had to play his cards right if he was going to make any kind of an impression on her. He tried humor, especially after she started with humor. He breathed a sigh of relief that his presence didn't send her running for the hills.

It was more than fate that had her working out at the very same gym where he worked. That was a sign that his first thoughts about her were correct. She was going to be his and all he had to do was wait until she came to the same realization. The fact that her boyfriend treats her like crap meant that he wouldn't have to try too hard. His mother and father had raised him to treat all women with the utmost respect and to treat them the same way he would want his mother treated. That's something his father always told him and it's something he would never forget.

The lady of his dreams walked into the deli while he was thinking about her. She looked lovely walking over to him in a black jogging suit.

"Good morning, beautiful," Kerrion said as Terri reached his table. He stood to pull her chair out for her.

"Good morning to you too. I see you came ready to work."

"Yes I did. Are you hungry?"

"Yes I am. I like this deli," she said looking around.

"I'm glad you like it. I come here often because I like the atmosphere and I can sit as long as I like and get work done. I think best when there is food in front of me," he said.

"You look like you certainly do eat right."

"Thank you," he replied. "I try, though I don't always succeed and for those times that I don't, I work out extra hard at the gym."

The waitress showed up to take their orders.

"You've done a great job on your business plan," she told him after they'd finished eating. They were now well into an hour of going over his plan while she shared with him ideas for her marketing strategy. A familiar voice turned her attention away from Kerrion as she looked to who had entered the deli. It was Daniel and from the looks of it, he was accompanied by a very, very young woman. She didn't look to be much older than twenty-one or twenty-two. Daniel's face turned ashen the moment he spotted Terri. They stared at each other as if neither was taking a breath in or out.

Daniel couldn't do anything, but stand where he stood, knowing he had a look on his face like a deer caught in headlights or more like a kid found with his hand in the cookie jar. It was too late to turn around because Terri had already seen him. What was Terri doing in this part of town so early in the morning? He thought to himself. To make matters worse, he had spent the night in a hotel with Shannon, the daughter of one of his partners at the firm and they had ventured out for an early breakfast before she got back on the road to college. He figured he was safe since the deli was quite a distance away from where he and Terri lived and worked. He needed to think quickly. An idea popped in his head and he headed towards Terri and some guy sitting at a table. He turned to his young friend and quickly said, "no matter what I say, don't say anything other than hi," he whispered to her.

"Hi baby," Daniel said, coming over to the table and giving Terri a quick kiss on the cheek. He stood so that he was partially blocking her view of his young, blond tag-a-long.

"Hi back. What are you doing here and who is that with

you?" Terri asked.

"I should be asking you the same thing," he said trying to turn the conversation away from Shannon hiding behind him.

"This is Kerrion Lee. This is the guy I told you I was working with to help with the marketing of the business he plans to start soon. My question still stands for you. Who is this you have with you?" she asked, noticing the young woman who was trying to hide behind Daniel. That may have been easier if she wasn't taller than he was. Here he was the only African-American partner in a major law firm and he was out traipsing around town with a young blond beauty. This couldn't be good, she thought.

"Oh, this is Bill's daughter Shannon and she's not with me. I was coming in to grab some breakfast and I saw her coming in this direction. She said she was coming in here so we started chatting while walking. She's home from school for the weekend or something I think, right Shannon?" Daniel asked, pulling her out from behind him. "She's kind of shy," Daniel added.

Terri noticed her looking to Daniel before responding.

"Yes. I'm in college out of state and I came home for the weekend. I saw Mr. Daniel when he was parking."

Kerrion smiled realizing this bastard has been caught with his pants down around his ankle with a young college girl. How old did Terri say this guy was? Forty-six if Kerrion recalled. He wasn't sure if Terri had caught on, but he sure did. He was going to enjoy this. The girl was in the shortest shorts he'd ever seen, that didn't appear to have any pockets and neither did her barely there top that barely covered the huge rack she had on display. Clearly daddy's money had paid for some very nice implants.

"You drove up Shannon?" Kerrion asked. "I don't see any car keys," he said, helping the conversation along to see how far the lie would go. Clearly they had come in together.

Shannon again looked to Daniel for an answer and Kerrion could sense that Daniel was a quick thinker. He figured he had to be since he was one of the best attorneys in town.

"No she didn't drive up. Someone else was driving."

To end the charade, Daniel ushered Shannon away.

"Tell your parents I said hello Shannon and tell your dad I'll see him bright and early Monday morning."

Daniel was definitely nervous and if Kerrion was correct, he appeared to be sweating though the deli was air conditioned.

Kerrion knew what he'd witnessed, but wasn't sure Terri caught wind of it. He looked at her and she definitely had her suspicions. He didn't want her to feel any more uncomfortable or embarrassed than she probably already was so he did what he could to dismiss the moment. He tried to chat a bit with Daniel and at the same time he watched Terri watch as Shannon went to the counter, ordered a coffee and then made a bee-line quickly for the door.

Still Terri hadn't said anything else. Now that Shannon was out of the door, all eyes turned back to Daniel.

"So Terri, you didn't mention anything about having breakfast this morning to discuss business when we had lunch yesterday," Daniel said, not taking his eyes off of Kerrion.

"You don't need to know every move I make Daniel. The last time I checked my license said grown ass woman!"

Terri bellowed a little louder than she'd planned. Other patrons turned to look at them.

It wasn't her plan to cause a scene.

"No need to be rude Terri and I don't want to keep you from your business breakfast. It was nice to meet you Kerrion," Daniel said. "Terri, I'll call you later on today. I was thinking we could check out the new Kevin Hart movie since I know you really like him."

"You do that Daniel. I'll be waiting for that call," she said with a venomous tone to her words.

To Kerrion, it was quite obvious Terri knew exactly what she had witnessed. He also knew they needed to get back to business. Any talk of what had happened would upset her even more.

"So shall we get back to your marketing strategy before breakfast turns into lunch?" Kerrion said, trying to lighten the mood.

Terri put on a fake smile to put a mask on her total and complete embarrassment.

"Yes we should."

Chapter Eight
TERRI

"Terri, please call me back," Daniel said on yet another voice mail message that Terri was again about to delete. She had managed to avoid him for an entire week.

How stupid did he think she was? Did he really expect her to believe that story about his partner's daughter? It was clear to her that something more than a chance meeting at the deli had taken place. She was disgusted to think that Daniel had something going on with her. On one hand she can't even imagine that he would do such a thing and on the other, it was clearly an uncomfortable moment for Daniel and Shannon, realizing they had been caught. When she got up the nerve, she would ask him. She hoped it wasn't what she thought, but she knew in the back of her mind that Daniel had shown up with that young woman and it wasn't a chance meeting.

She hit the delete message button on her cell and went about reading the manual for the new treadmill she'd ordered. For those days when she couldn't make it to the gym, she was happy to still be able to get some exercise in. Kerrion offered to come by her house to put it together and she was expecting him any minute.

For the past week, they had been talking on the phone non-stop. She'd even shared another conversation over smoothies after another day at the gym. She surprised herself that she had gone to the gym without her friends and was determined to get the weight off. That was part of the reason and the other part was because she was excited about her workout with Kerrion's help. He was turning out to be more than she could have imagined. Unlike Daniel, he encouraged her daily to keep up with her workout. Now she had to incorporate a regular workout schedule in her day. In a short period of time, she was already feeling better. She couldn't tell yet that she was losing any weight, but the fact that she was feeling better and had more energy was a plus.

Her doorbell signaled Kerrion had arrived.

When she opened the door to let him in, she could tell he was holding something behind his back.

"What are you hiding?"

When he showed her what he had, she became excited. No man had ever bought her flowers and the bouquet he was holding was beautiful. They were the prettiest bouquet of peach and yellow flowers she'd ever seen.

"For me?" she asked, taking the flowers.

"Beautiful flowers for a gorgeous woman."

"How did you know I liked the colors peach and yellow?"

She moved to the side to let him enter her house.

"The times you came into the gym you had those colors on. I figured they must be colors that you love," he said.

"Thank you so much," she said, taking a whiff of them. "Make yourself comfortable while I put these in water."

Kerrion walked over to the box with the treadmill, smiling that he was able to put a smile on her face. He knew from their conversations that she was struggling with what to do about Daniel and if for only a little while, he hoped the flowers would take her mind off of her troubles. He could easily advise her of the snake he knew Daniel was, but he didn't want to do that. He had to stay mutual if they were ever going to be able to be together, so he couldn't be the voice that told her to leave Daniel. She had to do it on her own. He loved the friendship they had developed and it was growing every day. He looked forward to the day Terri recognized her own true worth. She was worth more than even she thought she was and a whole lot more than Daniel apparently ever gave her respect for. She was not only lovely on the outside, but on the inside too. He could tell the flowers brightened up her mood and he felt good because that's what he'd set out to do.

"I can't wait until the treadmill is ready for me to use," Terri said, re-entering the room.

"I'll have this together in no time tonight. I'm glad you ordered the one I recommended."

"Thanks for suggesting this one. I was reading the manual before you got here so that I could familiarize myself with how it works and so far it looks pretty simple."

She sat down and watched as he took the various parts of the equipment out of the box. From her vantage point, she could see how in shape he really was. His muscles were bulging under his shirt and she wanted to reach out and touch them to see how they felt. She continued to scan his body, taking in the form of his strong, muscled legs and further up his torso at his tight butt. That was Terri's favorite part on a man and Kerrion had one that should go down in the record books for being the sexiest. When she stuck her tongue out and licked her lips at the sight of him, she became distracted from his purpose for being in her house, so she shook all thoughts of how good he looked off and tried to engage in conversation to keep herself out of trouble.

"So you're not working at the market tonight?" she asked.

"No, I have a friend who's celebrating a birthday tonight at a local club so I took off to celebrate his night with him."

"That sounds like fun."

"Would you like to come with me?"

When he didn't hear a response, he figured she was going to say no. He'd wanted to ask her for a few days, but figured she would say no since she was involved with someone.

"Yes I would like to come with you," she said, surprising them both.

When Kerrion looked over at her and smiled, Terri knew that her response had shocked him as much as it shocked her that she agreed.

"You'll have a good time, Terri."

"I'm sure I will and besides, I need to get out anyway. It's been a rough week at work. What time is this party?" she asked.

"It's in a couple of hours. Why don't you go get dressed while I finish up with the treadmill? I can drive so that we can stop by my place where I can change and then we can head to the party."

"Okay, I can do that."

Terri got up to find something to change into and turned back, not knowing the attire for the evening.

"Should I be dressy or casual?"

"The invitation said anything, but denim. I'm sure whatever you come up with will be fine. You look beautiful in everything."

"You say the sweetest things."

"It's easy when it's true."

When Terri emerged down the steps less than an hour later looking like a runway model, Kerrion lost all ability to speak.

"I swear, if you get any more beautiful, you'll send a brother into a heart attack. Wow," he said, checking out her black dress and high heel red shoes. "I'm going to have to beat the guys off with a stick all night long with you around. I should make sure I take along my boxing gloves to fight off any guys trying to get too close."

"No need for violence. Being with you, no one else even stands a chance."

Kerrion came and stood directly in front her.

"No one?" he asked.

Terri knew he was talking about Daniel and she meant what she said. She repeated it so that he knew they were both on the same page.

"No one."

No matter how much she thought about fighting her attraction to Kerrion, she was losing. He was an incredible guy and he made her feel special. She liked how he wasn't fake about his attraction and compliments. He genuinely liked her.

"Well your treadmill is up and ready for you to use. I'm ready to leave if you are."

"Yes I'm ready."

~~

Daniel waited long enough to deal with Terri. If he hadn't been so preoccupied with Tammy all week, he would have come back over to Terri's house earlier to deal with whatever issues they had going on. He'd had enough of Terri and it was time to put her back in her place. He assumed she was still angry over the incident in the deli, but he was sure his story was believable. He never thought he'd run into anyone so far away from town, but that's exactly what happened.

He knew he shouldn't have been with Shannon. As much as he tried to stay away from his partner's daughter, she was young and sexy and she wanted him. He couldn't fight his attraction to her and she did remarkable things in bed that kept him coming back for more. When she called to tell him she was driving into town, he knew he would drop everything to meet her at their usual spot. He was sure the story he concocted about showing up at the same time as her at the deli had worked on Terri. She was in love with him and believed everything he told her. The guy sitting across from her was a problem though. He'd caught on to the way he was looking at Terri and didn't like it. There was more than work going on between the two of them. He planned to be the only one with a side piece in his relationship with Terri. He needed to put an end to whatever business she had going on so that it didn't lead to anything personal. He and Terri needed to talk.

Daniel was about to find a parking space somewhere on her street when he noticed her front door was opening. He watched as Terri exited looking like she was going out on a date for the evening. His hunch was right when she was followed out by the guy he'd seen her with at the deli. According to her they were working and that was it. The way she was dressed didn't look anything like work. She was wearing a black form fitting black dress that showed more cleavage than he liked for her to show. He needed to remind her about that again. Terri's breasts were too big to be on display like that for anyone but him. The way she was dressed, she was asking for trouble. He also noticed she had on very high heeled bright red shoes and no stockings. Where was she going? He wondered.

Wherever it was, she was clearly not going alone. After the guy locked her door for her, he gave her back her keys and they got into, what he assumed was the guy's car and drove off. Is this how she wanted to play it, he thought to himself. Daniel reached for his phone to call Tammy and would deal with Terri another time. He wouldn't waste a night thinking about her when he could have Tammy wrapped all around him in all the ways his imagination could think of.

~~

Kerrion felt like the luckiest man in the club. Terri was not only beautiful, but she fit right in with his friends. He liked that she didn't feel uncomfortable or awkward knowing that his friends were all five and six years younger than her.

After introducing her to everyone as a friend of his from the gym, not wanting things to be strange knowing she was involved with someone else, he noticed that she relaxed and settled in to have fun. He liked that she sipped on the same glass of wine all night and wasn't a heavy drinker. One of his biggest turn-offs was women who over-indulged in alcohol to the point where they became loud and belligerent. Terri was a classy lady all night long.

They danced more than he'd danced in a long time. She laughed at the silly antics of his friends and even cracked a few jokes of her own.

Even though he and Terri had come to the club together,

they weren't a couple and the few friends that did ask, he was honest in telling them that he and Terri were only friends. After he picked up on the vibe that a friend or two of his was interested in her, he let them all down easy telling them that she was in a relationship with someone and that if she wasn't, he'd be the first to ask her out, so he alerted them to keep their hands off. He knew from the start that she was a great catch and any man in his right mind could see that.

While relaxing with his friends, Kerrion looked up to see Terri returning from the ladies room with a few of the other ladies who were in their group. She came right over to him to see if he wanted to dance. The slow dance that had begun playing was one of his favorite and when they reached the middle of the dance floor, he pulled her close to him.

"Are you having a good time?" he asked.

Terri almost missed his question. She was too busy leaning into the feel of his hard body pressed up against hers. She remembered what that body looked like glistening and hard from his workouts at the gym and she couldn't help but move even closer to him.

"Yes, I'm having a great time. I didn't realize how much I needed to get out. Thanks for inviting me."

"If I thought you'd say yes, I'd invite you out more, but I understand and respect your current situation."

"Yeah, my situation," she said softly. "I appreciate you understanding when it comes to Daniel. I know he has his issues, but deep down, past all the outer layer mess, he can really be a good person. We've been together almost a year and except for this hiccup in our relationship, things have gone pretty good."

Kerrion heard her, but he didn't believe any of what came out of her mouth. Unless she was simply blind to what was right in front of her eyes, she no clue as to the kind of man Daniel was. He peeped his game immediately and that was only from the first time they'd interacted at the deli. Terri didn't deserve being treated with disrespect. He hated guys who manipulated and used women. He made sure he always treated women well because he had a sister and nieces and he knew how he would want them treated by men.

Daniel's treatment of Terri sickened him every time he thought about it. Terri had shared a few things with him about some of Daniel's downfalls and he decided to not be judgmental. She needed to vent and he wanted to be someone who would listen and not judge, hoping it would make her feel better. What he was beginning to realize was no matter how much she vented or how angry she got at Daniel, she wasn't going to see or state the obvious, which to him was that they were not the perfect couple and everything probably wouldn't be okay. He wanted to insert his opinion and it was hard not to. He also didn't want to push her away so he held his opinion back; for now.

"Well you know if he slips up to the point of no return, I'm hoping you'll give me a chance to get to know you on a more personal level, business aside."

Terri knew that Daniel had already slipped up, she didn't want to imagine what he may have done. She thought back to the day at the deli when he walked in with the very young, busty blond. He told her the story of them running into each other by chance at the deli, but something didn't seem right about it and she was afraid to ask about it again, afraid of what she may find out.

She also couldn't forget the sounds she heard coming from the bedroom when Daniel took her to his friend's house to watch the football game. She knew the sounds Daniel made when he was aroused and if she were honest with herself, those were the sounds she heard through the door besides conversation. She couldn't imagine Daniel doing anything like that. She had dreams about where the path their life would take and she really wanted that. She knew he didn't always treat her the way she should be treated, but she had put in a lot of time to get the outcome she wanted.

Then here was Kerrion who was kind, sweet and handsome and knew how to say the right things at the right time without any hint of an ulterior motive. She knew he was interested in her, but he didn't push her. He saw the good in her and she didn't have to sacrifice any of who she was to be with him.

They continued to sway together to the music and she loved how slow and seductive he moved. Her mind started playing tricks on her as she began imagining other things about moving slow and seductive and it wasn't Daniel's face she was imagining; it was Kerrion's. .

"Terri, did you hear me?"

"Yes, I heard you. You don't make things easy on a woman do you?"

"Terri I'm not trying to complicate your life. I respect your relationship with Daniel, as strange as it is, but I won't hate on it. All I know is from the moment I met you and listened to you tell me about cleaning his place, I knew you deserved more than that. I can't really say there is anything wrong with helping your man out, but it was late in the evening and he didn't even go with you to the store.

I've listened to you confide in me and I don't want to throw your words back at you. You are an incredibly beautiful woman and any man would be grateful to call you his and treat you like the queen that you are. Don't think that I'm trying to lure you away from Daniel because that's a choice you and only you can make. I'm just saying, if that brother can't really appreciate you, don't think that someone else won't."

"I don't know how to respond to that. I know that Daniel has his issues and you aren't the only one who sees how he treats me and has commented on it. No one and no relationship is perfect and I've invested a lot of time and energy in my relationship with Daniel."

"Terri, I'm not asking you to second guess your choices when it comes to him. If being with him is what makes you happy then I'm happy for you. I'm not saying leave him and come to me. I'm not perfect either and relationships are hard work. I'm only saying make sure you're getting what you need and desire from your relationship and don't compromise on respect, trust and honesty. Those are the most important factors besides love. Now, I don't want to talk about Daniel anymore. I want to dance with you and have a good time, alright?"

She wanted to erase all thoughts of anything, but how good it felt to be out in public with a man who wasn't ashamed to be with her.

"Alright," was all she replied when he drew her closer as another slow song played.

Chapter Nine
TERRI

Daniel was livid. He'd come back to Terri's house a few times and she still hadn't returned. To top things off, he'd tried using his key to wait inside her house and it didn't work because it appeared she had changed the locks.

Anger like he'd never experienced surfaced when he spotted her leaving earlier and that sent him straight to Tammy's place where that anger spilled over into his visit with her. He left without the chance to see her naked, which was his plan. All he could think about was Terri and how he usually had her eating up anything he said, putting her back in check. Something was different and before it went on much longer, he needed to reign her back in.

She'd been suspicious of him many times and each time he was able to talk himself out of whatever she thought was going on behind her back. The close call the night of the football game was an example of that. He thought she'd heard him and Tammy having sex, but Terri had only heard them talking. He was able to talk himself out of that easily. Now there appeared to be another party involved in why Terri began pushing back.

There was no telling what kind of game this guy was running on her. It must be much better game than what he himself had been running on her for an entire year, keeping her exactly where he wanted her to be. Terri was easy prey because she had self-esteem issues when it came to her weight. Being desperate for the happy ever after life her friends were having gave him opportunity to dangle the love and marriage carrot in her face and she'd play along with whatever he had in mind.

Now, as he sat outside waiting for her to come home to talk so that they could work things out, he wondered if he'd pushed things a little too far. What he hadn't planned on was there being some other guy in the picture and not knowing what the so-called friendship between him and Terri would mean for the two of them. Tonight he'd find out.

~~

"Thank you for a wonderful time," Terri said, relaxing into the soft leather seat of his car with her shoes sitting on her lap. Having them on her feet was no longer a good idea. The pain from walking and dancing in them all night was too much to think about putting her shoes back on.

"I'm glad you had a great time. Everyone told me to tell you they enjoyed your company and they hope I'll bring you around more often."

"I liked them too. They were a lot of fun."

Terri did have a good time and the fact that Daniel called and left over a dozen messages didn't put a damper on her night. Tonight was not about him and she refused to give him any space in her head.

"I know it's late, but would you like to come in?" she asked when they pulled up to her house.

"Sure."

Kerrion looked around for a place to park. When he

did, he turned around as Terri was about to open her door to get out. He reached over to halt her.

"What are you doing?" he asked.

Terri looked at him confused.

"I was getting out since we're at my house. Why, what's wrong?" she asked.

"Sit tight while I come around to help you out. Don't men cater to you by pulling out chairs and opening doors?"

She was embarrassed to admit that the answer to his question was no.

When he came around to her side of the car and opened her door, watched as she reached down to try to get her shoes back on her feet.

"I thought your feet hurt to have them on?"

"They are, but I can't walk without shoes on."

Before she could utter another word, he reached into his truck and swooped her and her shoes up into his arms.

"That's why you have me with you tonight," he said, closing and locking the door and turning with her in his arms toward her house.

She couldn't help but laugh being carried in his arms. He was a true gentleman and she could see herself getting comfortable with this kind of treatment.

Once inside, Kerrion walked over to her living room sofa and placed her on it. The price of beauty was definitely a few aches and pains and tonight those aches and pains were in her feet.

He surprised her even more when he sat down next to her and grabbed her legs, swinging them into his lap. When he proceeded to massage the pains from her feet, Terri thought she'd died and gone to heaven.

"Why do women wear shoes that hurt their feet?" he

asked.

Terri laughed.

"We love looking and feeling pretty and if we have to endure a little pain, most times it's worth it. Tonight was one of those nights."

"Well let me see if I can help with that," he said as he began massaging her aching feet with deep, soothing rubs.

The foot massage was the best she'd ever had. Come to think of it, Terri had never had a foot massage before. Boy was she missing out on a lot and Kerrion was doing things that reminded her of that

"Oh my goodness that feels so good," she said while her body relaxed even more. "Your hands are magic."

"Where is the remote to your television? Turn it on, lay back and enjoy it. Around me, unless you really feel the need to, you never have to endure such pain for beauty. You are beautiful whether you wear heels like those or those cute sneakers you wear to the gym. I'm glad you don't have hammer toes. It makes this foot massage much easier," he said, laughing.

"Have you massaged many hammer toes?" she inquired.

"No not many, but yours are by far the prettiest."

"That's good because I see this as a job for you in your future."

Kerrion continued massaging not only her feet, but all around her ankles and her lower legs. He looked over at Terri, laid back with her whole body relaxed and even after a night of dancing until her feet hurt, she was still very beautiful. He was glad that she was relaxed because she seemed so tense and stressed out. Kerrion was more than happy to have a hand in her finally being able to let the stresses go, even if it was for one evening.

An hour later after his foot massage had put Terri to sleep, Kerrion knew it was time for him to leave so he shook her awake.

"Terri, come walk me to the door so that you can go up to bed."

"I'm so sorry I fell asleep on you. That was not a good host move on my part. It was the foot massage that did me in."

"Don't worry about it. I enjoyed watching you sleep. Thanks again for a great night. Get some sleep and I'll call you tomorrow to see if want to go for a run with me."

Terri wasn't a runner or even a jogger, but she didn't mind giving it a try.

"I'd love to as long as you promise to go slow because I'm no runner."

"Slow it is," he replied.

They walked toward the door when Terri walked into the back of him when he stopped suddenly in front of the door and turned to face her.

Kerrion seemed hesitant and she wondered if he suddenly changed his mind about the run in the morning.

"Is something wrong?" she asked.

Nothing was wrong and Kerrion knew it. He was hit with a sudden urge to kiss her. Disrespecting her was something he didn't want to do, nor did he want to cross a line, but he was struggling with dealing with the strong feelings he was developing for her and leaving without a taste of her didn't seem like a good option. He wasn't sure he'd ever get the chance again.

"Tell me right now if I'm wrong or going too far before I kiss you, Terri. You know I don't want to cross a line with you because your friendship means too much for me. I loved holding you in my arms tonight while we danced and being around you has stirred up feelings I can't deny. I know you're involved and dealing with issues in your relationship and I'm not trying to disrespect that so tell me no and I'll leave with no problem. We'll still do our run tomorrow and it won't change anything with our friendship if you don't allow me to kiss you."

As much as she'd like to fight her attraction to him, she couldn't, Daniel or no Daniel. She wanted the kiss as much as he did. Leaning in closer, she hoped he would pick up on her desire for the kiss.

Their eyes met as Kerrion leaned in joining their lips in a ruthless kiss. Terri felt like she was floating as his lips covered hers, tantalizing her to match his aggressiveness for an even deeper connection. The kiss was hot and laced with passion that traveled through her body, making her toes curl into the soft plushness of the carpet. Kerrion wasn't just kissing her, he was making love to her mouth and Terri never wanted the feeling to end as she reach up to grab and hold his head in place so that he knew she didn't want him to let up on his assault.

Kerrion knew kissing Terri would be this good. He continued plowing her mouth over and over giving as much pleasure as he was getting from her mouth. When he felt his body hardening and reacting to the kiss, Kerrion pulled away slowly, still holding her in his arms.

"Do you know how beautiful you look right now with your lips having that thoroughly kissed look? I better leave right now before I ask for more than the fiery kiss you gave me. Now I can go home and get some sleep."

He leaned down for a quicker kiss on her lips before opening the door to leave.

"Lock up and I'll talk to you tomorrow. Thanks again for going with me tonight."

Terri couldn't get her mouth to form words. She was still experiencing the kiss they'd shared. She wanted to hold on to it as she watched him get in his car and drive off. As soon as she'd shut the door her cell phone rang. She thought it was him calling from the car making sure she'd locked up after him. Once she'd heard who was on the other end, she wished she'd checked the caller ID and let it go to voicemail.

"Did you screw him?" Daniel asked her as soon as she answered.

"No, Daniel because I'm nothing like you and neither is he. What are you doing, spying on me?"

"Like me? What's that supposed to mean? For the record, I don't have to spy on you, you belong to me."

Terri pulled the phone from her ear and looked at it strangely not believing that he'd claimed her as if she was property.

"Belong to you? It's late Daniel and I don't feel like arguing with you. It's the middle of the night."

"I know what time it is. The time didn't seem to be an issue since lover boy just left. How old is he anyway?"

"You don't want to go there, Daniel. Trust me when I say, you don't," she said loudly.

"So is the relationship between you and me over? Let me know because there are plenty of women who are waiting for me and can appreciate a good man like me," Daniel said angrily, screaming at the top of his lungs.

Hearing his threats about other women didn't anger her, especially since she knew that there were already other women he was seeing. That reality was there for her to see all along, but she'd been blinded by the kind of relationship she desperately wanted them to have. Now, she was tired and over his mess.

"Daniel, you don't really want me do you? What you want is a pet that you can control and tell who to be and how to act. You want someone who will do everything you say and worship the ground you walk on because you're successful and handsome. You want someone who will be so submissive to you that they will forget about who they are and what their needs are and only focus on yours. I am more than what you give me credit for and I have allowed you to treat me like crap for a long time. I don't know what I am to you, but it's not what I should be. Do you realize the number of times I've said I loved you and not once have you ever said it back to me? That lame excuse that you don't need to say it because you show it to me is played out. A woman not only wants to know it, but she wants to hear it. I don't know what we are, but it's not a respectful, loving relationship. Here you are now trying to accuse me of the type of thing I have no doubt you're already doing. If fact, what are you doing, sitting outside of my house watching me come and go? How did you know anyone was here with me? That's pathetic, especially for you who claims he can have any woman he wants."

"No I'm not watching you. I came by to try and talk to you when I saw him leaving and besides that, what's up with my key not working? What the hell are you doing Terri? Are you trying to make me jealous? Well, I don't do jealous sweetheart because I don't have to. Here you are, involved with me yet you go out with another man tonight? I never pegged you for a cheating......"

Terri cut him off, knowing something disrespectful was

about to come out of his mouth as it usually did when he felt the need to put her in check.

"Pick your words carefully Daniel. Watch what you call me," she interrupted with disdain in her voice.

"What would you call a woman who goes out with another man when she's in a relationship with someone else Terri?"

"Yes I did change my locks and I decided unless I'm married, I'm not giving a man keys to my home to come and go as he pleases. That's too much control of my life that I'm relinquishing to someone else. Not that I have to explain anything to you, but it wasn't a date I was on tonight. I simply went out to a club, something you never do with me and I had a good time. I wanted to go out and have some fun for a change and there was no harm done. To answer your earlier question, no I didn't sleep with him and don't ever confuse me with the tricks you mess around with as if you think I don't know. I have been so wrapped up in you and your life and making sure you were happy that I let you get away with whatever you wanted."

"Well you get what you put out there," he replied.

"What's that supposed to mean? Are you saying, you mess around with other women because somehow I put the vibe out there that it would be okay with me? You are sadly mistaken. I may have overlooked it, but I didn't put out a vibe that it was okay to disrespect me. I deserve much better than that from a man I've clearly committed and dedicated myself to."

"So where is all of this coming from huh Terri? Your meddling girlfriends or that child you were out with tonight? What is he working his way into your panties by helping you point out all of the things that are wrong with our relationship? That doesn't sound like a business arrangement to me, which is what you said you had with him."

She'd had enough. Everyone had been right all along, telling her that she was wasting her time with him. She was about to tell him the relationship was over when he began shouting at her like a madman.

"Your self-esteem was in the toilet when we met. You could barely look people in the face because you didn't like who you thought people saw when they looked at you. Even with your size I was willing to take a chance on you and look where that got me; a woman with a whole lot of lip. You should be thankful that a man like me was even showing an interest in you. Since day one all you talked about was how there were no good men out here and how every man wanted a Beyoncé look alike. I looked past the fact that you were overweight and thought so little of yourself because of how men treated you in the past. I treated you good and you still complain. I'm successful, rich and was planning to one day marry you and make your life complete. I see that's not going to happen because you're not appreciative of a good man like me. Now I may reconsider my thinking if you apologize and stop acting like a little girl."

Terri heard him say apologize and she started pacing to walk off the level of anger boiling up in her body. She was ready to blow like a smokestack. He wanted her to apologize for telling him the truth? Never!

"You expect me to apologize for calling you out for the way you've treated me and the things you say to me? You think that's something admirable? It's not and you are mistaken if you think anything I've said warrants an apology on my end. What is it that makes you think you're so special? The fact that you're successful? There is nothing special about a man like you Daniel. All I see is one who doesn't respect me, who doesn't love me and no woman wants that. I let you control this relationship and me for a long time and I'm over it. Yes, my friends were right about you and you didn't like any of them because they could see right through you. I was too excited to be in a relationship that I thought was a good one, to see that it was the opposite. You are no different than other men I've been involved with. Your disrespect was hidden by a high powered job and a large bank account. The bling and the promises of what my life could be like being married to you had me blinded when what I really want is someone who will love me for me, fat or skinny, rich or poor or even younger or older. No, Kerrion never tried to persuade me to leave you or talked down about you because he's too much of a gentleman. Is he interested in me? Yes he is because contrary to what you may think, other men do find me attractive, as I am. There were a few times when I shared things with him that he could have used to get closer to me and convinced me to pull away from you, but he rose above that. He may be young, but he is more of a man at twenty-five than you have been at forty-six. I'm rising above this on my own. We're done," she finally said.

It was out there. She'd finally gotten up the nerve to end things with Daniel and it already felt good. He was silent for a few seconds and Terri wasn't sure what would come next after her declaration.

"Well you know what," she finally heard him say. "You don't deserve a man like me. I knew when I first started messing around with you that you weren't going to be enough. I wasted time on you which I can never get back. If what you want is some young buck, then so be it. He'll treat you like all of the other guys did before I came along. I was done with you anyway."

Terri interrupted him, no longer that naïve girl who he had been dating.

"I'm glad to hear that because the feeling is mutual. As far as my wanting a young buck, at least I'm closer to his age than you are to Shannon."

Terri planted her heels in to really let him have it with all of the things that had been on her mind.

"You should be ashamed of yourself for even touching that girl. She may be an adult, but you have no business messing around with your partner's daughter and there is no need to deny it. I would love to be around to see how Bill reacts when he finds out and I'm sure he will. I may not have wanted to believe what I saw that day in the deli, but I knew that day what it was, no matter what story you quickly came up with. You're a pig and a pig will have his final day at the slaughter. You are screwing his daughter Daniel! It was all over her face and yours. How old is she twenty-two or twenty-three? It really doesn't matter because there is a special place in hell for you. She may not be underage, but really Daniel? Oh and if you think Phil won't find out that you've been screwing Tammy, you are sadly mistaken about that too. Yes I knew about her too. I did hear you talking that day at the football party, but I also heard you screwing her. I know your moans of pleasure so no need in denying that either. I've overlooked a lot of things, but no more. I'm better than how you've made me feel, so do us both a favor and never call me again. No matter what you think or say about me, I'm a rose baby. I'm big, beautiful, bright and shiny for the world to see. I'm too beautiful to be held in the jar you've placed me in. Have a nice life."

She didn't give him an opportunity to respond to her rant. She disconnected the call and turned her phone off. It was the middle of the night and she needed some sleep to be well rested for her run with Kerrion in the morning. She had to remember to thank him when she saw him. In a short period of time, without even realizing it, he'd shown her the shortcomings in her relationship by how well he treated her. It's not that she didn't really know it; she overlooked it. Meeting him woke something up in her. He helped her see that she was living her life for someone else, going by someone else's rules. She now felt excited about taking her life back and living according to her own rules.

At one time in her life she thought she needed a man to define who she was, thinking that someone else's money and stature would put a stamp of approval on who she was as a person. Someone else's approval of her wasn't needed. Money, age or status of a man would not help her find the love and appreciation she deserved. Those things should come from someone unconditionally.

Never in her wildest dreams did she think she would ever connect with a man the way she was connecting with Kerrion. She was happy that she didn't let his age deter her from finding out what a great man he was.

Terri turned off all of the lights and headed to bed. She touched her lips where Kerrion's lips had touched hers and she smiled, looking forward to seeing him the next day.

Chapter Ten
TERRI

"Come on Terri, you only have a half a mile left. You can do it," Kerrion encouraged.

Terri couldn't respond. She was too busy concentrating on finishing her last mile. She and Kerrion had been running partners for a few months and she was getting acclimated to running with him on Saturdays.

After her breakup with Daniel she'd once again found herself and vowed to never let another man take her for granted. She and Kerrion weren't in a relationship, but they had gone out on a few dates in the time since her breakup. When she'd finally told him her relationship with Daniel was over, he was happy that she'd gotten up the nerve to walk away from a man who didn't respect her. When she mentioned her suspicions about Shannon and what she suspected, not surprisingly, Kerrion had already picked up on it when they saw them in the deli. Being able to share all of her thoughts with him, she shared what she knew happened with Tammy and a few other women she suspected he had been involved with. He didn't judge her naiveté, but shared that he was happy that she'd found herself and her newfound independence.

Jordan and her other friends were most happy for her. They never thought that Daniel was the man for her. He had a lot of superficial qualities Terri was looking for, but when it came down to love, caring and respect, he was lacking in all of those and those were the things that make for a successful relationship.

She'd gone to Jordan's wedding and was thankful that Kerrion agreed to accompany her as her date at the last minute. When she'd told him of her plan to go alone and felt good about doing so. The old Terri never would have thought about going to a wedding without a date. She didn't want to be pitied by anyone as people sometimes did when a woman was dateless to such an event. Kerrion told her to never feel that way and if she truly wanted to go alone, then she should do that or if she wanted an escort for the evening, he was more than willing to go as her friend. She accepted and he was the perfect date.

Daniel tried calling her a few times to apologize for the heated conversation they had where they both said things they regretted. Unlike him, Terri didn't regret anything she'd said and she was happy when he finally stopped calling.

When Kerrion slowed down, she knew she had reached her goal of running five miles without stopping. That's a first for her and she was excited.

"Congratulations Terri!" he exclaimed. "You did it. Five miles down and you're still breathing and you thought you wouldn't be able to do it. All the working out you've been doing and running every week and you're doing five miles like it's nothing. I'm so proud of you."

After catching her breath, she was proud of herself. Working out was her new obsession and it wasn't to be around Kerrion, but for her own health. She'd already noticed a difference in the way her clothes fit, especially when she had to go shopping to buy new things since her current clothes were getting to be too big for her.

"Thank you. It was hard, but not as hard as I thought it would be."

"That's good because that means our next goal is to get you up to seven miles."

Terri frowned.

"I see that frown. Don't worry, I plan to work you up to that, not right away," he explained.

"That's good to know. I was about to forget I know you if you were talking about the next run being seven miles," she laughed while they stretched.

Kerrion was happier than he'd been in a long time. He felt free when he was with Terri and he didn't have to be someone he wasn't. She'd finally started to accept him, twenty-five years old and all.

Now that her relationship with Daniel was over, he wanted to talk to her about taking their friendship to the next level, but he wasn't sure she was up for it. He knew what a toll the last relationship had taken on her and he didn't want to pressure her, loving that she'd found her new independence. Luckily they had become very good friends and were already spending a lot of time together. He was keeping things strictly friendship because he wanted to prove to her that he would never treat her the way other men had in her past.

Falling into a routine of doing fun things had been the norm for them over the past several weeks. They had gone to movies, out to eat and he'd even invited her to watch him play pickup basketball with his friends. They enjoyed movie and popcorn nights at his place and hers, growing closer without putting a label on what they were. Now he had to figure out a way to get even closer without scaring her off. He wanted more and he wanted her.

"What do you say we go grab some salads at your favorite spot?" he asked.

"That sounds great. Are we still on for later tonight?" Terri asked, hoping he remembered that she invited him to a game night Jordan and her husband were hosting.

"Of course we are. I love hanging with your friends and any day that I get to spend more time with you is a good day. I'll pick you up around seven."

Sliding up to him, she gave him a friendly hug to say thank you for being who he was. Sometimes the residual effects of her relationship with Daniel slipped in and she waited on pins and needles for the ball to drop and Kerrion would go from a Dr. Jekyll to a Mr. Hyde, but so far that had not happened. He was exactly who he said he was; a man who believed in treating a woman right. She didn't know what was in store for them, but she was hoping it was something good and that it would happen soon. Finally she felt like the perfect man had come her way, but she knew he was holding back waiting on her to let him know that she was ready for him. She was more than ready. Since that one night they'd kissed, he hadn't tried kissing her again except for pecks on the cheek. She didn't know why he was holding back since he knew that she wasn't involved with Daniel anymore. Maybe their time was coming, but she wouldn't push it for now. Things were going good and they not only spent personal time together, they continued working on his business and marketing plan and things were looking up.

Kerrion received the approval for the loan to start his business and now all he needed to do was find a location, get all of the equipment he was going to need and then build up his clientele using her marketing and public relations expertise. A lot of his clients at the gym where he worked now were planning to join him when his business opened. As soon as he had his location nailed down, she would begin working on mass marketing and promotion to really get the word out. Things were looking up for them both, for her on a personal level and for Kerrion on a business level and she was happy to be a part of his success.

~~

"Hey Ma, are you home?" Kerrion asked coming into his parents' house. He had a few hours before he had to pick Terri up.

"Hi," his mother said coming into the room.

"What brings you by on a Saturday?"

"Oh nothing, where's dad?" he said sitting down in the kitchen as his mother began washing the dishes.

"Mom, you have a dishwasher, why don't you use it?"

His mother looked at him strangely.

"What?" he asked.

"What is it Kerrion? I know when something's on your mind. You start rambling about crazy stuff and I hate dishwashers. They don't get dishes as clean as I want them to be so I prefer washing them by hand. Now what gives?" she asked.

His mother knew him well.

"I've met someone."

"You've met someone?"

"Yes, someone special."

"Someone special?"

"Are you going to repeat everything I say Ma?"

His mother smiled. He knew her smile meant she knew,

like he did, that he had never come to talk to her about a woman before. She knew he talked to his brothers and his father, but never her. To him, Terri was that special and he wanted his mother to know all about her.

"I'm sorry, was I doing that? You shocked me because you've never talked to me about a woman before. Is it the young lady you've been spending a lot of time with?"

How did she know that? He thought. Before he could ask, she answered.

"One of your brothers told me you've seeing someone. When he no longer asked me how your business plan was coming along and if you needed any money to help you out I asked him what was going on. He said the two of you had talked and you told him everything on the business front was working out good and that you'd been spending your free time with a nice young woman. So who is she?"

"Her name is Terri and she is beautiful Ma. Not just beautiful on the outside either. I met her a while ago and so far things have been moving pretty slow because she's recently out of a bad relationship. I didn't want to pressure her into another one so for now we've become the best of friends. Actually, that's not true, I'm in love with her."

Declaring his love for a woman was something his mother never heard him do before so she stopped what he was doing, sat across from him and gave him her undivided attention.

"She's a little older than I am, by five years. She's also a marketing and public relations specialist and she's been instrumental in helping me get my business off the ground by working on the marketing campaign. We've spent a lot of time together and I want her to meet you and dad. I don't want to push her too fast or too hard because she's been broken in the past by men who didn't appreciate her for the beautiful woman that she is. I know she knows that I'm far from being that type of guy. Her wounds are still a little fresh from her break-up and I'm ready for her, but I'm not sure she's ready for me. I don't want to keep her a secret though."

It felt good getting his thoughts out to his mother. He and his siblings could always tell her anything and she always gave good advice. He was hoping for that now, looking over at her with a look that said he needed her help.

"You know not to play around with this woman, especially if she's been hurt in the past, so if you say you're in love with her, you better mean it."

"I do," he quickly replied.

"Then tell her. I know that you're not the type to fall in love easily, so she must be something special. Your father and I have taught all of you, especially the boys, how you should love, treat and respect a woman. I think if you talked it out with her, showing her how genuine your feelings are for her, it'll work out fine, especially if you think she has feelings for you. Does she?"

Kerrion was almost one hundred percent sure she did.

"Yeah, Ma, I believe she does, though she's holding back not wanting to be hurt again. I think she's waiting on me to make the move, but I want to be sure she's gotten over any preconceived notions she has about men because of her past with them. I know I could make her happy and she already makes me happy. I was thinking of talking to her about it tonight and if things go well, I was hoping you'd cook one of your special Sunday dinners tomorrow and I could invite her over."

His mother smiled. He knew the wheels were already turning in his mother's head; planning for weddings and babies.

"Not so fast Ma. It's only dinner and I see the gleam in your eyes. I didn't say anything about marriage or babies. I said I wanted her to meet you and dad, that's it, okay?"

"Okay son, I hear you and I look forward to meeting her tomorrow after church. What about my pot roast with potatoes and carrots, some fresh greens and my homemade pasta salad? I think I may even make my famous French vanilla and strawberry preserves cake."

Kerrion knew he could count on his mother.

"Thanks Ma. I better get going. I'm supposed to pick her up soon for game night with some of her friends. Love you and I'll see you tomorrow after church and if things go well, I'll have Terri with me."

"Sounds good son. Good luck."

~~

"Terri, I know you're not calling me to cancel for tonight?" Jordan said before Terri could get out a hello.

"No, I'm not calling to cancel out. Kerrion and I are still coming. I was checking to see if you wanted me to bring anything while we're on our way. Why do you always think I'm going to cancel out on everything?"

"Because you do. You know you will flake out on getting together with everyone in a heartbeat. So Kerrion is still coming with you huh? How's that going because he seems like a really good guy. I watched you two at my wedding and he was very attentive and even with all the tail in the room, he only had eyes for you," Jordan chuckled.

Jordan was right. Kerrion pretty much stayed in the background at the wedding, but whenever she needed him, he was right there.

"It is what it is. We haven't said we're in a relationship or anything and there's been no more kissing since that night I told you he kissed me after that party I went to with him. There certainly hasn't been anything else, though I'm ready to jump him any minute now if he doesn't soon make a move."

They both laughed out loud.

"Now Terri, you've complained in the past that every relationship you've had was more about sex than really getting to know each other and spending time together. Now you have the chance to do that and you're complaining because he hasn't jumped you yet? Just go with the flow on this one. I think you have a winner and I'm going by all the good things you've told me about him, the few times we've all been together and on the interaction I've seen between the two of you at the wedding and definitely at the gym. What are you thinking when it comes to him?"

Terri didn't want to hear grief from Jordan if she told her the truth. Even though she'd expressed how much she liked Kerrion, she wasn't sure Jordan was ready to hear her truth. Here goes nothing, she thought.

"I think I'm in love with him Jordan."

She waited for all the ways Jordan would tell her she was moving too fast, that she always found herself in this trap with men or that she was only reacting to the person he was allowing her to see; all of the things she said when she told her about Daniel when they first started dating.

"It's about time girl!" she exclaimed, to Terri's surprise.

Terri was shocked by her response. She didn't expect that sort of reaction from Jordan.

"You surprise me Jordan."

"Why? Because you didn't get the speech you usually get from me? Girl, from the moment you told me about this guy I was hooked. When I saw it was the guy from the gym, I knew you had struck gold. I've watched woman after woman hit on him at the gym before and he never bit. They always tried using the wrong bait and you could see that's not what he was about. I've been hearing nothing but wonderful things about him, about how he treats you and I won't even talk about the flowers he sends you all the time to the office. He is a keeper girl and don't hesitate about the direction you're going in with him because he hasn't jumped you yet. Be happy that you've fallen in love and sex had nothing to do with it so your feelings aren't clouded. I have no doubt that he's in love with you too. He wears his feelings for you on his sleeve. Anyone can see how he feels about you and I'm glad you've taken things slow with him."

Terri hoped Jordan was right. She hasn't had the best of luck when it comes to men. She hoped this time was different.

"I hope you're right because I think it's time Kerrion and I had a talk. We've been avoiding and dancing around the attraction and I don't want to avoid it anymore. I'm thankful because I know he's patiently waiting because of what I went through with Daniel. He's been giving me time to find myself so that when I'm ready, I would be clear about his intentions. I love him so much Jordan. He has been incredible to me, always treating me like a queen and it's genuine. I don't know why I didn't see before that I was being mistreated and disrespected in relationships until they were over. Kerrion has got that old time upbringing of opening doors, entering a room first, walking so that he's next to the curb and not me and his heart is sincere when he speaks to me. Everything about him is so real. I can't tell you how glad I am that I went with you guys to the gym that day. I probably never would have used the number he slipped in my bag that night at the market. Running into him again gave me a chance to connect with him and really get to know him."

"Well I'm happy for you. Hurry up and do what you got to do to get your man girl and get here to the party. We're going to have a lot of fun."

Terri didn't doubt it. Jordan and the crew were a lively bunch. She was glad they hadn't given up on her with the many times she'd cancelled out on them.

"We'll be there in a little bit. My doorbell is ringing so Kerrion is here. I'll see you in a bit."

Terri hung up her phone and rushed to the door after checking herself one last time in the mirror. She smiled at herself, noticing the transition her body was making with all of the working out and running she and Kerrion have been doing. She also loved what she had on after being one of those women who happily hid behind all black attire. Tonight she was wearing a soft pink top with light gray slacks and grey and pink low heeled sandals. No more dull, dark colors for her. She flung open the door as Kerrion was about to ring the bell again.

"I'm sorry Kerrion, I was on the phone with Jordan. I wanted to know if she wanted us to bring anything before we got there. You look great," she said checking him out in denims and a mint green pullover shirt.

"Thank you. You look gorgeous as usual. You seem to get prettier and lovelier every time I see you."

"Thank you. You say the nicest things to me."

"It's easy when it's the truth."

Terri smiled thinking of how happy she was every chance she got to spend time with him.

"I'm ready to go if you are," she said.

It was now or never, Kerrion thought.

"Listen, do you mind if we talk for a minute?" he asked.

"Of course. Come on in and have a seat if you want. Is everything okay?"

Kerrion moved to take a seat on the sofa after she'd taken hers next to where he was about to sit. He turned to her to answer.

"Everything is fine. On the drive over here I was trying to think of a way to ease into this conversation with you without blurting it out, but I can't see another way to do it without making sure you would take me serious."

Terri didn't know what to expect. They had always been pretty open and she would be no different now.

"Whatever it is, say it," she said.

Kerrion hesitated before taking her hands into his. He made eye contact because he was about to give her all of him and he needed to see her reaction.

"Terri, I love you. I hope that doesn't frighten you or seem like it's sudden because it's not. We've been hanging out and spending a lot of time together and I've fallen in love with you. I wanted to give you plenty of time to work out whatever lingering feeling you had over your last relationship, whether they were good or bad. I want you to know that I want you and not only for now, I want you long term. I want us to give a serious relationship a try to see where it could take us. I've never felt for any woman the way I feel for you and I promise you that I will always respect, cherish and love you and never give you cause to doubt what we have. You will never feel anything but special around me. I want us to always communicate and say what's on our minds and be as open as we can about good and bad things. I hope that by now you can see that I'm not like any other guy you've dealt with who've taken advantage of you. No relationship is perfect and you have come to mean everything to me and I'm hoping the feeling isn't one-sided here. Making sure that we don't go another step without you knowing how much I love you and want to be with you is important to me. I want to be the only man in your life loving you like I do and I will make sure that you will always know that there is no other woman for me, but you."

Terri wanted to cry. Not only did she tell Jordan that she was in love with him, but he was in her living room telling her how deeply he felt about her. He was in love with her and it sounded like music to her ears as her heart overflowed with love for him.

This moment couldn't be more perfect. Before she lost her nerve, she took her hands from his grasp and reached them up to hold his face between them. She leaned closer and kissed him, pouring every bit of love she had for him into the kiss. She filled the kiss with everything she had in her, love, passion, adoration, lust, hunger, desire and anything else she could think of to let him know he'd made her the happiest woman in the world. The kiss went on and on, even when she felt herself being lifted up and into Kerrion's lap, she didn't stop plundering his mouth with her promise of love. He nestled her even more into his embrace and closer to him is exactly where she wanted to be. She settled comfortably on his lap while they continued to devour each other.

It was clear they knew how long it had been since they last kissed and were making up for missed time. By the time they broke apart, they were breathing heavily. It didn't take them long to catch a second wind before going in for a second round. This time along with the kiss, she moaned, he moaned and those sounds were the only noises they could hear, driving them even deeper into the intimate moment.

Terri's body temperature rose when he pulled back from the kiss to lick around her lips and plant soft kisses around her cheeks, across her jaw and down the slope of her neck. While he concentrated on that, she uttered her own affection for him.

"Kerrion, I love you too. I've been holding that back for a while now and I've wanted to tell you. I didn't want to scare you off."

He stopped his ministrations to look her in the eyes.

"Baby, you could never scare me off because I'm here to stay. I'm glad we're on the same page. I know we've only shared that one kiss, but I've been dreaming about the day I'd get a taste of those lips again. Now I'm mad we have to stop to get to the party with your friends because I want to stay here with you like this all night long."

"Well we could skip the party," she said.

Kerrion loved how she thought, but he knew how much hanging with her friends meant to her.

"No skipping the party. Didn't you tell me your friends always get on you for ditching them? I won't be the cause of that. I would like to make a suggestion though."

"Like?" she wondered.

"Like, we hang at the party to play a few games and then

high tail it out of there and go back to my place. I say you march your pretty behind upstairs, grab an overnight bag and spend the night with me. I want to make you breakfast in the morning."

Terri didn't even pretend to hesitate. She jumped right up.

"I'll be back in a flash. I would like nothing more," she said walking toward the stairs.

"Terri, wait. One more thing. I'd like for you to meet my parents. I told my mom all about you and it seems one of my brothers has already told her a little about you from a conversation I had with them a few weeks ago. She knows I'm in love with you and I couldn't wait for her to meet you whenever you're ready."

Now that's how a relationship is supposed to go. When you're in love, you meet the family.

"I'm ready whenever you're ready to introduce me to them."

"Okay, well how about tomorrow evening? My mom is cooking a special dinner. I asked her to in hopes that you were ready to meet them."

Terri walked back over to Kerrion and planted another steamy kiss on his perfect lips.

"I love you so much and tomorrow is fine. I'm thinking next Sunday, we need to take a trip to my parent's house since we're meeting the parents and all," she said smiling.

"I'm down for that. Your mom is going to love me. I already know it."

Terri had no doubt her mom would love him.

"I'm going to get my purse and my overnight bag and I'll be right back."

Kerrion watched her go and wondered how he got so

lucky. He finally found the woman of his dreams and there was no turning back now.

Terri grabbed all of the things she'd need for a night at Kerrion's including some sexy stuff. If they were going to spend the night together, she wanted it to be extra special. Before going back down to him, she said a thank you to no one in particular. She'd finally gotten the man of her dreams; the one she hoped would find her. She couldn't be happier because after all the frogs she'd gone through, her prince charming had finally arrived.

~~

Terri had been to Kerrion's condo on several occasions, but this was the first time she was coming to spend the night. She had no hesitation or reservations about doing so. It felt like the most natural thing in the world to her.

"I had a great time at your friend's house tonight. It also helped that we kicked their butts in most of the card games too."

"They're our friends now, not just mine" she replied.

"You're right about that. It seems everyone was happy to hear we are officially a couple."

Kerrion came up behind her, hugging her around the waist while caressing her neck with soft open mouth kisses.

"No one is happier than I am," she replied.

"No one except maybe me," he countered.

"Okay, no one happier than you," she added, loving their closeness.

Kerrion turned her around so that she was facing him as he pulled her into his strong embrace. "I love you so much Terri. You will never regret loving me back," he confessed.

"I love you too baby and the only regret I have is that I didn't tell you sooner."

"It's okay. I'm glad we both know now."

"So shall I make some popcorn while you find a movie?" she asked because it was a ritual they did a lot of nights over the past several weeks.

"No," Kerrion said before leaning down to steal a kiss.

"No popcorn or no movie?" she asked.

"No either. I want to bypass all that for now, go into my room and make love to you all night long. Now if you prefer popcorn and a movie, we can do that. I'm up for whatever you want."

He was so sexy and the way he lowered his voice and looked at her with bedroom eyes, Terri knew what she wanted. Being as close to him as she was, she could already feel what he was up for and she didn't want to wait either.

"I enjoy popcorn and a movie any time. Right now, I want you," she admitted.

"Then I am what you shall have."

Kerrion led her through his condo and into the bedroom, making sure to grab her overnight bag as he turned off all of the lights.

When Terri left him alone to slip into something sexy that she said she had for him, he went into action. He grabbed the bag of fresh white and red rose petals he'd picked up earlier from a local florist earlier, hoping they would make being a couple official tonight. Making sure to spread them all around, he made a path with the petals from the bathroom door where Terri was changing, all around the room and adding some to the bed.

He flipped a switch that opened a panel on the wall below the flat screen television on his bedroom wall that faced the bed and out slid his surround sound system. He put a few of his favorite Jazz CDs in the changer and set the mood for a night of lovemaking. He smiled when the music poured from the four speakers in the four corners of his bedroom, all focused on the king sized bed that was the center of the room.

He left the room after realizing he forgot to set the alarm and when he returned, Terri was laying like a vision from heaven across the center of his bed waiting for him. His mouth went dry as he took in her beauty. He hesitated for a second when he entered his bedroom, but no more than that. He went to her, joining her on the bed and pulled her close to him.

The look of seduction didn't scare Terri as Kerrion approached her. She was looking into the eyes of the man she loved and saw that same love in return for her.

"You look incredible Terri. You almost seem like a dream coming into the room. I can't tell you how many days and nights I've thought about making love to you. I don't want either of us to ever forget this night. We'll one day be old and gray, sitting on the deck of our home watching our grandkids play and still we will think of the first night we were together; the first time we both declared our love. It's important to me that you never, ever forget this moment because I love you more than anything in this world. You are my everything baby and I never want you to forget that."

Kerrion didn't give her a chance to respond to his declaration. He kissed whatever she was about to say right off of her lips. It didn't take long for the kiss to heat up and have them behaving like two starving maniacs who couldn't seem to get enough of each other. His desire for her matched hers for him as they both sighed deeply, allowing the pleasure of the moment to take them away to a place where they surrendered their all to each other, mind, body and spirit.

Terri's lips were warm and inviting and the more he delved into her mouth the more he wanted to drive them both crazy, by not stopping until they were both out of breath. When he felt Terri tugging on his clothing, he felt the need to help her divest him of every single stitch.

He moved away from her lips only for the few moments it took for him to get completely naked

"I don't want you to think that I don't love how lovely you look in this nightie you wore for me, but I need to get this off of you so that I can feel all of you baby," he whispered, raising her temperature a few degrees with the visual of the two of them joined intimately, making love until their bodies were exhausted.

"I want to feel you too," she replied while reaching to help him remove the one piece of clothing she had on that kept him from feasting on her with his eyes

"You take my breath away," was all Kerrion could get out once he had her naked before him. His dreams of her didn't do her justice because before him was a woman more exquisite than even the biggest diamond in the world. He couldn't wait another second to get acquainted with every part of her.

Situating her so that her body was flush against his, he laid down and rolled them so that they were laying on their sides facing each other. Without any pretense, he pulled her to him, so that he could caress the shape of her body. He felt her shiver and knew she was feeling the intense moment as much as he was.

"This is what I've dreamed of Terri. Being her with you

like this, holding you in my arms, whispering words to let you know how much I love you and thankful I am that you love me."

Terri knew their thoughts were the same.

"It seems like I've been waiting a lifetime for you and for this moment," she said, breathlessly.

"Our wait is over baby because here in this moment is where we will always be. I love you so much and if there is ever a time when you're not feeling my love, make sure you tell me because I'm going to make sure I let you know every day what you mean to me. I never want you to have to wonder. My love for you is not about us being right here, naked about to make love. It's about every moment we've shared together and every word we've said leading up to this point. This is the icing and looking at how beautiful you are, this is the best icing a brother has ever seen. Now all I need to do is taste and my day is complete."

Terri felt a twinge in her body that caused it to instantly prepare for him. She didn't want to wait any longer. She looked from his eyes to his mouth and she could imagine the pleasure those same lips would give to other parts of her body and she was ready. Before her mind could register what was happening, Kerrion rolled her over so that she was on her back and placed a kiss first on her lips and then traveled down her body stopping along the way to give her pleasure making her body rise up off of the bed to meet his mouth as he went further trying to place a kiss on every part of her body he encountered along the way.

"Turn over for me baby," Kerrion said.

When Terri was on her stomach, he continued pleasing her body. Kerrion could feel her reaction every time he touched her and he loved how responsive she was, letting him know that he was doing things she liked. He straddled her body and massaged her neck and shoulders, placing more soft kisses in all of the places that his hands had touched. Her moans were getting louder and louder and were arousing him to a level he'd never reached before without being intimately joined.

He continued further down her body until his hands came to rest on the rounded cheeks of her behind. She was a voluptuous woman and he loved every part of her as he continued to caress first one and then the other.

Terri began wiggling under his attentive caresses and he could see he was already taking her to the brink.

"Please Kerrion," Terri begged.

She wasn't sure how much more she could take if he didn't soon make love to her. It seems that she had been waiting an eternity for him and though she loved what he was doing and how it made her feel, she wanted to feel their bodies connected.

"I know how you feel baby and I feel the same way. I want to cherish this moment with you and I don't want one part of your body untouched by me at the end of the night."

Terri thought that any moment, she would leap off of the bed, especially when she felt his hands get replaced by his mouth. That sent her body thrashing around on the bed, uncontrollably.

Her reaction told him exactly what he needed to know and that was that she was more than ready for him. He turned her back over to continue his kisses from her feet all the way up her body until he had once again found her lips with his own.

"Now baby," Terri pleaded again.

"My pleasure, my love," he replied. Kerrion reached

under the pillow and withdrew a condom to protect them until they were ready for a more intimate connection. He opened the pack and in a second, he'd donned it and wasted no time sliding back between her legs where he entered her body and felt her shudder at his sudden invasion.

"It's me and you baby, forever and ever," Kerrion crooned as took them both over the edge, taking their love along with them.

When their bodies had finally calmed down, he lifted his head, looking into the face of the woman he loved more than anything and saw the look of a woman who had been thoroughly made love to.

"Open your eyes and look at me baby," he said.

Terri slowly opened her eyes, still reeling from her explosive climax and looked into the eyes of love.

"I love you," he said and she had no doubt he meant it.

"I love you too. Thank you for finding me and showing me what it means to really be loved."

Terri felt whole for the first time in her life, thanks to a man who opened her up to a whole new world where they were the center of each other's lives.

Chapter Eleven
TERRI

One Year Later

"Hello and thanks to everyone for coming out to support me in this venture. It's taken me a while to get here, but at least I'm here."

When the crowd who had gathered to help him celebrate the opening of his business had quieted down, he continued so that the ceremony could begin.

"This dream started back in high school when I played sports and even back then, I dreamed about helping other people become and stay healthy. When I was in college, I started working on my business plan and saving money to fulfill my dream of owning my own business. I'm thankful to my parents who paid for my education so that any money I made working several jobs was able to go towards the preparation for this day."

Kerrion looked around the room of his new personal gym at all of the family and friends who had come out to support him. Along with family and friends, he saw the staff that he was able to hire due to the overwhelming number of new clients he obtained before he even started business. All of the open slots for trainers had already been taken up and he was already in search of other trainers to employ due to the long waiting list of clientele.

He also looked around to connect with the one person who helped make his dream a reality.

"I can't let this opening continue without telling all of you about the love of my life."

He turned to be sure he was looking right at Terri when he spoke.

"This woman right here, that all of you know because I never stop talking about her, has been my rock. She started out helping with my marketing campaign and that turned into many late nights of listening to me complain when things weren't going the way I wanted. She encouraged me and never lost faith in what I wanted to achieve. She rode around town with me looking at property after property and when something didn't pan out, she never let me give up."

Terri couldn't be happier for Kerrion and nothing made her life more complete than being a part of his dream.

"She also became my first client, having faith that I could help her achieve the weight loss and body toning that she wanted. My baby even agreed to be my before and after shots for my promotional material. No matter what she looked like she was my baby and always will be. I love you Terri. I hope that I've shown you how much I love you each and every day that we've been together. My life is much better because you're in it. I'm a much better man because my parents taught me how to be that and you were open to let me prove that's who I could be. Thank you for loving me and thank you for agreeing to marry me," he said to the surprise and cheers of everyone in the room except his parents, her family and their closest friends.

"Now come over here and help me cut this ribbon. This place is for us, baby," he said.

Terri ran into his arms. The past year and a half with Kerrion had been the best time of her life. She looked forward to many, many more. After her last disastrous relationship, Kerrion coming into her life was a breath of fresh air and she never looked back.

She thought over how far she'd come in life and at how much she'd changed. She was glad that her once preconceived idea of what her dream life was supposed to be didn't keep her from being open to the life she now had, which was more than she ever expected. She once settled for whatever she could get because she didn't think she deserved more. For years she allowed herself to be treated in a way that made her seem desperate for a man and attention.

She shuttered at the thought of what she allowed to enter her space at earlier points in her life. She was thankful the day she got her wake-up call and was able to see what she was missing out on. Having the times she wasted on useless men behind her put her on the path to pure bliss and happiness with Kerrion. Her life had changed and it was certainly for the better.

She'd never heard from Daniel again after a few months of calls and messages from him. At worked, she asked to be reassigned from the marketing campaign for his firm and since she'd always been an exemplary employee, she had no problem being transferred to another project. The last she heard, his law firm had bought him out after he was caught with his partner's daughter. Terri knew that was inevitable. From what she heard through gossip, Shannon had confessed her love for Daniel to her father, unbeknownst to Daniel and when he was approached about it, he first denied any relationship to her until his partner confessed that Shannon had told him everything including dates, times and places of their meetings for sex. Since Shannon was an adult, it was illegal, but it was immoral for him to get involved with her.

He was offered a buyout and took it to move to the west coast, far from Virginia and she was glad about it. He had taken so much from her, that she didn't realize she had been broken and battered until Kerrion came into her life and showed her how a woman should be loved and cherished.

Not a day went by that he didn't tell her he loved her, showed her he loved her and continued to mean it every single day. They were planning the wedding of her dreams and she couldn't wait to be his wife.

As she helped him finally cut the ribbon for the opening of the gym, the ribbon cutting was more than the start of a new business; it was the start of a new life for them, together.

KARINA'S STORY

Chapter One
KARINA

Karina Joseph couldn't think of a better way to spend a Friday night than at home with her children, nine year old Tyler and three year old Kayla. At twenty-five, most women her age were out partying and having a good time, but she decided it was time she did the more responsible thing and spent more time with her children and less time hanging in the streets. That was until her cellphone rang and one of her best friends was calling to no doubt convince her to hit the streets.

"Karina, girl, get dressed and come out with us tonight and don't try coming up with any excuses to not go because we need you!"

"I don't know Robin. Tonight is not a good night because Kayla's got a fever and I haven't had a lot of time to spend with Tyler this week because I've been hanging out with you crazy fools. Even though you don't have any kids, you forget that I have two of them."

"Come on, this is a big night. Didn't you have a good time the last time I said those words? I swear to you girl, tonight is going to be our night, so get dressed and come out with us. It's Trina, you and I this time; a smaller crew. When I say big, deep pockets will be in the spot tonight, I'm not kidding."

Karina didn't know what to do. She wanted to get out and definitely wanted to meet a baller. At the same time, she was also trying to be a good mother to her children.

She paced back and forth in her bedroom of the three bedroom apartment she was able to get through public housing a few years ago.

Tonight, like most Friday nights, her friends were laying it on thick in their effort to convince her to hit the club scene. Robin was doing all of the talking, but she could hear Trina in the background backing up everything.

The three of them had been close since childhood and unlike her, Robin and Trina had no children to be concerned about, so club hopping several times a week was easier for them than for her. Life for her was not the same. If she wanted to hang like that, she had to get a babysitter. That wasn't difficult most times because her sister Tracie was always willing to help her out with watching the kids for a few dollars, something Karina didn't have at the moment.

"I hear you thinking through the phone Karina," Robin said. "If you need a few dollars to get a babysitter, Trina and I will help you out with that. Besides, if you play your cards right, you'll end the night with some nice cash in your pocket anyway."

Karina was tossed, not knowing what to do. She could definitely use a night out with her girls. She'd given up a lot having two kids at a young age and she would love to finally meet a guy with some serious paper.

She felt like she'd missed out on lots of things having her first child at the age of sixteen. Sometimes life felt like it was passing her by because she didn't have the type of upbringing she wished she could have had that would not have resulted in her having two kids so young. Kayla and Tyler were her world, but every now and then, she wished she'd waited.

"Girl you are always home with those kids and they'll be there when you get back. I'm telling you there are going to be some major ballers up in the club tonight. I even heard rapper JayMark and all his millions was coming through tonight. You know the place is always crawling with football players too. I scored us some tickets to this event tonight where you can only get in if you have these special invites. You don't want to know what I had to do to get them, so don't make me waste them."

Karina knew what she meant. They had all done things to get something out of life and from the men around them. She could only imagine how low Robin had to go to get her hands on the tickets and it definitely sounded like it was going to be the place to be tonight. They had all done a lot less to be with brothers who had nothing going for them, so she definitely didn't mind doing a little extra for men at the top of their game.

"Okay, let me see if my sister will watch Kayla and Tyler. She likes coming over here to get a break from the rat race that is the life of living at my mother's house. You know how she always has a lot of traffic in and out of there. I'll call you back in a few minutes."

~~

"This place is jumping tonight," Karina said as she and her friends entered one of the hottest clubs in Baltimore. Professional ball players and hip hop artists were known to frequent the club and from the looks of things, tonight was no different. Before they got inside, they peeped limousines and other expensive rides in the parking lot and knew they were about to hit jackpot.

The place looked like money with bottles of the best and most expensive liquor displayed throughout, especially in the VIP section which was where they wanted to be.

Making sure the night ended the way she'd planned, she went into full trap mode. She was looking to snare herself a man with lots of cash who didn't mind passing it around when his expectations were met. Giving a little to get a little hadn't worked in her favor so far, so tonight she was turning it up to get herself a lot with the hope that things would turn out different.

As they began checking the men out, the men were no doubt checking them out too. When they walked in all eyes were on them, three of the finest girl's in the place.

"Okay ladies, let's do what we do best and see what comes up," Trina said, flipping her long weave and going into full diva mode, increasing her level of hotness.

Reaching the bar, Karina faked an effort to get the attention of the bartender, waiting on the first guy to bite who would offer to buy her a drink. As she predicted, her first suitor flashed money and a smile along with his desire to buy her whatever she wanted to drink. She accepted his offer, entertained a quick conversation with him and then followed Robin and Trina onto the dance floor to a prime spot to be seen by those occupying VIP.

Karina added a little more sway to her hips, drawing attention to her behind, which to her was her greatest asset. She didn't have the Kim Kardashian kind of booty; hers was more the Jennifer Lopez, back in the day, video kind of booty and it drew men like a snake to a snake charmer. Her small waist and large breasts were one day going to get her the man of her dreams and out of a life of poverty. The fact that she was wearing a bright red, form fitting mini dress made her the center of attention in the room and before long, the ballers started to notice her.

She wore a long weave that she kept looking tight. Even though her own hair was long, men loved women with weaves so she had to play the game like the other women to stay in the race.

Her makeup was flawless, though she didn't need much of it due to her natural beauty, but she knew a little extra went a long way. Tonight her lips were a fiery red like her dress because red always looked good on her.

After a few minutes of working the dance floor with her slow seductive moves, she noticed one of hip hop's biggest rap artist's JayMark was checking her out. Game and set, she thought.

Now all she needed was for him to make a move and then it would be match. To give him a little more incentive to make a move, she continued dancing and turned around so that her behind was on full display for him to see. She then bent over a little knowing what it would take to really get him up and out of his seat. After a few shakes, drops, pickups and winds, simulating the act of sex, she got her wish. One of his bodyguards asked her and her friends to join him in VIP. That was the match she was waiting for.

Karina was reeling JayMark in; she could feel it. He was like a bee to her honey pot.

He was your typical hardcore rapper from the streets of New York who rapped about the struggles of a young black man doing whatever he had to do to stay alive and keep money in his pockets. His good looks were heightened by his thick, muscled body and the many tattoos that were prominently displayed, making him look hard and sexy at the same time. She remembered seeing photos of him shirtless and knew he was fine from head to toe.

She sat down and slid a closer to him.

"Thanks for the invite into your world for me and my girls."

Karina watched his eyes as they took her all in, especially noticing how high up on her thighs her red dress had slid up, which was all a part of her plan.

"No problem beautiful, considering you are the finest shorty up in here tonight. I couldn't pass up a chance to get to know you."

"Thank you. So what are you and your guys doing after the club?"

She could see from the way he was looking at her that he was imagining her naked, especially when she noticed how focused he was on her breasts which were more than overflowing over the top of the neckline of her dress. If she inhaled just right, the dress gave the illusion that her breasts were about to pop out any minute. When he licked his lips in true LL Cool J style, she knew she had him.

"I don't know about them, but I plan on spending the rest of this night chillin' with you. How does that sound?"

"That sounds like a good idea to me."

"Cool, let's bounce then."

Apparently he was a man who knew what he wanted and wasted no time going for it. She could relate because she had her own plan and saw no reason to waste time.

She stood when he did and whispered to her girls that she would call them in the morning. Robin and Trina looked like they were engaged in some plans for the rest of the night themselves.

Karina felt important walking through the club with

JayMark and his bodyguard with all eyes on her as they made their way through the crowd toward the front entrance.

When they exited the club and she saw the long white stretch hummer limousine waiting for her, she knew she was stepping into big time. She'd met a few ballers over the past few years, but none was rolling big time like JayMark. Her plan was to give him everything she had to guarantee that this wasn't the only time she'd be riding like this.

The bodyguard opened the door and she got in, sinking into the soft, gray leather seats. She knew if she played her cards right, this could be the first night of the best times of her life.

She looked up when JayMark entered. He had a look on his face like he was ready for some action. He climbed in and sat on the seat next to her. Once the door was closed shut behind him and without any pretense or warning, he pulled her to him for a hard kiss that was sloppy, wet and demanding. She could tell he was going to like it wild and wild was her middle name. She wanted to show him what she was all about in case he was testing her out. While he continued to vigorously attack her mouth with his tongue stealing her breath away, she reached down and unzipped his pants.

That move caught him off guard and by the look on his face, it was a welcomed move.

"Oh, so you really are game I see?" she heard him say, right before he leaned back in the seat and let her prove to him what her game was like. As her head went to his lap, her mind was already on all the things she could do with the kind of money he could throw her way if he made her his lady. That's what she was going for.

~ ~

"Karina woke in the morning hung over and not clear on where she was. The activities of the night before were still a little blurry to her. She remembered pleasing JayMark good in the limo and hearing him tell her she was the best he'd ever had. That led to him asking her to spend the night with him and of course she said yes; no woman in her right mind would say no.

Once they were in the hotel suite, which was bigger than any she had ever seen before, they'd indulged in a bottle of something that had her head spinning. After a few glasses, they dispensed with talk and he took her straight to the bedroom.

He wasted no time getting his clothes off and had her do the same thing. They got right to the reason why they were there. She had a plan so she went along with whatever he wanted and he wanted everything sexual known to man.

Now, in the light of day, she finally shook the sleep off and looked around for him, but her bed buddy was nowhere to be found.

She got up and grabbed the sheet to pull around her to quietly go in search of him in one of the other rooms in the suite. Maybe he was letting her get some extra sleep because she had put in work all night long, she thought as she went from room to room.

She was no longer sleepy and was hoping she'd locate him to see if he wanted to go a few more rounds and maybe take her out for breakfast before she had to get home to her kids. She couldn't wait for her neighbors to see her pull up and get out of his stretch limo. They would all be as jealous as she wanted them to be. None of them believed her when she said her stay in the hood was only temporary and getting out of a stretch limo would show them she was on her way.

An unnerving feeling came over her when she discovered she couldn't locate him. She went back to the bedroom and noticed something she hadn't seen the first time. He'd left a message for her on the nightstand. She picked it up and read it. *'Thanks for a good time shorty. You were all that with that banging body. I have a flight to catch so I had to bounce. I left something for you in the night stand.'*

Opening the night stand and counted out what he'd left, twenty crisp one hundred dollar bills. She was almost afraid to touch them as her hands began trembling at the meaning behind the money. The fear had nothing to do with the fact that there was money, but like in the past, another man had left her money after a night of sex as if she were a prostitute. He hadn't asked for her number, she didn't have his and he didn't wake her before he left. He slipped out as if the night they'd spent together meant nothing to him. Like always, it ended up being a night of sex with a man who had no interest in her beyond getting her clothes off. Her hopes were once again dashed.

Disappointment now led to embarrassment as she quickly got dressed and went in search of a cab. She tried not looking anyone in the eye as she made her way through the lobby and out the front door in an outfit made for a night out and not for the morning. She could only imagine what people must be thinking when they watched her do the walk of shame through the main lobby.

After the cab dropped her off at her apartment, she tried to slip inside without waking anyone, but her sister heard her as she was heading for the bathroom to wash off any residue of the night before.

"The infamous walk of shame I see," she heard her sister Tracie say from behind her.

Karina wasn't in the mood for her sister's sarcasm after the embarrassing night she'd had.

"Not now Tracie."

"It's not my fault you had your hopes up once again only to have them dashed by realizing you were just a piece for the night."

Sarcasm at its best, Karina thought. She loved Tracie, but right now she wasn't in the mood for her punches.

"I told you, not right now Tracie."

She could feel her anger rising the more her sister spoke.

"I'm not trying to be mean Karina, I'm saying that this is what always happens to you. You go out in your sluttiest outfit thinking a big time baller is going to make you his ride or die chick. Why can't you accept it for what it is, get what you can and keep it moving? Was he big time, this guy you spent the night with?"

Karina wanted to ignore her, but knew that doing so wouldn't work. Tracie would keep pressing her.

"Yeah he was. It was that rapper JayMark," she replied sounding defeated at not having the outcome she'd hoped for.

"Sis, I keep telling you you're putting out the wrong bait if you're trying to get a man who will stick around. You're the fun one, not the one he'd want on his arm for the world to see. You're all body to him because that's what you throw at him. Look at me and remember the things I've told you about me and man after man after man. That doesn't work, so you need to deal with the life you have, get what you can out of it and out of the men you mess around with. Tell me did he at least slide any money your way?"

She knew that was next. If she did learn anything at all from her mother and her sister, it was how to work her magic so that if she didn't end up with the man, she at least ended up with the paper he carried in his pocket. If she didn't do anything in life, she knew how to wrangle money from a man. It was the things she did to get that money that caused many sleepless nights for herself.

"Yeah he did. You can have it all because I don't want it."

"Girl, stop knocking the hustle. You're not gonna be down on yourself after last night are you? You had to know that's how it would be. You are like me and mommy and this is what we do to survive; we use guys to get what we want and need. If it wasn't for the fact that I'm pregnant yet again and walking around with this belly, I'd be out there running my game too. Look at us, we both have two children, we live on welfare and neither one of us has our high school diploma. With no hope for any real future, we do what we can to take care of ours. If mommy taught us anything, it was that."

Karina was sick of her sister always talking like they will never be anything more than what they are.

"It's not a hustle Tracie. I'm trying to have a better life for me and my kids. I don't want to deal with the situation I'm in. I really thought he liked me. We talked a lot in the club and he asked me a lot about myself and told me a lot about his life and his career. He showed real interest in me. I'm tired of these brothers in the hood who don't have any more than what I have and two wrongs won't make any situation right."

"Girl, you are preaching to the choir, but all this trying isn't getting you anywhere. This life is all we know and it's all we'll ever know."

If she had not been experiencing it herself, she wouldn't believe it. She'd had no luck so far in achieving anything so maybe her sister was right. Things were the way they were supposed to be."

"There has to be more to life than this. I was only trying to find something better."

"So what did you do, tell him you have two children, live in the projects and at twenty-five, you still don't have a high school diploma?"

Tracie laughed at her and her ridicule hurt.

"You thought he saw you as wifey material? What you need to do is stop dreaming because men don't want that in a wife. They want that in a trick and believe me he only showed that much interest in you because where you thought you were running your game on him, he was running his own game and that was to get in your panties, that is if you even wore any last night. Where's the money I need to leave. I have stuff to do."

Karina was more than ready for her sister to get out. She reached in her bag and pulled out the envelope with the two grand in it. She didn't let Tracie see all of it and gave her three hundred. She may have said she didn't want the money, but she and the kids needed things. She slid Tracie the envelope while hiding the fact that she slipped seventeen-hundred of it back into her bag. She watched as Tracie looked inside.

"Three hundred was all that million dollar rapper gave you? Damn, you've gotten more than that from guys in the hood you gave it up to. Well, thanks for the cash."

Karina followed her sister as she gathered her things to leave.

"Why didn't you bring my niece and nephew with you last night to play with Tyler and Kayla?" she asked as they walked.

"They both went with their daddies for a change. I have to go downtown today to use my independence card this month to score some cash and I didn't want them tagging along. I'll talk to you later," Tracie said before turning and leaving the apartment.

Karina stood in place thinking over the things she and Tracie talked about. All of their lives were going nowhere fast and she needed to do something different, but she didn't know what.

Feeling worse than she did when she first arrived home, she went into the bathroom and shut the door where she cried knowing she'd made a complete fool of herself.

After all the men that had used her over the years, she still didn't know any better than to think sex would make a man fall in love with her. She cried because she didn't know what else to do to find a man who would take her away from the life she lived and with the exception of her children, a life she hated.

Karina looked at herself in the bathroom mirror and hated what she saw. It was always the morning after, that made her feel dirty and trashy. She wished she'd feel that way before so that she wouldn't continue to make the same mistakes with men that she'd been making over the past several years.

Her mother had always taught her that you get nothing when you put nothing out. She was putting out everything she had that was worth anything and yet she still hadn't attracted anything but men who wanted to sleep with her. Once they got that, when she thought it would turn into something more permanent, she would never hear from them again unless it was sex they wanted. She cried harder when she asked herself when would a man want her just for her.

Chapter Two
KARINA

"Dr. Tanner, your patient in four thirty-eight has been prepped for his procedure."

"Thank you nurse," Mykel said. "Let's get him down to operating room number three and I'll meet you there after I scrub."

He watched as she headed off to follow his instructions.

"Mykel!" said a voice very familiar to him.

Mykel turned to see one of his colleagues from another local hospital coming in his direction.

"Thomas," he said as they greeted each other. "What brings you here?"

"I have operating privileges here today for a patient that couldn't be transferred to Hopkins. I'll be here at Sinai for most of the day. Maybe we can do lunch or an early dinner if you have time. We have much to catch up on."

"I may be able to squeeze in a quick late lunch. I have surgery today and it's my only one. I've been here since yesterday and I plan to get out of here after this is done to get a game or two of tennis in."

"Ah, so you still play tennis. I haven't played since the last time you murdered me on the court."

"In that case, we'll have to schedule another match soon

so that we can have more of the same. How are Kate and the kids doing?" Mykel asked.

"Everybody is great. Kate is having our third in about a month so we're excited about the new addition."

"That's awesome man. I think the last time I saw you, you mentioned she was pregnant again. Good to hear."

Mykel was happy for his friend and a little jealous.

"So what about you. Are you still the reigning bachelor? No wife, kids?"

Mykel knew Thomas knew the answer to that.

"Not yet, but there is still hope. I was dating someone, but it didn't work out. I'm amazed that when women find out I'm a surgeon, they start dreaming of big houses, big cars and glamorous expensive weddings. They forget about the dating phase and jump right to wedding bells. Keep hope alive though my friend," Mykel said. He needed to end the conversation because he knew what was about to follow was Thomas' offer to set him up.

"Listen, have me paged when your surgery is done and let's meet away from the hospital for a meal. I'm afraid if they discover I'm still around, I'll get called in to do an unscheduled surgery," Mykel said.

"Will do," Thomas replied.

He was glad to see Thomas. They had gone to medical school and when it was time to do a residency, they were once again united. He was glad that they'd both survived and had gone on to be great surgeons, him specializing in cardiology while Thomas' specialty was in pediatric surgery.

The conversation ended just in time before Thomas began asking him more about him not being married or having any kids. He wasn't prepared to talk about his struggles, even as a successful doctor, with finding that one person that completed his life. At thirty-two, he was surprised how hard he found it to have a nice long lasting relationship.

He either met women who were looking to get married right away even though they didn't have a real connection or he'd met those who couldn't hold his attention for more than a day. He didn't have a problem with the notion of marrying once he'd found the right woman.

He'd had his share of different types of women from the very well educated to those who didn't go to school beyond high school. He never judged any of them as far as using education as a condition for relationship material. What he really wanted was someone down to earth, who had a good heart and who was about family.

He'd come from a great family where his parents were still married after forty years. He was the oldest with a younger sister, Misha, whom he adored and one day he wanted to have the same kind of life being in love like his parents.

His sister Misha was currently in her last year of college at Stevenson University. Since her school wasn't far from his Columbia, Maryland residence and their parents lived close to Washington, D.C., she lived on campus and when she needed a break from school and hated the drive all the way home, he kept a room for her in his home, a home he hoped to one day share with a woman other than his sister.

His last relationship didn't end well. She wasn't the type of woman who could deal with the demanding and unpredictable schedule of a surgeon. After dating for several months, he caught her on a date with another man and ended things with her. What he would never tolerate is a woman who would rather cheat than to walk away when she's unhappy. He figured she was testing the waters to see what else was out there before she ended things with him. He ended up doing it for her and was glad he did. He knew they weren't compatible when they met, but she was a successful attorney looking to live a good life and have a family. What he didn't know was that she felt lonely on nights when he pulled all-nighters at the hospital and couldn't cater to her every need on demand. They had lucrative careers and he tried to be what she wanted and needed, but it wasn't enough so he moved on.

He wanted a woman he could love and who could love him back unconditionally. Someone that he could build a life with. He kept the faith that one day he'd run into her and when he did, he had a feeling she would be everything he was looking for. At this point in his life he was ready to finally settle down, not with any woman, but with the woman who would be perfect for him.

Chapter Three
KARINA

Karina woke to the sound of kids playing outside her bedroom window. Her sister had left early in the morning and Karina was able to go back to sleep before the kids woke up. She kept her eyes closed tight and daydreamed that she wasn't living in public housing, but in a big, beautiful house where birds chirped from nearby trees and her husband was in the kitchen feeding the kids while she caught a few quiet moments to herself before getting up to head to work as a nurse at a local hospital.

Dreaming was all it was when she finally sat up and looked around, knowing she was still in her apartment.

Her reality was a lot different than her dreams. If she could, she would change a lot about her life with the exception of her children. They are why she struggles hard to make sure they never feel the doldrums that could come with living in poverty. Poverty was definitely all around them, but it wasn't within them and she wanted to make sure her children never looked down on how or where they lived.

Any mistakes that led to them living in public housing, sometimes barely surviving, were all her fault. She still believed that one day she'd find a way out, able to provide for her children using money from a full-time job and not from public assistance. Right now, she was surviving and doing what she needed to do to be sure they were okay.

Remembering before she'd gone out the night before, Kayla had been suffering through an oncoming cold, she got out of bed to see if her baby girl was feeling any better.

As her feet hit the floor and the chill hit the bottom of her feet, she was reminded of how cold the uncarpeted floor was. She grabbed her old ratted slippers from under the bed before heading into Kayla's room. One of the first things she would do if she ever moved out of her apartment and into her own house would be to make sure they had carpeted floors.

Entering Kayla's room, she was happy to see her sitting up in bed, playing with toys, looking as if she was already feeling much better. She picked her up to feel her skin to see if it was still warm.

"How is mommy's baby feeling today? Are you feeling any better?"

Kayla gave her an upside down grin.

"Oh mommy, I'm not a baby. I'm a big girl remember? I'm is three now and not a baby anymore."

Karina smiled hearing that and hearing her daughter's attempts to speak like a big girl. She corrected her daughter's English so that she would learn early how to speak properly and not hood.

"Kayla, you will always be my baby and it's 'I am three, not I'm is three."

She watched as Kayla thought about the correction.

"Mommy, you not three, I am."

She couldn't help but laugh at her little princess.

"You are funny mommy. I'm hungry, can we have cereal today?"

"We sure can right after I take your temperature we'll have a good breakfast since Aunt Tracie said you wouldn't eat anything last night. Let's go see what your brother is getting into."

Kayla wiggled down from her mother's arms and took off at the speed of light looking through the three bedroom apartment for her brother. They found Tyler sitting in front of the one television they had watching his favorite Saturday morning cartoon.

Kayla settled in next to him as Karina went to the small kitchen to start breakfast.

Saturday mornings were the best, Karina thought. It was the one day she and the kids had to sit around the house and enjoy each other together. During the week, Tyler was in school and Kayla was home with her all day, but it was the time with both of her children that she cherished the most.

She loved them, but this was not how she'd wanted her life to turn out.

When she was in high school, she was focused. Her grades were good, she had been on the cheerleading squad and she was one of the most popular girls in school. All of the girls wanted to be her friend because she was popular and all of the boys wanted to date her because she was fine.

Why guys thought having long hair, big breasts and a big old round booty was fine, she didn't know and she didn't care. All she knew is that it got her more attention than any other girl at school and in her neighborhood. Guys were all over her no matter where she went, but back then she only had eyes for one guy and his name was Anthony, Tony for short, and he was the best looking guy at school. Every girl wanted him, but he only had eyes for her. He was the captain of the football and baseball teams.

Having the finest boy at school be into her when she turned sixteen, she thought she was all that and a bag of chips. She was envied by every girl in school because she was his girlfriend.

Even though she was bright and got very good grades, she didn't think about that as much as she should have. She was on the arm of the finest jock at school and to her, life was complete until she let him talk her into losing her virginity after the ring dance the November of her junior year. Two months later, she discovered she was pregnant. Seven months after that, she and Tony were parents to their son, Tyler.

They stayed together and tried to make it work because he was determined to do what he could for her and the baby they were going to have. Tony tried to find a part-time job, but that was impossible because of school and being a star athlete. All of his free time was spent in class, in practice or at baseball or football games. She didn't work and tried her best to keep up with school work while pregnant.

Her mother had also been living on welfare and after her sister had her second child at the age of eighteen, they were living in a three bedroom house in the hood with little to no money most months. They survived by money their fathers would give her mother or money from the many men her mother paraded through the house.

She and Tony wanted much more for themselves and baby Tyler, but being young themselves, there wasn't much they could do.

Tony was in need of money so he let some guys in the neighborhood talk him into dealing drugs to put money in his pocket. Karina knew it was bad news, but since she didn't have much in the form of money to take care of a baby, she didn't stand in his way. A few months before she had Tyler, Tony had been caught up in a drug sting and was sent to jail. Since he had just turned eighteen and with the high value of the drugs he was caught with, he was sentenced to four years leaving her to fend for herself and her son.

A few months after having Tyler, she tried to juggle school and taking care of a baby, but it didn't work and she ended up dropping out of high school during her senior year. For a year she sat around the house doing nothing, but looking after her son and following the same path as her mother and sister, she went on public assistance to help with Tyler's care.

Since her sister had already dropped out, it was nothing to her mother when she stopped going. Her mother never asked her why she was home all day and not in school. It became their way of life.

Once Karina had given birth to her son, the house they lived in became even more crowded. She and Tyler were in her room, her sister Tracie was in another bedroom with her two children and her mother had a room that she shared with Karina's two younger siblings, a little brother Tyrese and a little sister Ciara who was the same age as Tyler. It had been interesting being pregnant at the same time as her mother. She also had one brother, Caleb, who was the oldest of them all, who went to live with his father's family in Atlanta when he'd turned fifteen. Once he left, he didn't stay in contact with them. The last she heard, he had gone to college, graduated and was making a good life for himself. That was something Karina wanted for herself, but she didn't have a rescuer like Caleb did. Her own father was no help, being on drugs and going in and out of jail her entire life.

None of them had the same father and other than Caleb's father, none of the other fathers ever came around or did anything for their kids. Her mother was left to fend for herself and her kids the best way she could.

Karina thought she would be different from her mother and her sister and hoped that her other siblings coming up would have different, more productive lives. They certainly weren't getting a lesson on that by looking at the life she, Tracie and her mother provided as examples.

She didn't want to have a life of living on public assistance, waiting for a check to come each month that barely kept clothes on their backs.

When she first discovered she was pregnant, she assumed her mother would be upset, especially since it meant one more mouth to feed. That day sealed her fate. She thought back on it as she prepared breakfast for her munchkins.

'Tracie, how do I tell mommy that I'm pregnant?" Karina said to Tracie.

Tracie who was eighteen and already working on her second child, wasn't surprised to know that she and Tony had been having sex.

"I knew it wouldn't be long considering all the time you and Tony spend together. You need to tell her now and don't wait. She's used to it, especially from me, so you hitting her with this, won't be a real shock. She may be upset at first, but she'll get over it. Plus I don't think she'll care much since I think mommy is pregnant again too. All of the signs are there. It's your body and Tony is fine girl.

If it wasn't you, it was going to be someone else pregnant with his baby."

Her sister was probably right. If she had not had sex with him, he would have gotten it from some other girl. All the girls at her school wanted him and would have been more than willing to screw around with him.

Telling her mother went as easy as her sister said it would be. That may have been because her mother was pregnant herself and had no time to deal with Karina and the trouble she was in. The only comment she got was to not expect any help taking care of the baby because her mother didn't have any extra money.

That began the beginning of the end of her dreams. She decided to have her baby because Tony wanted it so bad. He walked around the school bragging about becoming a father. She was excited back then because she was in love and it wasn't until after she'd had the baby that everything changed.

Once he was finally out of jail the first time, Tony had become more distant and he never spent time with her and the Tyler. He was busy in the streets hustling to make money. In the beginning he was doing it for her and the baby, but when he started making lots of money, then came the fast car, more women than Karina could beat off with a stick and more money than she had ever seen in her life.

To keep her mother quiet, he would slide money her way so that she wouldn't go through with her threats to throw Karina and the baby out.

When she was old enough to apply for public housing, she did and prayed she would hear back soon. She was excited the day she got the notice that her housing had come through. She didn't have any money to furnish it, but Tony told her not to worry about anything. He would take care of it.

She'd had dreams of moving into her place, finding a daycare for Tyler and taking classes to get her GED. She'd had hopes that she wouldn't stop there, but would then take college classes toward getting a degree in nursing.

With the kind of street money Tony was making, she would be living the high life on the city's dime until she was able to do things on her own.

The week that she was scheduled to move into her new apartment, she came home to finish packing her things when a friend told her that she'd seen Tony getting arrested. She tried for days to get information on what happened and when Tony was able to call his mother, she was able to get the full story. The bottom line was, he wasn't going to be able to help her out financially like she'd hoped. They would not be moving into her apartment and living as a family with the baby. The place of course would only be in her name, but they had already discussed Tony living there with her and the baby.

Her heart sunk when she found out how much drugs he'd been caught with and if convicted he could get up to fifteen years. She didn't know what she was going to do. She knew that she could still move into her apartment, but the other part of her dream would have to be put on hold. She remembered there conversation from years ago when she was finally able to speak to him while he was in jail.

"Tony, what am I supposed to do now for me and Tyler?"

"Rina, listen, I don't want you to worry about it. You still have your place and I have some money at my mom's

house that you can have. I'll have some of my guys kick you some dough until I get out. I don't think it'll be all the time they said I could get. It will probably only be a few months since this is my first big offense. That first time was really minor which was why I got right out. I know this is a major bust, but my public defender thinks it won't be so bad."

"Okay," she replied.

"Now when we get off the phone, go into my room and the red shoe box on the top shelf has money in it. Take it, use what you need and hold the rest for me and trust me, everything will be alright."

She cried not knowing what would become of them.

"Where's my little man at?" Tony asked, changing the subject to keep her from crying.

"He's at the house with my sister. I was going to bring him, but it was raining hard and he already has a cold," she explained.

"That's alright. Tell him his daddy loves him and I'll be with both of you soon. I'll call again the same time each day so be at my mom's so we can talk. When the baby is feeling better, bring him too so he can hear my voice."

"Okay Tony. I love you."

"I love you too. Kiss Tyler for me and I'll talk to you tomorrow."

She did as he asked for a few days, but then she had to focus on getting settled into her apartment, which wasn't close to Tony's mom's house. She used some of the money to furnish her apartment and to get some things Tyler desperately needed. Since her food assistance had also kicked in, she was able to buy food without having to use too much of the money. She was going to have to figure out how to make it until Tony got out of jail.

Plans to get her GED were placed on hold and years later, after her second child, she still didn't have it.

The kids came running into the kitchen, snapping Karina out of her trip down memory lane and back to her current reality. As she was placing breakfast in front of the kids, her cell phone rang. It was no doubt Robin calling to find out how her night went. She had no plans of reliving the events of the night before and she was glad she didn't have a mirror in front of her to see how much of a fool she had been once again. She let it ring and sat down to breakfast with her children, erasing all thoughts of anything else.

Chapter Four
KARINA

Today was a big day, Mykel thought. For the first time in over a year, he was taking a vacation. He was originally scheduled to take time off a few weeks before on the day he'd run into his old friend Thomas, but some emergencies from a building that collapsed not far from the hospital postponed his planned time off.

Now that things had finally calmed down and he could get away from the hospital, he was happy to make time for some rest and relaxation.

Planning to go away wasn't on his list, but getting some construction projects done around his house and getting in a few games of tennis and possibly golf was.

He smiled knowing he was about to do his last surgery of the day before taking three weeks off.

"Dr. Tanner, you look very happy today," one of the other doctors said.

He turned around to see the Cardiologist who would be covering his patients for him.

"I am because in a few hours I am out of here for three whole weeks. This is the first time I've taken off in over a year."

"Are you taking a trip or any other big plans?"

"No, sticking close to home doing a few projects and

playing as much tennis as I can get in. I haven't been able to do that in a long time."

"I have a surgery I'm heading in for so I'll catch you in a few weeks when you return."

Mykel nodded in acknowledgement as he answered his ringing cell phone. It was his sister.

"Don't even think about it Misha," he said not giving her a chance to say anything.

"Don't think about what big brother? You haven't given me a chance to ask anything."

"You know I'm starting vacation today and you're starting spring break so I'm assuming you're scheming to either have me on a trip to some island somewhere or you're coming to my house for your break and the answer is already no. I don't plan on spending my time off going anywhere and you need to go home. Mom and Pop are still angry that you didn't go home for Christmas. It's bad enough I couldn't get home, but I worked so that doctors who had children could have some time off. You had no real excuse and I don't want them angry with me for not making you go home, so I'm not providing you with a place to stay for the week. So, did I answer all the questions you were thinking of asking?"

"You think you know me, but you don't. Well what do you have planned?"

"Playing tennis, some golf and some fixer up projects at the house."

"What, no hot plans with a woman? I mean you do have three weeks off."

"Stop digging for information Misha because there's nothing there."

"Why isn't there anything there? You're a handsome,

successful doctor and you're about to spend your three week vacation alone, unless that's a trick so that I won't come stay with you next week."

"It's not a trick Misha and I'm not seeing anyone right now, successful or not and there is nothing wrong with spending my vacation doing something other than women. I'm good, trust me."

"Still waiting on the perfect woman huh?" she asked.

"No, just the one woman that's perfect for me and when I find her, you'll be the first person I call. Now, go home, tell Mom and Pop I said hello and I'll be home for a visit soon. I have my last surgery and then I'm off. Be safe on the road."

"Mykel, please have some fun besides golf and tennis while you're off. Go to a club and have some fun."

"Goodbye sis."

Misha was right about one thing, he did need to get out and have some fun while he was off and it had been a long time since he'd hung out with his friends at a club to hear some good music and enjoy a few beers. He spends most his time working and had forgotten what it's like to have fun, especially the kind that involved a woman. He had a few female friends he knew he could call for some fun, but he was tired of the games and calling any of them would lead them to thinking he wanted more than fun. For now fun was all he was offering. Maybe a night at one of the local clubs was exactly what he needed.

Before heading to scrub in for his surgery, he decided to call a buddy or two to see if any wanted to hang out over the weekend.

"Travis, what's up bro?" Mykel said when one of his best friends answered.

"Not much, but it's nice hearing from you for a change. We were beginning to think you had permanently moved into the hospital. Do they ever let you out to play?" Travis joked.

"Real funny bro. Sometimes they let a brother out for some fresh air and contact with people who aren't sick. I'm actually off for a few weeks and was seeing what you guys were up to as far as free time to hang out."

"What? I must be hearing things. Dr. Mykel Tanner is taking some time off? The world must be coming to an end for you to finally take a vacation."

"So you got jokes?"

"Man I have tons when it comes to how much of a workaholic you are. What did you have in mind?"

Mykel didn't know what he had in mind. His sister got him thinking that he doesn't get out enough and he jumped on the idea to call a few friends.

"I don't know man. Remember, I'm the workaholic, so I'm clueless which is why I'm calling you, the party animal. What's going on around town?'

"Don't worry about it man, I got it all covered. I'll call the fellas today and get things jumping so don't make any plans for the whole weekend. We're taking you out on the town so that you can see how the brothers with regular jobs live."

"Yeah, you do that. I'm down for whatever you come up with, tell me when and where."

"Cool. I'll hit you back later. When does your vacation start?"

"It starts later today, in a few hours."

"Okay, well it's Wednesday so give me a day or two and I'll have our weekend of reinstating you back into the brotherhood all panned out."

"I'm assuming that's code for wild?" Mykel asked.

"Man that's code for wilder than you can imagine. Think back to our college days and you'll know what I'm talking about."

"Sounds like a trip to a strip club is a part of your plan."

"That and then some Mykel, but I promise it won't be anything that'll get you arrested."

Mykel laughed realizing he probably called the wrong friend first.

"Don't get your panties in a bunch Mykel. I can hear you thinking too hard about it already. Relax and get ready for some fun. The ladies won't know what hit them this weekend."

"Alright, I'm down. I have to get into surgery so I'll hit you later or sometime tomorrow. I knew you'd be on top of this if I called you."

"You know I got you man. Catch you later," Travis said hanging up. Mykel shook his head as he headed off to his last surgery before his vacation. He wondered what he'd given Travis permission to do

~~

Karina was tired, but she knew that she had a full day ahead of her. Wednesday morning came faster than she thought it would. She had been up late trying to study for her GED exam.

After weeks of finally taking the classes she needed, the day was finally here. After the nightmare that occurred a few weeks back with the rapper at the hotel, she decided to look into getting her GED. She didn't know what to do with it once she had it, but at least she'd have it.

After walking her son to school, she walked to her

mother's house to drop Kayla off so that her sister could keep an eye on her while she took the test.

She had been able to get Kayla enrolled in part-time day care while she took classes two days a week, but today she had a fever so she decided to not take her to daycare and her sister agreed to help her out.

She'd taken the necessary classes and though she thought it would take her a long time to prepare for the test, her instructor told her that she'd always passed every test in class with flying colors and that she didn't understand why she'd waited so long.

Karina told her that circumstances is why she waited, but now she was glad she did decide to finish. She knew she would ace the test and was excited to get it over with.

Having that GED in her hand could go a long way to putting in job applications at some of the stores that were on the bus route that she could easily get to after dropping Kayla off.

A few years back, before she'd had Kayla she tried signing up for GED classes and then on one of Tony's stints outside of the prison walls, she'd fallen for his charm once again and nine months later, Kayla was born, putting her back to where she started.

She had become lazy and content to have Tony back in her life. She was happy to have a man who really cared about her and not the sex. He wasn't even angry with her after hearing about all of the men she'd bedded while he was locked up, some of those guys being so-called friends of his. Karina did what she needed to do to survive. He'd filled her head again with lots of lies of getting himself together, getting a job and moving them all into a nicer place. Putting her dreams on hold, she believed him.

Kayla had not been born when he found himself back in jail once again and she was again back to doing things all by herself.

Tony had spent all of Kayla's life in jail and she'd confined herself to her own sort of prison, going from man to man thinking the next one was the one. She'd finally broken off her relationship with Tony realizing he was going to be one of those guys who did nothing but make a life out of going in and out of jail. She liked the money his street hustling provided, but in the end, it never resulted in anything positive. She still ended up alone with two children to raise by herself.

When she arrived at her mother's house, she knew she was about to get a speech from Tracie by her body language. When she told her sister she was going to get her GED so that she could get a job, she nor her mother were supportive. They didn't know why she wanted to make things hard on herself. All they thought about was how her benefits would get cut and that they didn't want her coming to them for help when she couldn't make ends meet. She decided to start the conversation about Kayla and then high tail it out of there before the speech could begin.

"Tracie, don't forget to give Kayla her medicine. She has the sniffles right now, but it will help her."

Karina watched as her sister picked up Kayla, snuggling her close.

"How long are you going to be? I have things to do while the kids are in school. If you're not going to be back to pick up Kayla by then, I have to change my plans," Tracie said.

If Kayla hadn't woke up with a fever, she would have

taken her to daycare.

"I told you I'll be back before lunchtime so you'll have time to do what you need. The test shouldn't take too long and then on my way back I'm going to stop at Walmart and possibly Target to put in a few job applications. I want to find a job."

"I still don't know why. Why would you do that knowing your check will get cut if you do?"

"Tracie, I know that, but if I pass the GED test today, I have to do something else besides sitting around all day."

"Girl, you are crazy. I'm not doing anything that will mess up that check I get every month. Plus you get more money from kicking it with guys than any retail store could ever pay you."

Her sister was always trying to make a living, like their mother, by lying on her back. Karina still couldn't believe the number of times she'd done that herself.

"Look, I'm running late. I promise I won't be long."

"Next you'll be talking about college or something," Tracie said.

"I'm not thinking about college. I can't afford to do that anyway. I'm trying to do something besides spreading my legs for money."

"Oh, so you're getting your diploma and everything so that somebody other than the brothers in the hood will look at you for more than just a roll in the hay? Whatever, but remember, you'll still be a girl from the hood, GED or not and like me and mommy, hood men are all you'll ever get."

Karina loved her sister, but hated her mindset. For too long she'd thought the same way.

"I'm out. I'll be back soon."

"You better not be late," she heard Tracie say as she ended any more talk and left.

~~

Karina passed the test for her GED and couldn't stop looking at the temporary notice she got that stated she'd passed. She also had time to stop at Walmart and Target to fill out applications. It wasn't much, but it would be something if she got either job. Kayla would soon be in daycare all day and she needed something to do with her time.

She'd made it back in time for her sister to still go where she needed to on time and she and Kayla were now walking back home. She wanted to be there when Tyler got home from school.

As they walked up to her apartment building, she noticed someone standing on the steps. As she got closer, she recognize Tony. It appeared he was out of jail yet again. The moment he spotted them, he lit up with excitement. Even though they were no longer together, she still wanted him to always be a part of the kids' lives so she put on a fake smile and greeted him.

"Hey Rina," he said as she walked up to him.

"Hi Tony."

He then looked down at Kayla who was holding tight to her mother's hand. He bent down to say hello to her.

"Hi Kayla."

Kayla shied away, not knowing for sure who he was. Karina urged her on.

"Say hello Kayla," she said.

"Hello," she heard her say.

"Do you know who I am?" Tony asked her.

Kayla didn't answer. She shook her head no.

"Sure you do. I'm your daddy. Remember you talk to me on the phone all the time?" he explained.

Kayla shook her head yes.

"Well that's me and I came to see you today instead of talking on the phone. I wanted you to see me."

He was greeted with silence and looked up to Karina for help when Kayla didn't respond in any way.

She reached down and picked her baby girl up.

"How about we go upstairs into the apartment. She'll probably be more comfortable there," Karina said. She was glad when Tony nodded his agreement. She didn't want a scene if she couldn't get Kayla to warm up to him.

As they entered the apartment, she tried to put Kayla down, but she wasn't having any of that.

"Have a seat Tony," Karina said as she took the seat across from him and sat with Kayla on her lap.

She wondered why he didn't tell her he'd be getting out soon. The few times she had spoken with him over the past year, he hadn't said anything about when he may be getting out. She didn't ask because she didn't want him to think that they would pick up where they left off. She decided to keep the conversation light in order to give Kayla time to warm up to her dad.

"You look good Tony. Are you okay?" she asked.

"Yeah I'm good. I see you're doing good too and Kayla is beautiful. Thanks for taking good care of her while I was away. Is Tyler still at school?" he inquired.

"Yeah. He'll be home around four. He walks with some of the bigger kids from the school a few blocks away," she said trying to lighten the mood, especially for Kayla. It didn't seem to be working when she noticed Kayla was still frightened of Tony.

"Kayla, why don't you tell your daddy about your new Dora dress?"

That got a rise out of her. Dora was the gospel to Kayla and she loved any time she got the chance to talk about her.

She still wasn't looking at Tony, but Karina was glad when she at least talked.

"I have a new Dora dress mommy got me. Dora is my favorite."

Tony took the cue.

"That's nice Kayla. I bet it's a pretty dress too."

Kayla shook her head and her long, thick ponytails shook vigorously along with her head. Karina even noticed a little smile.

"Why don't you go and get your dress to show your daddy."

She quickly got down from her mother's lap and ran to her room to get it.

That left her and Tony alone.

"You're still fine I see. Having the kids has thickened you up even more than you were before and I like it."

"Thank you."

When she looked at him, the look in his eyes told her what he really wanted; he wanted her.

Before she could shut his thoughts down, Kayla came bounding back in the room and rather than head for her, she went straight for her daddy and started telling him all about Dora and showing him her dress.

The two of them talked non-stop about Dora. Tony even brought up the conversations about Dora they'd shared when they talked on the phone. She settled back in her chair to let them have their time. After thirty minutes of non-stop talking, she told Kayla it was time for her afternoon nap since she hadn't taken one yet. Karina's heart melted when Kayla asked Tony if he would come visit her again so that they could play with her toys.

"I sure will baby girl. Anytime you want me to come over, tell your mommy and I'll come visit."

"Okay," Kayla said with extra excitement before heading off to her room with Karina behind her.

When she returned after putting Kayla down for her nap, Karina noticed that Tony was already sitting back, relaxed and flipping through television channels.

Her eyes took in the scene before her.

Tony noticed her reappearance when he spoke, he dropped his voice down to a sexy drawl.

"Come here Karina," he said, not taking his eyes off of her as he sat with one arm across the back of her sofa and his legs stretched out.

She went in his direction and sat down on the other end of the sofa.

"I don't bite. You can sit a little closer."

One thing she didn't know how to do was deny him. Since she was sixteen, he always seemed to have control over her. Even though they were no longer together and he knew she had been with other men, in his mind, she was his and would always be his, something he'd told her on many occasions. She went against her better judgment and slid over. When she did, the arm he'd rested across the back of the sofa came down to rest on her shoulder with the fingers coming to rest above her right breast.

"I've been thinking about you a lot lately, especially after I found out I was being released early. I couldn't wait to get out to see you and my kids."

"That's all good Tony, but you shouldn't be including me in that. You know we're over with, so you need to focus on your relationship with Tyler and Kayla."

"Yeah, I should have known you would say that, especially after I been hearing about all the guys you been kicking it with while I was locked up."

The air between them changed. The mentioning of her with other men clearly angered him and then add to that the fact that she let him know that there would be nothing between them, and the cordial atmosphere they'd started out with was now tension filled.

"Who I'm with is no business of yours. Don't forget we are not a couple anymore."

"So what, I'm not good enough for you anymore?"

"I'm not saying that. I'm saying I don't think we're good for each other. I'll always care about you and we have two children together, but that's it."

"So it's like that now, huh?" Tony asked.

"Like what Tony? You haven't been around for a lot of years. You can't believe that you could walk out of jail and walk back into how things were in the past."

"This must be about some dude or maybe even about several dudes. From what I've heard you've been spreading it pretty thin when it comes to guys and now you're saying the father of both of your children can't get any attention? Come on Karina, I've been locked up a long time."

She tensed up when he snuggled in a little closer to her. "Kayla is asleep and Tyler still has an hour before he gets here. I'm not asking for anything you're not familiar with. I know you still have some feelings for me. They didn't die away because I was locked up. Both of my kids look like me so I know every time you look at them, they remind you of me."

Before she had a chance to respond, Tony got up and stood right in front of her, placing his hand on his belt buckle.

"Don't Tony," she said, knowing what he had in mind.

Her turning him down upset him as he raised his voice.

"Don't what Rina? Don't get a piece of what's mine? I don't care how many men you've been with or are currently boning, as far as I'm concerned you'll always be mine. You remember what it was like with me. I know I do and no matter how much you want to fight me on this, I still love you and I still want you."

Tony reached down and took her hands in his pulling her up off of the sofa so that he could wrap her arms up around his neck.

She knew she needed to stick to her words and back off, but visions of them being together years ago and a combination of how good he smelled and felt confused her. "I don't want to fall back into this with you Tony. It never goes anywhere," she said.

"Rina, I'm going to get a job and take care of my family like I'm supposed to. I was given some good contacts when I got out on some jobs that hire guys who've been in jail. Let me prove to you that I can be the man you want me to be. I think we can make it if you give me a chance."

Karina knew her answer should be no, but when Tony began unbuttoning her top and walking her backwards toward her bedroom, she knew she was already falling back into the same trap she swore she'd never let happen again.

Chapter Five
KARINA

Mykel was enjoying his second week of vacation and after the wild weekend his friends had taken him out on, he had never laid in bed past noon on a Monday before. He knew he needed to get moving because his vacation was about to take a backseat for a few hours.

A patient he'd performed surgery on was back in the hospital and he wanted to look in on him and not have the doctor who was covering for him follow-up. It didn't appear to be anything too serious, buy Mykel wanted to check for himself. Right after that, he was planning on meeting Travis for a game of golf that he probably needed to cancel. He grabbed his cell to call him.

"Travis, listen I'm not going to make it for golf today. I have some things I need to do and I'm just getting up. I'm blaming it on the activities over the weekend and during the week that you and the fellas have been dragging me out to," he laughed.

"Admit that you have been having a good time since you've been off and hanging with us. It's been like old times again being out with some of the old crew. We have more in store for you this weekend coming up. You in?"

Mykel did have a good time. He also had to admit the

women were out in large numbers. He'd gotten a few numbers and wouldn't mind another weekend of hanging with the guys.

"Yeah, count me in. I don't want to admit it, but I had a great time. I should have done a lot less drinking last night, hence not getting up until noon today. Again, let me know when and where and I'll be there."

~~

Karina was excited because she was on her way to her first day of work at Walmart. A few days after putting in her application, she'd gotten a call for an interview and she was hired on the spot as a cashier. It was a school day for Tyler and she was rushing to get Kayla to daycare so that she wouldn't be late for her first day of work. She wasn't working a full day and wasn't scheduled to be there until two o'clock for a three hour training session. Luckily she was able to work with Tony's mother to pick up Kayla and Tyler because she would never make it in time after her training.

Thinking of Tony depressed her. It had been a week since he'd gotten out of jail and come home and for two days they'd fallen back into an old routine until she'd seen him selling drugs a few blocks from her place. She let him know she was through with him this time.

They'd had a bad argument and she hadn't seen or talked to him since. She thought she would be able to count on him to help her with the kids while she worked, but calls to him had been ignored. She was happy when she reached out to his mother who agreed to help her with the kids. She reminded Karina that no matter what her relationship was with Tony, she loved her grandkids and would do what she could to help, even while ignoring

Tony's grumbling about it.

After getting the kids to school and daycare, she had a little time to herself to get ready for work. She had several buses to catch, but after getting used to it, she would find the fastest route. She was happy that the store was willing to work around her availability especially when it came to the kids. She was going to be able to work during the day when they were in school and daycare.

Checking the time and the bus schedule Karina rushed to get out of the door to catch the first of three buses.

It didn't take too long for the first bus, but just as she'd gotten off of the first bus to catch the second, she saw it coming and knew that she would need to cross traffic to get to it before it passed her by and it was the last one that would get her to work on time. She never looked to see what cars were coming as she stepped off the curb and ran for the bus. The last thing she remembered before hitting the ground was the pain of what must have been a car hitting her. After the pain, there was total darkness.

~~

Mykel was making his way to his first stop of the day which was the hospital to check on his patient. Approaching an intersection, he never expected to see a woman dart out into traffic, especially when he had the green light. He did everything he could to avoid hitting her, but couldn't. In what seemed like slow motion, he slammed on the breaks, but not in time before the woman missed being hit by one car and ended up in the path of his car. He braked as hard as he could, but to no avail. He still hit her and she went flying in the air before landing in the street right in front of him. He leaped from his car and ran to her as others standing on the street also did.

"Miss, can you hear me?" he asked, trying to rouse her, but she didn't respond. He reached for his cell phone to call for an ambulance.

"Hello, this is Dr. Mykel Tanner and I've been involved in an accident where a young woman was hurt. I need an ambulance."

Mykel gave the operator all of the necessary information and then went back to tending to the woman lying in the street. He first checked to be sure she was still breathing and once discovering that she was, he tried to check her for any broken bones. Nothing seemed broken. He was concerned about any internal injuries she may have suffered because he knew he'd hit her pretty hard. Luckily they weren't too far from Sinai hospital where he worked. He stayed with her until the ambulance arrived and took over her care.

Mykel let the paramedics and police know who he was and what happened. Police took statements from others around who all confirmed that the woman had stepped out into traffic even though the light was green. There was no way anyone would have been able to avoid hitting her.

After giving the police his final statement, he jumped in his car and headed to the hospital to check on the woman's condition.

Mykel was happy to hear that she'd woken up when the ambulance brought her into the emergency room. He was told by one of the nurses that she did have a minor fracture in her leg, but so far they were unable to find any other major injuries, just a lot of bruises and swelling. He waited around until she was taken to a room and he went to check on her.

"How are you feeling?" he said coming into her room

after knocking.   She must have been groggy from the medication they gave her for the pain because she wasn't focusing on what he was saying.

"What?" she asked with slurred speech.

Mykel walked closer to the bed and looked at her chart.

"I asked how you were feeling," he explained.

"I've been better. It's not every day you get hit by a car."

"True, especially since I was the guy driving the car."

"You were?" she asked stunned to hear that. "Then why are you reading my hospital chart?"

"I'm sorry. I want to be sure you're okay. Have you given the hospital information to reach your family?"

"Yes."

"I'm really sorry about the accident. I didn't see you and wasn't expecting anyone to dart out into traffic when the light was green."

Karina knew it wasn't his fault. She was stupid for trying to cross traffic on a green light to catch a bus.

"I'm the one who's sorry. I was trying to catch my bus and I wasn't thinking. It was my first day at work and I didn't want to be late. That would have been the last bus."

While she lay in bed at the hospital, she'd forgotten about her new job.

"You should give your nurse that information so that someone can call them and tell them what happened."

"I'm less concerned about that and more concerned about my children."

Mykel became nervous.

"Wait, you had children with you? I didn't see any. What did they look like? None were brought in with you?"

Karina could see she'd frightened him.

"No, they weren't with me, they're in school. I was on

my way to my first day on my job. Do you know what time it is?" she asked, still groggy.

"Yes, it's eight o'clock in the evening."

"Oh no," she said. "I need to call their grandmother and let her know what happened. I was supposed to be on my way home by now and she'll be dropping my kids off soon."

Mykel reached for his cell phone for her to use.

"Here, use my phone and I'll give you some privacy," he said, handing her the phone and drawing the curtain to give her privacy to make her call.

Tony's mother was very understanding as she told her not to worry because she would keep the kids overnight. Karina assured her she would call whenever the hospital released her so that she could bring the kids home.

She must have fallen asleep right after that call because she woke to the sound of her mother and sister talking about law suits.

"I'm telling you Ma, Karina could get a lot of money out of this. I was told a Jaguar hit her and it belonged to some doctor."

"Yeah, that could be a big pay day for her and I'm sure she'd hit me off with a little bit of that. I did come up here to the hospital the minute I got the phone call that she had been in an accident."

Karina didn't want to open her eyes to let her family know she was woke. She heard what they were talking about and didn't want any parts of it. She opened them anyway knowing it was now or later and she knew it was best to get it over with now.

Tracie noticed her moving around first.

"Karina, do you know how much money you could get if you sued this guy that hit you?"

She should have known the first thing out of her mouth would be about some scheme she wanted to run. Like clockwork her mother chimed in.

"This could be your big pay day Rina. I heard the guy who hit you with his car is a big time doctor."

Talks of law suits and money didn't matter to her. She wasn't planning on suing anyone since she was at fault for the accident. She was lucky the first car had missed hitting her because she could have gotten hit by both cars and it could have been worse.

"Would either of you like to say hello to me first or even ask how I'm doing before you start calling in the lawyers and counting the dollars?" she asked annoyed.

Neither Tracie nor her mother said anything. They both gave her an inpatient look as if she should be grateful they were even at the hospital.

"You must have bumped your head talking to me like that," she heard her mother say. "I'll ignore it because I know you've been in an accident. I can see that you're okay or you wouldn't be talking."

She wished she didn't have to call her family, but the hospital insisted.

"Mom, I'm not suing anyone because it was my fault. I walked out into the street without looking or thinking while trying to catch the bus to work. I missed being hit by one car and jumped further into traffic to avoid it and walked right into the path of that doctor's car. It's not his fault and I'm not suing."

"See Karina, I told you all this work stuff was a bad idea," she heard her sister Tracie say.

"Where are the kids?" her mother asked.

"Tony's mother has them. She picked them up after

school and was going to bring them home after I got off."

She assumed that job was history now, especially since she didn't turn up for the first day. Maybe if she explained the accident to them they would understand. She would certainly give it a try as soon as she was back home.

"Do you need us to go get them?" Tracie asked.

"No, I spoke with her already. She's going to keep the kids overnight and take Tyler to school and Kayla to daycare tomorrow. She's got it covered until I go home."

"What about Tony? I heard he was out," her mother said.

"We're not on good terms right now, but he'll ask his mother why the kids are still there if or when he goes home tonight I guess. Right now I'm not thinking about him. I'm more concerned that I may not have that job anymore. Who knows how long I'll be out with this leg in a cast."

"That's why you need to get a lawyer and sue this doctor girl, for all of your pain, suffering and the money you're missing out on not working."

Leave it to Tracie to always take everything back to money.

"I'm going to call Manny who lives across the street from me and ask him for the name and number of that lawyer who helped him when he was in a bus accident a few years ago. He got paid big from that," her mother said.

"Momma, thanks for the help, but I meant it when I said I'm not suing the guy who hit me because it wasn't his fault. I told you I darted out into traffic trying to catch a bus. His light was green and I had the do not cross sign."

"Karina, you will be laid up in bed for I don't know how many weeks. You won't have the money from your job coming in so what will you do?" Tracie asked.

Leave it to Tracie for extra added drama.

"Tracie that is way too much drama. For starters I haven't even started working yet and for now I still get the assistance I've always been getting. That would not change until I start receiving a paycheck, so I'm not missing out on something I didn't even start getting yet. Like I said, I'm not suing anybody, especially not that doctor. It really wasn't his fault."

"Maybe you should listen to your family."

Karina looked up into the face of the doctor whose car she'd had a run-in with.

"Who are you?" Tracie asked before Karina could respond.

"I'm Dr. Mykel Tanner. I'm the doctor who was driving the car that hit Karina."

"Damn, you are fine!" Tracie shouted, shocking everyone in the room.

"Tracie, really?" Karina said, stunned by her lack of tact.

She looked at the doctor and saw that he seemed uncomfortable, not knowing whether to stay or go.

"I'm sorry for my sister, please excuse her," Karina said to him.

"So Dr. Tanner, it was you in the car that hit my baby huh?" Karina heard her mother ask.

Karina wished someone would pull a fire alarm or come in with some other type of emergency to stop the interaction her family was having with the doctor. They were embarrassing her.

"Everybody, stop it. I said I'm not suing and I'm not. Thanks Dr. Tanner, but please don't encourage them. They weren't there so they don't know what happened. I should be apologizing to you."

"No apology necessary. I was agreeing because that's what insurance is for especially if you'll be missing out on money earned from your job," he said.

"I'm not missing out on anything. I hadn't started the job yet. Did you come to check up on me again?"

"I did and I also came to get my cell phone back. After I gave it to you to make your call, I was called in for an emergency matter and I'm coming from wrapping that up."

Karina was really embarrassed now. She didn't realize she still had his phone. She looked around and found it under the blanket. She handed it to him.

"I'm so sorry. I forgot I had it and I think something they gave me for the pain knocked me right out after I made that call."

"No problem. I'll leave you with your family and again, I'm very sorry about the accident. I hope your recovery is swift," he said, exiting the room.

"Now that was one fine man and he's a doctor too," Tracie said. Did you see how sexy he looked in those jeans and that pullover sweater? Even that sweater couldn't hide all that sexiness under there. He can hit me with his car any day."

When she was about to respond, a nurse came in telling them that she would be discharged the next day. Though they were able to get her leg in a cast, they wanted to monitor her for the slight concussion she'd suffered.

"Well since you'll be here another day, there's no need for us to hang around unless you want to rethink the lawyer and I can get one on the phone," her mother said.

She couldn't wait for them to leave.

"No, that's isn't necessary. Mommy, can you get Mr. Charles to bring you back tomorrow to pick me up when they let me out of here?" Mr. Charles was her mother's boyfriend.

"Yeah, I can do that. You'll have to give him gas money if he does."

She already knew that. She also knew the money would be going to her mother and not to Mr. Charles. She didn't care because she needed a ride home from the hospital.

"Okay, I'll call you in the morning to tell you what time I'm being released. Thanks for coming to the hospital."

Karina barely got the words out before her mother and sister were already out the door.

In the peace and quiet Karina had a chance to think about all that had happened to her. She'd finally gotten a job only to lose it because she didn't show up for the first day. That was due to her carelessness.

She thought about a lot of things her sister always said to her and for once, she started to believe that Tracie was right. Maybe she was trying too hard for something she'd never get. This accident could be a sign that she was who she was and she wasn't meant to be anything else. It seemed like every time she tried to take one step forward, the two steps back she then took always pulled her further away from any dream of ever having anything.

She was tired and she wasn't going to call Walmart to tell them what happened. She would go back to what she was doing, sitting around like many others and letting the state take care of her. She was tired of all the setbacks.

Chapter Six
KARINA

Mykel laid awake, unable to sleep even though it was three in the morning. He hadn't been able to stop thinking about the young woman he'd been in the accident with. He used every excuse he could to continue hanging around the hospital so that he could keep checking in on her. He felt bad about the accident, though it wasn't the accident that kept his mind on her. He kept seeing her laying helpless in the hospital bed, not being able to forget that he was the cause of her current predicament.

Even though she continued to apologize for the accident being her fault, Mykel still couldn't help feeling somewhat responsible.

When he finally had to leave the hospital, he made one last trip to check on her after finding out that she wasn't going to be released until the next day. When he entered her room after knocking, but getting no response, he moved closer to her and saw that she was fast asleep.

He stood for a few moments looking at her. She was a beautiful woman even with the scars that covered her face. For some reason he felt drawn to her and he was intrigued.

The attraction he felt toward her was new for him. She had an innocence about her that he liked and he could tell from the interaction she had with her family about suing him that she had a heart of gold. She could have really dug her heels into his insurance company, but still she fought her family against doing so. He wasn't sure he knew of anyone who would genuinely pass up the chance to have a big pay day, as her family had put it.

He understood if she decided to do so. Even though it was true, she was at fault, he felt bad that she'd missed out on her first day of work. He didn't know anything about her situation, but he knew she had two children to take care of and if the accident would somehow put her at a disadvantage in taking care of them, he would not forgive himself. Maybe he would contact his insurance company to find out if he could submit some type of a request for monetary compensation for her.

At a minimum, maybe he could help with her medical expenses. He wanted to do something. He didn't want to wash his hands of it.

He left quietly knowing he would get up early the next day to check on her again.

~~

"Mommy, are you getting my texts and my messages? I've been calling you for over an hour. I'm about to be released and I still need a ride home. Call me back as soon as you can. I finally have my cell phone back so call as soon as you get this message."

Where was her mother and why hadn't she answered any of the messages she'd left. She'd gotten her discharge papers and any minute one of the nurses would be coming to the room with a wheelchair to wheel her out. She was supposed to have a ride home by now. It looked as if she would have to get a cab, the story of her life.

"Ms. Joseph, is your ride home here yet?" a nurse asked entering the room with a wheelchair.

"I've been calling my mother, but she must be tied up. I'll get a cab to take me home."

"Okay, why don't you sit tight for a few minutes and I'll see if there is one already available for you. If not, we can call one for you."

"Call her a cab for what? To take her home?"

Karina looked up and again, she looked into the light brown eyes of the doctor from the day before. She hated how her sister had blurted it out, but she had to agree, Dr. Tanner was gorgeous.

Without being doped up on so many drugs as she had been the day before, she could see him clearly now and her sister's sentiment had been on point.

Dr. Tanner was tall, at least six feet. His body was lean and he looked like a track star instead of a doctor. His skin was a dark chocolate and he reminded her of the actor Lance Gross who played in that Tyler Perry sitcom, House of Payne. She loved that show, mainly because of the character he played. His hair was cut close and he had the beginnings of a neatly trimmed goatee. What stood out to her the most were his eyes. They were electric to gaze into.

"Yes, Dr. Tanner. She was waiting for a ride that hasn't come yet."

Mykel looked from Karina and then back to the nurse.

"I'm going to look into a cab for her right now," the nurse said before leaving the room.

"You don't have anyone to come and pick you up? You have a fractured leg. Though it's not a solid break, you still will need some help," he said.

"I called my mother a while ago and I haven't heard back from her yet."

"What about your sister? A husband or boyfriend?"

Mykel knew he shouldn't pry, but that's exactly what he did. Besides, he really wanted to know if she was married or seeing anyone.

"My sister doesn't have a car and neither does my mother. She was supposed to get someone to bring her to pick me up, but I guess she got sidetracked. I'll be fine taking a cab. I live in a ground floor apartment so I won't need a lot of help. There are only three small steps out front. After that it's smooth sailing," she said, lightening the mood.

Mykel didn't like the sound of her having no one to look after her to be sure she got home okay.

"What are you doing back here again? Are you still checking up on me or are you concerned that I may sue like my family suggested? I meant what I said yesterday, I'm not suing you. No matter what family I may have come from, I'm not like that. I'm not trying to seize an opportunity for a big pay day for something that I caused. With the exception of the fracture to my leg, I'm fine. This could have been worse and I'm glad it wasn't and I'll be able to get home to see my kids later today."

Mykel couldn't help staring at her. He was hoping it wasn't obvious to Karina that he was a little smitten with her. She was more genuine than any woman he'd ever met and he liked her, though he didn't know much about her. He also didn't want her to think that he was hanging around to gage if she would sue him or not. He didn't care one way or the other because his only concern was for her.

"I came by because I wanted to see how you were doing. I was concerned and it has nothing to do with being sued. You do whatever it is you need to do and I'm going to provide you with the information for my insurance company if you need it. The police took the report and you'll need a copy of that. I came to check on you."

If Mykel didn't know any better, he would say she looked even more beautiful than she had the day before. She'd taken the time to fix her hair and put on a light touch of makeup, though he could tell she didn't need it. She was a natural beauty.

"Thank you Dr. Tanner. I appreciate you checking up on me."

"Mykel," he said. "My name is Mykel. I'm only Dr. Tanner to those I work with here in the hospital."

"Okay, Mykel it is," she said smiling.

Mykel couldn't stop the beat of his heart if he wanted to when she smiled at him. She had him hook, line and sinker. He was clearly taken by her and he couldn't figure out what was wrong with him. He'd never had such an instant attraction to any woman like the one he was having to her.

"Listen, if you don't have a problem with my driving skills, I'd like to give you a ride home. I really don't think you should be in a cab with that leg."

"Don't you have patients you need to see today?" she asked.

"Actually, I'm on vacation. I was yesterday when we ran into each other," he said making a joke of the situation.

"Very funny," she said laughing.

"Comedy is my part-time job," he joked. "I was making a trip to check on a patient on my day off when the accident happened. Now that you know you're not keeping me from anything, would you like a ride home?" he asked.

Karina would like nothing more considering it looked like her family had abandoned her, so she accepted.

"Yes, if you're sure it's not too much trouble."

"No trouble at all. Let's get you in this wheelchair and I'll have someone wheel you out to the main lobby while I go get my car."

Karina moved easily from the chair to the wheelchair with the help of the crutches that had been given to her earlier.

Once they reached the hallway, the nurse was coming toward them.

"I was coming in to get you Ms. Joseph. There are several cabs down by the main entrance that can take you home."

"No worries. I'm going to give her a ride home," Mykel said.

"You don't have any patients today Dr. Tanner?"

"I'm not on call today. Can you get someone to wheel her to the main entrance while I get my car?" he asked.

"Sure Dr. Tanner."

Karina remained quiet the entire time. She loved Mykel's take charge attitude. She'd never had someone look out for her the way he was doing.

As she and the aide that was pushing her wheelchair reached the lobby, Mykel was coming through the door to help her get to his car. As he wheeled her out to a waiting truck, Karina was shocked to see how big it was.

"Is this what hit me yesterday? I'm surprised I wasn't worse off."

Mykel grinned while helping her up and into the front seat that he'd already slid all the way back to accommodate the need for her to keep her leg straight.

"No, that was my car which is in the shop. There was a little damage to the bumper from the accident and it's being fixed."

"This is a nice truck," she said when he got in on the other side.

"Thanks. So where to?" he asked.

"Oh, right."

Karina gave him the address and they were off.

"Did you need to pick up your children or anything? I don't mind making that stop before taking you home."

"No, their grandmother will keep them for one more night so they won't be home until tomorrow. I told her I was coming home today, but she told me to get an extra day of rest before the kids came home. They'll be full of questions when they see my leg in this cast. I'm glad it's not a serious break, but a minor fracture. I shouldn't have this cast on for more than two weeks, if that long, as long as I stay off of it."

"How will you do that with two children around?"

"Well, my son won't be a big problem because he's nine and does most things for himself. My daughter is three so she'll be the challenge. The one good thing is the daycare where she goes can come and pick her up each morning so that'll give me a break during the day. My son already walks to and from school with friends so I'll be fine."

"You do not look old enough to have a nine year old son."

"I do and I am. I'm twenty-five."

"You still look very young and beautiful I might add, if that isn't inappropriate to say," Mykel said hesitantly.

"It's not and thank you," she replied.

When he finally pulled up in front of her building, she tried to decide how to handle not wanting him to come in. It was bad enough he had to see that she lived in a bad neighborhood where the neighbors still haven't learned how to pick up after themselves. Trash littered the streets and it discomforted her that he saw it. She could tell by the car he drove and the fact that he was a doctor, that he didn't live anywhere near a neighborhood like hers.

"Thank you for the ride, but I'll be okay from this point by myself."

She reached for the door handle and Mykel stopped her.

"At least let me help you out of the car."

She shook her head in agreement and watched as he exited the car and came around to help her. After getting her down, she thanked him again and assured him she'd be okay getting inside without any help.

"Okay, I'll let you take it from here. There is a copy of the police report in with your papers in case you need it. Please don't let my friendliness keep you from doing what you need to do. I know you'll probably have hospital bills and medication costs. Things like accidents are why we pay car insurance so if you need to, make sure you contact my insurance company. That information is also in with your papers. Again, I'm sorry about all of this. If you need anything or if I can be of service, call me. I put my business card in with your paperwork and on the back of the card is my personal cell phone number."

She thanked him and used the crutches to slowly make her way into her building and into her apartment. Once inside she looked out the window in time to see that he had taken off.

Finally alone, she winced at the pain in her leg and headed for her bedroom to lay down. She put all thoughts of the accident and the pain out of her mind and filled it with thoughts of the handsome doctor and went to sleep.

~ ~

Mykel had gotten a few blocks away from Karina's apartment and knew that no matter how much he tried to fight it, he was attracted to her. He wanted to know more about her and he wanted to spend more time with her. He hoped she'd use his number and give him a call because he would do anything to see her again.

His cell phone rang startling him.

"Hey sis. What's up?"

"I got your voicemail message about an accident. Are you alright?"

He smiled at how frantic she sounded, always worried about him.

"Yes I'm fine."

"What kind of accident were you in? The message you left wasn't very clear."

"I hit a woman crossing the street, but she's fine except for a small leg fracture. She crossed against traffic and walked right out into the street trying to catch a bus."

"Oh wow. Are you sure you're alright? I know how passionate you are about other people, not often thinking of yourself."

"I'm fine sis. I didn't want you to go by the house and both cars were gone. I know you'd wonder why. The car is in the shop with very minor damage to the front."

"Is this woman suing you or anything even though it sounds like it was her fault?"

"No she's not. Like I said it's a small fracture. I'm leaving from dropping her off at home and she appears to be doing better already."

"Wait, what? You took her home? What in the world is going on? Stop giving me the Cleland notes version to what

323

happened and tell it all to me."

Mykel knew he needed to start from the beginning to get to how he ended up giving Karina a ride home and since she was his sister and they were very close, he also wanted her to know that he'd met the woman he'd been waiting a lifetime for, a revelation that even shocked him.

Chapter Seven
KARINA

It was cast removal day and Karina was finally feeling like her old self again. She was on her way in a cab to the hospital to get it removed after struggling with getting around in it for two weeks.

She was supposed to go see her own doctor using the State insurance she had, but the doctor from the hospital called and said he wanted her to come see him to get the cast off. When she told him she couldn't afford a private doctor visit, he'd informed her that Dr. Mykel Tanner told him he would be covering the expense. He wanted her follow-up to be with him so that he could make sure her leg had healed properly.

Karina didn't know what to say. She thanked him and accepted the appointment and as soon as she was finished, she planned to call and thank Mykel for his generosity.

She arrived at Sinai hospital and went straight to the doctor's office to have the cast removed. She came out of his office to find Mykel sitting in the waiting area.

"Mykel, what are you doing here?" she asked.

"I'm here to check on you. You look good as new with your cast off. You even seem to be walking without a limp. Usually when you first get a cast off, it takes some getting used to having it off."

"I walked around the doctor's office on the leg back and

forth for him to see that I was okay. The x-ray shows the fracture is all healed. Thank you for making it so that I could see the same doctor to have the cast removed and get the x-ray. I was going to call you to thank you, but here you are. I really appreciate that."

"It was my pleasure. I felt like I needed to do something for you. How have you been," he asked as they walked out of the office.

"I've been great. It wasn't so bad being laid up for two weeks. Handling the kids was another story, but they worked with me realizing I was moving around on crutches. I had a time getting my daughter to leave me each day to go to daycare. She wanted to stay home to take care of me."

"I'm glad you're doing better."

"I am and I see you're in your doctor gear so your vacation must be over."

"Yes, it's officially over and I'm back to the daily grind."

"That's good."

"Listen, are you in a big hurry to leave?" he asked.

"No not really."

"Would you like to have lunch with me? It's just the hospital cafeteria food, but it's actually pretty good here."

Karina was feeling all giddy inside. The handsome doctor, it seems, may like her. She certainly did like him. She wouldn't get her hopes up because men like him weren't really into women like her. It was nice to be asked for lunch so she accepted.

"Sure, that would be nice."

He escorted her to the cafeteria where they ate sandwiches and talked about everything, but the accident and her leg. She learned a lot about him.

He has a sister whom he adores and his parents are still married after forty years together. He told her about his years of college, medical school and residency and how he knew since he was a young boy that he would be a doctor because he loved helping people.

She shared a little about herself. She answered the questions he asked her, but her resistance with providing extra information let him know not to pry so he didn't and Karina appreciated that. Her life was nowhere near as fascinating as his. His life was the kind of life dreams are made of. He knew what he wanted in life and didn't let anything get in the way of achieving it.

He had never been married and didn't have any children. He'd had a long-term relationship at one point that didn't end well and for now he was focused on work which left little time for dating and falling in love.

She didn't tell him anything about her personal dating life. She was ashamed at what she considered dating when it was actually spreading her legs when a man smiled at her and it looked like he may have had money or fame. That wasn't dating, but that was all she knew and that's all she'd had.

Mykel did ask about the job she was going to the day of the accident and she told him they told her they were holding the job for her when she got her cast removed. She was still deciding what to do about the job. She'd lost the zest she'd once had about working at Walmart. She told him she would make a decision soon now that the cast was off and she could easily get around.

Mykel noticed her looking at several nurses as they came in and out of the cafeteria and what he saw was envy. Something about the way she looked at them interested him so he asked her about it. She explained to him that as a young child, she'd had dreams of becoming a nurse. Once she'd had her son at sixteen that dream pretty much went out the window.

He noticed how sad the conversation made her feel so he didn't press anymore.

Lunch was over quickly when Mykel got called for an emergency. Before leaving he asked if he could call her sometime and Karina gave him her number, telling him to contact her anytime.

~~

Two weeks had gone by and Karina didn't hear anything from Mykel. She'd gotten the impression at the hospital that he was interested in her. Perhaps the little bit he did learn about her had killed any real interest he may have had in her which was why she hadn't heard from him. He may have even asked for her number to be polite.

When she'd mentioned to her sister that she'd run into Mykel again and that he'd shown interest in her, Tracie shot down any hopes she had that he may be interested in her by telling her that once again she'd leaned on false hope that a man like him would be interested in her like she thought about the rapper.

She thought about calling him a few times and each time she started to dial him, she never completed it.

Serves her right she thought. Maybe it was time she stopped her hopeless dreaming and dealt with reality. She needed a girl's night out. The kids were spending the night at her mother's house, it was Friday and she was bored. Those were never good combinations, but she was feeling a little down and needed a remedy. She was about to call one of her friends when Robin called. She hadn't spoken to her since the night they'd gone out to the club.

"Hey Robin. What's up?"

"Well I've been calling you for weeks and you haven't returned my call. I'm surprised you answered today."

Karina felt bad. It wasn't Robin's fault that she'd slept with JayMark and left feeling like a tramp.

"I know, I'm sorry. I've been going through something lately, but I'm over it. What are you up to tonight?"

"I'm hanging with a friend, but that's sort of why I'm calling you. Remember that rapper you spent the night with, JayMark?"

How could she forget that night?

"Yeah, what about him?" she asked.

"Well he's in town and checking for you. You know I've been kicking it with a friend of his since that night and he said JayMark has been trying to get in touch with you. He didn't mention that to me until tonight so I'm calling you to tell you he is feeling you girl. From what I'm told he had to rush out of town and didn't get your number that time when the two of you hooked up. He didn't realize I was still seeing one of his partners until recently and they asked me to get in contact with you. That's also why I've been leaving you so many messages. Next time call me back girl. This brother wants you and this is serious stuff Karina so take his number and call him."

Karina didn't know what to think. She thought he'd gotten what he wanted from her and never looked back. Now it seems he really was checking for her. Maybe the planets were lining up in her favor after all.

"He's in town and wants you to call him tonight. I think he wants to take you out or something. Do you have a babysitter for the kids?"

"Kayla and Tyler are at my mom's house tonight for a birthday party and Tony's mother is picking them up tomorrow for some play at her church so I'm kid free all weekend. Give me the number, I'll call him now."

To say that she was excited was an understatement. Her fingers were shaking as she dialed and her heart almost stopped beating when he answered on the first ring.

After telling him who she was, he told her that he couldn't stop thinking about her since the night they'd spent together and how sorry he was he didn't get her number before he left. They made plans to hookup and he gave her instructions to get dressed in her sexiest outfit.

As soon as they got off the phone and Karina told him where to pick her up at, she went to her closet for something hot to wear. JayMark told her to wear something like what she wore the night they met because he liked her in that and she had the perfect dress in mind. It was the same style as the red one she'd worn that night, but it was all white.

She needed to get moving. She didn't want him to pick her up at her apartment because she didn't want him to see where she lived. She wanted him to think she was more than where she lived so she told him she was going to be out anyway and she'd meet him downtown in front of one of her favorite restaurants.

After grabbing a quick shower, she got dressed in the sexy white number and called a cab.

She'd been waiting about thirty minutes when a limo pulled up and JayMark's bodyguard got out to help her in.

"What's up shorty? You are looking hot tonight, just like I remember and that dress is banging. Are you ready for some fun tonight?" he asked.

Karina was more than ready.

"Yes I am. It's good to see you again. I never thought I'd hear from you again after the way you left."

"Sorry about that shorty. I should have told you I had an early flight out for a concert on the west coast. I thought about you and I didn't have a number to contact you. It wasn't until one of my partners mentioned your girl from that night that I knew he'd been seeing her all this time. Us connecting again was meant to be baby. Now sit back and relax because we'll be there in a few minutes."

She did as he asked and didn't bother to ask where they were going. Wherever it was, she was down for it because he was checking for her.

The limo pulled up to a large mansion in a part of town she'd never been in before. The house was huge and there were several high end cars parked outside. Before they exited the limousine, she could hear loud rap music coming from the house. Something in the back of her mind was telling her this was not a good setup. She thought they were hanging out alone tonight and had no idea he was taking her to a party.

"Whose house is this?" she asked as they walked up to the door.

"It belongs to one of my label mates. Trust me you'll have a good time. It's the kind of party I know you'll love."

Something felt off about the party and she wasn't sure what his comment meant.

They entered the house and the party was in full swing. Taking a quick look around, she saw about thirty men and noticed that there were only six, maybe seven women, including her. Perhaps the other women were elsewhere in the house, she thought.

She leaned over to ask.

"Where is everyone else? All I see is a bunch of men and only a few women. Are there other women coming or are they someplace else?"

"No shorty, this is it. It's the guys, the ladies you see and you. You know what's up."

He walked her further into the room and when she hesitated, he took her to the side.

"Look, I'm sure you know about this type of scene. The way you put it on a brother that night right after meeting me, I knew this would be the perfect scene for you after I told my boys all about you. I can guarantee you a lot of paper if you do what you did with me that night, but on a bigger scale. I told them how freaky you were and they want to try you out for themselves. I told them I knew you'd be down so why don't you relax, get yourself a few drinks and loosen up. When you're ready, go ahead and mingle. These guys paid a lot of money to be at this party tonight and it all goes to you ladies. I'm going to go get a drink and have a few words with my man over there. Introduce yourself around and let the guys get a good look at the goods."

Karina was frightened as she looked around again. What was happening? What had she gotten herself into? He didn't contact her because he missed her or wanted her; he did so to have her participate in a sex party with a group of men.

Now that she paid a little more attention to what was going on in the house, she could see a few of the women were now topless moving around from man to man, getting groped and removing more and more of their clothing. She looked in another direction and saw another female who was now completely naked walking off in the direction of another room followed by several guys. Once the door was shut, she had an idea what was going on behind it and she wanted no parts of it. She was more scared than she'd ever been in her life. She'd had her times of sleeping with men that she regretted, but she was no whore. Several men were checking her out and coming in her direction. She needed to get out of there and didn't know what to do. There were several guys standing at the door so going back out the way she came wasn't going to be an option.

"Hey baby," one guy said coming up to her.

"Who me?" she asked, playing naïve.

"Yeah, you. My man over there said that your name was Karina and that you liked being down for whatever. What do you say to letting me and my friend here take a look at the body that dress is hiding, though it's not really hiding a whole lot? We can go to another room, a lot more private than standing right here at the door."

She felt dirty as he and his friend looked her over with eyes feasting on every one of her curves. One reached out and grabbed her behind and she jumped out of fear. This was a bad situation and she needed to think fast. She wanted no part of what they had in mind. She put on her game face as if she was going to play along.

"I need to visit the bathroom first and then I'll come back out and join you. Do you think you could get me a drink while you wait?"

"Sure baby, whatever you want."

"Anything is fine for me, make sure it's very strong," she replied.

Once the guys had turned away to get her drink, she looked around for the bathroom. After asking another guy where it was, she was pointed in the direction of one. Being sure that no one was looking, she slipped into one of the empty rooms and as luck would have it, there was a sliding glass door. Without thinking, she made a dash for the door and the minute she was outside, she removed her five inch heels and ran as if someone was chasing her. She had no idea where she was or how far from the city she was, but she didn't stop running until she could no longer see the house.

She found herself running so hard and fast that she failed to take in that she had no idea where she was. All of her life, she'd never even been outside of the city and she remembered that once they left the downtown area after being picked up, they drove another half hour or so to get to the house. Stopping a few times to catch her breath, she looked around and saw no one and nothing but long stretches of road. She didn't stop too long because she needed to get to an area where she felt safe until she could get a cab to get home. It was after midnight and after an hour of running and now walking she still wasn't in an area where she'd run into other people.

She had been walking for about an hour when her cell phone rang and she saw that it was Robin. She didn't answer it thinking Robin was calling her because JayMark had discovered she'd left the party. Robin was the last person she wanted to talk to. When she was less angry, she would let Robin know the kind of evening she'd help set her up for.

The night was getting cooler and it seemed as if there wasn't even light coming from the moon. She could barely see her own hands due to the darkness. She was scared and didn't know what to do. She pulled out her cell phone to call a cab. She dialed two of them and when she gave them the name of the street she was on, none would come that distance to get her. She'd called cabs who worked within the city limits. She didn't know where she was so she didn't know what company to call.

The tears came unexpectedly knowing her circumstance was dire. Anyone could come along and she'd be in even more trouble. Through the tears, she scrolled through her phone to see who she could call for help. None of her friends had cars and the few she did know didn't answer when she called. While scrolling she came across one number and dialed immediately.

"Hello."

She exhaled when he answered and tried to hold back the tears.

"Hello Mykel, it's Karina."

"Karina? Are you okay?"

Before she could get another word out, she began to cry uncontrollably.

"Karina, talk to me, what's wrong? Where are you?" he asked.

"I don't know," she answered.

"You don't know what? You don't know what's wrong or you don't know where you are?"

"I'm sorry for calling you so late," she said between cries.

"It's okay, tell me what's wrong."

"I can't because I'm too embarrassed, but I didn't have anyone else to call."

She cried harder.

"It's okay, tell me where you are?"

"I don't know." Her cries were now frantic.

"Karina, I can't help you if you don't calm down and tell me what's going on."

"I'm so stupid," she said. "I'm such a screw up."

"Karina are you near anyone who can tell me what's going on?"

"No, I'm out here by myself alone and I don't know where I am." She cried some more.

"Karina listen to me. Every road is a street and I need you to look around for the street you're on and tell me what that is? I'm coming to get you, but you have to calm down enough to tell me where you are?"

"I don't know how to tell you where I am."

"Give me the street name and I'll find it using the GPS in my car. Look around for the street."

Karina gave him the name and he told her to stay on the phone with him until he gets to her. She agreed, but she didn't want to talk.

Mykel didn't know what was going on, but he could hear what sounded like terror in her voice. Luckily he was off from the hospital for the evening and had just gotten home and hadn't fully undressed. He quickly grabbed a shirt and his keys and ran out of his house.

Whatever happened to Karina must be pretty bad considering she didn't want to talk about it. He couldn't let her hang up because he needed to know that she was okay.

"Karina, if you feel like you're not in a safe place, hang up and call the police okay?"

"I'm okay, I'm just scared and upset. Thank you for coming for me."

"I'm glad you called. According to my GPS, you're not too far from where I live in Columbia. What are you doing all the way out here alone?"

She didn't answer. She didn't want him thinking badly of her.

"Okay, you don't have to answer. Tell me that you're not physically hurt."

"I'm not hurt. I couldn't figure out how to get home. I called a few cab companies and none came out this far. Since I don't know where I am I didn't know how far out I was."

"Don't worry, I'll be there soon. Stay on the phone until I get to you."

She felt better knowing someone was coming to get her. She wished she didn't have to call Mykel, but she didn't know what else to do. It was the middle of the night and she was out roaming around on dark roads in a very short white dress and stiletto shoes.

Less than twenty minutes later, Mykel pulled onto the road where she was.

"Karina, I'm here. Do you see the headlights from my car? I'm blinking them."

"Yes, I see you. I'm at the end of the road, waving at you."

It was very dark, but Mykel could see her white dress. When he reached her, he saw that the white dress was extremely short and very tight. She must have been at a club or some type of party he thought.

He got out to help her in the car.

"Are you sure you're okay?" he asked once he'd gotten back in.

"Yes I'm fine."

"I'm glad you called me. This is a dark and secluded area and it would have been daylight before you would have found your way out of here and back home."

He turned his car around and headed for her apartment.

They rode in silence until he pulled up in front of her building. He waited for her to say something first. When she didn't reach for the door handle, he gave her a few moments to gather herself.

"Thank you for coming to my rescue. I wish I could tell you what happened, but right now I'm too ashamed and I don't want you to think badly of me. Not that you don't' already."

"I don't think badly of you Karina. Why would you think that?"

She turned this time before she spoke, to look directly at him.

"You didn't call. I gave you my number and you didn't call. I know I'm probably not the typical kind of woman that you usually associate with so I assumed you didn't call because after learning things about me, you didn't like what you found out and decided not to call."

Mykel felt bad because she was right, but only about the fact that he didn't call. He still liked her.

"I'm sorry for not calling you. It had nothing to do with not liking you. I actually like you a lot. I had every plan to call you, but work got in the way. I wasn't getting in some nights until the middle of the night and other nights I spent all night in the hospital, sleeping when I could catch a few hours during the night. Things have been crazy, but that's no excuse. Believe this or not, but I was planning to call you tomorrow. I'm off in the morning and was hoping to catch you to talk before I had to go in."

His explanation made her feel a little better. It didn't erase the events of the night, but it felt good knowing he didn't forget about her.

"No need to apologize. You're a doctor and your work comes first, so I understand."

"Now, as far as tonight, tell me or don't tell me, I'll leave that up to you, but no matter what, I like you and would love to see you again if you're up for that."

For the first time since her ordeal began, Karina smiled.

"Yes I'm up for that."

"It's late and I want you to get your rest so why don't you call me when you get up. I'm not due in the hospital until three in the afternoon. Before then I'll be free to talk if you want to."

"Okay, I'll call you in the morning. Thanks for coming to get me. I don't know what I would have done if you hadn't."

"Call me anytime. Now go ahead in so that I know you're safe inside before I pull off."

Karina got out of the car and ran into her building still carrying her shoes. Once inside, she turned on a light so that he could see she was inside. She saw him pulling off as she got to the window."

She went in her room and sat down on the bed thinking about the events of the night. No more foolish choices for her. Mykel had been her ram in the bush, as she remembered her grandmother saying many times when she was younger. Now she understood what it meant.

Chapter Eight
KARINA

Mykel didn't know what to make of the night before. After getting home from dropping Karina off, he laid awake the rest of the night. He still didn't know her well, but to hear her crying on the other end of the phone the way she was had frightened him like never before. He couldn't get to her fast enough to be sure she was okay. How she got way out in the middle of nowhere, he didn't know. Whatever the circumstance, she didn't want to talk about it.

He could tell by the way she was dressed that she was either out with friends who left her stranded or out on a date that didn't turn out so well. Either way, he felt helpless when she'd called him crying.

When his cell phone buzzed on his hip and he saw her number, he felt better, hoping she was able to get some sleep.

"Hi Karina," he said.

"Hi Mykel, were you busy? If so I can call you back before you go to work."

"No I'm not busy. I've been waiting, hoping you would call me. Did you get any sleep?"

"Yes I did."

"I'm glad. You were pretty worked up last night. I hope things are better in the light of day."

"Let me say that it was a wake-up call for me; it was

exactly what I needed."

"So how have you been?"

"I've been doing okay. Things could be better, but we have to lay in the bed we make right?"

"That's one way to look at life. I'm more of an optimist so I always see the good in every situation. Are things on your job okay? Are your children doing alright?" he asked trying to find out what has her so bothered.

"The kids are great. They are getting time with both grandmothers this weekend. As for the job, well I decided not to take it. It was at Walmart and to be honest, it's not what I want to do. I don't know what I want to do, but that's not it."

"What about nursing?"

"Mykel there is so much about me that you don't know. I don't think I'm cut out for that either. At one time I did want to be a nurse, but I have kids I need to think about and that means putting all these big dreams I have on the side at least until they are older."

"That doesn't have to be the case. People balance careers and children every day."

"True, but I'm sure they have a much better support system than I do. You've met my family and that's all I'm going to say about them. I'm doing this alone, pretty much, and it's already hard. I don't need to make things harder for myself."

"You do if you're in a place in your life that you're not happy with. Tell me if you could do anything right now to have the kind of life you wanted, what would that be?"

Karina thought about that. At one time she would have thought the idea of meeting a baller who could get her out of the lifestyle she was living and give her everything she wanted was what she desired. She no longer felt that way. She knew exactly how to answer his question.

"I'd like to go to college and work towards a degree in nursing."

"Then do that. I'll even help you."

"What? I can't do that. College is expensive and I don't have the time or money to do that. Remember I have two young children."

"Karina, you have two young children who are in school all day long. You could take classes during the day at the local community college and I'm sure you would be able to get money to cover your tuition and books. You're not working and I'm going to assume that you're living on public assistance?"

That made her skin crawl. It was such an embarrassing state of living.

"Karina?"

"Yes, you assumed correctly, though I'm not proud of it."

"Never be embarrassed or ashamed of who you are or what your circumstances are. You could be doing a lot worse, but you're not and I admire that. Now, how about you let me help you find a way to make this happen. The summer session will be starting soon so all you need to do is go up to the school and apply and they can also help you sign up for tuition assistance. When school lets out for your son, does he go to a summer camp of any kind?"

"Yes, he goes to an all day camp in the neighborhood. It runs from seven in the morning until six in the evening and even though I'm home, he likes to stay the whole day because of the activities. As for Kayla, as long as I'm either working on in school, she can go to daycare all day long.

Otherwise, she can only go part-time."

"Okay, so how about I pick you up one day this week and we'll go to the community college so that you can apply. You can get it all done the same day. No more thinking you can't follow your dreams because you have kids to take care of. I'll even help you study."

He was right. She needed to get up and do something about her situation. There was plenty of time during the day to get it done and there was no time for any more excuses. Again, she said to herself, Mykel was her ram in the bush.

"As long as you don't mind, I think that'll work out great."

"I don't mind at all. I have some time on Wednesday because I'm not due in the hospital until that evening. Why don't I come by to get you around nine in the morning so that you can have everything done in time to get back home before your kids get home?"

"Thank you Mykel. You keep rescuing me."

"I'm not complaining beautiful. I'm glad that I can hear you smiling through the phone. I was worried about you last night. Today, I feel better knowing you're doing better. I'm going to try and catch some sleep before I have to be at work. I'll call you later when I get a break."

"I can't thank you enough."

"No need to thank me."

Karina hung up her phone wanting to dance around the room. If what Mykel said was true, that she could get assistance to cover the cost of going to school, perhaps her dreams weren't too far away.

She spent the rest of the day cleaning her apartment while the kids were gone. She still hadn't returned the many messages left for her by Robin who was calling almost non-stop wondering what was going on with her. Apparently JayMark had called her to tell her she'd disappeared and Robin wanted to know that she was okay. Karina sent her a text telling her that she was and that she'd call her to explain. That seemed to satisfy her for the moment. For now, Karina didn't want to think about any of what happened the night before. She wanted to clean and daydream about the new path her life was about to take.

After cleaning her apartment until it was spotless, she was still on cloud nine when Tony showed up at her door.

"What are you doing here?" she asked opening the door to let him in.

"I came to see if the reason my kids are again with my mother is because you were laid up in here with some dude."

"I'm not laid up with anybody. I finished cleaning the apartment and I was about to go to the library to look up information about taking college courses and getting financial aid."

"For what?" he asked.

"I plan to take some classes to work towards getting my nursing degree. I've wanted to be a nurse since I was a little girl and I found out that I may be able to take classes and get financial assistance to pay for it."

"You are always dreaming about something. You never even graduated from high school. How are you going to take college courses?"

"I got my GED and because my scores were so high, I was actually given a high school diploma so yes, I can take college courses now. A lot happened while you were still locked up."

"Don't talk down to me Karina."

"I'm not talking down to you, I'm speaking up for myself."

"With all this dreaming and planning you have, don't forget you have my children to look after. Kayla is too young for you to be gone all the time."

"I'm planning to take classes while Kayla is in daycare all day and soon school will be out and Tyler will be in camp all day."

"Who has been filling your head with this school stuff? I never heard you talking like this before. You never mentioned anything about wanting to take college courses or becoming a nurse. Not since before you had Tyler."

She wasn't ready to tell him anything about Mykel. There really wasn't anything to tell since they were only friends and he was helping her find her way.

"No one. I decided I wanted to do something for myself. Now that you see that I'm not here with a dude, feel free to leave. I told you I'm going to the library."

"Wait, since we're here alone, why don't we spend a little private time together because I miss you. You've been treating a brother like a stranger lately."

"Tony, I haven't treated you any kind of way. I was in an accident and had a fractured leg and not once did you call or come by to check on me or to see if I needed anything or any help with the kids. If it hadn't been for your mother and the few times my sister helped me with them, I don't know how I would have made it. When you had the chance to do the right thing, you chose not too out of anger. You can't come up in here thinking I'll spread my legs for you because that's what you want. I don't want that. I'm tired of being a mat for you and any other man. I'm looking out for me now and my focus is on my children and finding a way to make these classes happen. As for you and I, we are over and have been over for a long time."

"Yeah, whatever," Tony said. "You say that now, but you'll come around."

"Not this time. Besides, what would your girlfriend say about you being all up in here trying to be all up in me?"

He looked at her with surprise wondering how she'd found out.

"Wondering how I found out about her? East Baltimore is a small community Tony and word travels. Now I'm not all up in your business and who you're with and I'm asking that you give me the same respect. I don't have anybody up here around my children, so you don't need to worry about that. If I do find someone that I want to be involved with and that I may want to introduce the kids to, I will let you know since you are their father. Other than that, my personal business is none of your business and the sex shop for you is permanently closed."

"I don't know who you are anymore. What happened to that girl who loved me more than anything?"

"She grew up and found she needed to start loving herself a lot more. I will always love you Tony, but I'm not in love with you and we can't play the back and forth game. I'm over it."

She could see he was hurt.

"Whatever you say. I'm bouncing and good luck with that school thing, if it works out."

"Oh it will work out. I want it too badly for it not to," she said as he was leaving. She was going for it and it was time to go to the library to do her research. She was looking forward to telling Mykel all about it when she talked to him later.

Chapter Nine
KARINA

Karina had never studied so hard in her life. She was in her second week of summer classes and she was already preparing for her first exam. Studying at home didn't work out when she needed to use the computer at the library. She was hesitant about taking the kids with her, not knowing how they would behave and how much studying she would get done trying to keep her eye on them.

Mykel, who had been her saving grace, told her about a new library out in the county that was right at the Metro station. They had a room just for kids where Tyler and Kayla could play and learn and she could keep an eye on them while she studied. She gathered them up and went to the library. Things turned out better than she'd expected. The kids busied themselves and she was able to get her paper done without much interruption.

She was excited all the time now especially with her classes going well. She was able to sign up for school full time three days a week which left her with two days while the kids were in camp and daycare where she could study in peace.

She and Mykel were also growing closer. They didn't do a lot of dating because she was still getting used to her schedule and balancing home life. Mykel was kind enough to understand, having a busy schedule himself. Whenever she needed help with her class assignments, he would help her without hesitation.

Her birthday was coming up and he'd asked her out on their first official date. So far they hadn't defined what was going on between the two of them, but Karina felt comfortable with the direction and pace at which they were moving.

She told her sister about the time she was spending with Mykel and when she told her about their date for her birthday, she enlightened Karina to what she thought the whole date was about.

"I think you're wrong Tracie," Karina said when Tracie showed up to watch the kids and help her pick out an outfit for her birthday date with Mykel.

"I'm not wrong. It's time for you to pay up. That fine doctor didn't do all this helping you out with school, helping you study, running you all around the place for nothing. To top it off, I get here today and find that for your birthday, he purchased you a brand new computer and printer. Girl do you know how much an Apple computer costs? A lot, and when I say a lot, I mean a lot of booty is what you're going to have to give up in return for all he's done for you."

"He's been helping me because he likes me and because he's a nice guy. He's not expecting sex in return. He hasn't done anything that would make me think that he had an ulterior motive for helping me as much as he has."

"Just because he hasn't said it, doesn't mean he isn't expecting it. Girl, men want one thing from women like you and I, especially men like the doctor who can get any woman he wants. Why would he want you just to want you? You're not new to the game. No matter who the guy is, the game is always the same. He's expecting you to drop it like it's hot for him tonight so be ready."

She didn't want to believe Tracie was right, but she did have a point. She'd never met a man who did anything for her who didn't want something in return and that something usually was sex. No matter how nice Mykel was, he was still a man and like any other man, she saw how he looked at her when they were together. She knew the look.

Karina continued looking for something to wear.

"What do you think about this dress?"

She held up a black, conservative looking dress.

"Girl, that's not showing any of your goods? Where is your short, peek-a-boo stuff? That's what men like."

"I don't know Tracie, I'm telling you, Mykel is not like that."

Tracie moved her to the side and started pulling other dresses out of the closet for Karina to try on.

"All men are like that, trust me. Go with this pink one. It's short, tight and very sexy. Where is the good doctor taking you?"

"He's making me a birthday dinner at his house. From his description it sounds really nice. He wanted to do something special for me and after he dropped the gift off this morning, he told me what he had planned and said to dress comfortably."

"Well you know what that means. That's code for don't wear too much that would take too long to get off of you."

Maybe Tracie was right, she thought. She gave the pink dress a second look before deciding to wear it. She appreciated everything Mykel had been doing to help her out and she had no problem paying the piper if that was what the night was about. It had to be, especially since he could have taken her to a nice restaurant. Her sister was right. He planned it so that they would be alone at his house. That game plan had sex written all over it.

"Okay, I'll wear the pink one."

"Good because if you plan to hold on to the good doctor, you know what you have to do. It's what all men expect from women like you, me and even mommy. Don't worry about the kids because we're going to be busy with games and movies most of the night. Try not to wake us up in the morning when you creep back in."

Karina ignored her as she gathered up her clothes and went to shower to wait for Mykel to pick her up. This would be the first time that he'd get to meet her kids. She'd asked him to come by a little early so that she could introduce him.

She now started to second guess that. If what he really wanted from her was sex then maybe she shouldn't introduce him to Kayla and Tyler. She had never introduced anyone to the kids before, but she thought perhaps things with Mykel was different then past situations. According to Tracie, she was still living in a dream world when it came to men and their expectations. Too late now, she'd already told him.

~~

Mykel checked everything before heading out to pick up Karina for their birthday dinner date. He'd spent all day with a local chef who agreed to come out to his house and walk him through a few recipes. He wanted to do something special and cook for her. They both lived busy lives and figured she would enjoy an evening relaxing.

He was preparing a meal of all of the things she liked.

He'd learned about all of those likes over the past several months of getting to know her. Tonight he wanted to talk to her about their relationship. They had not defined what they were to each other, but as time went by, he was falling more and more in love with her. He only hoped she was feeling the same way about him.

For the first time, he'd been spending time with a woman without sex being a major part of the relationship. He wanted things to be different with Karina. He had a feeling men had been using her for most of her adult life and he didn't want to be another one of those men. He wanted her to know he wanted her and not her body. She was definitely a beautiful woman and to him she was well worth the wait.

They would take the relationship to the next level only when they both thought the time was right and it wasn't something that Karina felt she had to do.

He'd gotten bits of information from her that told him that she didn't really know her worth beyond her beautiful body. He was serious about showing her that she was worth much more than that to him.

He looked around once more making sure the dining room was set up the way he wanted. He'd had an event planner come in earlier in the day to decorate for an elegant evening.

All of the food had been prepped and all he had to do once they got back to his house was to put the finishing touches on everything.

He got excited every time he was able to put a smile on Karina's face.

He will never forget the look earlier in the day when he'd stopped at her apartment to deliver the first of her birthday presents. He looked over and saw the other two gifts sitting nicely on the mantel in his living room. He loved doing nice things for her because she deserved them and much more.

She had been dealt a hard hand in life and if he had anything to do with her future, he would see to it that she never had to deal with another hard hand again in her lifetime. It was time to go pick up his lady.

Mykel grabbed his keys and checked his attire in the mirror. He assumed Karina was on the same page as him because she finally wanted to introduce him to Kayla and Tyler. They had discussed it before and had decided it would be up to her to decide when the time for that would be.

As he drove to her house, he thought over her explanation about the rocky relationship with their father and that whenever she decided she wanted him to meet the kids, she also said she needed to introduce him to Tony since he was their father and Mykel would be around them. He had no problem with that and he understood. Tonight he would meet the kids and they were planning on him meeting Tony a few days later when Karina could arrange it. Right now, he only wanted to think about Karina and the night of relaxation he had planned for them.

Mykel knocked on the door to Karina's apartment and was greeted by her sister. He remembered meeting her when Karina was in the hospital.

"Hello Dr. Mykel," Tracie said.

"Hello. It's nice to see you again Tracie."

"Oh, you know my name?"

"Yes, Karina talks about you all the time."

"Well come on in Dr. Mykel. My sister will be right out.

She saw you pulling up and went to get the kids together to meet you."

Mykel came inside and made himself comfortable while he waited. A few moments later, Karina came into the room followed by her two beautiful children. After meeting the kids and hearing all about Dora the Explorer from Kayla, they were finally off. When they got to his car, he told her how much he enjoyed meeting her kids. He wanted to ask why she was wearing a light trench coat, already buttoned up when he showed up considering it was warm outside, but he figured she may have on an outfit that she wanted to surprise him with since it was a special date night. He decided against asking and decided to wait and see.

They drove in silence for a few blocks as Karina sat nervously near the door, staring out at the scenery as they left the city, heading towards the expressway and out to Howard County where he lived. She had originally offered to take the bus to his house so that he wouldn't have to come and get her, but he explained there was no bus service where he lived so he would pick her up. Even if there was, he'd told her, he would never allow her to take the bus. This again set him aside from other guys. Most would have told her to get to them the best way she could and she would also have to get home the same way.

Mykel looked over at Karina and could see she wasn't as comfortable as he wanted her to be. He wanted her to have fun tonight and to learn how to relax and not worry about anything. He had plans to be sure she looked forward to being with him for many more dates in the future.

"Karina, are you okay? You look a little distracted or is it nervousness I see?"

She turned and tried her best to not let her nervousness show.

"No, I'm fine. I'm enjoying the ride. It's not often I get a night out without Kayla and Tyler so I'm taking it all in, especially the quietness," she laughed. "Having two kids who scream mommy all day and evening long, it's hard to sometimes get use to the quiet."

"Thanks for sharing your birthday with me."

When Mykel gave her a warm smile, she actually relaxed a little.

"Well we have a bit of a distance so enjoy the ride."

~~

Tony was still standing on the street fuming at the sight of Karina getting in a car with a man. He'd come by her apartment to wish her a happy birthday only to see her getting into a shiny black Jaguar with some dude. She told him she wasn't seeing anyone, yet here she was obviously dressed for a planned night out. Where were his kids? He waited until she'd pulled off before sending a text to her phone. Her only response was the kids were in the apartment with her sister. When he asked her about the guy he'd seen her get in the car with, he didn't get a response.

Whoever the guy was, it wasn't some dude or hustler from the neighborhood. The guy was neatly groomed and looked like he was about something. Karina had better not be hooking to make ends meet. This guy was definitely out of her league and that was the only reason he could think of that would have her getting in a ride with a guy clearly out of her league of dudes in the hood.

He knew that a lot of girls hooked up with big money guys to make ends meet and he had a feeling that's exactly what Karina had gotten into. That was probably the reason why she wouldn't let him touch her anymore. She was selling it out to higher bidders.

Still not getting any response to his numerous texts, he called her. His anger jumped ten-fold when her phone went to voicemail on the second ring. That meant she saw that he was calling and ignored the call sending it to voicemail.

He would have a few choice words for his children's mother when she returned. For now, he would call up one of his other jump offs to take his frustrations out on one of their bodies. They were always waiting for his phone call.

Karina saw that Tony was calling. From his texts, it appeared that he must have been on her block or nearby when she left with Mykel because one of his texts mentioned Mykel and the car he was driving. She didn't care and she didn't want anything to spoil her night with Mykel, especially not Tony and his drama.

"What are you thinking?" Mykel asked, breaking into her thoughts.

"I'm thinking about how special you always make me feel. I've never had anyone do anything this big for me on my birthday, not even my family."

"Well this is only the beginning of nice things for you. I enjoy doing things for you, especially when I can make you smile."

When they finally arrived at his home, the first thing Mykel wanted to do was give her a tour. Karina was excited because she'd never seen a house so nice before. She'd been in one recently, the night she'd like to forget about when Mykel had to come and rescue her, but that wasn't as pleasant a visit as this one.

They started first in the main foyer where staircases led up to the next level on the right and on the left of a round marble table with a big beautiful floral arrangement on it. Before going up to start the tour on the top floor, Mykel helped her remove her coat. She enjoyed his reaction when he saw the little pink number she'd chosen to wear for the night.

"You are truly a gorgeous woman Karina and pink is definitely your color."

"Thank you. I was hoping you'd like it."

"If you like it, I love it and since it's your birthday, I say make it what you want it to be. Shall we start the tour?"

"Yes," she replied taking his hand and going with him to the top level.

"Up here we have three large bedrooms. The one at the end of the hallway here is mine."

Mykel took them to the door of his room so that she could get a look inside. The room was magnificent and the biggest bedroom she'd ever seen. It was all male with lots of dark colors in shades of brown. She listened as he told her that his room also contained a huge walk-in closet and a Jacuzzi tub. They then went to the other two rooms where he'd turned one into a home gym and the other was a spare room for when his parents, who lived in DC came for a visit. After taking in the rest of the top level, they ventured back down to the main level, with each room being as magnificent as the last.

They did a quick tour of the lower level which is where his sister's room was when she stayed with him.

Now they were in the kitchen where Mykel started working on dinner.

He found it difficult to concentrate on dinner with

Karina dressed in a low-cut, short pink dress with matching pink and black very high heeled shoes. He'd never met a sexier woman and he found his body reacting to her in a way he was hoping to have better control over. She was gorgeous and his body recognized it.

"You look incredible Karina."

"Thank you. I wore this not only for my birthday, but for you too."

"Well I appreciate you doing so. Let's get this birthday dinner started." He needed to do something to get his mind off of her in that dress.

"So what are we having?" she said when Mykel began gathering covered dishes from his refrigerator.

"I'm making a few things that I know are your favorites. As he began uncovering dishes, Karina was shocked to see what he was preparing. There were mini shrimp egg rolls, mini hotdogs wrapped in biscuits and to top it off, he'd made mini crab balls. As he continued uncovering dishes she was even more shocked.

"Are those pork chops?" she asked.

"Yes and they are stuffed with crabmeat. I know you said you loved pork chops, but I wanted to do something special with them. I'm going to broil those on the grill along with some shrimp skewers and potatoes. We also have salad which I'll let you mix up. Grab the ingredients from the refrigerator. For dessert, we're having chocolate lava, red and blue velvet cupcakes. I know you love chocolate and you said red velvet was your favorite cake. I threw in the blue velvet cupcakes. There is a bakery that specializes in those and I think you'll love them.

"Mykel, you are too good to me. This is so special. Do you know other than spending my birthdays with my children, this is the best birthday ever? I feel like a princess."

"I want you to always feel like a princess around me."

Dinner was everything Mykel had hoped it would be. They both feasted well and were about to relax in his family room to watch movies and enjoy dessert.

Karina figured it was time to do what Tracie convinced her Mykel did all of this for.

"I need to use your restroom. Do you have one down here?" she asked.

"Sure. There is one right around to your left right outside of the kitchen."

Karina got up and went in to remove her dress. She exhaled several times before going back out to join him in nothing but her black laced bra and lacy black thong. She decided to keep the heels on for the extra added touch.

She exited the bathroom and went back to join Mykel. He was sitting on the sofa scrolling through the cable channels. Since his back was to her, he hadn't seen what she came back in the room in. She walked around until she blocked his view of the television. To say he was shocked was an understatement.

Mykel sat staring at Karina standing in front of him in only a very lacy bra that was clearly see through and a thong that made his mouth water. She was definitely a very, very beautiful woman, but he noticed she looked uneasy and uncomfortable. His reaction in seeing her was that he wanted her and he wanted her bad. He had a feeling there was more to her standing here like this than the intimacy they could share. They were having a great time and he could tell she'd been relaxed the whole evening until now. She stood before him looking as if someone made her take her clothes off and he didn't like or want that.

Karina watched the play of emotions as they crossed Mykel's face. She could tell he wanted her because she had come to know that look on every man's face she came in contact with. She wanted him to know how much she appreciated all he had been doing to help her and her kids. No one had ever taken as much time and patience with her and had shown as much concern for the path her life could take. When he looked his fill from her feet, slowly up her body to her face, she knew she had been right. This is why he had invited her for an evening alone at his house.

"Do you like?" she asked, trying to sound seductive.

Mykel definitely liked, but he didn't like what he was beginning to sense the reasoning behind this was. It wasn't that he didn't like aggressive women because he believed if a woman had a need, the best way to handle it was to be open and go after what she wanted. He sensed this wasn't the case here. Karina wasn't standing in front of him looking secure of what she was doing. She was terrified.

He reached for the remote, turning off the television. It was obvious they needed to talk.

"Karina, you are a gorgeous woman and any man in his right mind could see what you have in mind, but I'm not sure this is what you really want. You look scared to me. What's going on?"

He didn't want her. What she thought was want was apparently disgust. By now most men would have already undressed and had her in various positions. This man in front of her didn't make a move toward her. She watched as he leaned forward, looked up at her and questioned why she was standing in front of him practically naked. She was embarrassed yet again.

"Karina, did I say or do something to make you think you had to do this or that we had to have sex tonight?"

She didn't answer. She tried to cover herself with her hands, not being able to move her feet. She looked away not letting him see that she was about to cry.

"Please don't turn away from me. Don't think for one second that I don't find you desirable because that's far from the truth, but I'm confused because we haven't talked about taking our relationship to this level and I thought that if and when we would, we would talk about it first. If what you want is for me to make love to you, then have no doubt that I will, but there is something about the way you are standing in front of me that tells me you aren't doing this for you; you're doing it for me. Talk to me," he pleaded.

Karina finally found the words to speak.

"My sister told me that you were only being nice and doing nice things for me because you wanted sex and I believed her. I'm stupid and I'm embarrassed."

"Have a seat and I'll be right back," Mykel said.

Karina sat down and nervously twitched in her seat. She ruined everything she touched, she thought while she sat. It didn't take Mykel long to return and when he did, he came back with a pink and black sweat suit.

"This belongs to my sister. You look about her size. Go ahead and put this on and let's talk."

She put the clothes on and sat back down on the sofa as tears started spilling from her eyes.

"I'm sorry Mykel. I can't imagine what you must think of me."

"What I'm thinking is you need to stop listening to your

sister. You don't have to do this. I mean, I am a man and I can certainly appreciate a lovely woman such as yourself, standing before me in all of her glory and I can only imagine at this moment all of the things I would love to do to that beautiful body, but unless you are overly aroused and need release, which I can certainly help with, why would you do this because your sister told you too?"

"I was telling her about how you've helped me and the things you've done for me and she said you were doing them to get me to pay you back with sex. She suggested that when you offered to cook me dinner for my birthday and after buying me that expensive computer equipment, that it was time to pay you back for it all."

When Mykel didn't respond, she figured he was trying to come up with a way to let her know that she wasn't his type of woman after all.

"Karina, I meant it when I said you are a beautiful woman. Any man in his right mind can see that and would be crazy to turn down such an invitation, but an even better man would turn you down as I have. I don't want you because you think you owe me something. I don't want you trying to pay me back with your body. That's not who I am and I don't want that to be who you are either."

Karina looked down at her hands as she rubbed them in her lap.

"Why would you think you owed me anything? Hasn't anyone ever been nice to you before without looking for something like sex in return? I do what I do because I like you and I care about you. I don't do it in order to receive some type of payback with your body as the bounty."

She looked over at him, relieved that he wasn't looking at her with disgust, but with sincerity.

She wanted to be sincere in her response.

"You are not like any of the guys I know. Most would have jumped at the chance to have sex with me," she said.

"I am as much a man as any of those other dudes you know, but the difference is, I'm not with you simply because I want to have sex with you. I won't say that it hasn't been on my mind. I mean, look at you, you are fine. I would like nothing more than to take you to my room, or lay you out on this sofa and make love to you all night long. In fact, I hope that one day soon, we'll be doing that, but it won't be because you think I want it out of payment. It will be because our connection is so strong that we can't keep our hands off of each other. I'm picturing clothes flying all over the place, hearts racing, lips connecting, hands clawing, all to get as close to each other as we possibly can because of the feelings we share, not out of obligation.

Karina smiled. This was a big first for her. She always believed men had an agenda and it oftentimes had to do with her being naked, under them.

"I'm sorry," she apologized. "I know how this must look. I guess it's easy to take the girl out of the hood, but not so easy to take the hood out of the girl. I let my sister convince me that it was time to pay up for everything you've been doing for me and I knew deep down that you were not that kind of guy. I knew it, but I let her get in my head. She said no man did all the things you've done for me without expecting something in return. I let her make me believe that you didn't really like me, but that you wanted my body and I'm sorry. There are some old habits and old ways that I can't seem to shake off."

"Karina, its okay. I really do like you. I don't see a body when I see you, though as gorgeous as you are, it's hard to not see it, but I'm looking beyond that. I meet women all the time, but something about you stood out. The day of the accident when I stopped by your room at the hospital, you were so humble, so apologetic, very kind and sweet. Once we started talking I knew I wanted to know more about you. I didn't see you as some cause that I needed to undertake to make myself feel better or to do things because I was sorry about the accident. After talking to you, I wanted to spend time with you. I know our thinking on things are like night and day and I don't want to change who you are, but I want you to see that it's okay to take your blinders off around me. I'm not out to use or abuse you. I like you a lot and I want to show you things you've never seen before and share experiences in life that you are worthy to experience. If you'll let me, I think we could have a nice relationship without any pressure. How about we have some fun and when it's time to go to the next level, we'll both know it and there will be no pressure. When you're ready to make love with me because you want to and not because you feel an obligation to do so, I will be right here. I'm falling in love with you Karina and I want you to know that when you and I make love, I will be the last man you will ever make love to. I want that kind of commitment from you. No matter what has occurred in your past, your future is with me and I want there to be no traces of anyone else or anything you've done with them anywhere in your mind. How does that sound?" he asked, hoping she understood.

Karina smiled at him and he knew they were finally on the same page.

"That sounds like a good plan."

She watched as he reached for the remote to turn the

movie back on. She reached out to touch his arm as he did so, getting his attention again.

"Thank you. I've never met a man like you before. I can't begin to tell you what I have experienced when it comes to men. If I did, you would probably never return another one of my phone calls. I'm not proud of some of the things I've done, but thank you for letting me see that all men are not like those I've known so far. I guess I still have a lot to learn about men."

"It's not that you have a lot to learn about men, it's that you have a lot to learn about this one," Mykel said pointing to himself. "What I want you to do is erase any preconceived ideas you have about men according to your interaction with them so far. Start new with me and let me show you how a real man should treat you. There is nothing that you can tell me that would make me change my mind about wanting you in my life. Nothing Karina," Mykel said hoping his words were getting through to her.

She thought back to the night he rescued her. She wanted to be honest with him and share what happened.

"Mykel, the night you picked me up when I was stranded, I had been at a party given by a hip hop rap artist. He and I had hooked up before and I thought he would be my path out of the hood, so I went along with whatever he wanted. That night, I didn't know it, but he invited me to a sex party with him, about thirty other guys and a handful of women. I'd spent a night with him before and he thought I would be down for letting a bunch of men use my body. I didn't know what his intention was until I got to the party. I guess I looked the part when I got in his car wearing that dress you saw me in. It hurt that he saw me that way and I thought he was into me. When I found the chance before anything could happen, I ran out of there and kept running until I called you. That's why I was lost. I ran down street after street terrified of the situation I'd placed myself in. I have a past Mykel and it involves quite a few guys even though I'm only twenty-five. My path so far has not been a good one and it's one I'm very ashamed of. I guess I don't know how to move beyond it."

Mykel understood now what happened that night and why she stood before him tonight like she was offering herself as a sacrifice.

"We all have pasts Karina and though they may be different, it's still in the past. You have to let go of it. I don't feel any different about you because of what you've told me or because of anything else you've done. When I said I'm falling in love with you, I meant that and that still holds true. All of you is what I want, no just your body."

She was speechless. No one had ever said things to her like he was saying and did it without wanting something.

"Mykel, I'm falling in love with you too. I wasn't sure if I should feel this way because I've never really been in love before. What I felt for Kayla and Tyler's dad is not what I feel for you. Tonight you've shown me what it's like to be more to someone than just my body. I want to see where things can go for us. Thank you for a wonderful birthday."

Mykel leaned in and gave her a sweet kiss on the lips.

"Your birthday is not over yet. Let's get into some movies, grab the desserts and enjoy a nice evening doing nothing, but enjoying each other's company. I do suggest, however, that you not put the dress back on. I don't think my sister will mind having one less sweat suit. I'm not sure my heart can handle seeing you in that dress again, or out of it. Being a heart surgeon, I know how weak the heart can be," he joked while placing his hand over his heart, faking a heart attack.

That lightened the mood and they both fell into fits of laughter.

"You have a deal. You get the desserts while I change the movie. Since it's my birthday, I want a chick flick," she said smiling.

"Baby, we can watch anything you want."

Chapter Ten
KARINA

There was no better way to spend a day than lounging in bed. She and Mykel had been out the night before at a party at his best friend Travis' house. Karina was glad she was free to go with him. Tony's mother had asked to have the kids for the weekend because her church was having a fun weekend of events that included a trip to the Washington zoo on Saturday and a picnic at a local park for the kids on Sunday and she wanted to take her grandkids with her.

She missed her babies and wanted to talk to them before Mykel picked her up for what he called afternoon brunch and a day of fun activities. Dating was new for her. Calling what she'd done with other men dating was an untruth. The relationship she'd had with Tony didn't even compare. The fact that they would only go to the movies or some club didn't compare to the ideas Mykel shared with her for fun things he wanted them to do and she looked forward to every one of them. It wasn't often that he got a lot of time off, but he let her know that when he was off, he wanted to spend some of the time with her and often times, they included the kids. She tried to tell Tony about her relationship with Mykel so that he could meet him, but he didn't want to hear about it and every time she asked him to come by to meet Mykel, he would come up with an excuse of why he couldn't so she let it go.

She was enjoying her relationship with Mykel and her kids liked him from day one.

After getting her morning shower, she reached for her phone, noticing a missed call from Tony's house. She called back hoping to catch the kids before they left for the zoo.

Tyler answered the phone on the first ring as if he was waiting by the phone for her to call.

"Hey mom," he said.

"Hi baby. Are you and Kayla having a good time with your grandma?"

"Yes. We're going to the zoo today. She said if Kayla and I were good yesterday that we would go to the zoo with her church."

Karina listened as Tyler took her through everything he had done the night before and then he passed the phone to Kayla.

"Mommy, I miss you. Are you coming soon?" Kayla asked. Karina's heart melted. She loved her baby and knew she was a momma's girl.

"Mommy will see you tomorrow. I heard you're going to the zoo today. Don't you want to do that?" she asked.

She knew when Kayla didn't answer that she was probably nodding her head yes. She still needed to learn that being on the phone meant that the other person couldn't see her shaking her head yes or no.

"Kayla, you have to say yes or no. Remember mommy can't see you shaking your head."

"Yes, I want to see the bears and the monkeys."

"Okay, well I want you to keep being a good girl for grandma and she's going to bring you home tomorrow. I'll be right here at the door waiting for you, okay?"

"Okay mommy. Dora is on the television so bye."

Dora being on television meant the conversation with her daughter was over. She was about to hang up the phone when Tony picked up the line.

"Where were you all night Rina? I called you all evening and most of the night."

She wasn't in the mood.

"I was out Tony and I hope you're spending time with the kids and not leaving them solely to your mother."

"Don't worry about what I'm doing with my kids. Why aren't you home with them instead of out with some dude all night long? I guess you're still kicking it with this Mykel guy you've been trying to get me to meet for the past few weeks since your birthday."

"None of your business. I don't question you about the tricks you spend your time with, so don't question me about my life. I told you if I met someone serious that I would let you meet him since he'd be around the kids so you've had your chance. When you're ready to be a grown up and deal with this, let me know."

"Oh, so it's like that. I thought we were going to try and work things out. I guess my dollars aren't long enough for you now huh?" Tony said, clearly agitated.

"Tony, I'm not doing this with you today. We're not getting anything together. Things have been over between us for a long time now and I'm in a relationship with someone."

"You mean you're spreading it wide for this doctor guy, don't you?"

"Whatever I'm doing, it's not your business. If you want to meet him, fine and if not, that's fine too. It won't stop me from enjoying my relationship so either meet him or shut up about it."

The clicking of the phone in her ear told her that she had been hung up on. To her it didn't matter because no one could wipe away the smile on her face knowing that Mykel was on his way to pick her up for their day of fun.

She was putting final touches on her makeup and running a comb through her hair when she heard his knock on the door. She loved how she looked without all the weave in her hair. When she told Mykel she had been doing it because men liked it, he told her he liked her however she wanted to present herself and the one thing she wanted to do was to stop wearing weaves. Besides irritating, they were too much work. Her own hair was long and curly and she preferred it that way. She looked around her place, making sure everything was tidy.

Opening the door, she swallowed her words when she saw how sexy he looked in a black pullover sweater and jeans. He said they should dress very casual and he definitely was. She, herself, had dressed in jeans and added a canary yellow sweater along with her most comfortable sneakers.

"Hi, Mykel, come on in. I'm almost ready," she said heading back to her room to finish getting ready.

"Hey yourself. You look nice."

"Thank you," she yelled back over her shoulder. "So, what's this fun day you have planned for us all about?"

"Well if you must know. The hospital is having a huge carnival as a fundraiser for the pediatric unit and I thought we could go by to support. After that, you and I are going to take a trip to Atlantic City. I was able to get another doctor to cover for me this evening so that you could have me all to yourself. What do you think about that?"

Karina ran back in the room and jumped up in his arms thankful that he'd caught her. Before he could say another word, she kissed him and not one of those friendly little kisses either. The kiss was possessive, yet tender as they each wrestled for control of the kiss. The kiss that she initiated turned into Mykel attacking her mouth with an intensity that could only be described as fervent and passionate. She let him set the pace for the kiss that set her body on fire. Her excitement over having the evening with him to herself and doing it in Atlantic City, someplace she'd never been, but had heard about was more than she could have imagined.

As the kiss continued, she felt him stroking her hair with one hand as his other held her in place around the waist. Her own hands were caressing his head then his neck until he broke away from her, feeling the need to come up for air.

"Wow, I need to come up with fun things to do all the time if this is the reaction I'll always get," he said.

"I love you Mykel."

Those words were music to his ears.

"I love you too baby. This love between us is only the beginning. Let's go have some fun.

~~

Nothing could bring Karina down from the high of being in love. She and Mykel were wrapping up their last week of summer before school started for her and the kids. No one could have told her that she would ever be as happy as she was. She was finally able to put her bleak past behind her and she looked forward to the bright future ahead of her. She was enrolled for her next semester of classes, still excited that she'd received good grades from her summer classes. Tyler and Kayla had enjoyed a great summer of fun thanks to Mykel who took them to their first amusement park with a trip to Hershey Park. They'd gone together along with his sister Misha. Now she and Misha were like sisters because they had grown close over the summer.

She hadn't seen much of her own family because they didn't like the new Karina who was going to college and talking about a life outside of the hood. They told her that her relationship with the doctor wouldn't last and she'd be back to the same old hood rat that she always was. She was more than happy to prove them wrong. Even if her relationship with Mykel had not worked out, she was never going back to a life of mere existence. She saw that she could be whatever she wanted to be and she didn't have to settle for getting by anymore.

With Mykel's help, she was able to get a job working part-time as a nurse's aide at the hospital two days a week. Times when she would have to work over the weekend, Misha offered to help watch Tyler and Kayla and their grandmother also volunteered to help more, especially since she could see that Karina was trying to do good things with her life.

Things were looking up for her and she was thrilled. She Mykel and her kids were enjoying a visit to a local arcade with the kids when Mykel came up with an idea of how to close out the final week of their summer. The kids were playing games and the two of them were sitting, keeping an eye on Kayla as she played with other children.

"How would you like to take a small trip for a few days before school starts?" he asked.

"A small trip where?" she asked.

"I was thinking to an island for some fun and relaxation for the two of us."

"An island? I don't have a passport."

"We can do an island in this country, someplace like Hawaii. I've been dying to go there and I really want to experience it with you."

Karina thought of how nice a trip like that would be and going to Hawaii was something she thought she would only be able to dream about.

"This is last minute Mykel. I'd have to see if I can Tony's mother to keep them for a few days."

"Misha will watch them I'm sure of it."

Karina was suspicious.

"How do you know she'll be willing to give up a few days of her life to keep an eye on two children?"

Mykel had to tell her his plan.

"I've already asked her and she said yes. I wanted to be sure all of the worries you'd have were taken care of that would make you say no to going. I knew the kids would be a big issue and now that they aren't, how about it?"

Karina tossed the idea around in her head and she could see that Mykel knew she was struggling with going.

"Come on baby, soon you'll be busy with school, studying and working, I'll have the hospital and the kids will be back in school and so will Misha. It's now or not at all for a long while. Please, for me?" he asked, playing on her love for him.

Karina smiled knowing she wouldn't be able to deny him anything.

"For you I would do anything."

The happiest man in the world was sitting across from

her.

"I'll make all of the arrangements while you work things out with Misha. The kids will have a ball at my house while we're gone."

"Your house?" she asked.

"Well I thought it would be easier if the kids stayed at my house with Misha while we were gone. Do you prefer that they stay at your place? I'm sure either is fine with her?"

"No I don't mind them staying at your house. Are you sure you want two little kids running around your house, ruining things? Remember they are children, something you don't usually have at your house."

"Baby, the kids will be fine and Misha is good with children. You saw how we didn't have to do anything with them at Hershey because she took control and Tyler and Kayla love her. It'll be fine."

"Well as long as you think so I'm okay with it."

"Good, then it's settled. We'll spend four days and three nights on the beautiful island of Maui and it will be the best time of both of our lives."

Chapter Eleven
KARINA

Maui was more than Karina could have expected it would be. She and Mykel were returning from their trip and were leaving the airport to go out to his house to get the kids.

"Are you happy?"

Karina turned her attention away from thinking about her kids and on the man sitting next to her in the car smiling, as she was, from ear to ear.

"I've never been this happy in my life. What do you mean am I happy? Happy is a small word compared to how I'm feeling," she replied.

"Glad to hear that. I plan to make sure you feel this way every day. You deserve it baby and you make me very happy."

Karina blushed and thought of how lucky she was to have this gorgeous, successful and caring man head over heels in love with her.

"I plan to continue making you happy too. Who would have thought that getting hit by a car would result in me being in love and engaged to the driver," she laughed.

Mykel laughed along with her.

"I know it wasn't a good situation at the time; it was even a scary one, but I will never regret the moment that our path's crossed, no matter the situation. It's weird to say this, but that accident was meant to be. I, like you, had spent wasted time with one woman or another and it never seemed right until I met you. I can't wait until we say I do. Speaking of saying I do, when would you like to do that? Should we talk about setting a date?"

She hadn't thought about that since the engagement was still fresh.

While in Hawaii, Mykel had proposed to her and she'd said yes without hesitation. He loved her and wanted to spend the rest of his life with her. He proposed at night on the beach under the moon and stars and nothing could be more romantic. She wanted to get married soon and not waste any more time not being with him permanently.

"I've been thinking about that. I don't know about you, but I don't want a very long engagement. I don't see a reason to do that. I've waited for what seems a lifetime for a man like you and since my wait is over, I don't want to drag it out."

"I agree, so would six months from now give you enough time to plan everything you want to plan?"

Karina was excited that he was as anxious to marry her as she was to marry him.

"Six months is perfect. I don't want a very big wedding. I'd like to try to keep it to close family and friends. I'm thinking about the cost, so the smaller the better."

Mykel wasn't hearing any talk about cost.

"I want you to have the wedding you want to have and I want you to put cost at the back of your mind. Think of the day you want and focus only on that. If you want small, then we'll do small. If you want large, we can do that too. It's our day and I want you to do whatever makes you happy."

"Being your wife makes me happy, but I hear you. I'm

still thinking of a small affair. Kayla and Tyler are going to be crazy happy because they both love you. I can't wait to tell them," she bellowed, loudly.

Mykel laughed at her joyous reaction. He loved seeing her happy and it meant everything to him that she stay that way.

"Are we telling them today?" he asked. He wasn't only thinking about telling them, he was also thinking about how Karina was going to tell Tony, Kayla and Tyler's father. Even though he was confident in their love and the bond they shared, he also knew that Tony was still in love with Karina and wanted her to be with him. He knew Tony wouldn't be happy to hear that he and Karina were engaged to be married. As soon as they told the kids, he knew the next time they were around Tony, they would mention the fact that Karina and Mykel were going to be getting married. He didn't want Tony to find out through the kids.

"I want to tell them as soon as we walk in the door."

Mykel didn't want to interrupt her happiness, but he needed to bring up the elephant in the car.

"What about Tony? How do you plan to handle that?"

Karina's smile was replaced with a frown.

"I've been so happy since you asked me to marry you that I haven't thought about talking to Tony about it, though I know I need to. He is Kayla and Tyler's dad and since you and I and the kids will be a family, I need to work this out with him early. I also don't want the kids to slip up and tell him, so I need to do it sooner than later."

"I agree and if you need me to be with you, let me know. I think it would be best if we did it together so that we can keep things civil and also so that we can explain together that he will always be their father and that I'm not trying to replace him in their lives. I want him to always feel comfortable around us and to make sure that he knows there will always be a place for him in our lives as their father. He also needs to understand that any notion he had of getting you back is over and done with. His focus should be on being a good father to Tyler and Kayla and not you anymore."

Karina knew Mykel was right. She'd tried several times to let Tony know that they were never getting back together again. Sometimes she could tell that he knew she was serious; other times, she could tell he was planning and scheming to win her back because they have history and two kids together. She's explained to him more than once that history and kids do not make a loving family or a loving relationship. This engagement will upset him, but it was best to get it over with as soon as possible.

"I definitely want you to be with me. Do you have a problem with us stopping by his mother's house after we pick up the kids? I need to do this now and not let it drag on."

"That sounds like a good plan. Let's also wait until after you've talked to him to tell the kids. On the way back to your place, we can stop to get dinner and ice cream and tell them then. How does that sound?"

She smiled.

"That sounds great."

They pulled into the garage at Mykel's house and noticed Misha's car was also there which meant the kids were there.

Karina was hurt when she walked into Mykel's house. Her kids didn't miss her as much as she thought they would. When she and Mykel walked in, the kids came running to give them both a big hug, but that excitement over their return didn't last long. They were preparing to go swimming in Mykel's in-ground pool and right after a round of hugging, kissing and saying I miss you, they were running off toward the pool. Misha told them that the kids really did miss them, but that nothing comes before swimming with them. Karina knew that Tyler loved the water, getting lessons during a few summers of summer camp at the YWCA. She didn't know that Kayla also loved the water. She had been hesitant about how early to start swimming lessons for her. According to Misha, the kids had been swimming every day while she and Mykel were in Hawaii.

"You taught Kayla how to swim?" Karina asked her.

"She's not swimming yet. I've taught her to not be afraid of the water. I keep weights on her arms to help her stay afloat, but she loves the water. Come on out and see," Misha said, following behind the kids with Karina and Mykel in tow. When they reached the outside, the kids were waiting at the fence for Misha to unlock the gate that led to the pool. Once she did, Tyler jumped right in while Kayla held her hand out and waited for Misha. Karina was already impressed that Kayla had been taught to not go near the water without an adult. When Misha got in the pool with Kayla, Karina saw that she was a ball of laughs playing with her brother in the water. Leaving the kids with her while they were away was a great idea.

"Well it looks like we could have stayed a few extra days in Hawaii making love on the beach," Mykel said, pulling Karina close to his side, giving her a soft kiss on the cheek.

Karina remembered their time together and when he

mentioned making love, it was as if her body remembered and she began tingling all over. Thanks to him, she'd finally made love with a man and not just had sex. The experience was more than she ever thought it could be and making love with him erased the remembrance of all men she'd been with before him. His lovemaking was slow and intense in a way that made her feel like he was worshiping her body, not just loving it. As much as she missed her children, she saw no problem if they'd stayed a few more days making love all day and night like that did for the time they were there. Mykel's appetite for her matched hers for him and though they took in many sights and did a lot of fun things, her most treasured moments were the times being intimately connected to him.

"I see that. Now I know when you take me away, they'll be fine without me for a few days."

"Why don't we give them some time swimming while you go make your call to Tony?"

"Yeah, I guess it's time for that," Karina said worried.

"Don't worry so much. I'm sure everything will be okay. I know you haven't had good interactions with him lately, but we can't put this off, especially if you want to tell your family and friends and especially the kids, about the engagement."

"I know you're right. I'll try and reach out to him now," she said going into a quieter room and pulling out her cell phone.

Mykel gave her some privacy while he went to unpack his luggage from the trip.

"Hi Tony. I was wondering if you were home because I want to stop by with the kids."

Karina was surprised he'd answered the phone. He had

been ignoring her calls for a while.

"Oh, so you're back from your trip with the boyfriend I guess. Now I can see my kids?" she heard him say sarcastically.

"Tony, I asked you first if you could keep them while I was gone and you told me no. I couldn't cancel my plans to go."

"Sure you could have. You mean you didn't want to cancel your trip to go to some island with the doctor."

"I didn't call to argue with you. I wanted to bring the kids by. Are you going to be home in a few hours?" she asked again.

"Yeah, I'm here. Is the doctor bringing you?" he asked.

Karina had a feeling the conversation wasn't going to go well when she got to his house.

"Yes he is. Is that a problem?" she asked.

"Not a problem for me. You sure the doctor would be okay coming into the hood after dark? I wouldn't want him to feel out of place in his slick black shiny ride."

"Give it rest Tony. There is no reason to be cynical. We'll be by in a few hours after the kids finish swimming."

"Cynical? When did you start using words like that Ms. High and Mighty? You're moving on up in the world going to college, using big words and screwing a doctor!" he added, sounding like he was mocking her.

Karina didn't want to get into anything with him.

"We'll see you in a few hours Tony, bye," she said, disconnecting the call before he had a chance to say anything else. She went looking for Mykel to tell him about the conversation, wondering if telling Tony right now was a good idea

"Karina, we either keep it a secret from the kids right

now and not tell him either or we go ahead and get it over with, letting him take it all in whatever way he needs to. It doesn't matter what you decide, we're getting married in six months and I'm sure you'll want to start all of your planning soon. Not telling him is not the way to go. Let him be angry, pissed off or whatever and then let's move beyond it. We have a life to plan together and one of those additional plans is a bigger house so we have lots to do in a short period of time."

Karina looked at him stunned. She loved his house and to her it was huge. From where she grew up, this was a castle and she didn't see why they needed a bigger house.

"Why do we need a bigger house? This one is huge. I thought we'd be living here after the wedding." she said.

"It may seem that way, but once we get married and you and the kids move in, this place is going to seem mighty small. Besides, this house only has four bedrooms and right now one is being taken over by my sister and all of her things. I want to be sure I keep a room for her for whenever she wants to come over and I want Tyler and Kayla to also have their own rooms. Besides, once we have another baby, we'll want a room to decorate as a nursery."

Karina smiled. She couldn't wait to have his baby and was glad he was thinking early about it.

"How soon do you want children?" she asked.

"I want them whenever you want them. I know we have Tyler and Kayla and I love them like they're my own. Whenever you're ready, know that I'm ready too," he said kissing her and going back to removing the rest of his clothes from the suitcase.

"Well I do want to finish my classes first and then I'll think about it. Is that okay with you? I only have next year and I'll be finish."

Mykel knew she was talking about her two year degree as a certified nursing assistant. He wanted her to think bigger and wanted to be sure she knew she could if she wanted to.

"Karina, I was thinking about something. I know you're enjoying your CNA classes, but have you given any thought to going for your Bachelor's degree in nursing? I know it will take longer, but I want you to shoot for the stars baby. Don't stop at being an assistant."

"I have thought about it. That would take additional years and I wasn't sure how you'd feel about that. I want to be sure I'm being a good wife to you since I know how hectic your schedule can be. I don't want to be tired from studying or at school when you're here at home. I want to be here with you when you have time off."

Mykel loved how her first thoughts were always for him and her kids. He also wanted her to start putting herself first. He sat down on the seat at the foot of his bed.

"Come sit next to me," he said. They needed to talk a little more about how their life together would be. After Karina joined him he took a moment to gather his thoughts for the perfect thing to say.

"Baby, listen to me, our life together will not only be about me and Kayla and Tyler. It will also equally be about you. I want you to enjoy our life together as much as the kids and I will and it's not only about being my wife and their mother; it's being all that you want to be. If what you want is to further your education for however long you want to do it, I'll be here to support you and taking care of Kayla and Tyler will not only be your responsibility, it will be mine also. Yes, being a doctor comes with a very hectic schedule, but I think we can work it out where we'll have plenty of time together, the kids won't feel neglected because you're in school and studying and any moment with my wife will be special. It doesn't matter to me if it's five minutes. I want to help you make your dreams come true. If you tell me you want to focus on school and become a nurse, then that's what I want you to do. People do it every day baby, and we won't be any different. We will make it work. The kids will have full days in school so you'll have plenty of time to go to classes and study and if you need time in the evenings, we can always get some additional help around here as far as a nanny to help with the kids or someone to keep up with the housekeeping."

"Nanny? I don't know about that. I don't' want some strange woman around here, especially when I'm not here."

Mykel laughed at her, knowing that once everything came down on her at one time, she'll be begging him for some help.

"That's a big perk being married to not only a doctor but a doctor who is a well-respected and in high demand surgeon. Take the time and get your dream and we'll be here to cheer you on. I can't promise that my hours won't be crazy and I'm going to ask for your patience with that, so how can I deny you the time to do you?? This will work and we are going to be stupid happy together. I never, ever want you to put your own life on the back burner for the sake of us. We can do this together as a family."

Karina was about to cry. If anyone would ask her how her life was, she would say it was perfect. For so long, she wasn't sure she could ever see her life beyond where she grew up. It wasn't so much the location as much as it was the mentality. She never really thought she deserved more or that she could have more. Mykel came into her life like and showed her that she was more than she ever thought she could be.

"Thank you and I would like to get my bachelor's in nursing. It's something I've wanted to do since before I had any children. I always thought I would be a nurse and I'm happy to know that my dream was only sidetracked for a while and not stopped all together. Thank you for believing in me and loving me. I don't know where I would be or what my future would hold if you hadn't come along and showed me that I could be more than another pretty, flashy woman who didn't know her own worth was not tied to her body, but to her heart and her mind."

Before she knew it, tears did start falling down her face. She saw that Mykel was about to reach up and wipe them away when Kayla and Tyler came into the room, looking upset at the sight of her crying.

"Mommy, what's wrong?" Kayla asked.

Karina quickly put a bright smile on her face so that they wouldn't think that her tears were because she was sad.

"Nothing's wrong," she said pulling Kayla close to her and wrapping her arms around her, careful not to pull her on her lap because she was still in her wet bathing suit. "I'm fine. Mykel and I were having a good moment, not a sad one. Remember mommy told you before not all tears are sad tears? Well this is one of those times when my tears are happy tears. We'll talk more about that later. Are you both finished swimming?"

Tyler chimed in first. "Yes. Misha said we needed to get our clothes changed."

"Okay, well why don't you go do that and I'll go help

Kayla get dressed. We're going to stop by to see your dad before we go out to get dinner and then home."

Tyler ran off and Karina gave Mykel a tender kiss on the lips before she was pulled along by Kayla who was anxious to get dressed.

~~

"Grandma!" Kayla shouted, running into the house as soon as they pulled up in front of the house. Tyler wasn't far behind her. They both loved their grandmother and Karina loved that in spite of the way her relationship with Tony turned out, his mother was crazy about them.

Karina was visibly nervous as Mykel helped her out of the car.

"It's going to be fine," he whispered in her ear, trying to help ease the tension that appeared on her face and in the stiffness of her body.

She didn't respond. She took the hand he offered her and held on to it as they also entered the house. Inside she looked around for Tony, but didn't see him. She could hear the kids telling their grandmother all about time at Mykel's house with Misha. She was glad they hadn't told them about the engagement yet. She knew that both would have already spilled that bit of information in their excitement. As soon as she and Mykel entered the kitchen where the kids were, she noticed Tony through the back door on his cell phone. It was now or never, she thought as she turned to Mykel for support. He smiled letting her know he was with her. After introducing Mykel to Tony's mother Karina figured the time was right.

"Mykel and I are going to go out back to talk to your dad. Finish telling your Nana about swimming and I'll send your dad in to see you in a few minutes."

The tension was thick when Tony ended his call and turned to see her and Mykel standing in front of him.

"Where are my kids?" he asked, no hello greeting or pretense of pleasantries at seeing either of them.

"They're in the house with your mother. I was hoping I could talk to you for few minutes. Actually we were hoping we could talk to you for a few minutes."

Tony didn't immediately answer and that made Karina tense up even more. No one said anything and she didn't know how to proceed. She was glad when Mykel spoke up first.

"Hey Tony, it's good to finally meet you. I'm Mykel."

When Mykel extended his hand for a shake, Karina was afraid the tension would continue and Tony would ignore it. She was glad when he didn't ignore it, but reached out to return the handshake extended to him.

"Likewise. What did you want to talk to me about?" Tony asked calmly, surprising Karina. She thought it was amazing what a friendly handshake can do to an edgy situation.

Mykel looked at Karina to see if she was ready to tell him or if she wanted him to. Her smile told him she could handle it so he stood by her side for support.

"While we were away on our trip, Mykel asked me to marry him and I said yes. We're getting married in about six months. I wanted you to know so that you wouldn't hear it from anyone else."

Karina didn't know what she expected, but she thought anger or some not so nice words, but neither happened. He responded coolly.

"Is that so?" Karina saw Tony looking to her hand for an engagement ring.

"Nice rock. What about my kids? You planning on letting him adopt my kids or something?"

She responded immediately.

"No Tony, not at all. Kayla and Tyler love you and no matter what, you'll always be their father. I would never want to come between that."

"Neither would I," Mykel responded.

Tony's attention turned to him. Mykel could tell that though the history was between Tony and Karina, this was the part of the conversation he and Tony needed to have alone.

"Karina, why don't you let Tony and I have a few words alone. Go ahead inside with the kids."

She looked from Tony to Mykel who weren't looking at her, but at each other. She didn't know if it was a good idea or not to leave them alone.

"Congratulations Karina. I guess you're finally getting the life you've always wanted. I think Mykel is right though go inside and let us talk," he said.

Karina looked to Mykel again, not wanting to leave them alone.

"Its fine, I promise. Go ahead inside. We'll be a few minutes," he said, reassuring her.

When she was gone, Tony turned to Mykel.

"What do you want to say to me?" Tony asked.

"I want to let you know that I know you still love Karina and I can respect that. She's a remarkable woman. I love her more than I thought I could ever love a woman. You should know that I'm not trying to step in and get in the middle of your relationship with your children. They will always be your children; I will be their step-father. I know you and Karina have had a lot of tension between the two of you, but I hope that we can all co-exist. I don't want there to be any level of discomfort between the two of us. As gentlemen I think we can come up with a way that will make sure you are comfortable with this situation."

"Okay, I hear you," Tony responded. "I'm not trying to cause any problems between you and Karina. Actually I knew something like this was going to happen. When she told me the two of you were going away and asked me to look after my shorties, I didn't because I figured something like this would be going down. That's how it always happens in the movies. I'm cool though and like I told her, congratulations. As long as my kids know that I'm their father, I'm good with the situation. You got a good one in Karina. I never could seem to do the right thing and give her the kind of life she really deserved. I always felt like I ruined her life getting her pregnant at sixteen so I'm glad she's finally getting the life she deserves. My concern is about my kids and that's it. I can see that they are good around you and you seem like a guy on the up and up. No matter how pissed off I want to be that she's with you, I can't be. She's had a hard life and I'm happy to see her happy, though I don't want to admit it. Where are you guys gonna be living with my kids?"

"We're staying right here in the Maryland area and I'll work with Karina to be sure we drop them off here when you want to spend time with them. We'll work it out. I'm glad this isn't as awkward as Karina thought it would be."

"Yeah, well, Karina knows the real me. It was supposed to be awkward, but I can't knock a brother on his hustle, making sure the woman he loves is taken care of and like I said, my concern is staying in my kids' lives."

"You got that Tony," Mykel said, once again extending

his hand for a shake.

He was glad when Tony didn't hesitate this time to shake it.

"We're good Mykel. We're good."

Karina turned at the sound of the back door opening and Tony and Mykel coming through it without any blood being shed.

"Is everything okay?" she asked.

"Everything is good lil' mama," Tony replied. "Where's Kayla and Tyler?"

"Your mom took them next door for frozen cups."

Tony didn't say anything else as she watched him leave the room going in search of the kids. She turned to Mykel for an explanation of what she missed.

"So what happened? I thought I was going to need to call for an ambulance," she said smiling and going into Mykel's outstretched arms. She loved being in his embrace which made her feel so loved and safe.

"That was a father to husband and step-father to be conversation. Let me say everything is all good. How's that?" he asked, pulling her tighter.

"I trust you so that's good enough for me. I'm glad because now we can tell the kids when we go out to dinner. Before we leave I want to talk to Tony's mom alone and tell her also. I know Tony will tell her, but I want to be sure she hears it from me."

"Great idea baby. Let's go find everyone. I haven't had a frozen cup since I was a little boy growing up in the Park Heights area."

Epilogue
KARINA

THREE YEARS LATER

It was graduation day and Karina was a bag of nerves. She looked around at the other graduates from Towson State University and felt proud. Getting to this point wasn't an easy road, but it was a road well worth the travel.

After her wedding to Mykel, six months after he proposed, they'd settled into life as a family. There was an adjustment period dealing with the new surroundings for the kids, her class and study schedule and Mykel's ever demanding work schedule.

The friendship with Tony had even improved over the years. He became a strong presence in the kids' lives thanks to his girlfriend. Being on the sidelines while she married Mykel was a hard pill for him to swallow and in the beginning, he would disappear whenever she came around his mother's house with the kids. He never had a lot to say to her and she let him have the space he needed. Eventually he met a nice woman who kicked him into gear, getting him away from the life and friends who were holding him down. He picked himself up, got a job and he and his girlfriend had a baby boy and moved in together, far from the hood for a clean start. He'd finally moved on and was genuinely happy for her.

The crowd gathered for the graduation was full of

excitement, which included her own family. Her smile brightened when she spotted Mykel, holding Kayla up in his arms so that she could see over the crowd. Tyler was the typical boy, focused on playing a game on the new IPad he'd received from Mykel for his outstanding achievement in school, earning a place on the honor roll all year. She waved when she saw her mother and all of her siblings sitting together, proud of what she'd achieved. Even Mykel's parents and sister came to the graduation to support her.

She still couldn't believe she was graduating from college when at one point in her life she'd struggled with getting her GED. Not only was she graduating, but she was graduating at the top of her class all due to her hard work and the love of her husband who did everything in his power to make sure she stayed focused on school. Her life was everything it could be and much more than she ever thought it would be, learning that there was never a time when anyone should stop dreaming. She was an example that dreams did come true.

When her name was finally called and she walked across the stage on wobbly legs to receive her diploma, her life had come full circle. The young girl who years ago walked away from high school in her senior year was not only a high school graduate, but was now a college graduate. Never again would she ever question her ability to follow her dreams through to fruition. Her dreams and desires are within her reach as long as she never gives up on fighting for them.

Following the graduation, the family went out for a celebratory dinner and to her surprise, Mykel had arranged for a private room where they not only had dinner, but a small party for her that included more family and friends who were unable to attend the graduation. She had expected dinner, but not the surprise party. It topped off an incredible day. She'd received lots of gifts, but her favorite would come later. When Mykel asked her what she wanted most as a graduation gift, she told him a quiet evening alone with him. It had been three years of studying and sacrifices and all she wanted was an uninterrupted night with her husband.

Now that the partying was over and they were home alone, she was getting exactly what she asked for.

"Tyler and Kayla are with Misha for the weekend at her new house and everyone else has gone their separate ways. It's you and I for a night of nothing but peace and quiet."

"It sounds like the perfect ending to a wonderful day to me," Karina admitted.

"Me too baby," Mykel agreed.

"So what do you think of your college graduate?" she asked while they snuggled up in bed.

"I think I have the most incredible wife in the world and I'm very proud of her. I hope today was everything you wanted it to be."

It was that and more, she thought.

"Yes it was and thank you for my party with everyone. How did you keep that a secret?" she asked.

"I didn't tell Kayla!" he said. "You know she can't keep a secret."

"You're right about that."

"So what's next for you baby? I know you've received several offers for jobs at local hospitals. Do you have any idea where you're leaning towards?"

Karina knew she had decisions to make. Her

concentration on what he was saying was being sidetracked by the affection she was receiving. He may be talking to her, but his attention was on feasting on certain parts of her body, starting with her neck and making his way down from there.

"I've been thinking about it and I'm leaning towards the offer from the Pediatric Unit at Hopkins. I really want to work with kids, especially babies. That way I'll know how to take care of any ailments when ours get sick, especially the one we're having in about seven months."

"It will be great to have a doctor and a nurse that can tend to our sick children," Mykel said.

Karina knew that he clearly missed what she'd said when he made no reaction to her last statement, but continued kissing and caressing her.

"Mykel, did you hear what I said?"

"Yes baby," he said, not really focusing on words, but on pleasuring her. "You said Hopkins and I support you in that decision."

As much as she loved time alone making love with her husband, Karina wanted to be sure he'd heard what she'd said.

"Mykel, did you hear me?"

"What?" he stopped moving around her and asked. "Oh, we were talking about jobs. I said I heard you say Hopkins and I'm all for that," he said, going back to what he was doing.

"Well, that may be hard to do in about seven months when your son or daughter is born and I'll be home taking care of him or her."

Karina left that bit of information in the air and slid further down the bed reaching for Mykel and joining in on the kissing and caressing. She was about to remove his pajama bottoms when he suddenly stiffened, and not just that sexy part of him that she enjoyed being as stiff as possible.

"Wait, what did you say? Did you say son or daughter? Wait! What?" Mykel said, now sitting straight up in bed.

"Oh, you did hear me then?" she asked, playfully.

"Karina, tell me you did not say what I think you said? Are we having a baby?"

"So were you or were you not listening to me?"

"Karina, stop playing with me. I'm on the edge here."

She laughed at the look of fear and frustration on his face. Her husband's looks were priceless.

"Yes, you heard me correctly. We're going to have a baby in about seven months. Our family is about to grow."

Before she knew what was happening, she was being scooped up into Mykel's arms and being held tightly, almost cutting off her ability to breathe.

"Mykel, if you don't let me breathe, our baby can't breathe either."

He loosened his hold.

"I can't believe it. Thank you baby. I wasn't sure when we'd start working on having a baby. I guess you started before me," he laughed.

"I guess I did. I stopped taking the pill about three months ago thinking it would be a while before it worked its way out of my system and I figured we'd talk about it. Little did I know your little swimmers were Olympic champions and it seems we got pregnant right away. I'm glad you're happy because I am too. I know the kids will be over the top happy. Kayla asks me all the time when she was going to get a little brother or a little sister. Now I can tell her soon."

"I can't wait to tell my mom and dad. Their first grandchild is on the way. I can't even tell you how excited Misha will be. Let's call everyone now."

Before Karina could respond, Mykel forgot about the fact that she was naked and very much ready for something other than talking to family. She watched him as he looked around for his cell phone and stopped him before he could make the first call.

"Mykel, I think eleven o'clock at night is too late to call anyone. Let's do that in the morning. Right now, how about you come back to bed and finish what you were starting. I've waited all day to be alone with you and I don't want that interrupted by hours of phone conversations with family about a baby that won't be here for months."

Mykel calmed down and knew when he looked over at his luscious wife waiting for him that their family could indeed wait until the morning. Right now he wanted to make love to his wife, the woman he'd waited a long time for and though he couldn't wait to share their news with everyone, it was more important that he shower her with love and affection, thanking her for coming into his life. He knew that she thanked him for helping her to turn her life around, but it was him who was thankful for the day she stepped in the street. The memories of the accident still haunt him, but he also knew that if it hadn't been for that accident, he wouldn't be as happy as he is in his life now.